The Stratford Hunter

The Sixth Catrin Sayer Mystery

ALLAN JONES

ISBN: 978-1-9993813-4-9

Cover: The George pub (and its restaurant, The Pig and
Goose), the Strand, London. Author photograph

THE CATRIN SAYER MYSTERIES

*This book is a Kindle Direct Publishing paperback.
The series is also available as e-books from
Amazon Kindle eBooks and other suppliers.*

CONTENTS

FROM BOOK 5 (THE POWYS DEACON)

When Sayer and Coltrane arrived on the top floor of New Scotland Yard, they were shown into the commander's office. Catrin recognized the senior officer of Trident, the organized crime group of the Met, from her previous role working with Assistant Commissioner Hunt. He always came over as 'Mr. Imperturbable' on everything, at any meeting she had seen him at. Not someone who sought the limelight but always prepared, measured, capable.

He sat back in his chair, his eyes on Catrin, monitoring her.

"DI Sayer, I have a proposal that I ask you to consider carefully. Basically, I want you to help us from time to time; to work with Trident and other government departments dealing with security issues. Not for us, I should say; not change jobs. I wouldn't want to take you away from your role here; just ask for your help on occasion, on a matter of importance to, as the phrase goes, the 'national interest'.

"However, it is more logical to start with the background reason for approaching you."

He looked at the notes in front of him; or pretended to, Catrin thought.

"Our colleagues in SIS are in an operation to break into a triad group based in Hong Kong called Four Square. I think you have heard of them?"

Catrin responded, "I have come across the name. I read a lot about triad activity during the period I was under threat from the Ten Dragons group."

Barlow smiled. "I think you have more than read about them; you were chatting away not that long ago with one of their key people."

From his file he produced a photograph. It nicely showed Catrin in her bridesmaid's dress talking with Michael Yau at Li's wedding. He placed a second photo on the table showed the group drinking a toast together. She looked at them then turned to look at Coltrane who was staring at the photographs, his face impassive.

Catrin said, "This man was at my friend's wedding, yes. He is a friend of her father, Daniel Yeung, I believe."

"Indeed," said Barlow. "And this man's granddaughter is now in London, studying art and, I understand, you and your artist friends are mentoring her. Is that correct?"

Catrin just nodded, taking in that a lot of background work must have taken place besides the surveillance work that provided the photographs.

Barlow said, "It gives our people opportunities, routes of access perhaps. Four Square is a very difficult group to penetrate."

He smiled at her then turned serious, focusing on Neville Coltrane.

"DCI Coltrane, I think that gives a flavour, so to speak, of the type of support we are going to request, to accommodate our needs for some of Inspector Sayer's time. If you could leave us now?"

He was smooth, very pleasant, but the tone of voice left no doubt; Catrin's boss was being booted out.

The Stratford Hunter

PROLOGUE

Marcel and Francoise Cleroux loved their balcony in summer, particularly once the sun had passed its zenith and the overhang of the balcony above provided shade. They often spent a good part of the afternoon and evening there.

The balconies had been an attractive feature of the 'h'-shaped apartment block designed by a local architect; a woman who still lived in the complex. Exteriors that faced out of the site were largely tinted glass and concrete, but each apartment located in the fork of the 'h' had balconies that overlooked the rock outcrop left untouched in the middle. Only four stories high, it was a lot lower in profile than some of the surrounding buildings but its unique design ensured it was highly sought after; apartments here were never left empty for very long.

Across the expanse of the rockery and garden to the neighbouring arm of the building they could see movements of people on their own balconies. Some they knew and, if they spotted each other, would occasionally wave. But it was rare. One of the things about apartment living was the ability to ignore others, to create one's private space and give people their own. So it was coincidence, really, that Francoise had just pointed out the hyacinths in pots at of one of the apartment's opposite. They were healthy and spreading, whereas Francoise had not had success with her own for the last two years.

Francoise insisted, "It's the doctor; she must have green fingers."

Last year she had blamed the difference on the relative values of morning and afternoon sunshine. Privately, Marcel thought that if his wife bought quality plants from a decent supplier rather than the supermarket sources, the problem would be resolved.

He replied, "Professor Morin is a scientist, not a doctor. She works at the university, the article said."

"No, she's a doctor working on cancer," said Francoise immovably.

Marcel was referring to a piece in the local paper *Le Progrès* six months earlier. Vaulx-en-Velin was a sleepy suburb of Lyon and local people who achieved success were occasionally featured prominently in articles in the newspaper.

He made a platitude of surrender and returned to his crossword.

There was the sound first, the crack. Francoise leaned forward and peered down towards the road looking for a scooter with an exhaust misfire. But Marcel knew what he had heard and instinctively stood and pulled his wife back from the balcony wall. He had grown up in the era of national service and had joined the Chasseurs Alpins, the mountain infantry. He pulled them both into the shadow of the sliding door between the apartment interior and the balcony as he scanned the building opposite.

It was only when he saw Madame Morin on the balcony across, the one with the flowers they had looked at only half a minute before, he knew he had been right. She had been sitting reading a magazine. Now she appeared to be asleep with her head resting against the seatback and the patio window. If it wasn't for the splash of red on the left side of the face, and a spray of similar colour on the window behind, it would be peaceful.

As Francoise, surprised, asked him what he was doing

pulling her around like that, he slid the patio door closed and replied. "It was a shot, Fran. Sit down."

She looked at his face as she obeyed the tone of voice, knowing from both it was much worse than that.

He added, "Madame Morin."

He pulled out his mobile and called 112 to report the emergency. What he hadn't seen at that distance but expected would be there, was a hole in the glass. Its path, with the trajectory through the head, would give the police the angle of the shot. But he said nothing about that, concentrating on his wife. Like new soldiers at their first action, she had the look of disbelief, as if her world had turned upside down.

~~

Once the immediate fuss of the investigation died down and the police and forensic people left, the apartment stayed empty for some time. Problems of the estate settlement, the Cleroux couple decided.

It was some months later that the article in *Le Figaro* gave some insight into the scientist's death. It wasn't, as Francoise's friend, who worked in the student accommodation office at the university, had surmised. Francoise had told Marcel that the rumour was that Professor Morin's murder was attributable to a rival research group at the University of Albany in the infamously-competitive USA.

The crime reporter in Marseille noted in his article that Walid Rashid, the oldest son of Oussama Rashid, a man with his fingers in a number of illegal activities and who himself had spent two terms in prison, had just had a charge of manslaughter dismissed. He was accused of running down a woman on a country road and leaving the scene of the accident. The only witness to the event, the crucial piece of prosecution evidence, was the identification of the young man and the vehicle by another motorist. She had seen him get back into the car and drive off as she arrived. But the witness, a respected scientist identified as Professor Olivia Morin, had been assassinated in her home near Lyon only a week before the trial.

It wasn't American greed; it was Algerian criminal elements, albeit the third generation offspring, she explained.

"Les Algériens," exclaimed Francoise finally, shaking her head.

"Our cleaner when we lived in Lyon was Algerian," Marcel countered. "Her daughter Nour used to babysit for us."

"But we know them!" said Francoise, as if that was the big difference.

The media and politicians went wild and eventually the police officer leading the case was replaced, held accountable for failing to foresee the need to provide protection for the key witness. A home of a family in Marseille where the father was called Osama Rashid was torched; a case of 'mistaken identity' as one news report put it. Walid was sent to live with relatives in Skikda on the Algerian coast where the same Marseille reporter, not letting go of the issue, later found people who said the young Rashid had fallen in with 'not only criminals, but extremists'. That was good for more column-inches.

But in the months following the murder the Cleroux couple never heard any more news about the investigation into the person who had killed Professor Morin.

1 BARLOW

Lena Shannon came out of the Hackney Wick Overground station in East London feeling happy but trying to maintain the air of casual indifference to others and act like a local. She wasn't. One sentence from her mouth would tell anyone she was a Scot and anyone familiar with Scotland would type her as a born-and-bred Glaswegian girl who hadn't left home all that long ago.

There was a cold wind blowing, encouraging her to pull her lapels closed and turn her collar up to cover her neck and ears. Lena was nineteen, a student, wanting to show she was cool about living in London. A business student at City University, she was a little different than most other first-year students; she had her own flat. Not one she shared with others; not a cruddy wreck of a place like the ones others complained about, but a top-floor, one-bedroom flat close to this station in Stratford. Lena's mother had been on to her about sharing a place with other girls to build friendships, but she knew that the 'suggestions' were really about her mother's discomfort with the flat's landlord.

Walking along Chapman Road she reflected on the need to break the news to her mum that she would look for a job in London during the long vacation this summer. It made sense; more temp jobs were available in summer here than back in Greenock or Glasgow. Her mother's less-than-subtle hints made it clear she was missing her daughter and looking forward to what she recognized would be the last summer together for a while. "You are growing up, Lena, and soon will have no time to visit home for long, I know," she had said.

Lena had stayed quiet at that point. She didn't want to hurt her mother but that point had already been reached. But she would need to tell her soon.

The slight motion of the liquor bottle in her backpack as

she walked, the bounce of the fluid, reminded her that it wouldn't be today or tomorrow that she would face that hurdle. Not today because this evening was special. She and Malav were celebrating the quarter-anniversary of their first date. Having a local boyfriend who wasn't a student was another reason that her life wasn't locked into college and student friends. The vodka was a present for him; a brand she knew nothing about but hoped he hadn't tried. He was partial to vodka, she knew. And he, in turn, would bring her a present, she was sure. And tomorrow, she would probably be recovering from her night out, and in, so talking to her mother then would be off the list.

She turned the corner into Trowbridge Road and saw her block of flats come into sight. Home; her own home, for the time being. It still got to her and, ever-conscious of her surroundings, she made a special effort not look happy and excited.

~~

Detective Inspector Catrin Sayer finally emerged from Commander Barlow's office on the top floor of New Scotland Yard about half-an-hour after her boss, Detective Chief Inspector Neville Coltrane, had been asked to leave the little meeting there. The reason given for kicking him out had been that a 'need to know' discussion could be held with a visitor, who had walked straight in as Coltrane left.

As Catrin emerged into the outer office, Lorraine Adams, Barlow's executive assistant and the main gatekeeper to the commander's suite, smiled at her.

"They are still talking, I take it, DI Sayer?"

"Yes," was all that Catrin said.

"Are you alright?" Adams asked, seeing Sayer lost in thought. She looked despondent, not energized.

Sayer was not a particularly striking woman. About five foot eight inches, well-dressed, yes, but she was neither tall nor short for a female officer. She was trim and fit with dark blonde hair and features that would not stand out particularly in a crowd. The only item that could bring a second glance, Adams thought, was a thin, two-inch white line on her left cheek visible beneath the light make-up. Adams knew that it was a scar from a work-related incident years ago. She also recalled that the Welshwoman had a nice smile; Sayer had, until her recent promotion, worked nearby. But when she was pensive, like now, her face appeared serious, almost anxious.

Catrin forced a small smile. "They have given me some things to think about, Lorraine. You know what happens when you get summoned to the heavens."

'The heavens' was a nickname of the top floor, the location of various senior executives at the Metropolitan Police Service.

Adams smiled back. "As do you; you spent enough time working up here to know that there are days when it could be more aptly named the other place."

Sayer, as a uniformed sergeant, had recently completed a two-year appointment as an aide and security officer to an assistant commissioner, Sandra Hunt. Three months ago her promotion to detective inspector and her current role leading the Art Team came through.

But Catrin was now at the outer door of the suite. She just nodded and said, "Right!" as she left.

In the meeting she just participated in, part of the preliminary spiel by Commander Barlow explained that he had something to discuss outside normal police work, a request for Sayer's involvement in a matter 'of importance to the national interest', as he put it. Within a few minutes, Catrin had gone from enjoying a joke with her teammates in the Art and Antiques Unit to finding herself on sensitive ground; her friendship with a Chinese lawyer, Jian Li Yeung. Barlow had shown her and Coltrane photographs taken recently at Jian Li's wedding in Hong Kong, images in which Catrin had been chatting with a man called Michael Yau. He made it clear that this man was connected with the operation they had in mind.

After her boss left and the stranger had entered, Barlow

introduced him as 'Stephen Drew from SIS', the Special Intelligence Services. The Commander had then suggested a break for coffee, as Lorraine had taken the opportunity to bring in a tray with refreshments.

The two police officers and the SIS man had stood up and moved over to the conference table to get their cups and saucers.

In her role as an aide to Assistant Commissioner Hunt, Catrin had experienced many organized coffee breaks in meetings. She had listened to people taking civilly about nothing; cloud formations outside, the news on the front page of the Telegraph or who had died or retired. Ten minutes later the same people were back at the meeting table, sometimes at each other throats about budgets, manpower or operational priorities.

Now Barlow and Drew were chatting about a test match in Australia. Catrin didn't follow cricket at all and the whole thing, the sudden call upstairs, was starting to feel surreal; talk of cricket in November and triads in Hong Kong.

Holding her cup and saucer she stood quietly, taking in Drew's French cuffs and gold cuff-links. He looked archetypal 'establishment'. She wondered about the motif on them; a regimental or a school crest? If Coltrane was still here he would know, she thought.

Drew turned to her and said, "You are an artist yourself, we see, DI Sayer," jolting Catrin out of her thoughts.

She acknowledged the point. "Yes, a ceramic designer and decorator. I work with a potter, Jean Hughes, on pieces that we sell through a gallery near Harrods, one which specializes in contemporary British artists."

Drew nodded collaboratively. "I collect rare Wedgewood. Which bring us nicely back to the work in hand, I believe. Craig?"

He placed his cup and saucer back on the tray.

My stuff is a long way from what you collect, thought Catrin, as they resumed their places around Barlow's desk.

As he sat down, the SIS man automatically adjusted his cuffs to have equal lengths showing from the sleeves of his suit jacket. Fussy, thought Catrin, her eyes moving to his face. Drew was looking at the photographs on the desk showing Catrin talking with Michael Yau. The SIS man continued where Barlow had left off. He touched the top photo.

"The man here is a friend of Jian Li Yeung's father and a member of a Chinese triad based in Hong Kong, called Four Square. We are well aware of the friendship between Daniel Yeung and Michael Yau. It took us some time, but we worked out the particular nature of the friendship. Do you have that background?"

Catrin didn't like the way in which Drew said 'particular', as if it was sinister in some way.

She answered, "I believe they meet weekly or thereabouts with a third friend called Enlai Lin, in a bathhouse in Kowloon."

He nodded.

"A bathhouse, yes. Their meetings are in a private room. We can find no involvement of Yeung or Lin with our primary target, the triad; at least, nothing to tie them in, as yet."

Catrin switched her gaze to Commander Barlow.

"My friend's parents are devout Methodists. I have met them twice now during visits to Hong Kong. On my second visit, Jian Li's wedding was held at their church. My friend says her father meets Yau and Lin for company, for social interaction, as both men lost sons in a fire at an apartment in Kowloon many years ago. Daniel Yeung was working as a fireman at the time and was involved in the response to the fire. His leg was damaged severely trying to rescue the two boys. The weekly meetings of the three men started sometime after that."

"Six years ago I met Jian Li during the investigation into her missing brother, Han Yeung and that led to our friendship. As you may know, if it is in the file, Han was murdered in Wales. So all three men have lost sons now. It underpins the relationship. At least, that is my understanding."

Commander Barlow was giving little away but his eyes flicked to check Drew's reaction. Catrin got the impression that this was the first time the explanation had been given to the senior Scotland Yard officer.

Drew looked impassive. "Which brings me on to this," he said, pulling a multi-page memo from his file and passing it over to her.

Catrin caught the header and looked up, turning the document over, placing it face down on the table. She said, "It has a security 'flag'. I wasn't even entitled to read these when I worked in the office of Assistant Commissioner Hunt."

"You can read that one," said Drew.

She looked at Commander Barlow. "If so, please could you authorize this?"

She slid the document, face down, to the senior officer.

Barlow smiled, whispering to himself, "Quite right, really."

He turned over the pages, took out a pen and wrote something on the top page, then signed it and dated it, returning it to Sayer. Catrin started to read it carefully, taking her time.

It was a joint memorandum from DCI Coltrane and DCI Worsley, Coltrane's counterpart heading the Art Crime Unit, the ACU, in Serious Crime Command. Dated years ago, shortly after the close of the Han Yeung investigation, it went into some detail regarding a number of events indicating that someone in Hong Kong was interfering in the investigation. Whoever it was, the purpose appeared to be one of vindication, to show that Han Yeung was not involved with any criminal activity.

Catrin saw at the bottom of the second page an annotation, presumably by someone in SIS. 'Yau with Four Square most likely candidate'. That was dated about six months later. She wondered, hiding her apprehension as much as she could, what this man Drew would turn up next from his file folder. She knew more about Yau than she was prepared to admit.

But what she said was, "I never saw this at the time. I was new to art crime and the ACU. I was assigned to work with DI

Marshall and he and I talked about the fact that someone other than the Met or the Swiss police were flushing out the stolen paintings; that was clear. But we never put our finger on who did that during the investigation. The arrests of Parry and Williams were the closure point for us."

Drew replied, "I am quite aware of that. But it put the name of Four Square in front of us and we filed it. It came back in relation to another problem. Now, our proposal. I will explain in outline the job we would very much like you to do. And you won't get more than an outline unless you accept the offer, as you can understand, I am sure."

I am not sure I want an offer at all, she thought. I would be happy to leave right now.

~~

After leaving Barlow's office, Catrin first went to the cafeteria to get a cup of fresh coffee so she could drink it in peace and think for a few minutes before heading back to the Art and Antiques Unit area; back to reality. She was somewhat overwhelmed by the proposal that had been made.

When she returned to work, Coltrane's office door was open and there was no-one with him. Seeing her, he silently beckoned her inside and shut the door.

He said, "I suppose you can't say anything, from what Barlow said, but this is quite out of left field, Catrin. I had no warning. The man in the photograph is connected to Jian Li Yeung in some way, I take it?"

Catrin shook her head. "Not really; very peripherally at best. I met him only once at the wedding. I can tell you what I know about that, at least."

Meaning, of course, as Barlow had admonished her, she couldn't tell her boss anything else. They both understood that.

"I became friends with Jian Li during the Russian paintings' case tied to Han Yeung's disappearance, the one that brought me into Jane Worsley's team. Li told me her family story afterwards. Jane knows it already. Jian Li's father now co-owns a high-end tailor's shop in Hong Kong. But at one time after he left school he was a fireman."

She took him through the background of the relationship.

"I didn't say upstairs, but the man called Enlai Lin is a shipping executive and is very wealthy; probably Yau is, too. Lin helped Jian Li's dad enter the tailoring business."

She paused, sorting out her words carefully, deciding what to say. The meeting with Barlow and Drew was running through her mind.

"Daniel Yeung met them again by chance at a bathhouse which Lin and Yau use, one that's quite upmarket. The two men had stayed in contact after their sons died, despite their different backgrounds. Yeung had gone to the bathhouse by coincidence, Jian Li said; it was a recommendation from another fireman, therapy for his leg pains, the leg damaged in the fire. They all started meeting weekly thereafter; just to talk, not about business, just... about family and life. With the death of Jian Li's brother in Wales, all three have a more common bond now. It's a social meeting of three men, that's all; one a tailor, one a shipping executive and Yau, apparently a triad member. It is strange, but I think that is all it is."

She paused again and Coltrane waited.

"Commander Barlow knew about the intervention of someone Chinese in the Han Yeung case from an internal communication. That seemed to have reached SIS, who identified the possible link to Michael Yau, which would fit, of course. We knew someone was interfering in the investigation, if you recall?"

You should, she thought; you and Jane Worsley co-authored the memo back then which led to the problem I have now.

Coltrane nodded.

Catrin finished with, "Other than that, and what it has led to, I don't think I can say much more. I have to think about a proposal made to me and get back to Commander Barlow."

He looked at her. "But, whatever it is, you aren't happy about it, are you?"

It's that obvious, she thought. She wasn't sure what else to say to her boss.

"I'd better get back to work, think about this stuff later, once it has settled a bit."

He nodded.

As she stood, Coltrane said, "Have you anything special on the agenda today?"

Catrin was still thinking about the meeting upstairs.

"Mark is away now at his brother's wedding and Isabelle is out on a case assignment; I was planning to catch up on the developments in the Nahigian brothers' file, talking to FCO."

Detective Sergeant Mark Harper and Detective Constable Isabelle Howlett were Catrin's team members. A recent investigation had led to the prosecution of a pair of art thieves and smugglers, Kristoff and Jorge Nahigian, who owned a warehouse in Acton. It had come to a screeching halt as the two men, Armenians who had entered the UK on fake Polish passports, had broken their bail and fled. They were now holed up in the Republic of Moldova, outside the more workable Schengen country extradition arrangements. The discussions with Moldova were now bogged down at the Foreign and Commonwealth Office.

Coltrane wrinkled his nose and forehead.

"Ok, check it, but don't make a meal of it; you'll brood. Come with me later to Horseferry Road, to the Channel Four studios. I am on a panel interview there on the free port issue. I'm supposed to be representing the Coltrane Foundation, not the Met; but doubtlessly they will try to spear me on what Art and Antiques is doing or, in their eyes, failing to do about art being moved out of the UK into foreign bank vaults. A second set of eyes and ears would help."

The Coltrane family was wealthy and for decades had supported an art foundation. Neville Coltrane was heavily involved in its activity, as well as being a police officer.

Catrin's expression must have shown her wariness about getting involved in the media issue. "OK, if you say so. But what's that saying? Bad news comes in twos or threes?"

"Threes," responded her boss, promptly.

At which point, Vicky, Coltrane's administrative assistant, knocked and popped her head in.

"Sorry to interrupt, but I have had Gravesend call twice now this morning, Catrin. You were due for AFO re-certification today and the range is wondering where you got to. It will have to be re-scheduled."

As a trained personal security officer in her last role, Catrin was expected to maintain her Authorised Firearms Officer capability even though her current role did not require her to be armed. The Metropolitan Police Specialist Training Centre, MPSTC, was at Gravesend; it included firearms training.

Her face showed her surprise. "I didn't even have it in my schedule, for some reason: I must have missed the message. I'll call them."

"There!" said Coltrane, with an apparent sense of satisfaction. "Threes; like I said."

2 DREW

'The proposal' had been made as Stephen Drew interlocked his fingers and leaned forward towards Catrin, almost conspiratorially.

"The Four Square triad is mainly involved in commercial espionage; information theft. The biggest problem they have presented for us in the UK so far has been the Cramer-Moring debacle."

It was probably the talk of his club over folded Financial Times, she thought. I may have to tell him I don't have a club, just a pottery workshop.

But her non-reaction led him to explain more fully anyway.

"Moring Technologies Ltd. from Yeovil and an Australian company called Cramer Associates are in a joint venture; an advanced production process for greening the plastics industry, something about energy reduction. It took years of research. About the time you met Miss Yeung we found out that someone from the Four Square triad was working at Cramer's head office in Sydney.

"Less than a year ago, the Chinese revealed that they have a full-scale reactor built and operational while we and the Aussies are still sorting out the wrinkles in our scale-up plant. The Chinese are expanding the use of the technology and offering to trade it with others - and it's ours. The Four Square operation stole it and sold it to them.

"This triad has its fingers in a number of other pies, too, we believe. Unfortunately they are proving almost impossible to infiltrate. We need access."

If he thought he was explaining things clearly, Catrin's face showed to Commander Barlow that he wasn't.

She asked, "And how does that affect me?" just as the senior police officer, anticipating her, said, "They need someone trusted by key players in Four Square to assist with the infiltration of our people into their sphere; to provide a *bona fide* and help smooth the process at the entry point."

She could guess at possibilities but wanted it explained.

Drew nodded vigorously. "Right. First off, we have this man Yau's granddaughter now studying in England and, we understand, she will also work with you and your colleagues. One possibility is to provide another student for your studio who is also in need of mentoring, so to speak, to work their way into Miele Yau's confidence."

Catrin sat back, a little startled.

"I don't see how putting one of your people in touch with a student here will help much. My understanding is that Miele is passionate about becoming a professional ceramic artist. That is how we met."

Michael Yau had first approached Jian Li to introduce his granddaughter to Catrin and Jean Hughes, Catrin's artistic partner. Jean was the co-owner of a boutique pottery located in Spitalfields Market called the Cwmbran Kiln, shared with her partner in life and business, Melanie Farrar. Miele Yau wanted to establish herself as a ceramic artist and have a studio in Hong Kong, where she had been studying. Currently she had a placement for a year at the Royal College of Art in London.

The fact that Sayer and Hughes were a team, rather than an individual artist, had caught the student's eye; it was the way she wanted to set up her own studio once she qualified. That had led to a meeting between Jean, Melanie, Catrin and Miele during the visit for the wedding.

Drew smiled at her. "Our work is much more subtle than the world of fiction presents and we are in for the longer haul on this one. It will be up to the agent or agents to leverage the contacts."

He spread his fingers, stretching a little, offering enticements.

"We are also thinking about other things; such as getting you closer to Michael Yau. A secondment to work with art crime people in the Hong Kong Police, perhaps; ways to build on your reasons to visit your friend Jian Li more often, which we would fund behind the scenes, of course. Perhaps getting your art noticed out there; a gallery exhibition, for example. It will give you reasons to visit more frequently and we will guide you on how to build your relationship with Michael Yau and others while you are there."

Drew glanced across at Barlow and then focused again on Catrin.

"There could also be opportunities for more rapid promotion for you arising from all of this, don't you think, Craig? You will clearly still be a police officer; nothing undercover, nothing dangerous - well too dangerous; none of this is without risk, as you can appreciate. You won't be an SIS operative, in that sense. Just, from time to time, we will ask you to assist us in building relationships. It's as simple as that."

She looked at him then at Commander Barlow, who hadn't leapt into the breech to talk about promotion. He was quite unreadable. It didn't seem simple at all to Catrin.

Drew said, a little ruefully. "Getting closer to Yau and perhaps others, helping us introduce our own people to them along the way will be crucial work in our fight against organized crime."

He sat back, his pitch delivered. "Will you do it? Do you need to think about it a little?"

Catrin blinked.

"Yes."

Drew said brightly, "You'll do it?"

"No, sir. I meant, yes, I need to think about this... more carefully. It is a lot to absorb."

She was going to say 'a hell of a lot', not 'more carefully'. It was starting to horrify her; getting involved with a clandestine operation to use Li and her friends and Miele. The SIS man was looking a bit disappointed, she thought. He probably wanted her on a plane to Hong Kong tonight, complete with codebooks hidden in her underwear.

Drew said suddenly, "Of course, we could pursue other avenues, but this is a particularly strong opportunity. A police officer has certain training and experience that would assist a great deal. Moreso than, say, a lawyer, for example."

His gaze seemed to penetrate Catrin. She thought his expression was the equivalent of offering an enticement with one hand while holding a whip in the other. The import of Drew's comment hit her; 'a lawyer' as an alternative. Could SIS be thinking of trying to recruit Li directly as a fallback option? That chilled her even more.

Then his face softened. "We recognize that this is not easy; nor impersonal. In the Met, if you find yourself having a personal involvement during a case you have to declare it, right? A family member or a colleague suddenly appears to be the subject of an investigation and you are probably moved off it so there is no sense of conflict of interest."

He smiled at her warmly, even sympathetically, it seemed. "In my world it's different; deception or secrecy is called for and we need people to get close to those who pose a risk to our interests. It is harder, but our sense of duty has to carry us through it. I hope it will for you."

He stopped, waiting for any further comment from the younger police officer, to see if his words had tilted the balance in her decision-making. Other than she looked troubled, her face didn't change, he thought.

Commander Barlow suddenly sat forward, energized. He said, "Well, I think that about wraps it up unless you have questions now, DI Sayer? No? I will look forward to hearing further from you, then."

Drew said, "Let's say within a week, shall we? Take some time to think it through."

Barlow said tersely, "You made your case, Stephen; let's just leave the officer the time she needs. As you said, this is a long haul item. She can always come back with any questions of clarification, as well, before she decides. Through me, of course. We agreed that."

Catrin saw them exchange less-than-collegial glances. Then she stood up.

"Thank you for considering me..." was all she could think to say, although she didn't mean it. She would have preferred to let out stream of Welsh swearwords followed by a scream of frustration, but she wasn't a screamer anyway. She looked at Commander Barlow and beat a hasty retreat for the door.

3 HORSEFERRY ROAD

"I am sure that I have seen you here before, but I am trying to recall the context. Sorry, I should have said; I am Trish Douglas, part of the production team."

Catrin was standing with others outside the recording studio at Channel Four headquarters on Horseferry Road. They were watching the recording session on the free port art issue taking place on the other side of the glass wall, the sound within coming through a nearby monitor. Neville hadn't seemed bothered about it at all. Rather him than me, thought Catrin, as Coltrane had been taken away 'for preparation'.

The woman who had approached her was looking directly at Catrin's face. They were about the same age, Catrin thought.

"I am Detective Inspector Catrin Sayer. I'm here with Neville Coltrane; he's in there. You have a good memory. I have been here several times in uniform, as an aide to Assistant Commissioner Hunt. She has appeared -."

The program assistant nodded, interrupting her. "Yes, Sandra Hunt has been on the program quite a number of times over the years representing the Met. You were the officer with the gun; the security person with her. I recall now. The regular clothes threw me, but not the face."

She smiled.

And the scar on it, thought Catrin. You remembered the uniform, the scar and the gun. People do.

Catrin had been watching her boss. As he had predicted on the drive over, he was being set up as the villain of the hour by the host, Nicholas Foley. During the preparations for the recording of the panel discussion Foley had portrayed it as the 'sad state of fine art these days, with most of the good stuff not already in museums now being locked away in free port vaults by investors'.

Foley had prepped the panel members by saying, "Our researchers have identified the values, in millions, of art once on display here, in galleries, private homes and National Trust properties that has been sold or moved out of the country. Who owns it now is not the issue; that it is locked away in storage as investment capital rather than visible as art is the thrust. I will be asking you, Tim, as an artist, your feelings on that. For you, Mary, as a member of parliament with previous involvement in parliamentary committees on art, I will ask about what is going on to deal with this art exodus and you, Neville, as an art owner and art loss detective I'll ask for your view. It should lead to a fine discussion, should it not?"

Neville had just responded, "I was invited to represent the Coltrane Foundation; that's why I am here."

Foley had just smiled.

Douglas turned, looking back at Catrin. "Unfortunately your boss is going to be on the defensive a little, the way this has been set up, you understand."

We know, thought Catrin. A Labour Party MP who can claim her party is not in power, a bitter old painter past his prime with a score to settle against the establishment and a wealthy art collector who happened also to be a detective leading the elite Art and Antiques Unit of the Metropolitan Police.

"So why did you agree to participate?" she asked Coltrane, as they went by taxi to Horseferry Road.

"Because it is an important issue," he responded.

The artist, in his first round of comments, had already implied that the henhouse being guarded by a fox was part of the problem, clearly alluding to Neville.

The Labour Party representative was animated now, playing to the camera. What you see on television, Catrin knew from past experience, appeared artful or contrived when seen close up. Two years of media issues with Hunt had shown her that.

Mary Gallant said, "It's disgusting; all these national treasures being sold off by rich people to rich people. They keep them in bank vaults and no-one in authority is doing a damn thing about it. It's a scandal; totally against the national interest."

That's the second time I have heard that phrase today, thought Catrin; it's beginning to lose any meaning. A similar thought must have crossed her boss's mind, sitting in one of the fancy leather seats on the small stage where the panel interview was being recorded. Coltrane had let out an audible sigh as the MP finished her statement.

Foley, happy with the energy of the discussion, turned to focus on Coltrane, as cameras lined up on him.

"Neville Coltrane, you, or your family I should say, through the Coltrane Foundation, have a choice slice of valuable art hidden away from public view and you have the added insight of a being a police officer specializing in art crime. What do you say to assertions by Mary Gallant and Tim Colman about the lamentable state of things; the best of British art hidden away in tax havens, reduced to commodity items. Why don't the authorities do more?"

Coltrane didn't hesitate. "I completely sympathize with my friends here about the amount of art being stored away from view; it is very sad and, of course, it is counter to the original purpose of any artist."

His reply seemed to catch the other panelists and the interviewer by surprise. The MP actually smiled at him until he added, "Of course, fine art will always be a mix of works in publicly and privately held locations and one cannot generally tell a private owner what to do - unless the work is deemed of specific national value, precluding its export, for example.

"In my own case, or should I say, that of the Coltrane Foundation, we do not use free ports or their ilk. We celebrate the art we own, have the privilege to look after. We keep it in our own homes or loan it to galleries here and abroad for exhibitions. It is very fulfilling for my family to see these works enjoyed by many others."

He smiled, looking pleased with himself.

The interviewer, sensing he was losing his villain of the session, said firmly, "But the failure of authorities, including the police forces, to stop this drain of works of art into foreign vaults is true, is it not? Do you accept that?"

Coltrane's smile didn't fade. "Nicholas, you invited me on to the program to represent the Coltrane Foundation, as you know; not the Metropolitan Police Service. But I will give a personal answer, as a policeman with some experience in this area, one which I think is consistent with the Met's position."

"Nice," whispered Trish Douglas into Catrin's ear. "He made it clear he is not speaking for the Met then he does anyway!"

"The Metropolitan Police and government departments such as HM Revenue and Customs have to deal with specifics, not generalities. We must work within the laws that apply to customs warehousing facilities - what you would call bonded warehouses - in the UK. Items moved legally to storage in bonded vaults in, say, Geneva or Hong Kong become subject to foreign laws. We work on facts, on any basis for charges in UK law, as I said. And the Metropolitan Police takes this role very seriously given, as you said during the opening of this article, the high economic impact of art crime."

Nicholas Foley came back, "Do you have any specific examples to back up that assertion?"

He was sounding slightly argumentative.

Coltrane responded, "None that I can share; I don't represent the Met here, as I said. But if you want chapter and verse on a recent and very relevant example of art issues in free ports, you should have invited Jasper."

"Jasper?" asked the interviewer, with a sense of dread rising in his voice as he realised who Coltrane meant.

"Jasper Beaumont, your executive producer. He and other members of his family were recently featured in an article in ARTNews on the works they owned and stored in the La Praille facility in Geneva, as I recall. They have much more experience of the value of bonded warehouses than I do."

As one, the eyes of the two other panelists turned from watching Coltrane to stare at the interviewer. The MP fired off her inevitable question. "And why didn't you invite your boss, Nicholas?"

Catrin said to the program assistant, "I am not sure I agree, regarding your earlier comment about Neville being on the defensive…"

"Oh, hell," said Trish. "Jasper will be absolutely livid."

~~

There was some continuing argumentative discussion between the artist and the MP after the recording was over as they left their seats. Nicholas was thanking them for appearing, as was Trish, now in the studio. Coltrane said nothing but was all smiles.

It was evident that production staff now wanted the studio cleared; technicians were already disassembling the standard backdrop in preparation for the next use of the studio.

Coltrane came out and said to Catrin, "Not too bad, really, although I will probably hear about it separately from Beaumont. Let's go."

"You did sort of drop him in it." She smiled.

"He was the one who twisted my arm to appear. 'Nothing to do with the role at the Met, Neville, honestly', he said. Well, he didn't convey that to Nicholas Foley, did he? So he gets what he deserves. Now, I have had an idea."

She looked at him, unsure of the context.

"Let's go to the coffee bar on the mezzanine, I will tell you there."

Coltrane said, "About this offer this morning. I don't want you to let it fester. I know it can't be discussed but… you may want to mention something; what I don't know, but something to your old boss."

"AC Hunt?" She was surprised at his recommendation. Going above Barlow's head would only bring Hunt and Tom Sleiman, the assistant commissioner responsible for areas including Trident, into a discussion.

He laughed briefly, a joke she didn't see, and then said, "No, not her. I was thinking of DCI Worsley."

Her first boss after leaving the Brixton borough.

He said nothing more but his expression conveyed it wasn't an idle suggestion. Then she remembered that Jane Worsley's boss, Superintendent Jack Taylor, called SIS 'our slimy friends'. MI5 were his 'slippery friends', apparently a little more acceptable to him. Now she wondered why Taylor thought SIS to be 'slimy'. When she first heard him use it, she saw it as part of the 'Yorkshire blather' he put on at times. But perhaps there was more to it.

Coltrane suddenly looked up as someone approached.

"Jasper, how are you? Can I introduce my colleague, Catrin Sayer? She works with me at the Met and is an artist in her own right."

The tall, casually but well-dressed man who had joined them smiled at her briefly and said "Hello."

Then he turned to Coltrane and said, "Neville, thank you for appearing, but can we have a word in private, do you think?"

"About me dropping you in it, you mean?" said Coltrane, unperturbed.

Beaumont smiled again at Catrin, the message clear; he wanted her gone or Neville hauled away.

"I'll see you tomorrow then, Neville?" she said.

Her boss nodded, signifying it was fine; he didn't need her

any further.

"Think about what I said," was his parting shot as Jasper Beaumont gently steered him back into the labyrinth of Channel Four to exact his revenge, whatever that may be.

~~

Across London that same evening, in Stratford, Lena Shannon heard the front door of her flat open. It could only be one of two people who had keys; her 'landlord' Jalaj Ranjani or her new boyfriend Malav Rai. As she was expecting Malav and knew that Mr. Ranjani would never come without ringing the bell and waiting, she called out.

"I am in the bedroom, just finishing getting ready," she called out.

Rai was in his late-twenties and he considered himself to be smooth, capable and moneyed. How he came by the money, he would never say outside his business acquaintances these days, but there was a time in parts of Leytonstone when anyone in need of hard drugs could be given his name. Now he had progressed and ran others in that line of work. Lena was a user of his wares these days.

He remembered the first time she sniffed a line of coke, her laughter that, 'if her dad knew, he would give her hell'.

Malav was in two minds about it; he didn't want hell from her dad - or from Mr. Ranjani.

'I just want to try it', she had said. He had explained what she needed to do, provided the line and watched the result. Later, he told her the 'secrets', as he thought of them, of recreational use and steps to avoid dependency.

"Not everyone can, though," he warned her.

"I can," she said confidently.

On entering the bedroom he saw the trouble she had taken to look nice tonight, to celebrate. A meal, a club. Then back here. A good time ahead of them. His focus moved from her to behind her head, to the painting she had placed on the bedroom wall, making him recall his discussion with Mr. Ranjani about how much his boss had spent on it.

As they embraced he said, "It's still out, I see. You said - ."

"Tomorrow," she replied. "Look, I have the case for it out ready. Tonight is special."

Five minutes later, the front door closed.

4 MIST

The following morning, Lena Shannon regained consciousness sitting on the toilet. That she had been there for a while, blacked out, was self-evident; the cold from the porcelain had frozen the bare calf on her left leg and both her thighs were numb from the pressure of sitting on the hard toilet seat.

She stood up unsteadily, pressed the flush and pulled up her underwear. As the feeling returned in her legs, she limped for a step or two over to the washbasin. After washing her hands, Lena ran some cold water, cupping a little to her parched mouth, in the process soaking her chin and splashing her T-shirt on one side. She didn't feel too steady.

After a moment, she pulled the T-shirt off and put on the terry towel bathrobe hanging from the hook by the door. She was shivering from the cold or from withdrawal; or from both, most likely. She had traveled this road before.

Lena walked back into the bedroom and saw Malav sleeping like a baby on the other side of the bed. Sleeping or passed out, she wasn't sure. She went over to the dresser where, when they returned from their night out, she had the presence of mind to pour a large shot of vodka in a glass and place a bottle of tonic water and two pills beside it for exactly this moment. Her past experience had taught her to prepare well and last night had been wild. She needed to ease her way back, was her thought, not hit withdrawal hard.

The pills swallowed and the oh-so-familiar taste of the vodka and tonic in her mouth, she climbed into the still-warm bed, lay back and, on impulse, used her thumb and first finger to nip Malav on his shoulder blade to see if he stirred. Not a blink. She pinched him harder; too hard in fact, as the finger-nail cut the skin, a tiny line. It took a moment until blood came, a small line with a blob at the low end.

She lay there as the morning jolt kicked in and took in the painting on the wall opposite, trying to enter her magic place. It was a lake scene, Loch Lomond; not one she particularly liked; but a lake, nevertheless. It helped her at times like this, when she had to face reality again. When she was clean and sober she thought of the painting as too childlike; an image, with thick black lines accentuating the features of the landscape and the houseboats on the water.

The weak morning light of winter coming through the window was just catching the left side of the painting, heightening the colours. By late afternoon the effect would be reversed; the sparkles and reflections from the over-lit strokes of oil paint would be on the right. It was part of its meaning for her.

She half-closed her eyes and focused on the images of the two boats in the foreground. Knowing the scene was one her father liked was a component of it, she knew, and if his boat moved, then the chances were high that her mother's paler boat, a little further into the painting in perspective, would do so also. That was the great, secret pleasure; seeing them move closer to each other and eventually tie up side by side.

Sometimes it simply happened. At other times she mentally walked closer to one or the other, although she was a little leery of doing that. On more than one occasion she had found herself lying across the bed at a strange angle. Once she had come back to reality with a shock as she landed on the bed-room floor. It was best to stay still, she had admonished her sub-conscious.

One trick her imagination played was to conjure up a lake mist, rising along the water, billowing in thicker and thicker until the hull of each boat was obscured. Then she rose above it as if she was absorbing the scene over a band of cloud. The upper portions of the houseboats seemed much smaller then; little cottages in the soft ether as they edged closer to each other.

Today the light on the mist was wonderful, as if it wasn't reflecting from above but radiating from below. She looked across at the more distant houseboat, suddenly hearing her mother's voice. The voice was recognizable and saying something, words deep within her memory. But they floated in tantalizing fragments, a word here, a phrase or two there. She needed to get closer.

As she concentrated on the painting, Lena felt herself moving closer to it. The other houseboat was in motion so she was moving too, she realised abstractly. But it didn't matter.

The mist was uneven now, not dropping much but billowing up, covering her head and making her stretch to see and hear. But there was no impediment; it just needed a little effort. Part of her mind registered that her bare feet were moving across the hardwood floor. As she got closer and finally recognized the words, her hands and feet told her that she had opened the balcony door and was on the cold concrete outside. All she needed was to keep her head above the mist and listen, to concentrate on that something so special and precious deep within her memory.

She heard her mother perfectly as she climbed up a step, head above the mist, her eyes on the black outline of the houseboat door ahead of her. Then there was a noise behind her, a touch, as Lena Shannon took one more step and sank into the billowy mist.

~~

After a broken night's sleep, Catrin called Barlow's assistant on arrival at the Yard.

"Lorraine, could I get to see Commander Barlow sometime please, just for five minutes?"

Adams replied, "He is in meetings this morning and leaving for... well, it doesn't matter. He said I had to give you priority if you called. Come up now, can you? I will pull him out of the meeting he is in."

"Sayer. What can I do for you? Thought about Mr. Drew's proposal?"

Commander Barlow was looking at her as he entered his outer office from the corridor, signaling her to follow him into his inner sanctum. From the expression on his face, Catrin thought that he was assessing whether or not she had made a rapid decision. Barlow put down the file he was carrying and pointed to the tray with the coffee, inviting her to join him.

As she moved over, she said, "You said I could ask any questions of clarification, sir."

"Right, I did, I did. What do you want to know?"

He handed her a cup and saucer and carefully poured the coffee. "Milk? Sugar?"

"No sir, thank you. So would I be working on projects with you and your team, then? Seeing as you are working with Mr. Drew on this project. That's the first question. I only have two, sir. I won't take up much of your time."

He looked at her then glanced out the window, clearly thinking of the right answer.

"Probably not, Sayer, to be honest, but it is a good question and I can see the logic. A big team, Trident, with a broad role regarding organized crime. You are looking to the future I see."

I am stroking you for information, actually, Catrin thought.

He continued, "Unless an operational element has a local role for us; say this man Yau is transferred to London to head up the Four Square triad operation over here, for example. Then, of course, it would involve us. The honest answer is that the Met has no active investigation of this triad locally at present; the Cramer-Moring issue is the Avon and Somerset Constabulary's case."

Catrin said nothing, concluding that Barlow knew virtually nothing about the proposed 'joint' operation with SIS that Drew had referred to as 'we' several times. For example, he had no idea that Michael Yau had retired. She knew that from Jian Li; part of discussions in the past she had no intention of sharing with Drew or others.

"And the second question, Sayer?"

"What did Mr. Drew mean by 'more rapid promotion', can I ask?"

He looked at her and smiled conspiratorially.

"Ah, well, nothing promised, of course, you understand? No guarantees. But your co-operation would be noted by people here. There would also be feedback from SIS. Let me put it like that. It could help considerably at any interview, particularly if the position proposed not only filled the needs of the Met but that of our friends. For example, he mentioned the idea of a secondment to the Hong Kong Police. Coming back from that with a feather in your cap would automatically give you additional leverage for rapid promotion, I am sure."

He paused, assessing her, seeing if he had said enough.

"Does that help?"

She stood up, finishing her coffee quickly, placing the cup and saucer on the tray.

"Yes, it does sir, it helps a lot. Thank you for your time. But I still need to think about it more. I have a lot on my plate already with my new role with Arts & Antiques and… I don't want to over-commit and not deliver. And, frankly, my world is here, not Hong Kong, I feel."

Barlow nodded his understanding and was looking pleased that his answers had meant something to her.

"Well, let me know if you have more questions or a decision. Take your time, despite Mr. Drew pressing for an answer. It's a big issue for you, a decision like this. And it is your decision to make."

"Yes sir, thank you."

She returned to her office and took up Coltrane's enigmatic suggestion from yesterday; she called DCI Jane Worsley, the officer who had brought her from uniformed work in Brixton into the investigation of art crime. She left a cryptic message on her voicemail to set up a private meeting, asking if she was possibly available to meet after work.

As Catrin settled into her work, Isabelle Howlett popped her head around the door.

"There's a rumour circulating," she said, without preamble.

Catrin looked at her but said nothing.

"The boss is being reamed out upstairs for not clearing his appearance on the telly. I know you went with him to the studios so… forewarned is forearmed."

Catrin rolled her eyes. "He was representing the family foundation, not the Met; he made that clear. I thought he did well."

Howlett shrugged. "Well or not, he didn't clear it, the gossip is saying. You know what they're like; nobody speaks about the Met to anyone without authorisation."

5 STRATFORD

Ten minutes later Sayer was called into Coltrane's office almost as soon as he appeared from the corridor. Howlett watched, expecting some validation of the morning's rumour but, two minutes later, her team leader emerged and came across to her.

"You are with me; off to Stratford right now; a Trident case."

From the tone of voice, it was urgent.

"Which Stratford - ours?" asked Isabelle.

"Yes; Hackney Wick, not Shakespeare," was the response.

As Howlett gathered her coat and purse she said, "So it wasn't about the - ."

Catrin shook her head. "I asked him. Communications were laying into him about it, he said, when DCS Moore walked in and hauled him out. Saved by the bell, he said - or in this case, by a body and a painting."

~~

The gleaming silver BMW6 sat with its bonnet almost touching the 'Police: Do Not Enter' tape that had been stretched across the road. Catrin had parked further back on double yellow lines directly behind two patrol cars, one with an officer inside. He checked her out as the two female officers left the vehicle and Catrin showed her warrant card.

"I'm keeping an eye on the parking lot," he said. It wouldn't be the first time that officers had gone to the scene of a crime and emerged to find their vehicles stolen or vandalised.

As she walked past the Beemer, Catrin glanced at the well-dressed, middle-aged man inside. He was talking agitatedly on his mobile and glaring at her and the uniformed police officer keeping an eye on him. The wealth and luxury of the vehicle and occupant was a sharp contrast to its surroundings, a wall with washed-out graffiti hiding the 'wheelie bin' storage area for the three-story block of flats.

She looked up to the top floor balcony, where the white-hooded head of a scene of crime officer, a SOCO, bobbed in and out of sight. If Lena Shannon had landed on one of the bins, Catrin thought, she may have been badly injured but survived. But Coltrane had said that the woman had fallen directly on to the concrete, just behind another resident, a Mrs. Cluny, who was about to put her rubbish out. She heard the scream and looked up.

Once the older neighbour got over the initial shock, she told the police officer that she saw the woman come over the edge of the balcony backwards and, as she fell, two arms, a man's she thought, were visible. The noise of the girl hitting the floor was 'just horrible' she kept repeating.

The media were gathering behind another barrier, itself positioned behind the BMW. Catrin heard the clicks of camera shutters as she walked past the car and she felt more than saw the iPhones and video cameras following her as she entered.

They showed their warrant cards and said, "Art and Antiques" for the records officer, who responded, "Top floor; there are others inside. Suit up, please."

Once they had dressed in blue coveralls and overshoes, they went into a living area. On the wall were a number of engravings showing nineteenth century fashionable dress, male and female.

Howlett said suddenly, "I am not sure why we are here. If a violent crime has been committed, then shouldn't the ACU handle this?"

The Art Crime Unit supported other units in the Met when violent crimes involving art had taken place.

Catrin shook her head. "I should have said on the way over instead of talking about free ports; it's not about art involved in a crime. It's about assessing the art present at a crime scene. When Superintendent Lauder called for assistance, he said this flat is owned by a Jalaj Ranjani, a gang member who doesn't actually live here; that the deceased is a Lena Shannon, his mistress, he thought. The woman went over the balcony."

Isabelle was peering closely at one of the engravings. "So we are looking at where this Ranjani may play and work a little, too. Now I get it."

Catrin added, "Lauder is probably downstairs with the body. We are to assess the art in the flat and flag any findings before Ranjani's legal people raise objections. The man in the silver BMW is one of them, I suspect."

The authoritarian voice of the tall, thin man who entered the room at that point confirmed it.

"Yes he is and our time is limited on that score. DI Sayer? Superintendent Lauder. Be as quick as you can, but thorough. At some point we will be reminded that our search should be confined to elements relevant to the death of the young woman. You aren't after evidence related to Shannon's death *per se*, just look out for information that will help our work on the Bolan gang and Ranjani. Is there anything so far?"

"We just arrived," answered Catrin.

He nodded. "Well, I will leave you to it. See what you can find. They are going through her phone and computer now."

Catrin went into the bedroom, where a SOCO was carefully removing hairs and specks of… something from the sheets.

"Cake crumbs," answered the woman, seeing this officer's

gaze. "There is a half-eaten lemon cake in the kitchen."

The painting on the wall caught Catrin's attention. Her first thought was that it was by Leslie Hunter, a lake scene. It was one of his Loch Lomond houseboat scenes, Catrin realised, which surprised her for two reasons. If an original, it was worth a lot of money; this was top-end Scottish Colourist art. Secondly, it was positioned exactly where it shouldn't be. Given the window across, it would never receive an even lighting to view it properly. And it was too much in the direct light; over time it would damage the work. Hunter was an artist known for his focus on presenting the effects of light on objects, so it needed careful placement to get its full value. This looked as if someone had just said, 'here's a space', without any thought for artistic consideration.

She called out, "Isabelle, we need to photograph this and we will need the blind adjusting while you do."

Howlett came in with her camera. "Lovely choice of location, don't you think?" she asked, straight-faced.

The SOCO, thinking the question was directed to both of them, replied, "It's too much in the light, I think. Who did it, do you know?"

Catrin smiled. "George Leslie Hunter is the artist, a Scot. This is a very nice example of his work, if it's real. It looks it. Isabelle, let's check the back. Help me take it down."

"How do you know if it's real?" asked the SOCO.

Isabelle said, "A lifetime of training, years before the mast studying thousands of works of art and - ."

"We don't," cut across Catrin. "It looks genuine to me, but it will take more time than we have here to verify it."

By now they were studying the back, photographing dealer stamps and a number printed on the frame.

When they finished, the SOCO said, "Could we get the blind up again? I need all the light we can get to finish this bloody bed."

"Sorry," said Catrin, "We are finished here now."

The bloody bit, she thought, was the concrete outside, three floors down.

As they walked through the flat, they saw two detectives from Trident talking about an image on a mobile phone. Catrin didn't know either officer. Nor at the time did the comment from one of them, a man of Pakistani ethnicity, register with her.

"It's Malav Rai of all people, look! Shannon may have been Ranjani's mistress but she is all over Rai. What's the date stamp on - ?"

In the bathroom, of all places, they found a bronze by Frederic Remington, labelled 'Bronco Buster'. There was nothing special about it; these bronzes were sold in a lot of places in the USA and on-line. Several rings, two in gold with nice gemstones, were hanging from the raised whip in the rider's hand. The base was tarnished and the rings looked well-used.

Howlett examined the statue more closely.

"Why would you want to whip a wild horse while you are sitting on it?" she asked, rhetorically.

The painting, the engravings and the statue; that was all they found, from an Art and Antiques perspective. Only the Hunter was of significant monetary value. Catrin went in search of Superintendent Lauder, finding him outside talking to the well-dressed man who was now standing in front of the BMW. The man was holding a paper, a legal document, so she hung back, waiting. The camera shutters continued to click.

When Lauder had finished and moved away, Catrin approached and gave him a summary report, fully expecting to be released. He took a long look at her and said, "Just as well, the solicitor now has provided written authority to represent Ranjani regarding the flat, as he first claimed."

He paused, thinking. "Let your DC get back to whatever she was doing. She will be checking the background of the things you found?"

Catrin nodded. "That is our next step, yes."

"You come with me; we are going to see Mr. Ranjani. You can eyeball the art there."

From Catrin's face, he could see some concern arising. "You have something else to do?"

"No, sir; not at this instant, but I have an important meeting later on."

She had received a text from DCI Jane Worsley, as cryptic as the one sent to her by Sayer, giving a time and location to meet.

Lauder said, "You'll be free by then. The meeting with the Ranjanis won't take that long, I expect."

6 CINNAMON STREET

Catrin travelled from Stratford with Superintendent Lauder and a DC Loretta Hills to the Ranjani home, a large flat with views of the Thames in an upscale block off Cinnamon Street in Wapping. It was a half-hour drive. Lauder had a uniformed officer drive Sayer's vehicle to the location so she could get away to her meeting immediately afterwards.

Loretta Hills was young, black and of Caribbean origin from Finchley, it turned out. But she was slim and tall; as tall as Gerry Lauder. Superintendent Lauder, Catrin knew, was a long-serving member of Trident.

"We are breaking DC Hills in gently, aren't we, Loretta? Your second month now, isn't it?"

"Yes, boss, it is. Everyone is good to me; even the chief super, now I understand her."

Lauder responded, "You understand the mind of DCS Moore, do you, Hills? My goodness, that's progress!"

"Not that, boss; her accent."

Catrin smiled to herself. She had come across Detective Chief Superintendent Karen Moore previously while working for Hunt. She came from just outside Manchester and spoke very fast.

Lauder said, "Jalaj Ranjani supposedly runs a number of real estate businesses. His home is in a fancy renovated block with lawyers, doctors and bookies; and a proper villain - him. His wife is called Nirupa. She is cultured, if I can use that term. He isn't. In fact, I don't know what he is, to be honest, other than wooden, unreadable.

"They have some art in the home and the fact that you have found an expensive painting in his old flat struck me as strange. Why wasn't it in his home, I wondered?"

Catrin said, "The second flat is for what; just his other woman?"

"We think so. He has had women live there in the past. A couple of years ago the Vice Squad did a check, to see if we could leverage that against the man, but nothing came out of it. He is just a man who has an ethnically Indian wife and a series of Caucasian mistresses.

"The Stratford flat was his old home. He had his aunt living there until she died, then had it renovated and used it for his conquests, or whatever. His wife must be quite, what's the word…"

"Liberal?" asked Hills, trying to help.

Catrin smiled. "What does his wife think of all this, do we know?"

Lauder responded, "We've never asked; perhaps this is a good time to find out, seeing as the woman in his flat is dead."

DC Hills interjected. "Wait until you see the Ranjani place, it's a palace inside. I was there in my first week with Trident."

Catrin said, tongue-in-cheek, "I always knew there was a lot of money in real estate; enough for a fancy home on the Thames and expensive paintings."

Hills added, "It's all built on drug money. He runs Michael Bolan's operation while Bolan is in the nick. Do you have any background there, ma'am?"

Her voice was polite, but the undertone was didactic; two months in Trident and she was more than ready to explain the real world of 'hard' policing to the art detective, it seemed.

Catrin replied, "I spent three years in uniform at Lambeth

and Brixton, Hills, mainly in support of the drug squad. I knew of Bolan's gang; but he didn't operate in our turf. I don't recall any gang or crew member called Ranjani."

Lauder took up the background explanation. He knew more about Sayer. Hills sat back, realising she should keep quiet.

"Ranjani is from India; his wife is from Birmingham. I heard that they met at a party while she was at university. He had moved to London from Indore, in the state of Madhya Pradesh. His family was military. He tried it, didn't like life in the Indian army and fell in with some people over there who knew Bolan. What happened, we don't know, but he walked in to lead one of Bolan's crews."

"In Birmingham?" asked Catrin, surprised.

"Yes, Michael Bolan has part of the action there, too."

A crew was part of the sub-gang structure, the people on the streets that dealt drugs to the addicts, fought for territory and took the prison sentences, largely. Their linkage to the real drug operations, the gangs who imported and distributed, was always changing.

Lauder went on, "Nirupa Ranjani's maiden name was Sengupta. She comes from a strict family upbringing. Her dad's a teacher, I think. She was rebellious and Ranjani's patch for selling street drugs included part of the university complex. By the time he moved south as a full member of the Bolan gang he and Nirupa had married. Somehow he caught Michael Bolan's eye and, next thing you know, he has five years under his belt and becomes the caretaker for Bolan while the boss serves his time. We got Bolan on both tax fraud and the illegal import of Class A drugs."

Catrin recalled it. "That was the hearse arrest?"

"Right," said the superintendent. "It was the crash near the Dartford Tunnel with a coffin without a body but a lot of bags of white stuff; and with Michael Bolan driving the beast. For the fun of it, it turned out. He never was one for hands-on involvement during drug movement operations. But he fancied driving a Daimler hearse… for a laugh, he claimed later. We think he was showing his boys that he was still operational, so to speak. Fortunately for us he was a lousy driver."

He sighed.

"But Ranjani is Teflon-coated. We have nothing on him that amounts to hard evidence. We just have the informants and the tight lips on his people that we do pick up. He will probably be in a suit and tie, even at home. He could be working in the City, you would think."

They had just arrived at Cinnamon Street and the driver of Catrin's car drew up behind. They left him looking after both vehicles; not that this neighbourhood was one in which they expected vehicles to be vandalized.

~~

A muscular young Indian male opened the door and, once they had made clear who they were, he showed them in. He was quiet-spoken and his manners were faultless. Another man of similar build was inside. Catrin got the impression that neither of them were armed but they were there as guards. She wondered what a search warrant would turn up in terms of weapons.

From DC Hills' comment earlier, Catrin expected that the flat would be decked out like a maharaja's residence in India. In fact, the main area of the Ranjani flat would be closer to a formal reception room in an English stately home, she thought. The décor was English and French, in style.

Jalaj Ranjani was with his wife, him wearing slippers but no socks, with dress pants and a white cotton dress shirt, her in a pants and a silk blouse, both of good quality. The couple appeared to be stereotypical wealthy Indians in London. Both were in their late thirties and looked fit.

Superintendent Lauder explained the reason for the visit. Clearly they knew about it already if Ranjani had asked the solicitor to turn up there.

Lauder continued, "The flat is in your name, sir. Forgive me, but are you and the deceased woman involved in some way? She obviously lived there."

Before Ranjani could respond, his wife said, "My husband likes blonde mistresses, Superintendent Lauder."

She looked at Catrin, at the hair, at her scar. She added, "Some blondes at least; he prefers women who are golden blonde and cherub-faced."

I am neither of those, she is saying, thought Catrin. Somehow it didn't seem a slight.

But Jalaj Ranjani said nothing other than, "Yes the flat is mine. Miss Shannon is staying there. Was, you now say."

Lauder said, "When did you last see her?"

He replied, "I don't recall; not for some weeks, I believe."

He sounded vague.

Lauded pressed him. "Not earlier this morning, then? You weren't arguing with her?"

Nirupa Ranjani said, "He has been here all day. Ask the others, our servants and Keith Mattock, a neighbour. He came around earlier to drop off some items we left on the boat. He and his wife had been our guests, using it for a week. My husband and Mr. Mattock chatted for a good half-hour."

Hills asked for the address of the neighbour and added, "The boat is where, may I ask?"

"We keep it on the Blackwater, at the Horton Sailing Club."

Lauder said, "Thank you, we will check. It's simply routine procedure, you understand?"

He flicked a glance at Hills who went out of the room to find the others and he continued his systematic questioning of Jalaj Ranjani about the flat and his movements.

Catrin was looking at the art, mentally noting the works on display. She was inspecting carefully a small painting on the side wall as Nirupa Ranjani realised what she was doing. All that Superintendent Lauder could say later was the painting was an old one, with a medieval woman in a blue 'something'. It looked like velvet, the folds of her skirt, he said, when he briefed DCS Moore. But Sayer was on it in a flash.

"Are you interested in paintings or just looking around?" asked Mrs. Ranjani, her voice cutting across one of Lauder's questions to her husband.

"Is this a Sassoferrato?" Catrin responded. She was checking for a signature but didn't expect one.

Mrs. Ranjani answered, "No. A Pierre Mignard; bought for a song and restored for a fortune." Her voice was matter-of-fact.

Sayer said, "The ultramarine; it made me think of Sassoferrato, the paintings of his I have seen."

Ranjani replied, "That's a good call. Mignard was apparently an influence on the artist."

Catrin turned, exchanging glances with Superintendent Lauder and said to Mr. Ranjani, "It puzzles me; the Mignard here is well-placed and properly lit. Yet the Leslie Hunter painting in the other flat is in direct sunlight from the window. It will be damaged in a few years or will need restoration, which will make it worth a lot less at auction. You may want to do something about it."

She was exaggerating a little; oil paints were more resistant to UV light than most other media; it would probably be the areas of more lightly-coated canvas that would be susceptible to splitting. Her eyes moved to Nirupa Ranjani to gauge her reaction. Although fleeting, it confirmed her suspicions, but the woman recovered quickly.

Mrs. Ranjani asked, deflecting the implied question posed to her husband, "You are well-informed, I must say. Do you like the Scottish Colourists, Inspector?"

Superintendent Lauder said, "Detective Inspector Sayer is with the Art and Antiques Unit, not a member of my team. She is an expert."

Catrin moved closer to her. "I got this scar years ago chasing some Colourist paintings, in a sense; so I am not sure I do, emotionally, to be honest. Do you?"

The woman shook her head, "Not my period, no. It wouldn't fit here, I think; we should look at selling it."

Catrin asked, "And you, Mr. Ranjani?"

"Yes, Inspector, I do."

He didn't sound too convincing. She was going to prod him further on the matter but looked at Lauder who gave a slight shake of his head, so she left it there. It would be interesting to see what Isabelle turned up on the origin and history of the Hunter. It was his flat in Stratford, but she thought he was clueless about what he had on the wall.

Catrin added, "And Remington?"

His wife said, "Frederic Remington; that bronze? So that's where it is?"

She laughed. "My husband also likes cowboys. In fact, he can be a bit of a one himself."

It was a mirthless laugh. Catrin thought that the cowboy reference was more about the dead woman in the flat and her predecessors than the Remington. Whatever the relationship between the Ranjani pair, she wasn't the silent, obedient wife. Whether about the art or her husband, Nirupa Ranjani's face had a slight smirk at the end of each comment she made, as if she had some need to project an air of superiority.

Outside, by the vehicles, Lauder said, "Well, thank you for that. Other than have his wife declare that Lena Shannon was his mistress and he paid for everything, we didn't get very far. He wouldn't say who informed him about Shannon's death. If it turns out to be the man who was at the flat, I will look at charging him with obstruction.

"The brass of it; I can't imagine blithely talking about my mistress in front of my wife, even if I had one; a mistress I mean. My wife would hit the ceiling then pack my bags and throw me out."

DC Hills said, "The other people in the house and the neighbour sounded credible about him being there this morning. He does have an alibi."

Catrin added, "His wife made the point that Shannon was his mistress; he didn't say one way or the other, did he?"

"No," said Superintendent Lauder, "He didn't. Nirupa

Ranjani wasn't bothered by that, but she was bothered about that painting."

Catrin agreed. "Yes, sir, that was my read of her expression, as well. She didn't know about the Hunter. But she picked up on it fast, trying to cover her surprise. So I ask, if he has a valuable painting and is clueless about hanging it properly or how to look after it, is it in the flat for other reasons? Drugs and art…?"

The senior officer said, "You will be checking the painting, no doubt?"

"DC Howlett is doing just that."

Superintendent Lauder gave DC Hills a look and turned away a few steps, drawing Catrin with him by an arm gesture. He wanted a quiet word, was the message.

He said, "Well, let me know. The word around our shop is that you are meeting these days with Barlow. Are you looking to get into Trident? Should I put in a word?"

Catrin kept her face as impassive as possible. "No, sir; it's not that. I am happy in my role with Art and Antiques; I have only been there a few months and it's quite a stretch for me, being a DI and managing my own team for the first time. But thank you for asking."

He replied, "Well, you had better head off to your next meeting. Let me know what you come up with on the Hunter."

She nodded and took the key for her car from the uniformed officer waiting there; it would soon be time to meet up with DCI Jane Worsley to see what she had to say about Jack Taylor's 'slimy friends' at SIS.

7 WORSLEY

"Don't say anything; just listen."

DCI Jane Worsley was holding a glass of merlot slightly at an angle, pointing it at Catrin, as if admonishing her former team member to be quiet. Catrin had a large mineral water and a fiddly little teapot of hot water with an Earl Grey teabag steeping in it next to a waiting cup. They were in a bistro restaurant on Ludgate Hill, on the east side of London, well away from the watering holes used by people stationed at New Scotland Yard.

I have been listening, Catrin thought. She had met her former boss here as arranged and the woman had talked constantly during the seating and ordering stage. She's nervous, thought Catrin; I have seen it before.

Worsley had asked Catrin if she still went 'up the road'; attended services or just sat meditating in St. Paul's Cathedral, she meant.

"Yes, not regularly, just when I feel the need. You know."

In fact, being in East London already, she had done exactly that; the cathedral being only yards away. Earlier, by-passing the line of tourists, she entered and sat down in St. Dunstan's Chapel trying to find that inner peace she often found in these old walls. Sandra Hunt had been the first person to bring her to St. Paul's; the assistant commissioner was heavily involved in the cathedral community. That had been years before Sayer became her aide, shortly after the incident in Scotland.

Worsley had been meeting with someone in Barking on a case, so the venue of the restaurant was on her route as she headed back. She had said, "When your voicemail said you wanted to talk about 'slimy friends, informally' I thought we should do it well away from the office."

Catrin replied, "It worked out well; I was just in Stratford with Trident. Neville suggested it - but..."

"I thought he may have. Well, he knows a little, you see, but I can't talk much about my experience with SIS."

Catrin nodded. "You mean, I take it, your obligations under the Official Secrets Act? That's the frustration; that's what I can't talk about either."

'Ah," said Worsley.

That is when she told Catrin to just listen.

"Given your use of Jack's epithet I assume that you have been approached by them. Therefore they probably want you to do something and, as they do most of their damage overseas, that means something where you have connections they value. Just like I had in my former role in the Diplomatic Protection Branch."

She watched Sayer's face carefully as she continued, reading her.

"Knowing you, that is either something coming out of the Han Yeung incident and Jian Li, or more recently, the Ten Dragons issue, the threat from Nam Wu. So, it's probably to do with organized crime in Asia; hence triads, I would bet. They want help with some operation; probably putting microphones inside vases that you and Jean produce, making sure it finds its way into some Chinese gangster's home, to catch him talking about his secrets."

Catrin burst out laughing at the ridiculous image; she couldn't help herself.

"You have a wild imagination, Jane - ."

Worsley interrupted her, smiling. "Say nothing, I said. I was being a little facetious, but not much. They come up with some crazy stuff over at Vauxhall Cross."

She turned serious, looking away as she spoke, recalling things. "You are a police officer, so they won't be talking about money as the bait. They will play on loyalty, or duty, or the importance of the activity to the realm, that sort of thing. Noble deeds. And despite the sense that the decision is yours, I wouldn't count on them going away. By now, they will have put weeks of work into preparing this plan, whatever it is."

She paused.

"I am under similar restraints. Ironically, Jack talks about it more than me. All I can say is that, if you say yes, SIS will bring you more and more into the operation to meet their needs until whatever they want is completed - or it goes belly up. If the latter happens they will either do their best to get you out intact from the mess you may find yourself in or they will act as if you don't exist. If the latter, you will be on your own dealing with it. That's the way it is."

Catrin saw that her former boss was lost in her own experience. All Catrin knew was that Worsley had arrested someone while she was a DCI with the Diplomatic Protection Branch and it had political ramifications. Superintendent Taylor had appointed her in a lateral move to the then newly-established Art Crime Unit, even though she had no relevant specialist background. Worsley had moved from managing a sizeable team structure in DPB to head up the small Art Crime team; initially, it appeared, in competition with the much larger Art and Antiques Unit. It was not, in any sense, a career-enhancing change.

Jane continued, "So all I can advise is that you shouldn't do it unless you are really motivated by the purpose of their proposal, whatever it is; if success in that is sufficient in itself. And that's a tall order. You have to feel it personally. In your case…"

She stopped herself, realizing that she shouldn't be too

prescriptive; she was there to inform, not to direct Sayer's actions.

"But if you don't want to do it, you may need to go high inside the Met if they persist. Neville would need to get Matheson to go to Hunt or another assistant commissioner and bareknuckle fight it with senior people in SIS to make them back off. Hunt will be behind you, I am absolutely sure of that."

She smiled ruefully. "Not very positive, am I? Sorry about that but... that's the way I read it. And you have said nothing. As you should."

Their meals arrived as she finished and, until they could find a new topic of conversation more palatable, they ate in silence for a few moments. Then Jane started talking about a case Catrin was aware of.

"John attended a black tie dinner; I don't believe it!" Catrin responded, impressed.

DC John Obi had joined the Art Crime Unit when Catrin had first been promoted to the rank of sergeant there. He was a solid, steady performer but particularly hated the limelight.

Worsley said, "It took some doing. We needed someone to listen in to the Cavanagh brothers talk at an event; we are focused on them for the Maintree Estate break-in. They fancy themselves at black tie schmoozes with yesterday's pop stars, ever the big shots. John had the bright idea that they may even have one of the wives wear something at the dinner from jewelry taken at the robbery. It was a celebrity thing, with too much booze flowing, as usual. He thought I should go, or Keith. So I gave him the look. He took Aina as his dinner guest, for cover."

Aina Jinnah was the ACU's administrative officer. Her family was from Pakistan. John's parents were first generation Kenyan. DI Keith Marshall had been Catrin's first boss when she joined the Art Crime Unit as a rookie detective.

"His idea came home to roost, then. Did he do well?" Catrin asked.

Worsley laughed. "Depends on your viewpoint. They were

seated at a neighbouring table so that he and Aina could see and overhear the Cavanagh party. They did. Ozzie Cavanagh's wife, half drunk, started making strident racist remarks about some of the serving staff. Aina flashed at John that he shouldn't react - and he didn't, at first. Then, when another couple decided to leave the table, affronted, Ossie became verbally aggressive, and another person tried to intervene. It was getting out of hand.

"Aina said that John just got up, stood there like 'man mountain', put one big hand on Ossie's shoulder, forcing him back into his chair and said to him and his wife that they needed to behave or he would throw them out of the event personally. He didn't let it be known he was a police officer, but there is no way we can let him be seen by the Cavanagh lot after that. Keith is handling the case now.

"So, in one way, he didn't do well... but I am proud of him, anyway. Aina said they were awful. John couldn't do undercover work full-time."

From her expression, Catrin thought that the final comment had come from Worsley thinking about their earlier discussion again - and she had the same doubts about Catrin.

Later, as they finished the meal, Worsley said in a near-whisper, "As a last resort we could set Jack on his slimy friends, biting ankles or throats. He is retiring next year, he announced last week to some of us. Keep that under your hat."

Worsley adopted a broad Yorkshire accent, parodying her boss. "I'd rather go out with blood on my fangs..."

Catrin let out a peal of laughter, causing others in the restaurant to look their way.

"Oh, I miss working with you, Jane; for your sense of humour, not your knowledge of art. I have to say that."

8 BARSAR

Catrin's mobile rang at 1.48 a.m. the following morning. It felt as if she had no sleep at all.

It was Chris Treneer, her husband, who registered it first, seeing the digits as the phone screen illuminated. He simply sighed and switched on the bedside light as Catrin picked it up and answered. Telephone calls out of hours didn't produce exclamatory curses or questions.

It was a short call. Half-way through it Chris's own mobile rang and he took it into the bathroom to answer. His call wasn't much longer.

She said, "I have to dress and go into the Yard; right now."

"So do I," he answered. That was unusual, for him to be called in off-shift. He also worked at the Met, as a civilian computer and IT expert working mainly with PCeU, the police central e-crime unit.

Catrin added, "There's been an attack on an officer; one of the team who was at the crime scene I attended yesterday. There is a car on its way to collect me and we are not to go outside until it arrives. And I have to wear my stab vest."

Chris groaned. Catrin had an assigned vehicle, so he assumed he would ride in with her. The last time he had heard that sort of comment was shortly after they met, while she was under protection as a result of an incident in Malaysia.

It was a standard patrol car. All they learned on the way in driving along the relatively empty roads was that it was a detective sergeant who had been attacked and seriously injured; he may not make it, they said.

~~

At New Scotland Yard she was directed to an operations planning room as Chris headed off to his own unit. In the mix there she saw some of the officers and SOCOs present at the Ranjani flat the previous day. People were still arriving; some were as casually and rapidly dressed as she was but others were in uniform. Most were wearing or carrying their stab vests.

The same buzz was going around and the name Harry Barsar, a Trident officer, was identified as the victim. Catrin got some hot coffee from the urn that had been set up and had no more time to talk as the senior officers came in as a group. She saw Detective Chief Superintendent Karen Moore, Superintendent Lauder and three DCIs, including her boss Coltrane. Clearly they had come directly from a pre-meeting. In charge, however, was Commander Barlow. Just seeing him brought a slight shudder to Catrin, thinking of the Drew issue.

Isabelle Howlett arrived at the same time, saw Catrin and headed over to sit by her as Barlow moved to the microphone. He acknowledged the group and said he had a statement to make.

"At 11.45 last night, Detective Sergeant Harold Barsar was attacked by persons unknown as he arrived home. Reports indicate that two men of Indian ethnic appearance approached him in the street, where one of them produced a knife as the other grabbed his arms. He was stabbed multiple times and has undergone surgery at the Royal London Hospital. We are praying and hoping for the best.

"We suspect, but do not have any evidence at present, that it is related to the events at or following the search of the flat in Stratford at which a young woman called Lena Shannon died yesterday. Sergeant Barsar was caught on video coverage leaving the crime scene there and was featured in news clips, as were a number of you, so we are taking no chances. It could be retaliation by the Bolan gang for our actions yesterday.

"We are not ruling out the possibility that it may also be unrelated. Barsar is of Pakistani ethnicity and the perpetrators also seem to be of the same ethnicity or Indian. It may be racially motivated or possibly a terrorist action. Superintendent Lauder?"

Catrin recalled the injured officer; he had been the man talking with a colleague about someone he had identified on the phone found in the flat.

Lauder stepped forward a pace.

"Early yesterday evening, acting on the information we found at the Ranjani flat, DI Miller and DS Barsar went to a home in Hackney and arrested Malav Rai, who works for Jalaj Ranjani. We now believe that he was the person present when Shannon fell to her death from the balcony of Ranjani's flat. They were in a relationship, it appears. Whether that was a challenge to the woman's possible relationship with Ranjani, we don't know, but DI Sayer and I got mixed messages on that score when we interviewed the Ranjani couple yesterday afternoon.

"DS Barsar had already completed his duty shift and had gone home at around 10.00 p.m."

Commander Barlow took up the lead again.

"A police officer has been deliberately and viciously assaulted; an attempted murder, no less. Equally, we are not backing off on the pace or intensity of the enquiry that may have triggered the attack. All persons who were identified in the media coverage at the Stratford location will be required to wear stab vests effective on leaving the Yard. If you don't have one or yours is not currently to hand, see Constable Sellars; she is prepared accordingly.

"All officers on this investigation with current Authorised Firearms status will be armed on and off duty under Standing

Orders until informed otherwise. Those without firearms status will be accompanied by an AFO for the next day at least, until we have some sense of the scale of this threat or have arrested or identified the perpetrators. We want to maintain the momentum of this investigation but keep people safe.

"I personally will lead the investigation into the attack on Barsar during these initial stages. You will fulfil your duties, despite the circumstances and, if you are armed, or have responsibilities for a colleague who is not, you will take no chances. If approached by armed men or attacked in any way, you will neutralize the threat. No half-measures. Is that understood?"

He turned to face an officer standing to one side. "Sergeant Caswell?"

Catrin recognized the uniformed sergeant from the armory who stepped forward. He read out a shortlist of Trident officers with Authorised Firearms Officer status to go to the armoury at the end of the meeting for their equipment. Then he added, "DI Sayer, you are AFO and will be equipped first, I am told. We have also now rescheduled you for a refresher at the Gravesend range, subject to other duties."

Barlow looked at Sayer.

"DI Sayer, you will accompany Superintendent Lauder as he requires. You are under his command for the duration of this immediate operation."

Catrin nodded but glanced at Coltrane, who was looking grave; his brief nod back confirmed that he knew of this now. Catrin was now effectively commandeered. A police force was a quasi-military structure, after all.

Forty-five minutes later DC Anne Burrows was being issued her sidearm, clearly impressed at the speed of the process. She met up with her assigned partner, DS Tripp, who had also been in the video footage but had no weapons training. They were assigned to work together.

She said, "I'm surprised that art detective got assigned like that; it must be rank, her being a DI, getting to the front of the queue."

Tripp looked at her. "She was Assistant Commissioner Hunt's security officer until recently - and more. She will be looking after the Super; that's the way I read it."

"More?"

Tripp paused. "Just keep your eyes and ears open and keep me safe. I'm precious."

He had changed his mind about the comment that had occurred to him. He had heard that Sayer had not only been Hunt's security officer, she had first-hand experience in a weapons incident - and had taken out the assailant.

No-one said anything more to Catrin, but that was the way she read it too. She had always known that her training as a personal security officer could be called on again. The unprovoked attack on a member of the organized crime team had certainly raised security levels - and, as the leader of the investigation into the death of Shannon, Superintendent Lauder would be at the pointy end.

But by then Sayer and Lauder, with DC Hills, were about to knock on the front door in Ilford of a man called Donald Killam. He was the solicitor parked outside the flat yesterday. Travelling across London in a police car at four in the morning with lights flashing was a lot faster than at any other time.

~~

Lauder had told Sayer on the drive over that Killam was a sharp one to deal with. He had been Bolan's legal counsel for some years and, while the gang boss was serving his sentence, he acted for Jalaj Ranjani.

The home was a large, older home in Fairway Gardens, a street in which most of the homes seemed to be well kept and where front gardens had been sacrificed to make paved parking spaces. Hills started to get out of the vehicle as Catrin said firmly, "Wait!" She exited herself and first checked the surroundings before giving the all clear. Hills looked at her, recognizing belatedly that the art detective was acting in a different role.

As Hills rang the doorbell, the phone rang inside; Lauder was calling Killam also.

Donald Killam took in the dress of the officers; only the superintendent was in a suit. In fact, he was in the same clothes he had been wearing when they had last spoke together in front of Killam's BMW yesterday, the solicitor realised. The police officer hadn't been home.

The tall black detective constable who worked with Lauder was in casual clothes, as was the female officer he had first seen yesterday, but he noticed now the stab vests and the equipment belt with its firearm on the blonde woman, as she scanned the entrance hall behind him.

"You had better come in," he said, leading the way into his study.

Superintendent Lauder began, "Mr. Killam, we need to know who you talked to directly yesterday, after arrival at the flat. You witnessed officers and forensic staff entering and leaving."

The lawyer said in rebuttal, "So did a bunch of media there. They even took pictures; I didn't. So what's happened?"

Lauder said, "One of the officers involved was attacked by assailants late last night outside his home. He is in critical condition at present."

Lauder waited. He could see that the solicitor now understood the seriousness of the issue, at least from a police perspective. Injuring an officer in the line of duty was bad enough; to go after one off-duty was an order of magnitude more significant; it was predatory, a murder charge if the officer died.

Killam said slowly, "I spoke to Mr. Ranjani; he is my client. I informed him of my arrival and observations. I updated him on several occasions. I spoke to my legal secretary regarding your insistence that I provide documented evidence about my right of representation regarding the flat. She called me back with the courier information. Oh, and I called my wife to let her know I would probably be late home."

He stood still, sure of his facts, it seemed to Catrin. She was watching him carefully. Then the connecting door from a lounge to the office opened and a woman, his wife it appeared, entered wearing a dressing gown, pyjamas and slippers.

"It's four in the morning, I know. But can I offer anyone tea or coffee or something? Don?"

Both DI Hills and Superintendent Lauder shook their head, the senior officer saying 'No, thank you, Mrs. Killam."

No one else spoke as she said, "I have seen you before, Superintendent."

Lauder had been chasing Killam's clients for a long time, Catrin knew, so that was no surprise. Then she looked through the door the woman had emerged from and she responded.

"Not a hot drink, Mrs. Killam, but possibly a glass of water, thank you."

Superintendent Lauder gave her a quick glance. This was no routine visit and, anyway, it was protocol to follow the lead of the senior officer. Sometimes it was useful to accept offered hospitality and at other times like now, it was an unnecessary distraction.

And then he saw Sayer's glance.

As Mrs. Killam turned, Sayer said, "I'll follow you through; save you bringing it back."

Catching on, Lauder said to the solicitor, "If you would, sir, please allow DC Hills to check your mobile call record for the period. I saw you were using an iPhone."

The lawyer shook his head. "You have no right... as you know, superintendent. But..."

He took his phone from his dressing gown pocket and pulled up the phone call log. He said, "You can review the call and text logs for the last day, but not otherwise search the phone or take it away. Understood?"

Lauder nodded his assent as Hills checked the list, asked about one number to which Killam said, "That's my legal assistant's mobile; she was out of the office with the motorbike courier when she called."

Hills made a note of it and handed it back, just as Lauder's mobile rang and Sayer returned with the solicitor's wife.

"It seems to tally, sir," Hills said, as Lauder answered his phone.

Lauder identified himself, listened and said, "Repeat the name."

When he next spoke to Mr. Killam his voice sounded cold, brooking no leeway for evasion.

"Do you know a man with the name Arjun Sahota; yes or no, please?"

The phone was still held to the Superintendent's ear.

The lawyer hesitated. Lying to a police officer as a solicitor would bring him before the law society, he knew that.

"Yes, superintendent, I do. He is a relative of Malav Rai. Mr. Ranjani informed me yesterday evening that officers have arrested Mr. Rai. My colleague Lianne Mortimer is representing him, I understand."

"And do you have an address where this man Sahota may be found; yes or no?"

Again Killam couldn't easily bypass the question. 'I'm not sure' would only cause Lauder to repeat it or ask him to check his records. And Lauder had worded the question carefully, he thought; not asked for Sahota's address, but an address where Sahota may be located.

"I have a current address for Malav Rai and an old address of his. I heard some time ago, but do not know specifically it to be the case, that Rai has had relatives stay at that address at times. That is as much as I know. I don't say it is specifically this man's address or that I know him to be there."

Superintendent Lauder nodded, apparently satisfied with the answer and the delivery of it. "If we could get that; quickly, please."

The lawyer went to his desk and opened a file on his computer and showed Hills the address in Stratford. She read it out and Lauder repeated the address into the phone before closing the call. The lawyer said, "Can I ask why you said, 'quickly?"

Superintendent Lauder seemed to think about it for a moment.

"We are holding Malav Rai in relation to the death of Lena Shannon but we haven't, as yet, charged him with anything. DS Barsar, the injured officer, was one of my team who brought Rai into custody."

He signalled that they should leave. "Thank you for you co-operation, Mr. Killam."

He wasn't going to tell this man that the call he received was information from Commander Barlow himself. Barsar had regained consciousness and had given them the name Arjun Sahota to the colleagues waiting at the hospital.

In the car back to the Yard, Lauder closed his eyes, leaned back and sighed. Then after a moment he asked, "Sayer, the water trick; what was that about?"

"I saw another painting on the wall in the lounge as Mrs. Killam opened the door. Somewhere in the Hebrides, I think, but not one by the same artist we saw earlier, or even the same group of artists; it's by a painter called McTaggart. It turns out that Mrs. Killam sounds English but she was born in the Hebrides. Her parents moved to London when she was a young girl. Her husband gave it to her, she said, as a present.

"I am struck that two people we have come across in the last couple of days who are associated with the Bolan group have valuable Scottish paintings. So I will look into it further. It doesn't help your immediate concern, I know."

Lauder said, "But it may help our bigger issue, Ranjani and Bolan, which is why we wanted you to go over the Shannon flat anyway... so keep at it; when you aren't keeping Hills from walking into the same set-up as met Barsar."

Loretta Hills said, "Sorry, boss; I was just wanting..."

"I know, Hills," interjected Lauder, sounding tired. "If Sahota and his pal had come out of the ether, DI Sayer would have stopped them, I am sure."

Catrin said nothing. Hills looked at her, puzzled by the

different dimensions to this quiet Welsh woman.

They were arriving back at Scotland Yard just as Commander Barlow phoned Superintendent Lauder again. They all waited in the car until he finished the call.

Lauder said, "SCO19 went in, found two men and their partners at the address Killam gave us. They also found drugs and a number of knives, not of the kitchen variety. SOCOs are examining them now and say that the prelim UV check shows blood traces on two of the weapons, so far. We may have our attackers, let's wait and see."

~~

Catrin got to go home around dawn. Chris didn't. He told her, "I am covering through until normal shift change. We have a lot of CCTV and telecom work to do on this attack and we have been re-working the schedule."

By noon, when she surfaced from sleep, both the internal communications and the media were saying that charges for the attack on DS Barsar were pending against a suspect. These were made in the afternoon against the Sahota brothers and the Task Force was stood down. Catrin was formally released for normal duties. She was quite happy to return the sidearm to the armoury on arrival back at the Yard.

There she discovered that Arjun Sahota had actually confessed to the attack, a lethal combination of simple racial prejudice, Indian against Pakistani, coupled with a burning resentment of the man arresting his cousin.

There was also the element of coincidence; DS Barsar's daughter was in a dance class with Malav Rai's youngest sister, the baby of the family. Rai's mother, in her anger, had told Sahota that she knew Barsar lived nearby. Arjun Sahota had naively thought that Barsar was taking it on himself to pick on his cousin; a personal vendetta. The hatred of police in general, Pakistanis in particular and zero understanding of police procedure all contributed to the decision by the two men.

"Neither Arjun nor Pavar Sahota are exactly bright; they have no sense of reality, ma'am," DC Hills told Catrin, later. They had just learned that DS Barsar was going to make it, but there would be a long road to recovery.

"No sense at all, in them, or in what they did," Catrin responded. Her days working in a team based at Brixton Police station came back to mind; she had seen similar heartbreaking stupidity back then.

But, other than this new job to check on paintings by Leslie Hunter and William McTaggart, she could get back to her regular work, she thought.

It didn't take long to find out that was not the case.

She had settled in her office and called Lorraine Adams to schedule an appointment with Commander Barlow for a time, she thought, that would be days ahead. But she received a call back.

"He says right now, DI Sayer."

Five minutes later she was seated across from Barlow. He began by thanking her for the assistance with the Stratford case but went on immediately to say, "It's not about that, though, so, have you made a decision?"

She came straight out with it.

"I have, sir. Thank you for the opportunity to be involved in this joint operation with SIS, but I have decided not to do it. I can't work in the manner that Mr. Drew suggested, to be available on an *ad hoc* basis to facilitate contacts with Four Square.

"I am a police officer. And an artist. And I am married; my husband and I are talking about whether we should start a family and if so, when. I don't need a further complication in my life, one in which the timing, location and responsibility is so unclear. My work is policing, not undercover work related to the intelligence services even in the peripheral manner described by Mr. Drew."

Barlow nodded, absorbing her answer without revealing his own thoughts.

"Well, thank you for considering it, Sayer. You have made the reasons clear so I will pass these on, with your decision."

He gave her the impression that would be the end of it.

As she headed downstairs, she reviewed her own assessment of Stephen Drew from the one meeting they had and the advice she had received from Jane Worsley. Catrin had her doubts now, but she just hoped that it really was out of the way, behind her.

9 MOORE

Coltrane had been out of the office. He had simply sent her an email. "2.15 p.m. with Trident. We may need to re-visit assignments afterwards."

Catrin also learned that her firearms refresher training had been rescheduled now for the following week, with a flag that it couldn't be postponed further without senior officer approval. Having an officer who had experience and training in VIP personal security slipping off the maintenance schedule had caught someone's attention.

Coltrane brought her up to speed with the status of the interviews with Malav Rai.

"Trident is still deciding what further charges to bring; he has already been charged with possession of Class A drugs. They may go for 'unlawful act manslaughter' or 'gross negligence manslaughter', not a murder charge. From the autopsy and the trajectory of the fall they don't believe that Shannon was pushed. It looks more as if he reached her just as she went over and he wasn't able to get a hold of her properly."

Catrin mused on the possibilities. Neither manslaughter charge was a certainty. If he administered the drug to Shannon, it could be deemed an unlawful act. Alternatively, if he was awake and coherent, just watching while she was losing her balance on the balcony and he declined to help, it could be gross negligence. But each would have to be proven and there were no witnesses other than Mrs. Cluny at ground level.

Coltrane continued, "But your observations on the painting have stirred up Trident, I heard. At a particularly opportune time, in a sense, something that involved you previously."

She grimaced at her boss. "What now? I can't seem to get away from Trident, one way or another these days…"

"We'll hear more at the briefing. What I understand is that the National Crime Agency has been doing some retrospective forensic work - source fingerprinting they call it - of drugs imported into the UK over the last ten years. Their findings are redefining some of the transit routes and overseas suppliers, but they also recently came up with an interesting link. It appears that this man Bolan is closely linked to Dominic Connolly. You remember him, no doubt?"

"How could we forget - either of us?" replied Catrin.

Six years earlier, Catrin and DCI Worsley had been part of an investigation into a mysterious death of a retired Scottish clergyman, Andrew Gault. It led to the exposure of a fraud involving art painted by Gault's father, a former curator at the Kelvingrove Museum in Glasgow. During the investigation Catrin was injured and a bigger criminal scenario between two drug empires, the Connolly gang in Glasgow and the Milne gang in Edinburgh, was revealed. After Catrin's injury, Coltrane had volunteered to help; working with Police Scotland to bring down the key person behind the Colorist art fraud; Connolly's lawyer, Niall Irvin.

"So DCS Moore will be there and I understand that Police Scotland and in particular, DCS Strachan, will be linked in."

His expression said it all. Moore was a rising star at present, Catrin knew, younger than Lauder and half the officers in her command. As experienced as Gerry Lauder was, his boss was something of a firebrand who liked fast results. Catrin recalled that Moore had a reputation for either staying well under budget or, if she saw the need, going well over it, but she was very results-orientated. The Trident horses wouldn't be cantering on this one.

~~

It was indeed Detective Chief Superintendent Karen Moore who chaired the meeting. Her introductions were 'no nonsense' and without any grand opener. She simply ensured everyone around the table was known to her and others, and to the persons joining them via the speaker phone active in the centre of the table.

She said, "And on the phone is Chief Superintendent Eileen Strachan, Police Scotland. We have been talking a lot in the last few hours and she will kick this off."

Eileen Strachan's voice came out the speaker. Catrin hadn't had contact with the woman since Strachan had been a detective chief inspector, two ranks lower. Catrin had been a detective constable at the time. They had met on the operation that also led to her facial injury. Strachan began with an acknowledgement of the communications between the two police services and by introducing two officers in the meeting room with her. Then she got into the meat of it.

"The origin of this discussion goes back to a case only two of you were involved with directly. Neville and Catrin: how are you both?

The break in the formality caught both her and her boss by surprise, and clearly one or two in the room with them were similarly surprised that it was the two 'art detectives', not the Trident people, who were singled out. Coltrane answered briefly but far more elegantly than Catrin's, "Very well, ma'am; nice to hear your voice again."

Strachan went on, "Operation Finisterre was an action six years ago against the Connolly and Milne gangs in Glasgow and Edinburgh, an intelligence penetration operation coupled with a large drug shipment interception. It netted cocaine and other hard drugs worth eight million pounds. Even more importantly, largely due to a side issue with some paintings that involved a DC Sayer initially and DCI Coltrane later, it created the opportunity for us to provoke structural havoc in both gangs. Niall Irvin, a lawyer with the Connolly gang turned Queens Evidence and we -."

DCS Moore interrupted Strachan. "From the faces at this end, Eileen, everyone around the table has the background on that."

"Right," said Strachan. "Then we'll go straight to the issue. We knew we didn't get all of the Finisterre drug shipment. Some of it disappeared and we never found it. It was only recently, after some fancy fingerprinting by the NCA forensic people, that we could prove it went south to be part of the Bolan gang inventory. We never broke Shannon, Connolly's accountant, to give us access to the books or any information on asset distribution at all. He is in Barlinnie with another three years before a parole is possible."

The surname coincidence struck Catrin as Strachan continued, "Now Karen tells me his daughter went off the balcony of this man Ranjani's flat and Ranjani is the outside man for Michael Bolan. She had a valuable Scottish painting on her wall. So we want to stir the pot a little."

Eileen Strachan was a forceful, dominant woman, Catrin recalled, but Karen Moore was not relinquishing control of the meeting. She leaned forward, her voice focused on the speakerphone to cut off the sound as she spoke.

"Thank you Eileen, that sets the scene well. DI Sayer, you have an interim update on pertinent background information on this painting, I understand?"

Catrin began, "DC Howlett has been working this search, but our findings are still preliminary. Both the paintings, the one bought by Ranjani in the flat and the one now in the home of his lawyer, Donald Killam, went through the same dealer at a gallery in London. In each case there was an appraisal by the same man, the owner, a known and apparently reputable expert, but we have questions about that now."

Eileen Strachan's voice interjected, "A second painting? We don't know about that."

Superintendent Lauder spoke up, "My oversight, ma'am. DI Sayer spotted it in the early hours of this morning when we visited Ranjani's lawyer. She teased out the information on a painting by an artist called McTaggart from the man's wife. It was the middle of the night and... We will update you on that separately."

He looked at Moore as if it was his oversight but Hills was looking awkward. Sayer concluded she was the liaison with her opposite number on Strachan's team regarding information flow. Hills had dropped the ball. She liked the fact that Lauder took the responsibility himself.

Moore said, "Fine. But do I see you slumping down behind Gerry there, Loretta? Anything you want to confess to us, perhaps?"

Hills shot back, "Not when I have a good boss to cover for me like I do, ma'am, no."

Moore smiled and looked back at Catrin, who pressed on. "We have information from the Revenue and Customs filing. In Ranjani's case, the Leslie Hunter painting in the flat went through the same dealer, twice, a Richard Pennywell. He in turn obtained it from a man called Garrard. We think the purchase price was high; Ranjani paid the gallery partly in cash, partly by a bank transfer.

"Pennywell knew where the painting was located because six years ago he was the intermediary; he sold it to Garrard. He acquired it back then from Barhead Holdings Ltd. We understand that it is a company owned by Dominic Connolly."

"Right!" burst in Strachan. "Brodie Shannon works with Dominic Connolly and is now in prison, swept up in Finisterre. He looked after Barhead accounts, too."

Catrin smiled. She had been waiting to get this news out since she heard that Strachan was on the call.

Strachan added. "Barhead is a legitimate company owned by Connolly with another person. Connolly kept that one unsullied, so I expect all will be above board, in terms of the paperwork, taxes and so on. But an interesting connection, nevertheless."

Catrin, at a further prompt from Moore, pressed on.

"In the case of Ranjani's solicitor, Donald Killam, the painting is not by one of the Colourists, it is by the artist William McTaggart, a seascape. The lawyer's firm bought it at auction for a high price, but one that was reasonable for McTaggart's work; about £70,000. That was two years ago. Last year, Pennywell appraised it to be of much lower value, closer to £48,000. Killam then gave it to his wife as a personal gift and wrote off the difference between purchase and appraised value as a business loss for tax purposes. The painting's value at present, as best as we can estimate, is probably well above the original price at auction."

"Money laundering on the first one, perhaps; the cash Ranjani paid. Tax evasion on the second, really," Lauder said.

Catrin said, "Yes sir, the means being the highly arbitrary world of art appraisal and pricing."

Moore asked, "Do we know how long this gallery and the appraiser have been doing this, and the sums involved? There could be a lot more, I take it, if he has a larger customer base?"

Catrin replied, "Records say Pennywell has been in business by himself for seven years, but was in a partnership previously. Whether he has other transactions of this nature linked to Ranjani, Killam or others on our radar, it's too soon to tell… it's early days."

Her boss cleared his throat. "I know the man Pennywell slightly, as a dealer not an appraiser, so this is a surprise. Or I should say, I know more his wife. She is very active with various charity functions. And before Richard Pennywell set out on his own he was a junior partner at the Whitcomb Gallery. Very solid, the Whitcomb."

The Trident people looked at Coltrane as if they didn't think anyone in the art trade was as honest as he inferred them to be. Catrin was reminded that her boss may be a good policeman but he lacked the 'common touch' when it came to many people in the Met. It had been her own impression of him originally when she first joined the Art Crime Unit years ago.

DCS Moore jumped in.

"And that's where we need to plan our path forward. What we have now are two new findings. First, the Bolan gang, which operates in London and Birmingham, and the Connolly gang, which operates on the East side of Scotland, are not independent entities as we thought; they buy and sell from each other, it seems. Clearly, for some years, at least over the time that both gang leaders have been incarcerated and perhaps for some time before that. Police Scotland have offered full co-operation on this matter. A joint team will be looking into current and past supply routes, to see what we can find."

She named the two detectives that she and Strachan had agreed on, to lead this activity. Then she turned to look at Catrin.

"Also, we have just discovered a strange link between two gang members; Ranjani and Shannon, involving an unexpected development about art, loaning a flat to Shannon's daughter and a sudden death. How this relates, we don't know, if it relates at all. But Eileen and I want to stir the pot, see what comes out. Brodie Shannon must be in emotional turmoil. Ranjani had a member of his gang present when Shannon's daughter died so he must be thinking his way through this one, too.

"DI Sayer, we think that you are the right person to follow up on this second aspect. It could break open some new opportunities for us."

Catrin glanced at Coltrane. His face had clouded over. It's worth asking Ranjani, Catrin thought. He is just up the road.

She said, "It may be better, ma'am, for someone local to ask this man Shannon."

Moore responded a little more sensitively perhaps, despite never quite losing an argumentative undertone, "I am aware of your background on this; I have read the file, so I am not asking blindly. In a sense it's precisely that tension which may be necessary to provoke some disclosure."

Coltrane added, "And we have limited resources to look into it, as well."

Moore said, "It's only a visit of a couple of days or so, Neville. That's all."

The woman sounded so reasonable.

Coltrane was looking unsure. Coltrane continued, "DI Sayer was given security protection on her return from that case in response to a threat from the Connolly gang."

Strachan butted in. "That threat was dropped, we know that. I am sure Catrin will be pleased to come up and see us again; she and I can have a nice chinwag about the old days. As Karen said, having her pose the questions to Connolly's people will be more likely to cause a reaction in Shannon - and probably others who hear about it."

That's what I am worried about, thought Catrin.

DCS Moore chuckled. "Old days, Eileen? Really? DI Sayer is hardly at an age to have part of her career referred to as the 'old days' But I like the idea of stirring up things with Connolly's associates. I am sure it will get back south to Bolan and on to Ranjani. Anything which disturbs their sleep at night is a good thing for us."

But all eyes were on Catrin. She looked at Moore, recalling that the woman was a superintendent in Traffic Division at the time Connolly's gang member, Colin Cheney, was beating the hell out of her at Kinnington Church. She may have read about it in a file, but it wasn't the same. She felt more trapped now than when Commander Barlow had brought up the proposal about SIS.

10 POTTER

Isabelle was talking with HM Revenue and Customs. It was way after six thirty, late for bureaucrats but she knew her man and his timing. Howard Potter; 'her man there', as she put it to Catrin the first time they had to talk to HMRC after Sayer's appointment.

"Your man?" Catrin had asked.

"Ma main man," parroted Isabelle. "My taxman friend who tells me everything."

She had got the basic information for Catrin's brief to Trident from available records and a quick call to someone in Potter's office. Howard, her co-conspirator on defeating the silos of bureaucracy, would tell her more, she was sure.

At six thirty in the evening Howard would be finished work but waiting for the rush hour to wane a little. He would answer her call.

"So what's the Acton warehouse up to now?" Potter asked as an opener.

He meant specifically the value of the items recovered, not the progress of the recent investigation into the Nahigian brothers.

"£18.3 million and counting, all in, including the jewelry,"

Howlett answered.

She knew that something like that would probably be his first question.

"That's good," said Potter. He was always one for monetary value, not the art.

"For a grubby little electrical warehouse hiding stuff, yes, Howard. We are quite pleased with it. If we could extricate the Nahigians from their life of leisure in Moldova and put them back in the dock, it would be even better. How is your Barnstable case?"

She listened to the man detail the value of tax recovered and fines from an import-export scam that was working its way through the system. After a pause, pleasantries and inter-departmental courtship over with, he asked her what he could do for his friends in the Art and Antiques Unit.

"Can you tell me anything you have about a dealer called Richard Pennywell? We see he is registered as a High Value Dealer. Secondly, is there anything active on him? There is nothing in our system, no flags. Melissa gave me the basics on two paintings he handled."

She automatically read out the full name and current business address without being asked.

"Hang on."

She could hear his raspy breathing; the man was overweight, she knew.

"Yes, he is registered as HVD under the money-laundering regs; there are a number of reported transactions all appearing normal; taxes paid, documentation checked off, at least according to the summary page; no he has not been audited since registration. One moment..."

"His company was set up eight years ago; formerly he was with a place called the Whitcomb Gallery. Is there something we should know?"

Isabelle said, "No, we are just checking on two paintings at present, the Leslie Hunter sold to a Mr. Ranjani and a William McTaggart sold to a Mr. Donald Killam, as I said. They are in our sights. The dealer's name came up and I was just covering all the bases."

Potter said, "Those paintings are both listed here. The Hunter exceeded the cash threshold for reporting under the regs; the cash payment was £25,000 of the total price. VAT was paid. Pennywell has been quite busy, it seems, but most of the transactions were bank transfers - of fourteen recorded in the last reporting year, two were cash, the sale of another painting to a Jalaj Ranjani, presumably your man, for £38,500, a full payment.

"If I go back... hang on. It looks as if he did more transactions with Ranjani in the last three years; another three paintings and, let me check another file... two more in the year before. So seven in total to the two people you named over nearly five years, all but one of those to Mr. Ranjani. Some cash was involved on those but not much, not to cause us to worry; but some big money overall. Do you want the list?"

"Yes, please. Can you check any sales he made to a person called Bolan, if any, also; just in case? And Howard, I don't want to flag anything with Pennywell or Ranjani, so don't get interested from your end yet, if you would? If we see anything funny I will let you know. If we don't, I'll still let you know and then you can do what you want. At present there are some boats settling in the water."

Potter replied, "Fair enough. Anything else?"

They talked a bit more then closed the call.

~~

When Catrin arrived at the office the following morning, she called her team into her office.

Mark Harper had been on holiday, a quick trip to Ibiza. Mark's brother Dylan and his fiancée had taken an all-in wedding package at a resort there. Their own parents would have preferred a London wedding and the bride's parents were really hoping for a wedding at their village church, but they all flew over to have a beach wedding in Spain. After a long engagement, the run-up to the marriage had been stressful on the couple.

The best man became ill the night before the event with a stomach bug and Mark spent a frantic hour working out nice and humorous things to say about his brother, as the stand-in at the reception. Then the pasty-faced best man turned up in time for the wedding anyway, looking exhausted. He didn't eat but did a good job otherwise.

But it all went well.

Sayer brought them up to date with their workload. She and Neville had talked yesterday evening.

"We are taking on the free port file monitoring; Neville needs to show he is a little more 'arm's length' on it with the fuss after the interview. The next step is an international coordination meeting being held in Paris next week. He will bow out of it and I can't go."

"He's passing on the Holy Grail, then," said Howlett. She was sounding impressed. "I always thought he would be hanging on to the free port file. The international links; you know?"

That Coltrane was not only well-connected and wealthy but that he liked his visits to Europe was well known. The man spoke French and Italian fluently. The coordination work on free port crime had been his bailiwick, albeit that he often had Isabelle or other staff members do the tracking and detail work.

"Mark, you are with me, on a trip to Scotland on Sunday. Isabelle, you will be going to Paris the same day; or Saturday, if you want to play tourist, to cover for me at the coordination meeting. Get Vicky to do the re-ticketing and logistics for Paris. Mark, I've already made travel arrangements for you with me."

Neither of her team said anything, just looked at each other. Then Howlett said, "Me; to Paris for an international meeting; by myself?"

"I like Paris," responded Harper.

"I only went once years ago, but it's on my list, to visit with my friend," added Howlett.

Isabelle's life revolved around her work, her cat, an aunt on Canvey Island and carefully-planned trips with a friend (gender and relationship otherwise unknown, according to the departmental gossip) to devour foreign art galleries, a city at a time. These epic travel events seemed to take place once every eighteen months and each was planned like a wilderness trip to the remotest parts of the planet.

Catrin just nodded. She looked at Harper, who appeared to be similarly surprised. He had assumed that he get the Paris assignment if Catrin couldn't go.

"Next week we will be in Bonnie Scotland, Mark, for a few days; there is nothing like the fresh air of Scottish prisons in the company of your boss to make you feel alive."

She didn't give an explanation for the assignments. If questioned, she would have explained that she wanted both her team members to be able to pick up any of the work assigned to the Arts Team; it was too obvious that each saw their own role defined. But beneath it was a deeper personal reason.

She was going back to Scotland, to talk with people she had no wish to see again. Despite the comments of Moore and Strachan yesterday making light of the visit, she was disturbed. Harper was a big, fit man, young and well-trained. If anyone started anything physical with her she didn't want to be alone this time.

She couldn't have told anyone else that was the reason for her choice, other than her psychologist. But she hadn't seen Dr. Herrington for a long time now and she saw no need to call him - at least yet. She would see what her dreams were like after this set of interviews. Last night's nightmare had brought it all back.

Catrin stood up, signaling the meeting was over. She said, "But I am just off to Gravesend now. My much-rescheduled firearms refresher is brought forward again. I was told I had to get it out of the way before I go to Scotland, as I told them it can't be next week now."

She looked at the expression on Howlett's face. "Just

routine, Isabelle; they found out I was overdue, that's all."

"Glad to hear that, ma'am. It gives me great comfort."

Her voice lacked sincerity. She had heard about the things her boss had got up to in Scotland previously.

"And the latest on our friend Pennywell?" Catrin asked her.

"Puzzling, at present. The prices for the art sold to the Ranjani couple don't seem right; some are too high, some are too low. I am still looking into it. I'll summarise it for you later."

Like Harper, she was surprised at the assignments; she, after all, had been working on the Stratford case.

11 MORLEY

The hotel was in La Défense, not Paris, as Isabelle thought of it; new, not old. There had been no time at all to do any of her regular planning for an overseas trip; nor was there the possibility to involve her friend Maureen, with whom she went on holiday.

Normally they would spend time preparing for their trips; evenings or lunches together sharing what each had discovered as they planned their time and activities. But this was business, not pleasure, and she had been up to her eyes finishing the background information on Pennywell for Catrin.

The thought of sitting in an international meeting and presenting the Met update intimidated her.

In a sense, she was also reluctant to leave the Pennywell case; it had pulled her in. The additional information that Howard Potter had provided and the results of her own research intrigued her. The prices paid for the group of paintings sold to the Ranjanis were all over the map; they made no sense. She had said as much in the covering note she left with the file for Catrin to review, but they had no time to discuss it further.

When Isabelle talked with Vicky about the travel arrangements, she chose to go on the Saturday, not the Sunday. She had checked the weather, at least, and decided on the mix of clothes she would take so she could explore Paris a little.

She took the Eurostar from St. Pancras. Vicky had said she should take a taxi when she arrived at Gare du Nord; that's what Neville did. At heart Isabelle was a public transport person in cities and knew she needed to learn the Paris Metro systems for when she and Maureen visited for a holiday. She took the RER and only got lost for a minute or so in the Chatelet Les Halles station while transferring to the line for La Défense. On arrival there it was a short walk in a modern area, nothing like the Paris she recalled, to reach the anonymous-looking hotel organized for the meeting participants.

As she checked in, she was told her room would be ready in 'about an hour' and they would bring her coffee or tea in the lounge while she waited, if she wished. Standing there, deciding what to do next and how to get organized to see some of Paris, she suddenly saw a man waiting, looking at her. He was vaguely familiar, serious-looking, older than her and balding, with a moustache. When he spoke, it was obvious that he was an American.

"Hello, I'm Morley Kerswell, part of Agent Klintz' team; you and I are the only ones here today, I just found out. Most others are either staying in central Paris during the weekend or are arriving tomorrow. I couldn't be bothered staying in a different hotel for one night then change. Apparently your boss informed my boss that you would be subbing for her."

After she introduced herself, she said, "I know your face from a couple of the videoconference calls that I participated in. But I also know your name from correspondence, of course."

They shook hands formally.

Morley said, "This is your first time at the meeting?"

She nodded, "Yes. And only my second time in Paris; I had a holiday here years ago. I came early, to see Paris a bit more. But I am sorry; I don't know my way around very well."

She assumed that the American was hoping for a more

knowledgeable guide. She remembered him because he never spoke in the videoconferences but seemed the man that other FBI agents turned to for facts.

Morley said, "Well, I do, a little. So if you want to check in and sort yourself out, we can go out and sightsee together, if you would like?"

Isabell responded, "My room's not ready yet and I need somewhere to freshen up so… you shouldn't wait. I want to go out and see some art, actually, but haven't decided on anything."

Kerswell spoke in what she thought was competent French to the reception clerk and soon had a response. The man disappeared and came back with another man, obviously a more senior staff member, who said in English, "Miss Howlett is it? Yes, indeed. We are giving you a different room available now, a very nice room, with a view from the window over to the centre of Paris."

Morley said, "I will wait in the lounge. Take your time but, but if you agree, please let me take you to the gallery I was planning to visit today, anyway; Musée de L'Orangerie."

He never said a word in a work context in the past, she thought, but now he sounded like a tour guide. She, at least, knew the world inside the galleries and L'Orangerie was on her own list. Things were looking up.

~~

Almost," said Catrin Sayer, picking up her own brush.

She made a stroke along the neck and upper section of the almost identical olpe-shaped vase in front of her, finishing the uniform line with a tapered point.

"You have to force yourself to create a two-dimensional curve in a three-dimensional plane, accepting that your hand is going to give you feedback that the curve is wrong. Your eye and your hand will tell you different things. On vases that are meant to present a primary image in one direction, you have to work a little differently."

Miele Yau was nodding, getting it intellectually but her face showed that she was unsure of her capacity to emulate her teacher.

Catrin smiled at the student from Hong Kong. "But it is all about understanding and practice. I used eighteenth century Japanese woodblock print designs for practice early on. You can trace each one to begin with then try doing it freehand. It's all line work and requires care, but you can see when the image on the ceramic surface has not been true to the original print. I'll show you."

She pulled out her iPhone and tapped away at it until an image came up and she picked up a platter; an unglazed, near-white bisque, slightly bevelled.

"This is Utamaro's 'Lady with the Mirror'; it's a formal Japanese female head viewed from the rear, with the top of the kimono providing a colour contrast to the black formal hairstyle. As a series of curves in line work, it seems straight-forward, doesn't it? But getting the proportions on the curve of a platter to appear the same as the flat image is a little tricky. I'll send you the link.

"Be very light with the pencil marks, so errors will burn off in the first firing. When you have it, use the bisque pencil for the final outline, drawing fine lines for the hair contours and then give the sections light washes of colours, letting them bleed into each other in places. See how it goes."

The student was nodding, seeing the issue more clearly. "I will try that one next. It is a good idea to use these sorts of line images, I can see. Thank you."

It was Saturday morning in the Cwmbran Kiln, a boutique pottery in Spitalfields Market in London. In the months since Miele Yau arrived from Hong Kong to start her year of study at the Royal College of Art, the time at the Kiln with the owners, Jean Hughes and Melanie Farrar, had been as valuable to her future plans as her formal studies. On the Saturday mornings when the artist Catrin Sayer worked there and gave her tips or insights were also precious. Miele wanted to be a ceramic artist in her own right. Catrin generally appeared only on Saturdays and sometimes Sunday afternoons.

Miele said, "I am learning a lot from all of you. I really appreciate it."

From the shop area at the front Melanie let out a squeal.

"Jean, if Miele thanks us one more time please throw her out, or something. Give her some absolutely boring job to do. Send her to clean our flat; anything!"

Miele burst out laughing; it was not the first barrage of false annoyance from the co-owner of the pottery.

She replied, "I will try to remember. I will just say it to my aunts and grandfather and think it silently here."

At the mention of her grandfather, Catrin quickly pulled her brush off the surface of the piece she was working on herself. Long practice and experience had taught her that it was better to stop half-way than 'wing it' when she was distracted in the middle of a delicate part. It wasn't the banter. It was the word 'grandfather' - Michael Yau. It reminded her of Stephen Drew. While that was not the fault of this student, her Saturdays working with Jean on new art were not so enjoyable these days.

"I'll be away next week, in Scotland," Catrin announced suddenly, "for part of the week anyway."

Jean gave her a look but said nothing. From the front of the boutique, the shop area, Melanie said, "You haven't been back since the... no, that's right; you went back as a witness, at that murder trial."

Miele gave a quick glance but concentrated again on her work. She knew that Catrin was sensitive about the fact that she was a police officer and members of her own family were criminals, in the baldest sense. Sometimes, although she tried to show her gratitude, she wondered if it had been an error to persist with her request once she found out that there was a link, however tenuous, between her grandfather and this woman.

Melanie came through to the workshop area. "I had a call

from someone in the British Council this week asking for our current artist inventory and profile. She was Scottish, from Manchester."

Miele looked uncomprehendingly at her, working out the English.

Jean said, "The British Council office is in Manchester and the employee had a Scottish accent. And what that has to do with Catrin going to Scotland, I just can't translate."

Miele laughed. "You are funny, you two; always funny."

"What did they want?" asked Catrin.

"Our web info, our artists, did we sell abroad? They had questions on that sort of thing. She had some form to fill in. I told them and said we had a simply marvelous student from Hong Kong with us at present."

She pulled a face at Jean and smiled at Miele. Catrin smiled also at the interactions but didn't say more about it.

Later, at home after her regular Saturday run she showered and changed then met up with her husband for dinner. He had been playing five-a-side football that afternoon. Dinner out together on Saturday, unless they invited friends over or were similarly entertained, had become a regular pleasure.

As they walked back afterwards, she asked, "Do you know anything about the British Council?"

Chris shook his head, "Just what you would know; they liaise on arts and cultural exchange internationally, I think."

She said, "Melanie was contacted by someone asking about the Kiln, Jean and myself. They wanted some update on our art. The enquirer was a Scottish woman at the headquarters, she said."

Chris asked, "You think it might be SIS?"

Catrin pursed her lips. "I hope not. I wondered, while I am away up north, you being such a nosy telecom and computer geek…"

He smiled, "Could I pop round to the Kiln, check their call log then penetrate the deepest parts of the British Security Service? No. The first bit, yes; and I will see if it's legit."

"You are a wonderful man. I knew I could count on you."

She put her arm around his waist at the back and gave him a hug.

Chris replied, "You always can, you know that. Just stay out of trouble north of the border this time."

"You know me."

"That's what I'm worried about."

~~

Isabelle Howlett and Morley Kerswell had spent some time circulating in the two elliptical rooms with Monet's 'Waterlilies' - Les Nympheas. Then Morley waited, taking in one particular canvas in detail after Isabelle had spotted a space freed up one the seats at the focal centre of the second room. She sat absorbing the monumental paintings, sitting next to an Asian student lost in her iPhone. Even from a distance, Kerswell knew she was also looking into herself.

He had taken the British detective from La Défense by taxi to the L'Orangerie museum. As she hesitated and glanced in the direction of the Metro, he said, "This way we get the drive down the Champs Elysees and around the Arc de Triomphe; you will like that."

After a while she stood up, walked to see an element of one of the other Monet canvases where he saw her move a tissue to her face, after which she joined him. The bustle of other visitors circulating continued.

"Thank you for not rushing me," she said.

He smiled. "Ready for more?"

She nodded. "You were spot on with your choice of the first stop. To think…"

She let it go. To think that Monet was so old when he toiled away painting these huge canvases, a national treasure.

He said softly, "They used to be downstairs here. That's where I first saw them. There are other Monet waterlilies in the world, but none like these."

She took a deep breath. "Utrillo next?"

"Follow me," he said.

Later, they were walking in the Tuileries Gardens on the way to a small restaurant he knew.

"The Jeu de Paume museum is just there," said Isabelle.

"Yes, it is. But it houses photographs now - ."

She responded more sharply than she meant. "I know that. No, I don't want to go in just now; I am saturated with the works we have seen. I would like to see a plaque there."

Morley said immediately, "Rose Valland?"

"Yes," replied Isabelle, surprised. "You know it - and of her?"

"Oh, yes," replied Morley.

He led the way to the plaque on the side of the 'sister' museum to the L'Orangerie on the north corner of the Tuileries Gardens. It was a large stone tablet, a memorial to the woman who had been instrumental in saving thousands of France's art masterpieces from the Nazis. He translated the text aloud for her, assuming she had no French. It wasn't totally true, but her school French had long been abandoned and suffered from disuse.

"Thank you. She is something of a hero of mine. But how come you speak French so well?" she asked.

Morley laughed. "All Americans are unilingual, you mean? American English or loud American English for foreigners? I thought that characterization started with the Brits. My grandfather died as he arrived in France and my father came here a lot, sometimes with us, so it was natural to take an interest and for me to study French."

She said, less as a question, more a statement, "World War Two?"

He nodded, "D-Day itself. We need to head over to that exit now and cross over."

She sensed that he didn't want to go deeper on that one. After all, they hardly knew each other, so she talked about the meeting coming up; it was safer ground. But in Rose Valland, they seem to have a common interest.

The restaurant was as she thought it would be given Morley's prior experience of Paris. It was not that visible or expensive and its clientele was mainly local rather than tourist. If she had been alone it would have fulfilled her worst fears of travel abroad, her ability to cope feeling like an outsider. But with him there she was able to relax.

She told him a little of her previous trips, her travels with an old school friend who came back into her life a few years ago.

"Maureen works at the Law Courts in London. We both have long hours at work, so we plan our time off. We like the planning stages of our trips and getting together and enjoying the memories afterwards. I do a lot of preparatory work on the art we want to see; she likes dealing with the logistics and finding the right hotel, that sort of thing. I mean, I knew about the waterlilies at L'Orangerie; but the experience... that's what we go for, that sort of experience. I didn't get a chance to do my research on the Utrillo works beforehand."

Morley was quiet. She thought from his face that his viewpoint was different, but he didn't want to say anything.

At one point she said, "We all meet up at the reception tomorrow evening."

Her implication was that there was another day of tourism ahead.

He replied, "Unfortunately, I have things to tie me up most of tomorrow afternoon. I have to do the final compilation of our input with our team."

She knew that the FBI had three attendees and a lot to report, so preparatory internal meetings were on the cards.

He said, "But if you are free and up to it, we could go to Notre-Dame tomorrow morning early."

"It's Sunday and I am not religious, so..."

Morley replied, "It doesn't matter - and actually, it is better to be in the service than stroll around at the edges. It's about the experience. And we can grab a brunch somewhere. If you would like, I could work out some suggestions for you for the afternoon?

She was about to say yes when, instead, she replied, "Thank you; the morning sounds a good idea, but I think I will simply play it by ear afterwards."

Their discussion turned to roles and work. She was surprised to learn that Morley had no formal art training, he had an amateur interest in the subject.

He said, "I came into the team four years ago from other FBI work. There is so much coordination needed with other federal departments, state agencies, you name it. We are tied up with red tape in the US with so many overlapping jurisdictions. That's my job; to sort the coordination aspects of all our cases. I am mainly in the office these days."

It sounded boring, she thought. Isabelle realised that was the reason he never spoke up in conference calls and others kept checking with him.

"So what -?" she stopped. It was the expression on his face which told her that asking what he did previously would result in him saying he couldn't talk about it.

He deflected, finishing the sentence, "-about dessert? Good idea."

12 KINNINGTON CHURCH

On Sunday morning, allowing for the time difference, Catrin called Jian Li Yeung to find out that she wasn't in Hong Kong, she was in a home in mainland China with her husband, James Hoi. People were talking in the background.

"We are visiting some of my grandfather's relatives. James says we need to learn more about my family roots ourselves but the plane is delayed, so we are waiting to hear about its replacement."

"You have work tomorrow?"

"We both do."

A minute or two into the call Catrin mentioned she would be in Scotland for the next few days. She was leaving shortly. "I am in Euston right now."

Jian Li's reaction was, "Well, stay safe. If I have to visit you in hospital there again it will be very expensive; it's not as if I am in Bangor this time. Are you OK with it?"

"I'm fine! You sound just like Jean, as if going to Scotland is asking for trouble."

Li said, "For you, it's a possibility. For others, no… but be careful; whatever it is."

~~

Later, on the plane to Hong Kong, James said, "I heard part of your conversation with Catrin, but how is she?"

Li paused a moment. "She sounds well. She has to go back to Scotland; I told you about that experience while I was studying in Wales, going up there after she was injured. This time it is to interview one or two prisoners, she said, so there wasn't a safety issue."

James said, "I also overheard your comment that 'people in prison have brothers and friends'."

There was a moment or two of silence between them then Li said, "The timing of her call was awful, wasn't it? We had been told Daiyu dislikes 'foreigners' but her comments as I left the room to talk to Catrin… wow! Just because I mentioned it was my friend from London."

James gave a smile. "Well, she's old. Her knowledge of foreigners was all from her own parents. With life in China then, the European sense of superiority, it's understandable. Your mother said Daiyu was sensitive on the subject. Well, she doesn't like Christians much either, so she and your parents don't get along well, that's evident. But I enjoyed the talk with her. While you were out, she said that she was frightened of Europeans still, because their minds work differently."

Jian Li said, "Catrin's mind doesn't, I know her so well. If there is anything different, it is that she is a police officer. That affects people."

James said, "So was there a specific reason for the call then, other than just catching up?"

"She didn't say."

Li had already come to the conclusion that Catrin had called to check her out; to see if there was any flag regarding their need to talk clandestinely. She hadn't said so and Jian Li had no specific signal to tell her that; it was intuition. But if that was the case, it would probably be something involving Michael Yau.

James changed the subject. "Chris is a good guy, but he is a bit of a surprise at times."

She knew that Catrin's husband and James kept in touch

regarding sports interests. They had hit it off really well during the visit for Li and James's marriage.

Li asked, "How?"

"He has small boat sailing experience, it turns out, but he lost interest in his late teens. I'm not even sure whether he has mentioned it to Catrin as she has no interest in boats."

Li and James were both involved in short course racing; the sailing club was where they had first met. They had rented a larger sailing yacht for a leisure cruise during their honeymoon.

Li replied, "He never said! Well... he grew up in Cornwall, so thinking about it, I shouldn't be surprised. We will have to work on it; if there is only Catrin to convince..."

Her mind moved away from the thought of triad issues to the prospect of meeting up with Catrin and Chris for a sailing holiday.

~~

The train ride north was grey and overcast, with rain showers all the way up to the Lake District, where the sun broke through.

"The weather is looking up!" said Mark, as they left Penrith.

By Glasgow, the world outside was more colourful and warmer than anywhere on the route through England. They were in first class, in a pair of single seats across from each other. Both Catrin and Mark had been largely silent on the journey so far. On Friday they had gone through the work expectations and planning so there was no need to regurgitate it on the train. The compartment was fairly full all the way from London until the Lake District, which discouraged work talk anyway. At Penrith a group of people sitting near them left the train and the area seemed almost empty.

Mark looked around before speaking.

"Catrin, I have a question; it may be out of line but... now is as good as any time to ask, I suppose."

She looked up from what she was reading and smiled. "Ask. I'll tell you if it's out of line."

"What am I getting into? I know you got the scar in Glasgow and you say DCS Moore wants you to stir the pot with people close to this man Connolly. We will have local people looking after us, driving us, but... why am I here, not in Paris? In line of command I should stand in for you at the Paris meeting. I've done as much, if not more on the free port file as Isabelle... I don't know even what happened between you and the people up here other than you were injured during an arrest of one of Connolly's people."

She looked at him, deciding. "It's fair game to ask. In part, I want someone capable with me if something does go wrong, not that it is likely to. In part, Isabelle needs to stop running automatically for the role of backup, the 'coordinating in the office' that she likes to do."

She put her iPad down. "What happened here when I got injured? Yes, you should have the background, considering the people we will meet."

She told him quietly and matter-of-factly about the incident outside Kinnington Church that had given her the scar on her cheek.

It had been an under-resourced stakeout of a church in Glasgow where a painting was located, one they believed that a member of the Connolly gang wanted, she began. At dusk, a parishioner entering the supposedly empty church suddenly collapsed in the main doorway at the same time as her assigned partner was away for a break.

"The man in the church doorway had been hit with a steel baton, but I didn't know that at the time, it could have been a stroke, or anything. But I was suspicious that the break-in we were watching out for had taken place after all."

She had called on her mobile for help as she ran over to the church to check the man out, bending over him just as the gang member who had downed him burst out through the door, hitting her in the face with the same baton.

"His name is Colin Cheney; he is now in Barlinnie, where we are going. He was an enforcer for Connolly. But we aren't seeing him."

She paused, recalling it. "I didn't know my cheek was so badly damaged at the time; I was off-balance at the moment I was hit, anyway, so the force sent me rolling down the steps. Cheney slipped on the torch I had brought over with me; I had dropped it. He went down himself, flat on his face. I got up, grabbed the torch and hit him hard. When he tried to get up again, I kicked him between the legs, kneed him in the back and cuffed him."

"And then?" asked Mark

"While that was happening, a car drew up with Connolly's lawyer, Niall Irvin; he later turned Queen's Evidence. He was with Cheney; he was the one who really wanted the painting. He didn't attack me, he just wanted Cheney to punch me out, grab the painting and get in the car. But handcuffing Cheney put a stop to that and then knocking Irvin's phone flying with the torch put a stop to him calling anyone.

"I passed out as my shift partner came running up. After that, it was hospital and surgery. By the time I was through that, Jane Worsley and two of her former team in Diplomatic Protection were whisking me south. They had heard that Connolly wanted me dead.

"Afterwards, one of the psychologists that the Met uses, Dr. Herrington, picked up the mental pieces. I was a wreck. Damage to my face, the death threat and our team being thrown off the case all overwhelmed me.

"I remember my first meeting with him, telling him I just needed to get back to work. My face was half-covered in dressings and… I really meant it at the time. But with him, it took time to get sorted out; to let me heal."

Mark said slowly, "So we are going to see members of a drug gang, one in which you played a part in their downfall. And you helped put one of them away. We are going to stir it up a little? With a gang that wanted you dead?"

Catrin said, "Well, Eileen Strachan heard afterwards that Connolly relented on that one, she believes. And it happened a few years ago."

Mark shook his head.

She added, smiling a little. "It's teamwork, that's why you are here. And we are going to see an accountant, not one of the heavies."

He said mock-formally, "Ma'am, you may still be in need of this Dr. Herrington, for taking this one on."

They arrived in Glasgow in time to check into their hotel, the Grand Central, located beside the train station. They then took a taxi to the Kelvingrove Museum. The Kelvingrove was one of the premier museums and art galleries in the country and a city landmark; an impressive piece of architecture set in its own grounds near Glasgow University.

Susan Hetherington, still the security director of the museum and Cory Robson, one of the curators, had agreed to meet up and show them their Colourist section.

They talked about paintings as they wandered through, technical details and facts, specifically giving the officers more background on Leslie Hunter's works on houseboats in Loch Lomond. It was only after thanking Robson and watching him depart that Susan asked if they had time for dinner with her; the visit arrangements had been set up at such short notice.

Catrin said, "I'd love that. Mark?"

Harper made his excuses, wanting to 'get the feel' of the city, mooch around a bit. In part that was true; in part he sensed that the two women had history and had things they wanted to catch up on.

~~

After ordering their meals in the restaurant that Susan Hetherington had selected, the talk turned to the past. Catrin had been injured mid-operation and had heard the rest second-hand. Worsley's unit had been thrown off the case; it was Coltrane, ironically now her current boss, who volunteered to work with Police Scotland to help them close out the investigation. Hetherington had worked with Coltrane and

Strachan on part of it.

"Neville came over to me as a… loyal gentleman. That's it, I think."

Catrin said, "Gentleman, I get; he has always been that. Loyal?"

"To the Metropolitan Police; he wanted, I think, to bring down the people who had injured you and take on those trying to damage the reputation of the Met. He doesn't seem the normal sort of policeman, but he is very committed to the organisation."

It was interesting to hear it from a third person; that was Catrin's recall too, but over the years had thought herself too emotional at the time to see it clearly.

She just said, "He's a good boss."

Susan sighed. "And now you are back here for work. And about something to do with a Colourist painting by Leslie Hunter, I gather. Will you be seeing Eileen? We stay in touch, not a lot, but... she's a chief superintendent now. To me she still seems under a lot of strain."

Catrin nodded. "Yes, we will see her after a meeting tomorrow morning. We talked on a conference call recently."

The talk turned to the people they had worked with during the Connolly operation. DCI Eric Sinclair, who had led the investigation that brought in Worsley and Sayer, had retired, Catrin knew. She had lost track of him, as had Susan.

"And the Gaults, do you stay in touch?" asked Catrin. Hetherington said she had more contact with them.

Mary Gault's husband, the Reverend Alexander Gault, had died of a heart attack in the museum. It was the finding that his heart pills were placebos that started the whole investigation.

Hetherington told her that Mary Gault had died recently but her daughter Elizabeth and Susan stayed in touch. The paintings by Elizabeth's grandfather, Alistair Gault, a former employee at the Kelvingrove, had been part of the invest-igation. The museum director had arranged a temporary summer exhibition of works by several Kelvingrove current and former employees who were also artists and had included Alistair's paintings in it prominently.

"It pleased Mary and Elizabeth; they came to see the exhibition and we made a big fuss. We felt we owed them that."

13 GREENOCK

"We are sorry for your loss," Catrin began, trying to break the silence in the awkward moment after being introduced. She meant it and sounded as if she did. Anne Shannon's husband may be a drug gang accountant but neither the wife nor the daughter had been involved, Strachan had said. Anne had believed that her husband's secrecy over his only 'client' was just that; good business practice.

It was Monday morning at a small, older home in central Greenock, twenty-five miles west of Glasgow. Catrin and Mark had been driven there in a police vehicle to meet up with a local officer who had the unenviable job a few days ago of breaking the news that Shannon's daughter had died suddenly and violently in London.

Mrs. Shannon said nothing for a moment, then murmured, "Thank you." In a quiet, calm voice, she asked, "Do you have more news?"

Catrin had her script. The mother had come down to London as soon as she was contacted but had returned home two days later. The body wasn't going to be released for a while and she couldn't have access to the flat, as it was still a crime scene. It turned out that she knew no-one else there other than Nirupa and Jalaj Ranjani. Since her husband's arrest and conviction, she had no further contact with them and she didn't want any now. She would return shortly for the coroner's inquest and to bring her daughter's body back but in the interim, she wanted to be at home.

Catrin replied, "The investigation is on-going. At the last briefing we received the final results of the toxicology tests on Lena's blood, confirming what was indicated previously. It appears that Lena had significant levels of a number of street drugs and alcohol in her system. Enough, the pathologist feels, to make her disorientated and lose her balance, as one theory suggests. But we are still interviewing the man who was arrested. He has now admitted to being present at the time of death and said they were in a relationship; that he woke up and saw her on the balcony, staggering and went to get her, hold her. He, too, was under the influence of alcohol, he claims. The rest... we don't know.

"I am told that the pathologist will complete his report this morning and it will be reviewed very quickly by the senior investigating officer, probably today, so the inquest can proceed quite soon. It will then be a matter for the coroner to release Lena to the funeral directors that you arrange, but we see no reason for further delay."

The woman was nodding; more to indicate that she was listening.

Shannon said, "I want to get her buried, of course, and organize that. It's such mess, such a waste. I can't blame her about the drugs and drink; she's dead, but she has been so independent in recent years. Since her father's arrest she was... struggling. I hoped that being in London would be a chance for a new start for her. I think Malav, that's the man you are talking about, is probably telling the truth; they got along well, I know.

"I can blame Brodie, though, for starting all this. And that man Ranjani wasn't there, I hear, even though it was his place that Lena was staying at."

She shook her head then asked, "Are you going to talk to him?"

Catrin said, "Yes, we have already done so, on the same day as we received the news of Lena's fall. I attended that interview with Superintendent Lauder. It may require further interviews."

The mother shook her head. "Brodie's world; it's so different, I found out. He went off to work like a normal person with a job. But it wasn't. He worked for a gang. I thought at first he had just fallen in with a bad crowd, he could be straightened out. It took a colleague of DCI Strachan's, as she was then, to explain it more clearly to me. He had crossed a line and was in that world for life."

Catrin didn't say anything. She, too, recalled the first time that organized crime had been explained to her accurately; the families and groups who control it in the UK; the ways they worked; their hierarchies, territoriality or specialty interests. They lived in a different world from normal people, the ways in which they formed allegiances or fought, depending on their interests.

In her first year on the job, based in Lambeth, she had been really troubled by a comment from a woman about her age, a mother of a one-year-old. The woman had just witnessed her husband beaten so badly he was in a life support unit and yet she refused to provide any information to the police to assist the investigation. Despite being distraught, she was also matter-of-fact about it. 'Howie broke the rules; he paid the price; that's it, isn't it?' She wasn't going to break them herself.

Anne Shannon said at last, "I don't know why you are here, really. PC McKinnon has been very good about explaining the situation."

She smiled at the local officer, with whom she clearly had a rapport. The officer specialized in family liaison work.

Catrin said, "We have a few questions. Hopefully they will touch on something you know a little about that may help us shed some light on all of this. Lena went to London just over a year ago. Other officers tell me that she was enrolled in a business and commerce course there but she lived at Jalaj

Ranjani's flat. It must be hard, but we would appreciate any insight you may have as to why she was living there?"

The woman looked lost, Catrin thought. She had lived all her life in Greenock, Strachan had said. Her father had been a town councillor when it had been a burgh. Anne had been a librarian when she met Brodie Shannon; her husband an accountant who became increasingly successful, until the truth emerged.

Anne Shannon said, "When it happened, when Brodie was arrested, Lena and I were both… shocked to the core. I stood by him at first, so did Lena. But I think, looking back, whereas I felt betrayed, Lena didn't. That was the difference. It was embarrassing for us and particularly difficult for her as the details came out. Over time, it seemed as if she accepted it. I thought at times she romanticized it."

Catrin prompted her. "She met Mr. Ranjani through visits to your home, then?"

"Ranjani had been in contact with Brodie and visited Glasgow on occasion. Once Brodie and I had dinner with the Ranjani couple in the city. That's when I met his wife - just the one occasion, but that was enough. Another time he visited our home; that was when he met Lena. I cooked dinner. He seemed nice enough, I thought, until I found out the nature of Brodie's work. Before that I thought Ranjani was simply a younger businessman. But there was always a suspicion of… something."

"Such as?" prompted Catrin.

"At the dinner in Glasgow, a man in the restaurant spotted him and came over; French, I think. Ranjani didn't introduce him, just smiled, excusing himself and taking him away for a few minutes, for a chat. He said nothing about it when he came back. Normally, you explain, don't you - say something, anyway, or introduce the person? Ranjani didn't. Secrecy, that's what I was suspicious about, reflecting on it."

She paused, thinking. "Lena wasn't having an affair with him, as far as I am aware. You asked me that indirectly, didn't you, just now? No, I don't think so, but I don't know."

Catrin replied, "After the report of Lena's fall, I was part of the team visiting the flat and later, the Ranjani couple. The flat had apparently been used as a place for him to keep other women in the past and his wife seemed to assume Lena was in a relationship with him, too. He neither confirmed nor denied it but I got the impression he wasn't having an affair with her either, to be honest. That's just my impression."

Shannon nodded, understanding. "No, I think it was just a favour between the men, a - what's the term - payback of some sort from Ranjani to Brodie. Perhaps Nirupa was trying to hide that by sullying my daughter's reputation still further. I don't like her, to be honest, from that one meeting we had. Cool as cucumber, she seemed; no warmth to her."

She took a breath. "We went from being very well-off to... I kept the house at first then sold it and we moved here. I didn't want to leave Greenock, start again somewhere else. But living expenses and college fees add up. I'm back working part-time at the library, which helps, of course.

"Lena wanted to study in London and then told me that she had talked to her dad. She had found Ranjani funny, more amusing really, when he came to visit. Through Brodie, Ranjani offered her a place he wasn't using. I knew it wasn't a good solution, deep down."

She sighed.

"We rowed about it then. I didn't want her to run off: I couldn't have taken that after losing my marriage so I accepted it was part of life - and her argument that it saved money was true. I went to see her down there. When I visited it was just her there but... you have seen the flat, you said? It wasn't a student place. I even wanted her to get another girl to share the place and have more normal student company."

Catrin glanced at Mark. He was to ask about the painting, they had decided. If it went off the rails, she would try to bring it back.

Mark said, "That's part of the reason we are here really, Mrs. Shannon. There is a puzzle about a painting in the flat. It's an original oil painting by a Scottish artist, one of a group called the Scottish Colourists; quite valuable, a view of -.''

The woman's face crumpled. Mark stopped as the tears appeared and her hand went to her mouth. Mark's expression showed that he was unsure what he had said to bring her to tears.

Mrs. Shannon said, "Sayer; I just realised who you are now, mentioning art and seeing your face. You are the lass injured in the church in Glasgow; am I right? Inspector Strachan told me about it when she interviewed me back then. I knew so little, to be honest."

Catrin nodded.

Mrs. Shannon went on, "To think my husband was tied into so much violence. When I heard of a young police officer being hurt, it was the last straw. It was all too hard to bear."

Catrin said softly, "My injury is not yours to bear, Mrs. Shannon."

Mark jumped back in, trying to get things back on track. "The painting is a view of Loch Lomond, one with house-boats."

Shannon sighed, wiping her eyes. "I know it; I saw it there, in fact, on the last visit, in Ranjani's flat - and before, when Brodie brought it here. He told me it was originally a present for the lawyer chap who turned Queen's Evidence; Niall Irvin. Brodie had it here for a week or so a few weeks before he was arrested. He told us he wished it was his, he liked it so much. I didn't. He passed it on to someone else, but I don't know who. Brodie took it away in his Volvo with a bunch of file boxes he had in his home office. Next thing I knew was that he had been arrested at his business office and a team of people were searching our home."

The stress of recalling that time was playing in her voice, Catrin heard. Anne Shannon stopped a moment to regain her balance.

"When I saw the painting in Ranjani's flat I was surprised. Lena said that Ranjani had bought it at her request. She wanted it. When I asked why she did that, she wasn't very forth-coming, but eventually she told me it was in hope there would be a time when we are all together again, as a family and that her dad really liked it."

She shook her head. "I have no idea where she got that from, but she obsessed on us getting back together. Brodie and I are finished. I wasn't leaving Greenock, despite everyone knowing, as I said. I needed something real, you see? I think it was harder on Lena, at school, the taunts. She was glad to get away to London. It's valuable, you say?"

Catrin said, "Yes, quite valuable. It sort of stood out as we went through the flat…"

Anne interjected, "From the junk? Yes, I thought so, too. The scene on Loch Lomond is close to where Brodie was born, near Tarbet."

Catrin kept her face neutral. Dominic Connolly had bought the painting for Niall Irvin; that was something new. But he changed his mind and sold it. She wondered when that decision had taken place.

Mrs. Shannon's final comments were to encourage Sayer to speak to Nina Trew, a student at Glasgow University.

"Nina was her closest friend all the way through school. She went down to London this year to see her twice, I know, and made a comment about the painting after the second visit, when I talked to her. But she didn't go back down and I got the impression that they had fallen out."

Catrin made a note to talk to Lauder about the friend, see if he wanted Mark and her to interview the student while they were in Glasgow. It wasn't why they were here; their job was to stir the pot with Connolly and Bolan, not solve the Shannon case. But the painting had been mentioned.

She looked at the uniformed officer and signaled that they were done. Another car was going to take DI Sayer and her sergeant to their next appointment. They wouldn't tell Mrs. Shannon, but they were off to see her husband, locked away in Barlinnie Prison.

14 BARLINNIE

The large, blue letters of the prison name loomed above them as the police car dropped Sayer and Harper outside Her Majesty's Prison, Barlinnie. As they slowed to a halt outside the tan brick building, Harper felt his boss's shoulder shudder next to him.

"Prisons do that?" he asked.

She replied, "This one does; it's where the man I told you about is held, Colin Cheney."

The name clearly meant something to one of the two police officers in front, the older man. He looked round at Catrin briefly but made no comment. After a second or two he said, "We are here, ma'am. I see Chief Superintendent Strachan outside the door over there, watching for us."

Catrin said, "I see her. Having a smoke, you mean."

The officer laughed. As he exited the vehicle, he opened the rear door like a chauffeur or doorman would do. Catrin was surprised but said, "Thank you."

Strachan came forward as they approached and Catrin introduced Mark Harper.

"A Scottish Harper, sergeant?" she asked, pointing in the direction of a door away from the security check.

"No, ma'am. My father is American; his family tree goes back to Germany. The name became anglicized as Harper in the early eighteen hundreds."

Strachan smiled. "Pity. You aren't entitled to the Clan Buchanan tartan, then. This way. Catrin, how are you in yourself? I have followed your meteoric rise in rank, I must say."

Catrin laughed. "You and Eric Sinclair were both DCI's, ma'am, when I was here; now you are a chief super. Talk about meteoric rise!"

"Attrition, girlie, I am a survivor; as are you."

"And Eric?"

"Let's talk later."

That was an answer in itself, Catrin thought.

They spent two hours in a meeting room in consultation, catching up on the interview with Lena's mother and in a call to Moore, Lauder and DCI Coltrane.

Regarding the news about the transfer of the painting, Strachan said, "I always thought Connolly had a sixth sense. When Niall's attempt to steal paintings by Gault failed, I think Connolly decided to distance himself from the art fraud around Colourists. Getting rid of Niall's present, a genuine Colourist painting, would fit that."

Lauder said, "If you could fit in the interview with this friend Trew, it might help."

Eileen Strachan said, "We'll check on her whereabouts. Perhaps we can make it tomorrow, early, before we take the big decision."

The outcome of the meeting with Lena's father this afternoon would tell them whether it would be of value to talk to the gang leader himself, Dominic Connolly. He was in a high-security prison east of Glasgow, HMP Shotts.

They reviewed how much Police Scotland had told Brodie Shannon about Lena's death.

"He will know more, no doubt, through others," Strachan said.

Lauder responded, "Well, he needs to know officially some-time that his daughter most probably died as a result of drugs; this is as good as any and may help get something out of him."

Lena Shannon had been high as a kite when she went off the balcony.

~~

Brodie Shannon was a mild-looking man in his fifties. If he was dressed normally and was with his wife in Greenock at some function at a club or church, you wouldn't notice him. Yet he had been the cold-blooded accountant of an operation which brought devastation to many lives in Scotland.

As the guard brought him in and seated him, he asked, "Why are you here? And who are you with?"

They hadn't spoken yet; he was straight out with it.

Catrin said, "The Metropolitan Police in London. This is DS Harper, I am DI Sayer."

He sounded worked up, tense. "Sayer, Sayer... yes, that Sayer! Well, you are popular with some people I know. In here and out. Thanks for letting me see the scar. I will tell Colin, it will make his day. He talks about you, you know? Still. And others in here do, as well. You were in at the start of the rot that Strachan started."

They sat impassive, letting his anger seethe, watching it get higher then wane; it was one of three possible reactions they had previewed.

Eileen Strachan had said, 'Shannon won't say a word in my presence; he just gives me the look of hate. He was probably one of the main brains of the Connolly mob, watching his people go down. But he hid the books; we never got those, I am sorry to say."

He stopped, shifted in his chair and spoke to the prison officer standing on one side. "I'm done here."

The man didn't move; he had been told not to, first time at least.

Catrin said, "I was in the flat shortly after Lena died, Mr.

Shannon, while her body was still on the concrete outside. I am sorry for your loss."

He swallowed, put his hand to his mouth stopping his lips from moving for a second.

"You come questioning me now... you pair of - ."

He stopped himself. "Did you see her... was she badly - ."

"No, Mr. Shannon, I didn't. It was an active crime scene and I wasn't there for that part of it. Was she badly injured in the fall, you ask? They believe that death was instantaneous. I think they told you that. She landed with the back of the head first so... there was severe trauma to the body. But the pathologist thought she didn't suffer."

He asked, "Who did it? All I heard was it was a possible murder investigation."

"It's an investigation into a suspicious death at this stage. Someone else appeared to be present when Lena fell from the balcony, but wasn't there when the responding officers went in. But it wasn't Mr. Ranjani, the owner; he has an alibi."

"I didn't think it was."

He looked at them, waiting for more.

Catrin said, "We are holding a man called Malav Rai, who we think was there, but at present he hasn't been charged with anything other than drug offences. He works for Ranjani we believe and he and Lena were in a relationship. From the results just received, Lena appears to have taken a significant mix of street drugs and alcohol; most probably she would not have been in control of herself, either her balance or her whereabouts. It will be a factor in the investigation."

It would be news to him, they knew. His daughter was one of the casualties at the other end of the lethal business he ran with Dominic Connolly. He hadn't given a damn about the hundreds of others.

They sat quietly waiting, while the man cried his heart out and swore. Arrested for an eight million pound drug haul, his sentence rendered him a Category A status prisoner. Home Office rules meant he would not be entitled to a special licence to attend the funeral of his daughter, even if his wife would allow him there.

"So why are you here? The people here could have told me," he asked, finally.

His voice sounded more normal now. Catrin knew that this was the critical point. They had talked about it. He would either bail on them with some curses or get involved at this point.

"We are art detectives, Mr. Shannon; the Art and Antiques Unit. It's about a quite valuable painting by the artist Leslie Hunter that we found at the flat, a scene of houseboats on Loch Lomond. At first we thought it belonged to Jalaj Ranjani. We now understand, from a message on Lena's laptop, that it was bought by him but given to her."

Shannon was listening intently.

Catrin continued, "Our boss asked me to find out more. We think it's your daughter's possession, or part of her estate, but there is no documentation."

He interrupted, ever the accountant. "What does Jalaj say? It's his flat."

Mark sat up straight. "Well, we haven't asked him yet. I thought up the idea of asking you first."

"Why?" he barked

"Well, I, well… I talked with someone I know in Trident on the investigation and he said that Lena was your daughter and… I looked you up in the database and saw that you were born in Tarbet and the painting is by Leslie Hunter, one of Loch Lomond scene, and…"

Catrin interjected, "Sergeant, we are asking the questions here, not explaining."

"…thought there was a link," finished Mark lamely, glancing at Catrin.

He had handled that bit well, she thought. She looked directly at Shannon and said flatly, as if it didn't matter a lot to her, "If it belongs to your daughter, it goes to her estate. If not, it goes to Ranjani. We were asked by Trident to try to find out."

Brodie Shannon suddenly looked suspicious. "Your friends in Trident want to play games; to piss off Jalaj Ranjani is what I hear, behind what you said. That's why you're visiting me now. Well, ask him. I liked the painting, yes. If my daughter - ."

He paused, swallowed, but went on in the same tone. "If she wanted it for me well that would be understandable. She saw it after I acquired it for Dom. He wanted it for Niall, seeing as he was getting into the Colourists. You know all about that, I am sure. But this was a real one for Niall, as he was busy forging others, was the joke. Well, the bastard didn't get it.

"As to who owns it now, ask Jalaj; I trust the man. If he bought it so she could give it to me a present, he will say that. If not, it's his."

Catrin sat looking impassive then said, "Just before you were arrested you supplied this painting directly to a Richard Pennywell, an art dealer, who sold it to a man called Garrard. Pennywell also bought it back from the same man for Ranjani. Did you drive it down to Pennywell or send someone? Life was getting busy around then, wasn't it?"

She thought he was going to walk away but he stopped himself and smiled. "No, I didn't take it down to Pennywell; someone else did. I was busy, you see. We all were that day. Niall and Colin had screwed up badly the night before at some church and news of the shipment from France getting seized had reached us. You may recall something about that yourself - or not. You were probably drugged up to the eyeballs if it was a bad as Colin said."

Catrin ignored the taunt. "We are going to check on a lot more than the Hunter painting, I assure you; the Ranjanis have quite a collection of art. We will find out if more of them came from Dominic Connolly."

He made no comment at all this time, but they caught his expression. Look all you want; it has nothing to do with Connolly. But her job was to stir him up; provoke him. So she stuck it to him, saying with conviction, "Of course, you won't get the Hunter, even if that was Lena's wish."

"Why?"

"It goes to her estate. There is no will. The normal bene-
ficiaries for an intestate death of this sort would be your ex-
wife and yourself, so she has at least an equal say. You are an
accountant; you will know that a court of probate, if it comes
to that, will probably rule that she has more than an equal say
under the circumstances, don't you think?"

He leaned forward, his anger visible, realizing the difficulty
he was now in.

"You can look at Ranjani's painting all you want; they are
nothing to do with us. You don't have any understanding of
trust, do you? Think you can pull information out of me to use
against Dom or Michael Bolan? No way. Trust, as I said."

Catrin got the impression that the smile was a little too self-
congratulatory, as if he was pulling a fast one with her. But his
expression changed again and his voice turned increasingly
vindictive.

"Colin exaggerates about his violence, of course, he always
did. In here we can call him on it generally and he backs off;
but about your face, he won't back off. The cheek was a real
mess, he claims. Wide open."

His eyes were fixed on her scar now, as if he was imagining
Cheney's description. Catrin felt Mark inhale, ready to say
something and she instinctively touched his forearm resting
next to hers to silence him. But the movement didn't go
unnoticed by Shannon, who stopped his invective.

He sat back in his seat.

"So that was the day. Dom bought that painting legally and
disposed of it legally, that is all I will say. I am done here."

Shannon turned to look at the prison officer, signaling he
wanted to leave. He stood up, staring at Catrin's face again. He
shook his head. "As I said, this will make Colin's day."

Catrin had sat through his mini-tirade without comment.
As he moved back she said, "You asked me earlier, Mr.
Shannon, who was responsible for your daughter's death."

He stopped and looked back at her.

"Unless the coroner comes to a different conclusion, Lena

was high on street drugs when she went over the balcony; so I suggest you go look in a mirror."

He grimaced, his distaste for her comment evident as he turned and left the room with the prison officer.

Harper looked at the empty doorway as Shannon turned in the corridor. He let out a small sigh and glanced at his boss. It was fleeting, and only momentary, but the side profile he saw with her eyes closed and her lips compressed conveyed the impact of the interview on DI Sayer, exposing her vulnerability or fragility, he wasn't sure. He glanced back at the table and his notebook and picked it up. When he next looked at her, as DCS Strachan came in, she was her normal self.

Strachan said, without preamble, "Well, we have the history now, and the day it went south. Catrin, I will be bringing this recording back to haunt him come his first parole request. Nasty bastard."

Catrin just gave a big blow of air from her cheeks. "I think Anne Shannon is well rid of him. Did you get that strange look though, when he started on about trust? I don't know what to make of it."

She looked at Strachan then at Harper, catching Mark glancing at her face, probably envisaging the wound as described by Brodie Shannon. Eileen Strachan caught him doing it too.

"He seemed smug," Strachan said. "It could be about the accounts never being discovered, but it seemed... more personal, as if by using the word he was pulling one over on you for the pleasure of it."

Her voice turned bright and breezy. "Well, that went a bit like the plan, didn't it? Let's go back downtown. I'll drop you off at the hotel and we can meet up for dinner later."

Mark said, "Well, thank you, but -"

Strachan arched her eyebrows, "Do you not think I can drive well, young man. Is that it?"

"No, it's not that, it's - ."

Catrin was smiling.

The chief superintendent continued, "Do you not want

dinner with two attractive women?"

Now both Mark and Catrin were smiling.

"I would love to have dinner with my boss and your good self, ma'am."

"That's better; a little gallantry suits a man. Besides, do you like alcohol? You may not know it, but your boss is a right pain, she doesn't touch a drop. I need someone who can talk about the wine list or the whisky; someone civilised."

She was eyeing Catrin as she finished.

Catrin said, "Speaking of which....?"

Harper sensed that his boss and Eileen Strachan had already been discussing something in private.

Strachan looked serious. "Eric is struggling but was sober a few days ago; I know that. He should be at his AA meeting tonight, the one you eyeballed him attending during that first visit, near the hotel. It starts at seven, so he could arrive early. Let's say seven fifteen at the hotel for us to meet for dinner. That should give you time?"

Catrin nodded.

Mark, catching on at last, said to his boss, surprised, "You are in Alcoholics Anonymous, ma'am?"

Catrin laughed. "No, Mark. I just don't drink. But I come by the knowledge honestly; it's a family disease. Seven fifteen will be fine."

15 SINCLAIR

She had asked Harper to wait, to watch her back while she went across the road to the church. "Just in case; there's nothing I can see out there to worry about, but... I won't be long."

Mark stood there looking through the glass of the side hallway of the hotel, his eyes on her and the people, mainly men, standing smoking near the entrance to the church basement steps along the side road. His boss changed direction slightly, seeing one man as she gave a small wave.

The older man who approached her was in an overcoat, a little old-fashioned, Mark thought. If it was smart it would be distinctive, but it looked well-worn and in need of dry-cleaning. He threw his cigarette away as he reached Sayer. This man was the retired policeman Detective Chief Inspector Eric Sinclair, now a struggling drunk according to Strachan, Mark concluded

Sinclair's voice was raspy, probably from too much smoking, she thought, but he sounded the old Eric Sinclair.

"You are looking well, Catrin! God, this is a surprise. I talked with Eileen a few days ago; she never said..."

His face was haggard, a lot older, she saw now that she was standing closer to him. He'd put on weight. Sinclair had been

113

trim; a smart dresser. His former brush cut had grown out a little and was uneven.

She wasn't going to fall for the 'you are doing well too, I hope' routine. "I'm well, Eric. I made DI a few months ago. I'm married now, a nice guy from Cornwall. I came really to say something, though."

She needed to get straight to it, she knew. This meeting was already bringing back emotions from the worst days with her mother. Sinclair looked at her, knowing this would be hard for her, seeing him in this state.

"How is your mum doing?" he interjected desperately. A few seconds of delay before his own reality was aired.

Catrin said, "She been sober ten years now. Still active as hell in AA and scared that if she doesn't stay so, she could slip. And you, how long?"

"Four and half weeks now, this time. A day at a time. It got a bit rough after I retired."

Catrin remembered her mother's words; don't sympathize even once, just keep it honest. She had talked with her last night asking her advice about this meeting.

Catrin said, "I wish you well, Eric; I truly do. But if any of your burdens are to do with the Kinnington Church stakeout and me being injured, drop them right now, please; let them go. That's what I came to say. I said it on the phone to you at the time; now I am saying it to your face so you can see I mean it. I really do. I wish you the best and hold no resentments about that assignment."

"I know," he said. "It's not just that, it's … everything."

His face showed how lame he knew that response to be.

She nodded, "It's not to do with any excuse, is it? You have a disease and have to work at it constantly, like my mum does."

He nodded. "I do. And I do. I still get a little cocky about it from time to time and then I fall flat on my arse. Now one of my former sponsees is my sponsor; a bloody Irishman, to boot."

He smiled at his own joke.

"At lease he's not Welsh," she responded, returning the

smile.

The group he was with as she approached had now turned and started going down the steps to the basement. Sinclair caught the movement and then looked back at Catrin.

"You could come in if you want. It's an open meeting tonight with a speaker, so we can have anyone attend; there's an anniversary. Bring the young guy who is keeping an eye out for you in the lobby over there. Your sergeant, I guess? He could learn a thing or two about drunks perhaps."

She replied, "Thank you, but no, we have other things we have to do. With Eileen, as well, so I can't say no to her can I?"

He laughed. "Eileen would come in the church, interrupt the speaker and drag you out. She's quite a tornado, as you know. Well, thank you again. It's great to see you, lass."

Harper startled as the man suddenly moved forward, but he only hugged his boss briefly, then he turned round and went down the steps, not looking back. Sayer turned round and walked back slowly. As she reached the door to the side lobby, she checked her watch and increased her pace.

She said, up-beat, "We are in good time to meet Eileen in the main lobby, aren't we?" as she sailed past him, taking the lead.

She was avoiding looking at him, he concluded and the wind must have developed a chill, making her eyes water. Or something.

~~

Strachan was high on the story rather than the wine, Catrin thought. Her own sergeant, though, had consumed his share and was relaxing, at least, hearing his laughter in response to Eileen Strachan's comedy act.

Strachan continued, "So there we are, building the camel of Police Scotland out of eight independent police services with the help or hindrance of a tribe of politicians, bureaucrats and consultants. We had innumerable secret meetings on structure and 'what we can't talk about' to the poor sods who were being kept in the dark, like mushrooms. The internal politics were awful.

"And in the throes of the great transition, I am trying to run a drug gang penetration bigger than any I had participated in previously. Then in walks Eric Sinclair saying he has Lady Jane Worsley and this Welsh girlie here coming up from London, helping with a suspicious death involving art. It was drug-related peripherally; it had some issue of a placebo being substituted for a heart medication. Could one of my team sit in on it, he asked? Nothing onerous, he said.

"I thought, sideline it; all I have to do is keep my operation quiet until the trap is sprung on Connolly. Then a week or more later, I get the call."

She pauses for dramatic impact, mock-glaring at Catrin, as she took a sip of her wine.

"Eric tells me that he is on his way back from the Oban stakeout and the girlie has taken out one of Connolly's enforcers at Kinnington church. Kicked him in the whatsits. We had put her with Peter McPherson watching a damn church of all things. I thought she would be sleeping or praying. 'She's hurt', he said. Oh, and she made Peter, the poor sod, arrest Niall Irvin as well, whom we knew was a complete shit, but half of the key people in Glasgow at the time thought he was walking on water, a hotshot defense lawyer."

Her arms went out, mocking her shock at the news.

"How? Why?" I asked. "The only answer I got from the man was him blathering on that she is good and she's Welsh. 'You know, Eileen, they are tenacious, the Welsh'. Can you credit it?"

"Peter?" Mark asked, laughing, trying to keep up.

"DS Peter McPherson, on Eric Sinclair's team at the time. He left the job afterwards," explained Catrin.

Strachan gave her a warm, conspiratorial smile. "But you kept the damn church thing contained didn't you, Catrin? Without that, Operation Finisterre could have gone west. I thank you for that, I really do."

Eileen Strachan readied herself for the next chapter of her story of how she met the 'girlie'. Catrin was smiling at the act, hearing Strachan's perspective. It hadn't been funny the first time.

"So I am up all hours calling people, trying to get Eric straightened out, getting Angus off his arse and trying to avoid the -."

Catrin butted in, her voice reflecting her surprise. "Angus Leiss, the surgeon? You called him?"

Her question, or the tone of it, had broken the jovial atmosphere and Eileen Strachan said more seriously, "His wife is a Strachan. Clan Strachan. I know anyone who is anyone in my clan in Glasgow. See what you miss out on, Mark; not being a Scottish Harper?"

She looked at Catrin, her face confirming it. The secret was out, so she stopped her spiel. Mark thought DCS Strachan was sounding slightly defensive; as if his boss's question had broken through the wall of Strachan the tough police officer to Eileen Strachan, the woman; one who would understand how difficult a facial injury would be for another woman.

Catrin said sincerely, "Thank you; I never knew that. No-one said."

She turned to Harper, happy to bring the conversation back to earth a little. "He is a fine man, the cosmetic surgeon who fixed my face, one of the best. He came in specially, I heard. He wasn't on call."

There was a moment's silence. The meal was over really; no-one had wanted dessert or coffee; Catrin had just asked for a fresh tea after the main course as the other two had emptied the wine bottle.

Strachan looked at her watch, all business now. "Enough fun and games. I'd better be going. Call when you finish with Trew and you will be collected and brought over to Govan. I'll see you both then. It has been good to catch up, really."

They said their goodbyes at the door and Strachan disappeared in the opposite direction from their short walk back to the hotel. She had parked at home, she said, wherever that was, but it wasn't far. So she could have a glass. Or two.

As they headed back to the hotel, Catrin looked at Mark. "OK?" she asked.

Harper smiled. "Yes, it was a good meal and… informative. She has such energy. And you ma'am, well; today has been an insight. While you were in the loo she said that everyone had been told to steer clear of Eric Sinclair and the Met visitors after the incident at the church, despite you being injured. It was politics. But on your way back south every copper with a marked car who could get on the motorway was flashing his lights at the vehicle taking you back, saying hello and sticking the finger to the messengers higher up."

She smiled and he saw the tears in her eyes; hopefully the wind again, not him treading too close.

Catrin responded, "It seemed that way, but I was largely out of it. Jane had her Diplomatic Protection people she had pulled in and we had my friend Jian Li with us. But I slept a lot on the drive south."

She let out a sigh. "And it's time we got some sleep, because tomorrow we have to decide whether to see Dominic Connolly or not. And that won't be up to us really, it's between Trident and Strachan's mob to sort out."

Mark said, "We have this Nina Trew first. She is coming to the hotel; Eileen's person said it would work best, she has classes all morning. And a chance of free food for a student…"

16 TREW

By late-afternoon on Monday Isabelle was tired. The day-long meeting of the free port analysis group, in which she had no background on most of the cases, was all new to her. There were only three cases in which she had been directly or peripherally involved. She realised that it would be a slog for her boss to get on board with this team, in the same way.

She gave the updates from the Art and Antiques Unit. But it was mainly listening to others; building a composite of the current status of known art crimes (under investigation, solved or unsolved, or no further action) linked to free port tax havens. The chairperson was Senior Agent David Klintz, the head of the FBI Art Crime Team, who closed the session with a summary and the comment that, 'tomorrow, we will review which areas we feel we are able to work on together, going forward."

After the meeting, Klintz came up to her. "DC Howlett, I hear that it is only your second time in Paris and you are by yourself; would you care to join our team for dinner tonight?"

She saw that others were sorting themselves out in different combinations for the same purpose.

"Thank you, sir. It is very kind of you to offer."

He had headed straight over from the chairman's seat to

ask her. She wondered if Morley Kerswell had said something, or her boss.

At dinner in a more upscale restaurant than the Saturday evening with Morley, the Americans talked about anything but work, but mainly about sport. Not that Isabelle followed sport in the UK other than the general status of London football clubs, but American sport was Greek to her.

Both David Klintz and another agent, Walkley Ballard, made attempts to talk about the state of things in the UK with Isabelle, but each time it petered out, not having a natural dynamic.

She realised that neither she nor Morley Kerswell were good conversationalists in this forum, although he would occasionally make a comment that fitted exactly the topic. But it came over, too, that he was not main league in the larger FBI team hierarchy.

Both Klintz and Kerswell spoke French, it turned out. The others were oblivious to it, just bursting out in American English to the waiter. She ordered her courses in her school French but the waiter responded to her in English. She was already missing the atmosphere of the meal on Saturday; simpler, but more friendly.

A couple of times they talked about art in general, which brought Isabelle back into play at the table. On one item Morley made a simple error, mixing up two painters with the same surname. David stopped the thread of discussion to explain it to him nicely. Neither Morley nor anyone else in his team seemed embarrassed and she got the impression that this was a routine practice.

They ended up dividing the bill individually, which didn't seem to faze the waiter at all. Isabelle was a bit surprised at how high it worked out to be and hoped that it didn't make waves with her boss. On the way back to the hotel, Morley fell in step with her, talking more easily one-on-one. On Tuesday they would wrap up and she would be heading home by train.

~~

Nina Trew had taken the trouble to look good this morning, Catrin thought, perhaps because the hotel was up-market and something of a Glasgow icon. She was nervous, which was to be expected, so Catrin took the time to put her at ease.

"We are part of the team investigating Lena's death, but we work for the Met's Art and Antiques Unit. We know you weren't in London when she died but we would appreciate some background information on her to help us understand better Lena's motive in acquiring a particular painting."

She left it there, wondering if Nina would ask why art detectives were involved. But the student gave a nod and said nothing for a moment.

"Tell me about her. Let's start with the last time you saw Lena," Catrin began.

Her answers were staccato. "It was three months ago. She wasn't well; the drugs she was taking. Lena knew it; we talked about her using them but she wouldn't do anything about it. I think the decision to go to that flat and sponge off that man Ranjani was all part of her illness, frankly. Just my opinion. She started to fall apart on the day her dad was arrested. Her mum told me you were part of that investigation."

During the preliminaries, while ordering the breakfast and choosing tea or coffee, the girl had looked a couple of times at Catrin's scar, but she carefully avoided doing so as she spoke now.

Catrin nodded. "Peripherally I was part of it, yes. It was an overlapping investigation involving paintings. But what do you mean by 'fall apart'?"

"Well, they went from a normal family, but a lot wealthier than mine with her dad an accountant, through the shock of his arrest to her parents not just separating but actually divorcing. Her mum was in a daze that her husband was involved in gangs and drugs and Lena was totally lost about it all.

"She and her mum moved into a smaller place and endured; that's probably the term. They had to deal with the press coverage and the comments, locally and from people else-where. When it quietened down, Mrs. Shannon went back to work and stuck it out, but Lena continued to receive a lot of cruel comments at school, I tell you. People were convinced she knew all about it. Some were sanctimonious about it; others were sure she had her own drug supplies and was using but not sharing; but she wasn't using then, I know. I am sure Lena didn't know about her dad either."

Catrin said, "So Lena was under a lot of pressure. What happened?"

"She isolated a lot, didn't get involved in activities, despite Helen, another friend, and I trying to get her to join us. I think that carried on at university, too; she didn't get involved there, other than the study courses. And she was a little weird, at times."

"Weird; how?" asked Catrin.

Lena responded, "She started fantasizing that if she could get her parents back together, even with him in prison, things would get better in the long run. There was no way that was going to happen, I knew. Lena just got worse and she and her mum fell further apart. But I don't know what Mrs. Shannon could do, really; Lena was hell-bent on trying to control her parents. As I said, it wasn't normal."

Mark said, "Mrs. Shannon said you saw the painting in the flat, the one with Loch Lomond and the houseboats. That's partly why we are talking to you."

Nina nodded, "Lena got Mr. Ranjani to buy it. Her dad liked it, he had seen it before, she said. It was painted near to where he grew up."

Mark asked, "Why would Mr. Ranjani do that for her? Were they sleeping together?"

Nina wrinkled her nose in distaste. "No. I thought that at first, when I made my first visit. The place didn't look like her, it was too fancy, I thought; money wasted on showy fittings that were a bit trashy to me. But it wasn't so; she wasn't paying him at all; in money or with sex."

"How do you know that?" asked Catrin.

"She told me. Ranjani had been clear to her that it was a place he used for other women; he would do so again after she left, he said. His wife wasn't against it. Making it available for her was a payment to her dad in some way. No strings attached. As was the purchase of the painting. He paid for it. It cost hundreds, perhaps thousands, she said. I was amazed."

And the rest, thought Catrin. Inwardly she smiled. Trew would be more than amazed at the purchase price, if she knew, unlike Neville Coltrane. After a call from his counterpart in Italy on a work recently recovered there valued in the millions, he said, "Despite Trident, I am not sure how much time and effort we can really put into this, Catrin; we have our own priorities to deal with."

Priorities set by the value of the art itself, he meant and the Hunter wasn't in their major league.

Mark continued. "Did she say why he was so generous?"

Nina shook her head. "No. I didn't ask, either. I just assumed it was drugs-related. Ranjani may own some office buildings but he was into street drugs big time; a gang leader, she said. That's how she met Malav; through Ranjani."

Catrin said, "She had drugs in her system, the post-mortem found."

Nina said immediately, "Mrs. Shannon told me when she called. It's just one more blow."

They waited her out.

"The second time I went to London she wasn't just drinking, she was using. She said it helped her cope with stress. We quarreled about it and I think it was clear we weren't the same friends anymore; I wanted to help but she was so different. I didn't want to go back to London to see her like that."

Mark said, "About this painting, why did she want it? Just for her dad? He liked it, you said? But it was hanging on her bedroom wall across from her bed, not wrapped away. Did she like the artist, too?"

Nina said, "No, it was the boats in the water; she dreamed

about them. It was all part of her illness, I think. She should have been seeing a doctor or a counsellor, but she wasn't having any of that and, when she wanted, she could sound as normal as you and me."

She explained Lena's fantasy as best as she could.

"Nina told me that she fell out of bed once when she imagined the boats moving, getting her mum's boat closer to her dad's. Weird, don't you think? I wondered if she had been dreaming, sleepwalking, when I heard about her death."

Catrin asked, "Did you meet this Malav Rai?"

"Yes, he collected us when we got drunk together on my first trip down to see her; a big night out. She was just drinking then. He seemed a nice guy; he had a good car. Second time, I knew he was supplying her. He didn't use, I gather, he just liked high-end liquor. He would have been chucked out of his group if he used drugs - what's it called, not a gang?"

"Crew?" suggested Catrin.

"Yes, that's it. Like they were a work team, or in a boat race."

"What was he like?"

Nina replied, "He was steady, I would say, quiet; but he drank a bit too much."

Mark asked, "Would he be the sort to lose his temper with her?"

"I doubt it. He seemed pretty easy-peasy, really, in one way; hard in another. And he really liked her. But I wasn't there. And if he was supplying others, then there had to be a hard side to him, didn't there? I just wasn't exposed to it."

She shook her head.

"We lost one of my classmates to a drug overdose in my first term here. Now Lena. I just signed up for training for a volunteer thing, a night line for people who need help. I thought I would do it to remember Lena, in a sense, and to remind me not to get tempted. Have either of you been through this sort of thing?"

Catrin nodded. "I worked on street drug work in Brixton when I joined the Met. I saw a lot of people in the situation you saw Lena in. I know what you mean when you said earlier that she was so different."

Mark just looked impassive. He exchanged glances with Catrin, who nodded.

He said to the student, "Thank you for your time."

Nina said, "Thank you also for the breakfast. I can't say I have eaten breakfast in too many hotels. And not in the Grand Central. It's fancy here."

Catrin said, "That's enough of the questions from us. Let's finish our breakfast in peace. But I am interested in this volunteer thing you mentioned, if you want to talk about that."

The meeting with Nina proved to be the better of the two interviews they held that day.

17 SHOTTS

The big man now sitting across from Mark was his height and frame, but with plenty of muscle and fat evident. It wasn't his physical presence, though, that made Mark Harper feel apprehensive, nor was it the man's behaviour. His clothes were casual and good quality, as prisoners wore their own clothes in Shotts. Given his wealth, they were not even ostentatious. Dominic Connolly had simply come in quietly, sat down and said nothing, waiting.

Whatever it was; the way in which the man looked at him and his boss or his demeanour in sitting back in the chair, there was a sense of authority and power in him. Mark was still adjusting to the idea of the person sitting across from him fitting the description of a drug baron, with huge sums of money stashed away, still running his operation from inside a high security prison.

Mark glanced briefly at his boss and her stone-faced stare at the prisoner, not seeing or sensing in her the same discomfort. He was to begin the questions, he knew.

He said firmly, "I'm Detective Sergeant Harper, Mr. Connolly; this is Detective Inspector Sayer. We are with the Metropolitan Police. I have a couple of questions for you about a painting you used to own."

Connolly looked at him then smiled. "You seriously want to ask me questions without my solicitor present. You are from where in the Met?"

He was mocking the younger man.

"The Art and Antiques Unit."

"It must be a different world south of the border. No lawyer, no answer. No advance notice of a meeting, no chance to organize my lawyer. Simple really. Have a good trip home."

He stood. Mark had to fight every instinct not to say something but DCS Strachan had been adamant in the prep meeting. "Act like you don't give a monkey's uncle. He won't go. He will be pissed that Catrin hasn't spoken to him yet."

As per plan, Catrin was simply looking at Connolly.

The gang leader looked at him for a moment and moved from the table. Then he looked up at the CCTV camera in the corner of the room before sitting down again, this time turning his chair slightly to face towards Sayer.

"It healed nicely, I see. But, it's a few years now. You have been under some strain though, I can tell. You should find an easier job."

Catrin remembered photographs of Connolly from her visit to Glasgow years ago. If anything, facially he looked younger and less careworn. But Strachan's last words before they left her to go to the interview room had been, "Fire him up, if you can." He had given her a perfect opportunity, right at the outset.

She retorted, "It's a stressful job. Particularly when I am under the impression that for a while you were paying someone to kill me off; yes."

Mark remained impassive but he was alarmed. That comment wasn't in the game plan they had discussed. He glanced at his boss and saw the anger on her face directed fully at Connolly. He tensed, waiting for some sort of reaction from the man.

Connolly simply said, "Not true, despite the rumour out there. And you knew that, anyway, I hope."

He looked again at the camera. "You heard that afterwards, Eileen, I know. So I hope you didn't keep Detective Constable Sayer, as was, in the dark all this time."

Catrin ignored his comment. He had started talking, which was what she wanted.

She said, "You sold a painting of Loch Lomond by Leslie Hunter to a dealer called Richard Pennywell. Would you tell us what you paid for it, did you have it appraised at all and what was the selling price? That's all we want to know."

He laughed gently. "Didn't you just hear me? No solicitor, no answers."

She fired back, "I was under the impression that you had a reputation for looking after your people and their families. Pity."

The amused look left his face. "I do."

Catrin replied, "Lena Shannon recently fell from the bal--cony of a flat in London. You know about that, I'm sure; you seem well informed about everything else. We are trying to determine if the painting belonged to her or to a Jalaj Ranjani. He owns the flat. If the Hunter is Lena's property, it's her estate, so it could go to her parents. Mrs. Shannon, at least, could use the money, I think. We talked to her as well yesterday.

"However, Jalaj Ranjani's wife seemed interested in selling it but, at present, we have said we are holding it pending clarification. There is a note on Lena's computer saying that Jalaj bought it for her, so she could give it to her father. But your name came up in the sales history, which complicates it further, as you may gather. We have to ensure that there aren't other issues; like those with Niall Irvin's knock-offs that got me the scar you seem to think has healed nicely."

He said nothing for a moment, absorbing the information. "Anne Shannon won't take any of my money, I know that. Tainted, she said. But coppers don't sort out the estates of the deceased; private solicitors do that. So what else?"

Catrin looked at Mark and nodded.

Mark said, "Why Ranjani bought this one and left it at the

flat is still unclear to us. His other paintings are in his home. He is in your line of business, he and his wife have a nice art collection and we are the Art and Antiques Unit. You can read between the lines. We just thought we could clear this one out of the way if we could, despite your name and Ranjani's being tied to the work."

Art and Antiques were looking into Ranjani's paintings, was the message. Connolly kept his face impassive but something about him, a new tension, told Catrin that the man was in some way disturbed about the news. She wondered why. But he got the picture; that was evident.

Catrin said, "It's an opportunity to help us confirm the provenance of the Hunter painting as legitimate. Certainly, when we found out it was linked to you we questioned that, so yes, we talked to Police Scotland. DCS Strachan invited us up to ask."

They waited as Connolly considered what to say.

"I had it bought for Niall Irvin. It was all above board, through one of my companies, Barhead Holdings. Brodie handled that and you saw him yesterday, I gather. But I changed my mind about giving it to Niall some time before he sweet-talked Eileen. I would have regretted giving it to him even more then. But that was weeks later.

"At the time I sold it, I had no more interest in Niall's fraud using Colourist forgeries; the ones you were investigating when you crossed paths with Colin. Niall was getting too obsessed about the whole thing. I didn't want to encourage him further and so my planned 'surprise present' of a genuine Colourist was dropped. The painting went south without him ever knowing.

"Then Niall put me in here. I wasn't happy with him after that, so I am even more chuffed to have sold it on. I still don't feel charitably towards him, actually."

Mark said, doggedly, "So you don't recall any details of the purchase price or the sale price?"

Connolly replied, "It was around forty thousand I paid, roughly. And the sale price wasn't far off that, one way or another. I was in a lot of problems, sorting things out, so I simply don't recall. Brodie dealt with it, moved it on."

He took a moment to consider.

"It was all legit and it's a past issue. If it goes to Anne or Brodie Shannon I am happy with that. I think this is the limit of my informal co-operation on this one, DI Sayer, so yes, I look after my people. If you have more questions that relate to my interests, I think I would want my solicitor here."

Catrin said, "Well, thank you for the information you have given us, anyway."

He stood up and the prison officer moved nearer to escort him out. Connolly stared at Catrin then said deliberately to her, "Just think, I'm in here and the man who put me away, the man who really wanted you dead on the steps of that church, is given immunity for it and everything else. Niall told me he wanted Colin to finish you. That's where the noise that I had threatened your life in the days afterwards derived from, if truth be told; from Niall. I never called for it or acted on it, though, as I said; even though others were saying it was coming from me. By then I was up to my eyes with much bigger problems. Did Eileen tell you that part of it, that it was Niall? He told her too, I am sure."

He looked away at the camera after a split-second.

"No, Eileen, you didn't, it seems. You don't keep your friends south of the border very well informed at all, do you?

He looked back at Catrin and she could see he was speaking openly, emotionally. "Colin's blood was up and he was in a fight; fair enough. But Niall was standing there, willing him to kill a police officer. He was deadly serious about it, then and after, pressing me to have you eliminated. And Eileen gave him the keys to some other kingdom."

The resentment of his situation and of Niall Irvin, the lifelong friend who sold him out, just flooded the room. The guard moved closer to Connolly but the man just walked to the door and went out first.

Mark stole a sideways glance at Catrin. She sat totally still and again, he saw her eyes close and the expression of distaste or pain cross her face, as it had after the interview with Brodie Shannon. Irrespective of her demeanour during the interview, these sessions were proving to be hard-going for his boss.

He switched off the recorder and stood himself. "Ma'am. Let's go."

His tone of voice, rather than the comment itself, revealed his concern, his wish for this phase of assistance by Art and Antiques to DCS Moore to be over with.

Catrin stood and faced him. "Yes, we should. Let's leave, but go home. Call Vicky to cancel the hotel and change the train reservations for this afternoon, first class. We will go back now and pick up the bags at the hotel. I will talk to DCS Strachan alone when we get outside.

"It went to plan, mostly. Connolly will be on to Brodie and others and probably be in touch with Ranjani or Bolan about our interest in Ranjani's paintings. We had to help Trident, but I will be damned if I stay in Scotland a day longer to do it."

From what he had heard about the Kinnington Church incident, Mark understood that Niall Irvin did nothing to help her and had wanted his partner in crime that night to get away from Catrin so that they could get out of there. To explicitly hear that the man wanted her dead was another level. His boss, from her tone of voice, had had enough.

He wondered what the conversation between Catrin and Chief Superintendent Strachan would be like.

~~

"How are you doing now?" he asked, as the train passed Motherwell.

Sayer had been largely silent since leaving Shotts. He had watched her through the window of the lobby area there as she had spoken on her mobile to Strachan. Then she had checked her messages, stiffening visibly as she read a new one before they entered the Police Scotland car that was taking them back to the hotel and station.

Catrin looked at him, registering his concern. Before she thought of an answer he said, "I know that they specifically chose you to stir up Shannon and Connolly about the painting, because you had 'baggage'. I didn't really understand how much or how heavy that baggage was."

She smiled. "Well, there's that. It was a little harder than I expected, but I am not really mulling it over. It was a bit of a shock hearing Connolly, but not too much of a surprise. We heard back then that Connolly had called for my death and the death of the undercover agent from the French police. He didn't mention the second person, did he?

"Eileen told me when I called her that she knew what a mess I was in physically and emotionally around then. Irvin was unloading so much evidence about the Connolly operation on to her team it was just part of the flow; that the threat against me came from the Connolly gang, but it was Niall who was pressing it. She decided no value would come out of going into the details with Jane about it, just let her know that I was in the clear. Things were pretty polarized between the Met and Police Scotland at the time."

She paused.

"Strachan is a good copper; I am OK with her. I never had any time for Irvin, anyway. He swapped his grandfather's heart tablets for placebos, so the man died during his next heart attack, in the Kelvingrove. To me he is already a murderer who got off when he shouldn't have.

"It's another thing, a personal matter. I had emails; one from my artistic partner Jean Hughes and another one on the same theme from our gallery. We've been invited to fill in at short notice to replace another artist at a cultural reception tied to a conference; to display and talk about our art. The people who invited us will pay travel and accommodation, seeing as it's so close in timing, and also pay for the transport of the pieces we choose to display; the insurance; the lot. It possibly gives us a new client group."

Mark's eyebrows rose. "Wow; you don't hear much of that. Good luck, you should be happy but... ma'am, you seem really bothered by it. It must be the timing, with everything else going on."

She nodded. "It's at the end of next week at a British Council diplomatic event hosted by the Deputy Consul-General in Hong Kong."

Mark replied, "Hong Kong! Well that's a big turn up. I thought you meant in London or somewhere else in the UK. Someone will be paying a lot in expenses. And exposure to Asian art collectors… they are hot at present, as we know. Well done."

"Yes," said Catrin, "it's a big opportunity."

She went silent again, occasionally checking business and personal emails and, to Mark, obviously declining incoming calls on both mobiles. After about twenty minutes she gave a sigh and sat up straight, coming out of her reverie. She has made a decision about something, Mark thought.

Her office mobile rang again; she looked at the number. "Isabelle; I didn't answer her earlier when I was in my black fugue."

She listened, said 'OK' a couple of times then added, "I see no reason why not; I will flag it to Neville, but go ahead. Relationship-building with the FBI is always on the cards; they hosted us well in Washington."

Catrin and Mark had attended a Task Force meeting hosted by the FBI Art Crime people for UK, French and German colleagues almost a month earlier. Chris had taken time off to join her and they had the weekend in Washington DC playing tourist before the meeting. Klintz had invited both Chris and the German lead's wife, who was also visiting Washington, to the informal team dinner.

After telling Howlett she would be back in the office tomorrow earlier than scheduled, she closed the call.

"Morley Kerswell, the data management guy on David Klintz's team, as I think of him; Isabelle wants to invite him to the Yard to see our operation, as he is already visiting the UK after Paris. He is always on the videoconference calls."

Mark asked, "The balding guy with the moustache, the one who says little except to feed his colleagues info?"

"Yes, him."

Mark looked at his boss. "It's business, right? Not case work specifically but…"

He trailed off, his face revealing his meaning.

Catrin replied, "I don't know. They've been together in a meeting in Paris for two days, that's all. He is a little older than Isabelle, I think, but we'll see, I guess; being hotshot detectives we can probably read a clue or two."

Suddenly she smiled properly, for the first time this trip. Mark thought his boss looked really attractive when she smiled like that. It didn't happen often.

18 INVITATION

Catrin briefed DCI Coltrane in a call on her arrival back into London. The following morning she was in the office bright and early to meet him. They were still locked away when Mark and Isabelle arrived and compared notes on their respective trips. About nine-thirty Morley Kerswell turned up and still the door to Coltrane's office remained closed.

Isabelle had given Kerswell a quick tour to meet the team and had just left for the Black Museum by the time Coltrane's door opened.

DI Kit Madder, Catrin's counterpart leading the Antiques Team, said to Catrin and Neville, "I was a good host for our FBI friend; Kerswell is being given the history tour with Isabelle."

The Black Museum, as it was called, the Crime Museum of Scotland Yard, contains artefacts and evidence from major crimes in the United Kingdom. A private museum, it was generally only open to police officers.

Coltrane responded, "Thank you. We'll say 'hello' when he returns."

Vicky came running along after them.

"Commander Barlow can fit you in, but it has to be right now or after four, sir."

"Or not." he added, to Madder. "Now," he said to Catrin and Vicky.

~~

Barlow said, "I agree, this invitation to go to Hong Kong is probably linked to the proposal from SIS, but I don't know that formally - or informally. I called our contact as soon as I received the information from you, DI Sayer. He has not returned my call yet."

He emphasized 'our contact' by looking sharply at Sayer as he spoke those words, assuming that she had not revealed the name of Stephen Drew to others.

He continued, "And I take it that the proposals we discussed in this room have not been shared further?"

Catrin just shook her head and said, "No, sir," quietly.

Coltrane, clearly more annoyed now, said, "DI Sayer simply flagged to me that she may need, at short notice, to attend a British Council meeting in Hong Kong. It was clear that she wasn't exactly the originator of this wonderful interruption in our casework and I came to my own conclusion, particularly as you mentioned a Hong Kong triad before ejecting me from the meeting which started this matter."

Barlow looked surprised at Coltrane's remark and his tone of voice; a DCI was three levels in rank below a commander in the Met and for Coltrane to be visibly annoyed was a rare sight.

He responded, "I will try again after our discussion, if you would wait outside then. Sayer, what do you want to do about it, that's the thing. Any thoughts?"

Catrin said evenly, "On the train back from Scotland yesterday I decided to accept the invitation, subject to getting the time off. My artistic partner is bowled over by it, as is my gallery owner, for her to be included. It provides visibility for our art with an Asian audience, a new area for us. For my friends, the pottery business they own is doing fine in general, but costs are high, being based in London. So this opportunity is cost-free and can't hurt their business. For me, well, for more people to see my art is always welcome. To be clear, sir, I will not engage in anything else of a security nature while there, if you understand me."

Barlow nodded. "That is entirely reasonable and I fully support your position. I was accurate in my representation of your response to SIS. If our contact is trying to pull a fast one he will hear that exactly from me also. If it isn't truly a British Council initiative, SIS may end up paying for nothing and, if so, it will serve them right."

His tone indicated that the matter was resolved, for now.

"If you would?"

They waited in his outer office while he made a phone call. Then his door opened and he stepped out to say, "I left another message but..."

Catrin stood and pulled a piece of paper from the file folder she was carrying, passing it to Commander Barlow. Coltrane had already been shown it but looked away as if the document was between his DI and this senior officer.

She said, "I'll leave this, sir. Note my highlight."

He looked at it, noting the yellow area. It was a photocopy of the formal invitation from the British Council. The highlighted section specifically stated that they would welcome 'one work included in the items on display from a current student, highlighting knowledge transfer in the area of artistic skills'."

Then he recalled that Sayer and her artist friend had only one student; the granddaughter of the man Stephen Drew had mentioned. Commander Barlow decided to talk his boss, Assistant Commissioner Sleiman, run it by him to see if he had any suggestions. It was hard to raise an issue regarding an SIS operation involving a Met police officer when there was no operation identified and no liaison established.

He wondered what the hell Stephen Drew was doing.

~~

On returning to the Art and Antiques area, Catrin and Neville said their hellos and made the right pleasantries to Morley Kerswell. He was happy to have the opportunity to visit, but without a shared case for them to discuss he appeared to be more a tourist than a police officer.

Catrin pulled Howlett to one side. She asked, "When do you plan to finish with Agent Kerswell?"

Isabelle replied, "I was going to take him to lunch at the George and leave him to get back to his hotel from there; then get back here."

For some reason, Catrin knew, the George was a favorite venue for Isabelle to meet people, an old pub on the Strand across from the Law Courts.

Catrin said, "Ask someone else here to do that, will you? You take him out tonight if you want to, for dinner; charge it to expenses. I would like you to come with me now. I am going to see Ranjani's lawyer, Donald Killam, about his painting; the one I only saw briefly and I need another set of eyes on it. If his wife is there, we will talk to her. Mark is tied up preparing the formal report of our interviews in Scotland for DCS Moore."

In the car Catrin briefed her team member.

"Neville and I talked this morning with Superintendent Lauder about your analysis of the other paintings Ranjani bought through this dealer Pennywell. I had reviewed them on the train up north and we both agree with you; they don't make sense for an operation that needs to launder cash from drug sales.

"Trident is happy with our trip north, stirring the pot, but they are now more puzzled about the paintings. They are looking to us for possible answers. So we are to prod the lawyer over the obvious tax fiddle on his painting, to stir it up some more. Then Lauder wants Neville and me to go through your findings with Moore. Neville and Gerry Lauder are meeting today, to hatch up a path forward to recommend to her."

Howlett asked, "Is there anything new on the Shannon death? Are they pushing that one, too?"

Catrin replied, "Not quite the way we thought. It seems more and more likely that the man Rai will only be charged with supplying Lena Shannon with drugs rather than with involuntary manslaughter. It's clear she took the final dose herself, from the fingerprints on a glass found by the bed. His statement said he woke up or came to, I am not sure, and he saw her on the balcony just stepping on to the stool, as if in a dream. He reacted as fast as he could seeing as he was hung over, he claimed, but she was over the edge before he actually touched her and he couldn't get a hold ... she was gone."

She paused while working her way through a difficult left-hand turn then she continued.

"Rai had a fresh mark on his back in an area he couldn't reach, a pinch mark where her nail had cut the skin. She used to pinch him playfully to get his attention at times, he said. It was only on examination when he was brought in that it was spotted. He thought she may have tried to get him to wake up earlier that morning but he had no other explanation of it."

"Doesn't sound like the marks of a fight, then."

"No. But they have him on solid ground about supplying her. He started her on drugs, he admitted. He is in it up to his eyes with Ranjani, as is Ranjani with her dad Brodie Shannon. We shall see."

19 MCTAGGART

"My husband is not here; he is at his office, Inspector."

Catrin and Howlett had arrived at the lawyer's home in Ilford to find Mrs. Killam alone. She had invited them in; not this time into the home office her husband used but the main drawing room.

Catrin said, "It may well be you that we need to see. You mentioned that you are the current owner of this painting."

She pointed and moved closer to it, with Howlett following suit. As Sayer re-focused on Mrs. Killam, Howlett did the same on the painting.

The lawyer's wife replied, "Yes, I think we talked about that in the middle of the night, during your visit with Mr. Lauder. My husband gave it to me. He bought it for the office - the one where he is at now, not his home office - but decided to give it to me when I saw it was the Hebrides."

Howlett added, "It's in excellent condition. McTaggart did a number of paintings of the same area, I recall."

Mrs. Killam smiled at the older detective; a woman of similar age, she thought; one who understands.

Catrin said, "We are looking into another painting owned by Mr. Ranjani, one of your husband's clients. In checking the regulatory filings on that, we came across the information that the same dealer had sold Mr. Killam your painting. May we just check something on the back?"

"If you are careful, yes. This is not a fraud thing, I hope? I know vaguely about the role of Art and Antiques."

Catrin and Isabelle were carefully lifting the painting off its mount. On turning it round, Isabelle said, "Ah yes, I thought; the gallery stamp and the date was…"

She noted it in her book. They then returned the painting to its place.

Mrs. Killam asked, "And the significance of that?"

Catrin responded, "The dealer, Mr. Pennywell, is a gallery owner and an art appraiser. To answer your earlier question, neither of us have any basis to say that this is anything other than genuine. The provenance on it is good through to the transfer to your husband's business. But I suggest you should consider having it appraised again for insurance purposes, at least. We think it may be considerably more valuable than the price now on record."

"That makes very good sense, Inspector. I will talk to my husband about it."

They moved on to questions about the dates the painting was acquired by Donald Killam and later transferred to his wife. Mrs. Killam knew the date she received it, but not the other details. They asked also about the reason for the transfer, getting her to talk about the link to the Hebrides. For the Scotland Yard detectives, it was simply padding; window dressing.

It was only after they left that Laura Killam thought that the detectives had not actually clarified fully the purpose of their visit. Then the phrase, 'through to the transfer to your husband's business' struck her. It was her painting; DI Sayer had known that, but she had chosen her words carefully at that point. She pressed the speed-dial number on the phone to put her through to Donald's private line, to see if he could make any sense of this enquiry.

~~

"And tomorrow?" Isabelle asked Morley that evening, during dinner at the Pig and Goose, the restaurant above the George pub.

"I have a visit to Southampton, to a friend. His grandfather was killed on D-Day too, same landing beach, different unit. We met in France doing research. He and his wife are taking me to Portsmouth and the area. He is very knowledgeable about the departure points for Operation Overlord. After staying with them and seeing more of that part of England it's back here and an evening flight home."

"Right," said Isabelle. "Well, it's been very nice to meet you and spend time with you in Paris; you really made it easier for me. I feel like I can go back with Maureen... or by myself."

She dried up suddenly, not sure what else to say, then added, "Maureen and I often meet in the pub downstairs; it is just across from where she works."

The conversation lulled until Morley came to a conclusion of sorts.

He said suddenly, "I really enjoyed your company and... would you be open to staying in touch personally? Not work. Perhaps even meeting in Paris? I ask, because I am a bit of a loner, not good at this. But I don't want to appear pushy."

Isabelle said, "Staying in touch, yes; I would like that. Paris, well, that's a bit of a... stretch, I was going to say. But I am a bit the same way; self-reliant, I think of it as, not loner."

She took a deep breath.

"I'm divorced. My husband was a police officer who met someone else. Since then... well."

Morley said, "I talked with David, about talking to you. Made sure it was OK."

"David? David Klintz. Why?"

His words came quickly, as if he wanted to get something off his chest, but was unsure about doing so.

"I was in an FBI unit based in Chicago looking into interstate killings. Not serial murders; you know; the TV drama diet. Our team was focused on killers for hire, contract killers."

She didn't say anything. It's a long way from art work, she

thought.

"It got too much for me, the clinical nature of homicides like that, ones that people will do for money. I had a breakdown and... the Bureau is very good with that sort of thing. I always liked art so when I came back they asked David, I guess, about a less stressful role. I have been with his team in Washington ever since."

She nodded, seeing now the reason that no-one made fun of his gaffs about art and why they tried to help him. They hadn't worked on the raw side of FBI work in the way Morley obviously had. Looking at him, she saw he needed to reach some sort of closure on this revelation, so she waited.

He went on, "In my time with my former team, we tracked down fourteen contractors. We were able to arrest only five; four really; evidence is really difficult with professionals like that. The last one I went after killed himself as we raided his apartment. We had traced eleven known killings to him, five in the USA, the others abroad. It was that fact that he escaped justice that gave me my breakdown. He was dead, but there was no justice to it."

She thought for a moment. "Are you married? Divorced?"

He shook his head. "I had a long relationship with a woman while stationed at the Chicago office, but it was never going to be marriage, I think. It definitely wasn't when I became ill."

"And why did you ask David about talking to me, can I ask? About telling me this?"

He looked uncomfortable.

"It's hard to talk about my past and I don't socialize a lot. I told him I really liked talking to you and he said, "Morley, just tell her. Stop being a closed book. Have some faith in people! David's Jewish."

That explained the advice, he meant.

Isabelle burst out laughing, which surprised Morley.

"What?" he said.

She replied, "I think I knew that, the last bit. I am an art crime detective and he is one of the top people in my field. I've read his bio."

She reached over and touched his hand. "Let's stay in contact, see how it goes. And think about somewhere other than Paris, perhaps."

His face clouded over. "What's wrong with Paris?"

She smiled. "Nothing. In fact, I think I am going to talk to Maureen about doing a gallery visit with her there, now I know my way around a bit more. If things develop between us, we can meet in other places, can't we?"

He nodded, smiling. "And Paris too, you can go more than once, you know!"

"Oh, I don't know about that," she said severely, "I have my list of cities with art I want to see; it only allows for one visit per location. I have already made an exception for my earlier holiday in Paris, long before Maureen and I started our quest. I would have to break my own rules."

Then she realised she was making a joke about herself, something she hadn't done in a long time.

20 BOLAN

The fact that two men in different high-security prisons could not only make phone calls from illegally-held mobiles, but could schedule the call as if they were city businessmen reflected the power they held and the people they controlled. But they didn't waste time on pleasantries.

Dominic Connolly said, "Michael, a matter of our mutual security. Two days ago Brodie was interviewed by the Met. The same people visited me yesterday, part of the Art and Antiques lot. We think they were just fronting for our respective oppositions, as I know Strachan was involved at this end. But the focus was a painting that I once owned, that Jalaj bought."

Bolan was an older man than Connolly and his voice reflected it. But God help the man who dismissed him as an old fool. He replied, "We are aware; I have already had a message delivered to Brodie with our condolences. Jalaj meant well in buying the painting; you know that."

"It's not that particularly; that's not a worry, but you know me."

Michael replied, "Like a cat with a six and half senses and ten lives."

They both laughed and a moment of silence hung between them.

Bolan said, "The police officer who came up, Sayer; she has history with you, I hear. Not on-going, like Strachan, or Lauder with me, but…"

"Yes she does. And it's not the Hunter I am worried about. Nor the accounting."

He didn't say what it was; he didn't have to.

Again, they wasted precious air time in silence.

Connolly said, "I'll leave it with you. Perhaps it will not turn into anything, but if it does…"

Bolan recognized that Connolly was being respectful about the issue being on his patch, not one for him to deal with in Scotland. He just said, "I will sort it. Without repercussions. But this copper who came up to see you has set you on edge, I think?"

"After the Kinnington Church fiasco, she probably has. She was the one who picked up on Niall's little game. I know, you told me at the time not to play stupid with the Milnes, but that's water under the bridge."

Bolan laughed quietly, "As is me driving a bloody Daimler. But, duly noted, Dom. I will pay attention."

On that happy note they closed the call.

Tony, Dominic's phone man and number two on his team in HMP Shotts, popped his head back in the room, closing out another call on another mobile. Dominic could see one of the lookouts behind him.

"Liam is getting back with an update on the Dundee problem in two, Dom."

Tony had a scar above his right eye, a difference of opinion with someone inside on a previous prison stretch. It made him think of that Welsh woman. She had some go about her to take down Colin, he thought. It reminded him of Joan, his wife, who was doing sterling stuff keeping everything together for him on the outside.

He hoped Sayer wasn't as energetic on the Ranjani issue as she had been on the Gault forgeries back then but, if so, he had just done the right thing for the relationship with Michael.

He nodded to Tony. Back to work.

21 DECISION

Coltrane and Lauder had spent about twenty minutes so far with DCS Moore, explaining the case that Sayer and Howlett had put together and their conclusions. Catrin just watched, making sure no errors were made. That had gone relatively smoothly until Neville Coltrane proposed the next step.

Moore said, apparently unconvinced, "I think you are on to something, Neville, but why do you want to hold off dragging in Pennywell, interviewing him and charging him? He has no priors so it should be easy; he won't be used to this."

Coltrane responded, "Because he won't tell us much during the interview. And he won't sit there saying 'no comment' repeatedly, like members of Bolan's gang after a drug bust. He will sit quietly and wait for his solicitor to guide him, after which he will be out on bail talking to his friends in high places. Something is going on with these paintings; the price issue, the reaction by Connolly we saw on the interview recording. We need to get to the bottom of it."

Moore responded, "Being part of some society elite doesn't give him immunity from being questioned, with or without bail."

She sounded snappy, not liking the inference.

Coltrane replied evenly, "No. But it provides him with top-line lawyers that will make life very hard indeed for us to get information. I think this is a better way forward."

She paused, musing. "Bob, what do you say?"

Coltrane's boss, Chief Superintendent Matheson, was her counterpart.

Matheson said, "I go along with Neville's proposal but I told him Art and Antiques will support your operation, which-ever path you choose."

He smiled, adding, "I told him not to make it sound as if it's an 'Old Etonians Protection Society'; it wouldn't go down well."

Catrin pursed her lips hard, trying not to smile. In fact, it was her boss who broke out in one. "Did I do that?" Neville asked Moore.

The Trident DCS deigned not to answer and looked at him. "You went to Eton with Pennywell?" she asked, with obvious distaste.

"No, of course not," Neville replied, apparently insulted. Catrin knew he had gone to Charterhouse, which would have been as bad in Moore's eyes. Catrin suspected that the plain-spoken Mancunian wasn't too impressed by elite public schools.

Moore looked at her. "And you, DI Sayer; where did you go?"

"I went to Pontypridd High School, ma'am. We don't have a protection society either."

Moore quipped back, "London Welsh is one vast protect-ion society if you ask me, hiding behind the sport of rugby."

She held up her hand to stop the discussion.

"See if I have it all."

She focused on Sayer, the most junior officer in the room.

"This highly respected Old Etonian art dealer, Richard Clark Pennywell, Esq., gallery owner, man of substance and influence around town, has for some unknown reason, probably money, gone off the rails - but with only one client group that we are aware of so far, Bolan and the Ranjanis. Otherwise, he would be a run of the mill - forgive that term,

Neville; I know fine art is not run of the mill - art dealer, no different from the rest.

"First you find that he sold two paintings to Michael Bolan in 2006, just prior to the money laundering regulations coming into force. The prices for them seemed high, even for the hot economy back then. You suspect some flow-through; some of the dirty money paid for the painting returned as clean cash to Bolan with more than a standard fee retained by Pennywell.

"Later, when the regs were in place and Pennywell had to report the specifics, you find seven moderately expensive paintings that he sold to the Ranjanis over an eight-year period. No big deal other than they were also valued wrong - but seriously wrong. Two bought in the UK were significantly over-priced, which we can rationalize in the same way as the Bolan paintings, the cash components probably being drug money which our friend Pennywell laundered. Now for the funny bit."

"Funny peculiar," interjected Lauder, growing a bit tired of the soliloquy.

It didn't stop Karen Moore.

"Five paintings came from overseas. Everything was above board in terms of their last owners, you say, other than the prices were consistently low. Not a bit; a lot. Forty thousand euros low on a two hundred thousand euro painting, on average. Not just once, which could be explained as an aberration, but it happened consistently across the bunch. Payments by Ranjani were clean, it appears. In each case a numbered company in Europe made a separate down-payment for the work directly to each seller. Collectively it's about quarter of a million euros that appears to have been paid by someone else. Is it drugs-related or not, you ask?

"Finally, weirdly, there are the recent sales to Killam and Ranjani of two paintings by Scottish artists and, of all of them, the Hunter at the Stratford flat appears to be the only honest-to-god, regular transaction above sin, a sale of absolute purity shining out from this motely mix. How am I doing so far?"

Catrin said, "You have it, ma'am."

Moore said, "Now the proposal. Rather than simply haul Pennywell in and ream out the explanation for his list of sins, your boss wants to set it up so that he turns voluntarily into an informant. This will take longer, as Trident will have to bring some pressure to bear, but it could be more productive. You think once he starts talking openly about the reasons for these variations, it will reveal far more about the workings of Bolan and Ranjani than would ever come out of a formal interview if a charge was looming. What was implied in this most erudite and circumlocutory proposal - ."

She smiled warmly at Neville Coltrane in her shift in the level of English; she was a smart one, Catrin knew.

"- is that I am a 'get stuck in and give it to them' sort of copper, who would prefer to put the fear of God and a miserable prison existence to Pennywell in a loud voice at ten-thirty at night. You also warn me that this more complex approach could go off the rails and get nowhere. Have I got it all now?"

Catrin smiled and nodded, not saying anything further. Coltrane and Lauder tried to look as if they hadn't hatched this plan between them and Neville hadn't drawn the short straw to deliver it. Bob Matheson simply looked entertained.

Moore scanned the group. "It sounds great; let's do it. Have I ever been known to be difficult on things like this? I am a reasonable person, after all, aren't I?"

Back in the Arts and Antiques Unit area, Coltrane said, "So now Gerry and his team will spend some time with their informants, listening and sending messages. By the time you get back from Hong Kong we should be ready to talk to Richard Pennywell."

Catrin said, "Will that be a freezing cold interview room with him dressed in baggy coveralls while his clothes are being gone through?"

Coltrane resisted the temptation initially. "No; it will be lunch somewhere quite nice. To begin, at least. Then I will show him a photo of DCS Moore looking reasonable at us;

that should bring him out in a cold sweat, confessing everything."

Catrin said, "And all I have to do first is stir the issue of the paintings with the Ranjani couple."

~~

Superintendent Lauder did the talking initially during the second visit to the Ranjani home. He had started asking questions about the relationship between Malav Rai and Jalaj Ranjani.

"Is he an employee, sir? Did Lena meet him through you, perhaps?"

"I run real estate businesses, superintendent. As far as I am aware Mr. Rai isn't employed there."

Lauder let that one slide. He went on, "We have reason to believe, contrary to the impression Mrs. Ranjani left with us last time, that the deceased was not, in fact, in a relationship with you, was she?"

Ranjani didn't answer but his wife did. "It's his love nest, superintendent, so why else would she be there?"

From her voice Catrin thought the woman knew the answer; she was part of the cover up.

"That's why we are asking, Mrs. Ranjani," Lauder said tersely. "Lena Shannon's mother and best friend separately told DI Sayer that Mr. Ranjani provided the flat for Miss Shannon's use but he wasn't in a relationship with their daughter. It was a favour; a payback, they said. Like buying the painting there. Payback for what, I wonder?"

Nirupa Ranjani said, "We have decided to sell that painting, superintendent."

It sounded as she, rather than Jalaj, had made that decision.

Catrin watched the woman's face as Lauder responded. "I don't think you can do that as it doesn't belong to you. It is part of the estate of Lena Shannon. Mr. Ranjani gave it to her, didn't you, sir?"

Ranjani said, "Well, I may have said that I was thinking

about it…"

Lauder replied, "More than that, I think. Lena made notes of the conversation. It is quite clear."

"A conversation, purely that, superintendent." Ranjani was trying to pull it back.

Lauder added, "Which she also recorded, on the same laptop."

Ranjani looked pensive, deciding not to say anything.

Lauder waited a moment before continuing. "Well, it's a conversation we mentioned separately to both Mr. and Mrs. Shannon. And, I gather, to a Mr. Dominic Connolly in Shotts prison. Isn't that right, Sayer?"

"Yes, sir. He was interested in that. A painting once bought by Mr. Connolly being returned to Scotland."

Ranjani looked as if the news of Connolly finding out about it was more troublesome for him than the rest he had heard.

Catrin had moved nearer to the Mignard painting, looking at it again. Mrs. Ranjani said immediately, "That is definitely ours. We bought it!"

Catrin smiled. "As I said last time, it is very nice."

Superintendent Lauder said, "Yes it is. You bought it through the same gallery as the Hunter painting."

That was Sayer's signal. She asked, "Do you know a Mr. Pennywell at the Broughton Gallery, Mr. Ranjani?"

Ranjani seemed surprised at the change in topic.

He said, "The name is familiar; I can't remember who we dealt with at the gallery. Can you, Nirupa?"

She said, "I have more contact there than my husband. Yes, we know Mr. Pennywell in a business capacity quite well. He is very knowledgeable and helpful. And we did buy the Mignard through his gallery, yes."

Catrin moved towards her a little. "Did he handle the communications with the seller of the Mignard alone, or did you have direct talks with the owner?"

Nirupa Ranjani thought for a moment. "I heard about the Mignard independently and mentioned it to Mr. Pennywell. He secured it for me."

Catrin asked, "So, do you find that the Broughton gallery - or Mr. Pennywell, I should say - gives good service for all the paintings you acquire through them?"

Nirupa Ranjani stared at her coldly. "My husband bought the Hunter, Inspector. He will have to say whether he thought the price to be fair."

She chose not to comment on the other paintings. But her face signaled to Catrin she had not missed the comment about multiple works bought from the gallery.

Lauder returned to questions about Malav Rai, how he had been seen in the company of Jalaj Ranjani. If he wasn't an employee, was he a friend? Did he know the man was having a relationship with Lena Shannon? Did it annoy him?

As he pressed on, Jalaj became more careful and un-cooperative in his responses. But he was a seasoned criminal. He knew not to lose his temper or curtail an interview that was simply 'helping the police with their enquiries'. If he did, he would be taken to a police station and would definitely need his lawyer.

When Catrin and Superintendent Lauder left the Ranjani home and drove away, Lauder seemed pleased. "They'll analyse that lot to death and back. And the one thing they will remember is your questions about Pennywell."

Catrin said, "Hopefully they will give him a call, share their worries with him; work at getting their respective stories straight. But the Ranjanis are weird, don't you think?"

Lauder asked, "What do you mean?"

His expression seemed to indicate he had similar thoughts.

She answered, "The flat is sumptuous. They have a great art collection and two bodyguard-type servants and - nothing! There is nothing 'everyday' around the house. No mess. None of the normal things. It's like visiting a show home. It tells us so little about them. I recall your comment on the previous visit; that you found them 'wooden'. I agree, as if they are devoid of the common elements of life."

Lauder nodded. "It's always been that way with them. The first time I took him in for questioning, they were living at the Stratford flat. It looked back then as if Nirupa and Jalaj were living in a hotel suite. There wasn't even a family photograph, I recall. I was struck by that at the time. Weird, as you say."

22 HONG KONG

Catrin was sitting in a window seat and had a particularly good view during the descent and arrival into Hong Kong airport. The British Council had sprung for business class travel on British Airways, given that the trip was both at short notice and brief; they were staying only two full working days.

As their contact person told Jean, "It will be a lot of travel time. We want to show our appreciation for your cooperation. And we have arrangements with a number of British carriers which helps."

As the Boeing 777 came in over the outer islands, Jean leaned over the aisle from her seat to peer out the window. "It's really exciting, coming back so soon," she said.

Only months ago, Jean and Melanie had flown into Hong Kong to attend Li's wedding. Neither of them were aware of the issues surrounding Michael Yau or that, as Catrin had worked out, it was Yau who engineered their airline tickets through a travel agent. Jean and Melanie believed that the tickets were a fortuitous outcome of an 'exchange of labour' with the owners of another boutique in the Spitalfields Market. It made Catrin think how sensitive and devious the world of Michael Yau and Four Square was; and how she had no idea what SIS may have planned for her during this visit.

She replied, "I'm looking forward to seeing Li and to the reception, to see how our art is perceived here, I must admit."

She pointed out the window at the skyline. "Years ago the airport was in the centre of Hong Kong; the planes had to fly in right over the buildings and turn on to the runway."

Jean cringed a little. "It sounds dangerous."

Catrin just watched the view, wondering if this visit had any dangers of its own. While working as Sandra Hunt's security aide she had been trained in counter-surveillance and was going to be on full alert while she was here, she told herself.

Liz Marshall, the gallery owner that sold Catrin and Jean's works, had flown in separately with Miele Yau on Cathay Pacific. Jean had spoken to the British Council contact who indicated that they would arrange an invitation for Liz, as she had the job of sorting out the available art and loaned items. They would provide also a hotel room for her but not pay for her flight; and they would only pay a discount economy airfare for Miele, 'as a student who would have a work featured'.

Liz had said that the trip would in any case be a business cost for her, meeting potential new clients. Miele just said enigmatically, "Leave it to me; we can travel together."

Catrin studiously avoided overhearing Liz's remark to Jean the following day that, "Your student comes from wealth; we knew that, I think. I have just had it demonstrated."

Like the SIS, she thought, she could indulge in some 'plausible deniability'. She suspected that Miele and Liz were not travelling at the rear of the Cathay Pacific aircraft.

It was early evening when they arrived at the airport, to be met by a woman called Iris Chan, a local employee of the British Council. She confirmed that the correct number of boxes had been delivered to their offices yesterday and Liz, who had arrived earlier that morning, had been through them to check their contents. Chan had a car to take them to the hotel.

In fact, a text from Liz to Jean confirmed the fact that the art works had all arrived safely. She said that she was having a quick meal with Miele and having an early night. She needed sleep. Miele was heading off now to see her family.

Jian Li arrived at the hotel after work and the friends spent the evening talking and eating in a nearby restaurant. Throughout it all, Catrin kept her eyes open for any signs of Stephen Drew or his ilk. If we are being watched or monitored, she thought, I can't see it.

"It's such a short visit," said Li.

Jean said, "It's a business trip - in and out. You know about those. In fact, after the Kuala Lumpur issue, you came to London for the same amount of time, as I recall."

"Right!" laughed Li, but in the glances exchanged with Catrin she conveyed a different message. That trip hadn't been about business, it had been about friendship.

"I am looking forward to the show tomorrow," she added, changing the topic.

They weren't expected to put in any appearance at the day-long conference being held at the British Council before the reception. According to the schedule, Jean and Catrin had been asked to have breakfast with someone else from the Council team locally.

"Just a quick word with Miles, to talk about the event and yourselves. A walk through, to make sure it goes smoothly," Chan had said in the car.

When they were alone Jean commented, "It's to give us the 'once over'; to make sure we can speak properly and don't have 'Free Wales' tattooed on our foreheads."

In reality, it became clear that the man, Miles Parsons, was simply looking for input; he had the job of writing the note announcing the reception, to be read at the main conference session after lunch. He also had to script a few words for the Deputy Consul-General, who would formally open the event.

He said earnestly, "We normally do this well in advance. I looked at your web site but those things are so formal. Seeing as you agreed to come all the way here at such short notice, it seemed easier to chat about what to say."

Catrin liked him. He appeared genuine.

Jean and Liz went shopping late morning and Li, Miele and Catrin went for a run. "I'm not acclimatized; not too far or hard;" Catrin said.

Li had chosen Bowden Road, a jogging and hiking trail along a road that was car-free, a relatively flat four kilometre trail not too far from the hotel. It was a quiet oasis for running early morning, but later on it was busier.

In suggesting the run to both women, Catrin thought this would be the time, if ever, that some approach by SIS would be made. What would happen, she didn't know, but it was ideal - her and Miele together in Hong Kong and easily accessible. It made sense.

It was half-way along, as they stopped to drink water, that Miele said, "My grandparents were pleased with the invitation to the reception."

Catrin said nothing, taking it in, as Li said, "You asked them last night, I take it?"

"No," said Miele. "They received an invitation from the Council, with a handwritten note that one of my works would be shown. They move very fast at that office, it seems."

Li gave Catrin a searching look, which she avoided by dropping down on one knee to re-tie a lace. In any event, no one bothered them during the run.

~~

The reception was held on the first floor of the British Council building, adjacent to the British Consulate-General; two pale grey, dissimilar office blocks joined by a connecting unit on Supreme Court Road.

The visitors went along to the closed-off room in the Council building early-afternoon to open the transport boxes, consult the floorplan and decide on the placement of the works among the three display tables. These were nicely draped to floor level and were very sturdy, much to Liz's pleasure. Each table was a different shape, well suited for its location and around each were posts and ropes to prevent people getting too close.

"They've done this before, obviously," said Jean, agreeing with Liz.

"Probably had too many people in the past colliding with a table," said Catrin. "But, I agree. It looks good."

Once they finished placing the pieces, Liz said, "I am pleased that Mr. Kyriakos agreed to the loan of the figurine, Catrin. We were just about to ship it to him."

Catrin smiled. "Having met him a couple of times now, he will be delighted to talk about art he owns being sent to Hong Kong to be part of an exhibition."

"It's hardly that, really," said Miele, "Just an afternoon reception. But still, it's exciting!"

She was looking at her own work, the Utamaro-style design on a medium size platter, her pleasure very evident about its inclusion. "Truly, I would love it to be a longer exhibition and just turn up every day and hang around, talking to whoever is interested. Whomever, yes; must get my English right."

Liz said, "I should have you working in my gallery."

Miele's look seemed to indicate that it wouldn't be the same at all.

Jean replied, "I just want the wait to be over with, or at least, the thing to start. Miele, Catrin and Liz are professionals at the schmooze… my stomach just churns until I get started. Look how relaxed Catrin is!"

Catrin thought that she must be covering her anxiety pretty well.

She said, "Shall we get some tea or something before the conference session finishes? We won't get the chance once they arrive; it will be nothing but talking for us."

As the people moved into the reception room following the close of the afternoon session, the cultural attaché at the consulate and Miles Parsons attached themselves, one to

Catrin, the other to Jean; each artist was aware that they would be guided to meet different participants. The group assembling was now examining the art, talking among themselves and being served drinks and canapés. The reception was scheduled to last about ninety minutes, but would probably be less, they had been told. The attendees were on their own for dinner.

Within minutes, Catrin found herself moving from one person to another, being introduced and talking about the works until there was a chink of metal on a glass. Miles Parsons spoke up, announcing that the Deputy Consul-General would like to welcome participants to the reception. Catrin and Jean were led over to stand by the man as he spoke.

It was a set piece. The senior diplomat must have done this sort of welcome a thousand times. He was glad that the attendees had participated in the conference and stayed on to join the reception and he was appreciative that the artists had made the time to join also and show some of their works. He introduced Catrin and Jean as "Welsh artists living in London, brought to the attention of the Council as being 'on the verge of joining the major league'; whatever that meant. Then he added, "And Ms. Miele Yau, a student at the University of Hong Kong, now at the Royal College of Art this year, joins us also. Miss Yau is working with these artists while in London. One of your own works is on display, I gather."

Miele, standing in the crowd, beamed at receiving the recognition, as others looked at her. Then Catrin noticed Michael Yau and his wife were standing close to their granddaughter.

Catrin had past experiences that whenever introductory speeches end, the stillness of a polite audience is released, the noise level goes through the roof and people move around as if suddenly unchained. Miles led her directly over to Miele and a man in a suit who had just joined her, talking about the work, a tall European who turned suddenly to focus on Catrin.

"Catrin, I don't know if you remember me? Peter Griffiths. I was a friend of David's at university. Congratulations on your success as an artist."

He held out his hand and she shook it automatically, smiling, trying to recall the man. She remembered the name but didn't recall the face or voice. The mention of her former boyfriend David James, the person she had thought she would marry during her student days, always threw her.

"Thank you. It has been a while since Aberystwyth; how are you?" she said, smiling at him.

"Very well, thank you," Griffiths replied. He was beaming at her, his recognition of her apparently much clearer than hers.

Miele said, "You know each other, from university?"

"Yes," said the man firmly still looking at Catrin, as if she should comment also. But she didn't say anything.

Afterwards, Catrin blamed it on the whole momentum of the reception, the number of new people she was meeting. It annoyed her that it took her that long to realize that this man was Stephen Drew's plant.

Parsons, standing by Catrin, said, "Mr. Griffiths is a trade attaché at the Consulate, but very interested in the activities of the Council, I am glad to say."

A trade attaché; just the sort of role that a commercial espionage organisation would naturally focus on, Catrin realised.

Griffiths turned his lantern smile on Parsons. "Art always interests me, even if my career took other turns."

He focused again on Catrin. "You left Aber to become a police officer, I recall and now, this. Wonderful! A much more enjoyable occupation, an artist, I would think."

"I still am a police officer, as well," she replied, trying to keep her voice neutral, thinking that this man Griffiths would be well aware of that from his briefing.

Catrin glanced at Michael Yau. He was taking it all in, she saw. She was wondering how to extricate herself from the situation when Jean solved the problem, waving urgently from across the room. Parsons saw it and whispered to Catrin.

"If you will excuse us," he said, and without waiting, led Catrin over to Jean and Liz, standing with the cultural attaché and two Chinese men close to one of their works of art.

Jean said breathlessly, "This is Mr. Joe Chung and Mr. Desmond Chung; Joe just bought the 'Brecon Black'."

A year ago Catrin and Jean had created a series of vases and bowls decorated with abstract elements developed from images of the Brecon Beacons, a mountain range in south Wales. The 'Black' vase was the last unsold item, so they had brought it along. The two men were elegantly dressed in good suits; one was slimmer than the other, Catrin noticed and they appeared to be about the same age as Jean and herself.

Catrin smiled. She was still reeling from the encounter with Griffiths. The two men were smiling back.

One said, "Pleased to meet you; I'm Joe." The other said, "Likewise, I'm Desi."

"Desi?" repeated Catrin.

"Easier to say than Desmond for us Chinese," the man replied.

The cultural attaché said, "Joe and Desi are brothers and entrepreneurs. They started up the regional commuter airline Clearwater Air. They are great friends of the Council."

Jean broke in. "Desi asked the price of the 'Black' and then said he would buy it after Liz told him. Joe upped him and Liz looked after the short bidding battle, for want of a better word. They took it up to HK\$ 30,000! Joe is the winner. I think it should go to the first offer at our asking price; it's not an auction."

"So do I," said Catrin quickly, getting a glare from Liz.

"It's no big deal," said Desi. "We do this all the time, Joe and I, but not about business, just about art and fun stuff."

Miles Parson was laughing, clearly well aware of the two brothers. Catrin wanted to ask, 'do this all the time; waste money?' but held her tongue.

Jean was looking shell-shocked, Catrin realised, and probably the adjustment to the numerically larger Hong Kong dollar price wasn't helping; the vase had been sold for nearly three thousand pounds. Instead, she said, "Well, thank you. It is very nice to be so appreciated. Jean and I have been collaborating for -."

"That's not it, the problem," interjected Liz, as the two men stared at Catrin, assessing her. "They would like to commission miniatures of the piece, to be given to their passengers."

Desi said, "Just for our top tier clients in our rewards program, at our airline. Not many copies, probably about three hundred pieces. We haven't decided on the number, but probably something small like that. We need to put our client communication people in touch with your marketing agent."

We don't have one, we are artists, thought Catrin, looking first at Jean and then at Liz. Liz's contract covered all sales of Sayer-Hughes pottery made in her gallery, with an exclusivity arrangement for the UK. Hong Kong was a little further afield.

Liz spoke again, "I said that each of your works was unique, so any copies, however made, could not be the same size or be an exact duplicate … but I may be speaking out of turn."

Clearly she was looking to Catrin for guidance as Jean was appearing out of her depth. Catrin wished that Melanie was here; she liked this sort of discussion.

Catrin responded, "Mr. Chung, Liz is quite correct. We have undertaken commissions on occasion for specific pieces for a client, but have never copied our original art. I think we could talk with you further on your proposal, but I am not completely comfortable at present with the items you purchase being copies of this particular piece. As an artist, I need to think it through and talk with Jean. I'm sorry."

She looked at Jean seeing her friend was lost in the dilemma of the sales opportunity on one hand and the Sayer-Hughes agreement about original art.

The brothers looked at each other.

Catrin added, "If this means you wish to cancel the offer for our vase, we quite understand. We would still like to work with you on a solution."

Joe Chung smiled. "Miss Sayer, Catrin. Can I call you that? I am happy with our purchase and also your idea for a solution.

It is quite understandable. Desi, we need to put Mona in touch with Catrin and Jean's representative and take it forward. My only stipulation is that they are left to do the design as their own work. I don't want Mona jumping in with her artistic flair; it's great what she does for our corporate image but these should not be items with a Clearwater Air image. It is something unique, but taking account of the design elements in this work that I am after."

As he explained, Catrin could see his brother was in agreement with him. Almost simultaneously they produced their business cards as Liz, ever capable, pulled out cards for Jean, Catrin and herself.

"You leave tomorrow?" Joe said.

Jean said, "Yes, back to London. We will be in touch before we go, though, to give you our representative's contact details. But you have our own contact information there."

They all shook hands and the brothers made their departure. Parsons said, "Even by Council standards, this has been an incredibly fast networking success. I think they all came out of the afternoon session quite energized."

Jean started responding as Catrin looked around. Griffiths was still with the Yau group, just handing over his business cards to Michael Yau and Miele.

Miles Parson said, "Miss Sayer, if you could come and meet Mr. and Mrs. Choi, they asked me to introduce you. His wife is a collector. He may also buy a work, I suspect."

It was later, as the flow of people died down and the stragglers finishing the drinks and conversations, that Miele came up to Catrin and Jean with her grandparents.

"It was such fun! My Utamaro-style platter sold, even though I told the man it was mine, not yours. He called it an investment. My first sale!"

Jean responded, "But you didn't call it that, I hope. I told you, we never sell our art indicating that it is a financial investment."

Miele laughed. "I know. Even if your works always seem to

be increasing in market value."

Michael Yau spoke up. "Miss Sayer; Miss Hughes, thank you for taking Miele under your wing so carefully. It is very much appreciated, I assure you."

Jean said, "We love having her, don't we, Catrin?"

Catrin nodded, wondering what had transpired between Michael Yau and Peter Griffiths. But she said instead, "It is a pleasure to meet you again, Mr. and Mrs. Yau."

She let the conversation flow among the group, watching rather than participating until Miele suddenly asked, "How do you feel?"

Catrin replied, "To be frank, I really need to rest a little. With the long trip and all this excitement, I am quite worn out."

Mrs. Yau said, "I can quite understand. I would be, too."

Jean said, "And me. I am not even sure if I will make it through the Council dinner."

Miele said, "We have to. We are invited guests. I will go afterwards to my grandparents' home, but - can I say the words I am not allowed to say?"

"No," said Jean firmly and Catrin just laughed.

Catrin watched Miele explaining the exchange to her grandparents as they walked away.

23 GHOSTS

Shortly afterwards, the British Council hosted a dinner for both the speaker panel from the conference and the visiting artists from the reception. It was held nearby, at the Conrad Hotel across the road, a set menu in a private room. Catrin found that Li had also been invited, in the same mysterious manner as Miele's grandparents had been invited earlier to the reception.

The Deputy Consul-General spoke at the dinner, where he thanked various people, including Jean and Catrin, reserving his final appreciation for the representative of an investment company. It had co-sponsored the two day event and the dinner itself.

Catrin found herself sitting diagonally across from the man posing as Peter Griffiths, but the long dining table was also wide. Initially, conversation with people on either side of it predominated rather than across the table. Catrin wondered if the Council was simply being used by SIS or had been involved in some way. Once she saw the seating plan she was sure it was the latter. Sitting next to Griffiths, on his far side, was Miele Yau. She was glad that the student would be returning to London. For the remainder of the academic year, at least, she would be out of the loop, away from it.

As an aide to an assistant commissioner, Catrin had plenty of experience at this sort of formal event and was able to hold conversations on her side of the table as well as monitor from time to time the activity of Griffiths. She saw the man was carefully balancing his time between Miele and the guest on his other side, an older Chinese man, as he should.

It was this man who started the interaction. The dinner, with wine adding to the drinks consumed during the reception, had become more social and energized. Conversations across the table had started.

"Miss Sayer?"

She smiled at him, understanding that he was a member of the organizing committee of the conference.

"Mr. Griffiths said he knew you from college days in Wales, I heard."

Griffiths looked up sharply, first at the man then at Catrin. She replied, "Yes, Mr. Griffiths is a friend of someone I knew there; he mentioned it to me earlier."

The man said, quite seriously, "I wonder if I could hear you speak Welsh to each other? I don't know the language and I am by profession a language teacher."

Catrin looked at Peter Griffiths, her expression indicating she was open to it. She was interested in what he would do. She wondered if the man spoke Welsh at all.

"Of course; let's," he said, in English, raising his hand to invite Catrin to start.

"How is David these days?" she asked in Welsh.

She had followed from time to time news of her former fiancé, even though they didn't stay in touch.

Griffiths responded in the same language. "Doing well, I gather from Hugh. Do you remember Hugh Owens? He said David is teaching in the Vale of Glamorgan. David and his wife now have another child, a baby born a few months ago. I last saw David briefly before I left for my first overseas assignment. But not since. You know; the life of a diplomat…"

He smiled, leaving it open.

Catrin replied, "Like the life of a police officer, never quite predictable, I am sure."

She looked at the questioner across the table, asking in English how he found the language. Soft and flowing, the man replied, compared with Chinese. It was very pleasant to listen to. The conversation moved on and Catrin avoided any subsequent eye contact with Griffiths, as he seemed to do with her.

If she had any doubts, the Welsh discussion confirmed it. He was spot on with information about David Jameson and she recalled Hugh Owens clearly. She didn't recall many things about David's university friends; his friends were his whereas her friends seemed over time to become theirs. It was just the way it was. But she recalled that the small group all came from North Wales, as did David. This man's Welsh accent and intonation was from South Wales, Pembrokeshire specifically. She would have remembered that.

~~

Later, gathered in Liz's hotel room after it was all over, shoes off, they connected on Skype to Melanie, who was in the shop in Spitalfields. It was early afternoon, her time.

"You will be our marketing representative," said Jean. "We decided just now."

"Me?" Melanie said, shocked, "I got jet lag when I came over for Li's wedding. I would be no good. Who will manage the Kiln?"

"We will bring in someone for the shop, filling in; we've done that before," said Jean promptly. "You have the business head for this deal."

"This is different," said Melanie promptly. "We can't make that number very quickly; we would need to sub-contract possibly, if they would accept that approach. We need to know their timeframe. If we sub-contract, there is the quality control, the supply logistics and approvals, it's…"

Liz butted in. "I am on the phone with William; he says he will help."

"I agree, let William do it," said Melanie instantly.

Liz said clearly, "He will mentor you on the logistics, Melanie, work with you on the deal from his end; not do it for you. He will even be available on your schedule, if necessary, a phone call away while you are here. Then he can go back to lolling around my gallery."

She was speaking to them, but also to her husband, William Esquith, on the phone. William used to work in the city, but they knew he did a lot of the logistics for the gallery sales domestically and internationally.

"Well, I... guess I am going to do it, then. What next?"

Jean said, "I am so glad we came; this is so... different. It's our good luck that the Council thought of us."

She sounded both tired and happy.

Catrin stayed silent. She was still lost in the events at the reception and dinner, rationalizing them. Was all this effort worth it? The reception 'fix', the travel and event costs, all just to get Michael Yau and Peter Griffiths together? They would have had to persuade the artist already booked to back out as well, one would presume. Then she realized that the answer was yes; a few thousand pounds for a solid access opportunity to a key triad member; all it involved was high-jacking an existing event for a couple of hours. To SIS, of course it was.

Melanie answered her own question saying, "So I will be coming over to Hong Kong within... days, I suppose?"

Li had been quiet in the background throughout the discussion on Skype. Now she said, "It's a hot deal, so yes, you should. And I can help, or at least sort out arrangements. I will get better deals than you would on your hotel, for example."

Melanie replied, "Let's talk later, I have a customer waiting, she says she wants to buy some more mugs, Jean, for her set, before I go running out the door to Hong Kong. Bye for now."

The line disconnected.

"I need my bed," said Liz, pointedly. It was her room.

"So do I," chimed in Catrin, slipping her shoes back on.

Jian Li stood, to leave also, when she suddenly thought of her earlier discussion with her husband about Chris's sailing experience.

"Now Catrin, I have a big bone to pick with you! You didn't tell me," she said, mock-seriously.

"What do you mean?" asked Catrin, surprised, now alert again.

"Your husband is a sailor."

"He was. He isn't. I forgot," she responded.

Li smiled. "No, he isn't now, but James and I are. He could be again and that leaves only you... James and I are thinking about us meeting up for a sailing holiday next year?"

Catrin smiled, now realizing the purpose. "And I can't think any further than getting to my room and having a good night's sleep. Let's talk about it tomorrow. See if I can get over my fear of open water in a small boat."

As they left Liz's room together, Li needed a lift going down to the ground, Catrin and Jean needing one to higher floors. As they waited, Li asked Catrin if she was OK. She sounded concerned.

Catrin said, "I am just tired, Li; why?"

Li said, "It was in the reception, when that man introduced himself, it was as if you had seen a ghost. I wondered if it was because he raised David's name. It was an intense relationship, I know."

Catrin said, "Probably. I didn't know that I looked so surprised."

Li said, "Did he talk to you again? Leave you his card? He was giving them to people."

Catrin said, "No, it was so busy. We talked briefly at dinner. It doesn't matter. David... a friend of David's... it's over with."

She wrinkled her nose.

Jean said, "Best put behind you." She remembered the heartache her friend went through when Catrin and David split up.

Catrin repeated, "It doesn't matter at all, really."

Li looked at Catrin, wondering why her friend was concealing the fact that it did matter. She and Catrin had a very open relationship and things had seemed to go well at dinner. She had looked like she had seen a ghost when she first met Peter Griffiths. And she had that same look again when Li made a joke of her 'not telling her something'. It wasn't about the fact that Chris was a sailor; it was that she had suggested to Catrin that she was hiding something.

She obviously was; and it was about something more important than sailing.

~~

The following morning, Catrin, Liz and Jean had worked on the repacking and transit details of the remaining items being shipped back, finalizing it with Iris at the Council.

"We could almost take them with us, what's left," said Jean, "but, best not to, with the paperwork."

Iris Chan smiled. "It's part of our offer, to manage the transport. We were really pleased with the reception - and that people took an interest and actually bought some of your works. Sometimes the people are lost in post-conference session talk and hardly notice the works of the artists, but this one worked well."

"You do this regularly?" asked Jean, as Catrin joined them, finishing an email on her phone.

"Yes, from time to time. Normally with a British artist already in the region visiting, teaching or studying. When Jim Kerry had to cancel at the last minute we were glad that you came through for us."

"How did you find us? We never did hear," asked Catrin.

"Our planned artist for the event teaches in Taiwan but he got called to an interview in London to explore a possible new university position. Miles asked our contacts at headquarters if they knew of an appropriate replacement at short notice. She said they had been updating the database and... you were also ceramic artists. Miles said it was urgent and we should go for it, ask you. HQ covered the expenses which we are thankful for; but it was a surprise as they don't normally do that."

"It was all Melanie's doing, then," concluded Jean, recalling the conversation. "She told us about the contact with the Council."

Catrin kept her face neutral. They all looked up as James and Li arrived. They were having lunch together before driving the visitors to the airport. Catrin remembered she had to talk about sailing holidays.

~~

On her return to London, Catrin called Commander Barlow, intending to leave a message. Though it was early evening, he answered himself. All she said was that she was back from Hong Kong and something had happened there. He asked her to come to see him at 8.45 a.m. the following morning.

In his office, she said, "After speaking to you I did nothing on-line last night, just went back through personal photographs. The man calling himself Peter Griffiths looks similar to my former boyfriend's college friend, but he isn't the same man. I didn't want to take any actions there or here to jeopardize him, if I am correct. Just in case."

"It is a few years, DI Sayer; people change. How sure are you?" asked Barlow. "As my earlier voicemail said, Stephen Drew eventually got back to me and denied that the invitation had anything to do with SIS. After speaking with you, I texted him again last night. This morning, I received this email."

He had printed it out and Catrin read it quickly.

"Drew said he had looked into it further and heard that you and your artist colleague had made substantial sales at the reception. He claimed it was simply a successful event by the British Council."

Catrin replied, "Yes, it was an amazing experience, in that sense. The buyers were interested and I don't regret going. But it is still an issue of concern."

He smiled. "Stephen Drew is deflecting, I feel. He is going to too much trouble to deny it; so I think you are right. But I have no idea where to take this next. I can't raise a nonexistent operation with others in SIS. I have already informed Assistant Commissioner Sleiman, so he may decide to make some waves - or not. Relationships with the security services are delicate at times. I will bring him up to date and it will be in his hands."

He had clearly finished with the issue and Catrin moved to leave.

Barlow said, "Have you spoken to DCS Moore, by any chance?"

"No, sir."

Popping into the offices of detective chief superintendents wasn't a habit she had, she thought; particularly Moore. It would probably mean more work.

"Your visit north seems to have stirred things up. The day after you saw Connolly, Bolan summonsed Jalaj Ranjani to see him, we heard. It was only two days after his regular scheduled visit. Word was that Bolan didn't look too happy about it."

He looked happy about it himself. Catrin didn't question how Trident knew these things; informants were stock-in-trade for organized crime investigations.

She replied, "Thank you for letting me know."

He added, "And Neville will tell you, no doubt, that we are well along the way to having a little talk with the art dealer Pennywell."

24 UTAMARO

For two days following her return Catrin was kept busy at work in the preparations for the Pennywell interview. Outside work she was engaged in the follow-up actions arising from discussion with the Chung Brothers.

Jean and Catrin spent some time on several designs, ideas different from the work purchased by Joe Chung but which had similar elements. It took no more than a day after submission of several proposals before Mona responded with a choice, their final decision on the production run subject to first inspection of the original art. By then Melanie was in Hong Kong.

She was very effective in her meetings there, but wanted to keep Jean and Catrin informed and involved with the key decisions, even if it was out of phase in terms of time zones. It turned out that Mona, the Chung's design team leader, was Swedish, not Chinese, and worked all hours.

Meanwhile, Jean had brought in temporary cover for the Cwmbran Kiln, someone who had experience already at working in the shop. She contacted another potter, a man she knew who did good work and he agreed to split the workload, if required.

Catrin started to suffer from broken sleep, her nights disturbed either by bad dreams from the Kinnington Church incident six years ago or irrational fears about demands from SIS. At first she wrote it off as jet lag and effects of time change but Chris wouldn't have that.

"You cried out softly, last night; it woke me."

Catrin hesitated, then said, "Was I intelligible?"

He nodded. "All you said was, 'my face', but it sounded so distressed. You seemed to go back to sleep, so I did, then woke up to find you out of bed up early - again."

She nodded. "I'll talk to Dr. Herrington. I am able to call him anytime, he said."

Chris didn't ask when; he got the impression that she wasn't quite ready to do it yet.

Melanie also returned from Hong Kong pleased with the outcome and the path forward. They were in the Cymbran Kiln, meeting up on her return.

"Joe and Desi are great to work with, as is Mona," Melanie said. "She took me sightseeing one evening and to a club. A guy tried to pick me up but I told him I was engaged. I quite like the life of international marketing. Where to next, boss?"

Her question was directed to her partner with an impudent smile. The thought of Melanie clubbing brought a smile to Catrin's face.

"Probably to the front of our shop for a while; to do some dusting, sell a dinner service or two, get that urge for nightlife out of your system," Jean said.

Out of the carry-on bag from which she had unloaded her laptop and the business papers, Melanie produced two slim boxes.

"These are for you; not from me, nor Miele. She assured me she took the dreaded and banned words of 'thank you' to heart. But her grandparents didn't. They were very happy with the reception at the Council that your international marketing expert missed. Miele heads back here next Tuesday."

Jean's present was a silk scarf that was intricate and expensive. Catrin's was in a similar size box but wasn't cloth. It was a woodblock print, a Japanese nineteenth century art print, in very good condition. She turned it to show her friends.

"By the artist Utamaro," she said.

In each box was a note from Michael Yau thanking them for looking after Miele so well. He said that he and Mrs. Yau were overjoyed to see their granddaughter so happy and these were simply small tokens.

Jean said, "I saw this scarf in the display in the shop next to the hotel, with Miele. She must have told him. And yours? It's a good choice given Miele's platter that sold over there."

As Jean spoke, she saw her friend smile. 'You like yours, too," she added.

"Yes, said Catrin, "I do."

It wasn't the print she had pulled up on her iPhone when she had demonstrated its use to Miele. This was rarer, she knew. She understood the message - it was that which caused her to smile. She wasn't sure why, but she felt relieved.

"You really do like it, don't you?" Melanie asked, looking at it a little suspiciously.

"I do, indeed."

Melanie said nothing; her own preference by far was for the image Catrin had first shown to Miele.

Catrin sent a text later asking to see Commander Barlow again when convenient. On Monday morning Lorraine responded, saying it could only be the following Wednesday at the earliest, if it wasn't an operational issue. She didn't push it, she waited. Neville's big date with Richard Pennywell was taking place on Tuesday lunchtime.

But that evening she sent an email to Miele, acknowledging the gift and asking her to pass on directly to her grandparents her appreciation, particularly for the print chosen. 'It is very good quality and the image is very clearly defined', she wrote.

25 SIMPSONS

Neville Coltrane had chosen the Grand Divan Room at the restaurant Simpsons on the Strand as the venue for lunch with Richard Pennywell, knowing it would likely be crowded and busy. Simpsons, the archetypal traditional English restaurant established near the Savoy in 1828 had, some said, lost many of its high-end clientele to the more modern, international restaurants. It was now the focus of the tourist trade, they opined ominously.

Coltrane was unfazed by the gourmet gossip. He had first been taken there as a boy by his grandfather, who was a 'known gentleman' there. Neville, in turn, had kept up the family tradition and was known by name there too. He used the restaurant often for Coltrane Foundation work. But its large dining room was also a venue where two men could talk in confidence - and do so without giving Pennywell any advance warning of his dilemma.

Catrin was sitting in the front passenger seat of Superintendent Lauder's car, parked on double yellow lines in Burleigh Street, around the corner. They were both listening to a feed of the conversation and drinking coffee that DC Hills had brought along from a nearby sandwich shop. Loretta Hills was outside, drinking her own and smoking, an earpiece connected to her own radio.

"I've never been to Simpsons," said Lauder. "Must try it sometime. In the old days, they didn't take credit cards. You needed a wodge of fivers, a cheque book or an account with them. Your boss probably still has one of the latter."

He glanced across, testing his humour, baiting her a little. "They even let women in now. Had to break down and change the rules in the eighties, I recall."

Catrin looked at him. "Alone, together, or only in the company of a man?"

"Oh, I don't know that and we can't exactly go in now and find out, can we?"

They sat in silence for a while, listening to the conversation being transmitted over the radio. Coltrane and Pennywell were past the discussions of braised pork cheek and steamed mussels for starters.

Lauder turned to Catrin and said, "You know why we are really doing this, don't you? I saw it on your face at the briefing."

She looked at him, assessing her response.

She said, "It's not Ranjani; it's Bolan. His sentence was fourteen years, so he should be eligible for parole in two. You are going to milk Pennywell but string it out, save the charges against Bolan until the months before his parole hearing, make it really solid. It will sway the hearing and, if it goes all the way through, add to the length of his total sentence. You will hold off on the critical charges until then."

He nodded. "Not exactly by the book, I know."

Catrin responded, "I spent two years in Brixton dealing with the customer end of the likes of Ranjani and Bolan, so they get no sympathy from me. And in Scotland…"

She paused, deciding how open to be.

"When I was injured there, one of the consoling thoughts was that at least I had been part of a large-scale drug operation against the Connolly and Milne gangs. The thing which galls me coming out of this now is that Niall Irvin really wanted me dead when I was in that fight at the church. Dominic Connolly made a specific point of driving it home."

"We are on. They are into the roast beef," interjected Lauder, picking up the developments on the radio.

The waiter serving the two men had noticed that in the largely upbeat atmosphere, Mr. Coltrane's guest had suddenly changed from a sunny disposition towards a roast beef lunch to a man who had been hit with bad news. Mr. Coltrane's guest had eulogized over the menu as they ordered. This was the best of British food, he had said. It must have been an aspect of their discussion which had upset him, the waiter thought, as he cleared away the plates from their first course. People shouldn't really mix difficult business with meals, was his personal opinion.

"So this is not about an invitation to the committee that you alluded to on the phone."

Neville said, "No, Richard, it's about my other hat, I am afraid. About certain irregularities in sales made by you over a long period to people with criminal connections."

Pennywell's face went ashen, as if a weight he knew was hanging over him had suddenly fallen. "I see. Do I need my solicitor? Are you going to arrest me or something?"

Coltrane looked at him neutrally. "That will depend. If it happens, it will be our organized crime people, Trident, who do that, not me. They have bigger issues to deal with."

And if you don't cooperate, thought Coltrane, it will happen sooner rather than later. I am not letting you swan off, heaven knows where.

He watched the art dealer absorb the blow as the waiter returned bearing two plates with the main course, talking about the fare. Neville thanked him as they went through the ritual of selection of accompanying vegetables and sauces. Pennywell appeared to have lost his appetite.

Coltrane went on, "I thought an informal talk was in order. This is not an interview."

He reached into his inside pocket, brushing past the microphone and pulling out the folded single sheet of paper, a table listing works, dates and currencies. He placed it between them, finger resting on the edge. The man wasn't going to be able to keep it.

He waited for the reaction then said, "The people who will deal with this are the organized crime group, as I said. I see all manner of art theft and fraud in my work, and these sums, while not trivial, are not up there at the top end, the millions. You understand that."

Pennywell nodded. From his expression, it seemed to be good news.

Neville continued and the man's face fell. "But when they told me about the names; Ranjani is a drug boss, as is Bolan. So is this man Connolly. It's the drug people that should worry you, not Trident."

Pennywell's voice was audible but less clear in the car. "Are we 'off the record', Neville?" he said.

"We are in Simpsons, not Belgravia Police Station," was Coltrane's non-answer. He went straight on, "It took some discussion with my Trident colleagues, but I said I felt I should speak to you first, to see if there is a path forward. These are serious criminals running large drug gangs. The art crime aspects are secondary, frankly."

Catrin let out a snort of laughter, "Oh Neville, if we played this back ... art crime is not that serious."

Lauder said, "I'd think it was Colonel Blimp talking to me but Neville knows his man, it seems."

Coltrane was still talking. "Drug bosses give no leeway to people cheating them. And Trident tells me they are already hearing noises as a result of our own investigation. One of my people went up to Scotland to do the routine enquiry on this painting by Leslie Hunter. She had been involved in a previous operation against Connolly and caught his attention. Ironically it seems that the Hunter was the only one of these you didn't fiddle - allegedly fiddle, I should say, until you are tried and found guilty."

Pennywell's face changed noticeably at the mention of the name Connolly.

He said, "Ah… that would explain several calls I have had recently which, frankly, have left me a little uncomfortable. About the Hunter painting; that was entirely above board, as you say. And, frankly, I didn't cheat anybody, despite what you think of the prices."

Coltrane didn't respond. He just cut himself a small slice of prime rib.

After a moment Pennywell said, "These alleged business discrepancies; it is art valuation we are talking about. Neville, you have expertise here, too, I know. These are minor irregularities at best compared with the things going on else-where. I saw you on Channel Four a few weeks ago talking about the economic losses in art sold through free ports."

Coltrane stopped chewing and swallowed.

"But this happened here, on British soil, with British laws and taxes; that's the difference. You are not hearing me, Richard, I think; it's the personal risk you face with these criminals; cheating them, as I said."

The man's face was looking increasingly worried.

"Oh I am Neville, I am; I am thinking about it. I am also thinking about Sir Joseph's wife persuading that corporate idiot to bid on her little Birger Sandzén piece last month. You were there. It was at a far higher price than it was worth and the man was more than half-cut. That was daylight robbery, but no-one will go after her, will they?"

Neville said nothing, sipping his glass of sparkling water trying to hold his expression of concern. He was thoroughly enjoying this. Pennywell was getting desperate if he was dragging up that sort of thing.

He stuck to his theme. "These gang leaders deal very severely with their own people when crossed. I know you are not one of them; but will they care, I ask?"

Lauder said softly, "If Pennywell storms out early, we have lost it. If Neville walks out early, the same. If they come out together, well, we will see. A lot's gone into this."

He had said as much already, back in the Yard in the briefing. His comment in wrap-up then to his team was, "Keep sharp, no blunders. Art and Antiques have done their bit and DCI Coltrane is ready for the finale. He is good at this. Eileen Strachan said so, not him."

At that point, Neville was in a Coltrane Foundation board meeting being held at the Courtauld Institute; Pennywell had been invited as his guest and he was taking him afterwards to lunch.

All Lauder and Catrin could hear was a silence punctuated by the sound of cutlery on plates. Catrin kept thinking that one or other would say something more. The waiter was heard checking with them but no response was given. She wondered what sort of expression Pennywell had on his face.

Lauder said, "Neville is waiting him out. Good."

About thirty seconds later, Pennywell said, "You said earlier, 'a path forward'. I should say that I won't do a thing without my solicitor's advice, but… what are you thinking of?"

In the car, Lauder said to no-one in particular, "He's there. Careful, Neville."

Coltrane put his knife and fork down carefully on his plate.

"I'm serious about the risk of violence. Perhaps being somewhat over-reactive but not out-of-field on this. It does happen."

"So what do I do?"

"Tell us all about it. The lot. Leave nothing off the list. We'll get your lawyer to work with CPS and…"

Pennywell interjected, "God, no. They will kill me for sure then. Or I will have to go into a new identity and… what's it called?"

"Witness protection, but no, Richard; now you are being

over-dramatic. Frankly you don't have, I suspect, anywhere near the level of knowledge on their operations to warrant that; you aren't exactly supergrass material, are you?"

Pennywell responded, "Not at all. We just discussed paintings and sculptures... art."

Coltrane tagged on, "And money; means of payment; and timings. Didn't you?"

The dealer replied, "Well, obviously; sellers needed to be paid, I needed my fees; naturally. Sometimes it was a lot of work, I tell you."

"The paintings that were over-priced - these."

Coltrane, looking at the sheet upside down, used the hilt of his dinner knife to flag the paintings he meant.

"Was there money flowing back to Bolan and Ranjani? Were you doing their laundry, so to speak?"

He wasn't expecting a straight answer, but wanted to see Pennywell's face while he responded. In fact, Pennywell sounded genuine.

"No, Neville; I never paid anything back 'under the counter', if that's what you are referring to."

"So why would they pay more than they were worth? And why don't you see my point on your risk, if these people feel you have cheated them?"

Pennywell looked down at his meal and after a moment pushed the plate away; only about an inch, but it signified a lot to Coltrane. Pennywell now accepted this wasn't a pleasant lunch meeting; it was all business - police business.

"Some things don't get written down. For example, Simone and I have a small villa near Cannes, more a house with a garden, really. Nice place; my grandfather bought it. Let's say a client may choose to be generous about a payment on a painting. I may choose to offer the use of our villa rent-free to people I feel generous towards myself. No-one was cheated."

Neville noted it and moved on; that would be a can of worms for Trident to unravel. He stabbed the blunt end of his knife down on the paper, highlighting other paintings.

"But some of your valuations, quite frankly are... all over

the place. Your fees are a percentage of the sale price. For some, you lost out a lot, didn't you? I can't work out why."

Pennywell looked a little embarrassed. "No. Actually, I got my fees and... other funds for those."

Neville looked at him. Now Pennywell knew he had crossed a line, admitting undeclared income, at least. Again, he resisted going into depth about the reasons.

"Who set the prices then? I know your competence; this doesn't tally, frankly."

Pennywell replied, "To be honest, Nirupa Ranjani did, for those. I just told her what they were worth and developed the excuse for each price she chose to pay, ones that we could use with others including the tax people. I gave the justifications. Someone else made up the balance of the selling price each time, but I don't know who that was."

He stopped talking, looking at the expression on Coltrane's face, the disbelief; that he allowed a gang leader's wife to set lowball prices.

"Well, well, well, that's interesting. Nirupa sets the prices. Why?" asked Catrin.

Lauder replied, "Where now, I wonder?"

He meant, where now would Coltrane lead the questioning? They hadn't planned for this eventuality.

Hills got back into the car, the back seat, asking, "What does this mean, boss?"

"Shush," said Lauder.

Coltrane said, "Richard, I hadn't realised that it was as bad as that!"

Pennywell looked perplexed. "But, I told you, I haven't cheated either Mr. Bolan or the Ranjani couple."

Coltrane took off his glasses and polished them on a white cotton handkerchief, thinking of the next step. He gazed across at Pennywell as he put his glasses back on.

"No, but you have involved yourself in a conspiracy to move monies around the world. If Ranjani underpaid for these paintings, someone else was paying the seller the differential, right? You said so. In money, in drugs, who knows? You are part of a bigger conspiracy than I thought. And at the time Trident is prizing open this can of worms."

He leaned forward. "At some point the drawbridges will close and those on the outside will be left to fend for themselves. In the worst case, if they have information that could open those drawbridges, they are at risk of blackmail, extortion or elimination."

As it dawned on Pennywell he turned pale. "God, it's a mess isn't it? What do I do?"

Coltrane said, "Tell us openly, clear the slate and we will sort something out. Nothing you give us will be attributable to you directly. When it is used, if it is used, it will come out of other areas than art transactions. I can't guarantee you will get a deal that gets you off scot-free, though. But - who is your solicitor?"

"Belinda Strickland at Strickland, Jarvis and Strickland."

Neville said, "I know her; Jeremy Strickland's daughter; they are both very good. I would insist on her or him during the discussions, not one of the lower ranks, some criminal litigation junior who will want to micro-manage the detail of our list of charges. You need a 'big picture' person at this stage; after all, you haven't been charged with anything yet."

"Can I sail through this, Neville, if I do, do you think? Honestly now?"

Coltrane said, "Belinda would advise you. She may have to settle for something light, perhaps some fiddling you did outside the window of Mr. Ranjani and this man Connolly, something which will be seen to give you a light sentence and take you out of the field. Probation won't be that bad once your family gets through the shock of your behaviour. The dust will die down, take it from me. But I must emphasize, it's not up to me. I can put in a word, but I am only a chief inspector. It has to be your call."

Pennywell replied, speaking more to himself, "And Belinda will advise me about the value of... what I know, I am sure.

Perhaps, if it is valuable enough to the Met I could keep out of it completely?"

Coltrane said, "It would have to be very useful indeed to Trident. But if Belinda convinces them and CPS, well... I doubt Art and Antiques will be in a position to follow up on this list. We would be overruled. But you will need to talk with others in the Met and your solicitor."

Pennywell replied, "I don't relish it, but... what next? I am totally torn on this."

The man pushed his plate away still further and moved his chair back. Neville thought he might bolt; that he had over-played it. The waiter hurried across.

"Is there anything wrong, sir?" he seemed concerned.

Pennywell smiled briefly at him. "No, not with the food. It's... me."

The waiter leaned in, closer to his ear to give him the directions to the washroom, just in case.

As the waiter took the plate away, Coltrane forced himself to sit still.

Pennywell said, "I need to think about this. It's a lot to... swallow."

Neville nodded. He eventually said, "Take your time. Not my recommendation, by the way, to drag it out. One is either going to do the right thing, or not. But I understand."

He sipped his water and leaned forward.

"This conversation never took place. The dice will roll..."

He forced himself to pick up his knife and fork again.

Pennywell let out a sigh of defeat. "I don't know... what the hell; from what you say they will be talking to me at some time anyway. Let's do it. But where?"

The knife and fork clanged as Coltrane put them down.

"At Scotland Yard, not a police station. Call Strickland now. Just tell her that you are helping with enquiries and you must have her or Jeremy represent you; no if, ands or buts. Mention my name, if you must; that may help. We have a car standing by, just in case you were open to this. As I said, Trident wasn't too happy that I was having this frank discussion with you, but they are prepared. Strike fast, I suggest."

Coltrane flagged the waiter.

"Mr. Coltrane?"

"On my account, Paul. My guest needs to leave and I apologize for our rush, but lunch was superb as usual."

The waiter said, "Mr. Seeley will get you a taxi, Mr. Coltrane, if you need one."

He was referring to the guest manager in the lobby.

Neville stayed one step behind Pennywell as they walked up the paneled dining room to the lobby. The Maître' D was engaged with others, Neville saw; thank God for small mercies. A wave and a mouthed 'thank you' and they were at the front door.

It was a matter of a minute, no more, as Coltrane stood there, supposedly on his phone calling for the car with Pennywell beside him. The unmarked vehicle with a driver and someone already in the back seat drew up and Neville opened the rear curbside door.

"You aren't coming, Neville?"

"Yes, Richard; I will be there, I promise. I will follow along behind directly."

Pennywell suddenly thought that Coltrane would be driving back in his own vehicle. "I left my car at the Institute," he said. "I need to -."

"They will sort it all out, Richard. I will see you in a few minutes."

He could hear DS Mahon talking to him, introducing himself; a steady friendly voice from someone young wafting across the doorframe as Coltrane pushed the door closed. He gave a deep sigh. In a moment, the car was out in the traffic and he waited for Lauder's car to appear.

Lauder had driven along Burleigh Street to work his way back around to the Strand. He said, "There's Neville seeing him off. And Sayer, the Irvin issue. I will talk to Karen and give you a call."

"Sir?"

"Something that can help you, and us, no doubt. Perhaps even help him."

She knew Lauder was a Baptist; someone in Trident had commented on it. It was probably the only way that he could stay so long in this job, she thought; hope for salvation for even the worst offenders. But her mind wasn't on that, it was on Coltrane and Pennywell. She was not sure what Lauder meant and didn't process it at the time.

Catrin climbed out as they shuffled seats; DC Hills scooted across the back seat as Neville climbed in next to Lauder and she got in the back. In the dance around she said to her boss, "Well done, Neville."

His first comment as they set off was, "I thought he might bolt at one point. But we got there."

"He's over the threshold. Thank you." said Lauder. "And that bit at the end, where he is hoping to be free and clear of the charges; that should make him very co-operative."

Catrin thought, by the end of the day Richard Pennywell would probably be back in his own home, but his world will have changed. Over the days and weeks ahead he would be interviewed and re-interviewed. His lawyer would be talking about deals for his client. And out of the mess of detail, they would hopefully tie in a number of drug money transfers. As the car sped back to Scotland Yard, above the quiet conversation between Lauder and Coltrane, she put her head back and closed her eyes. She was still out of phase, hit by moments of jet lag and, if she was honest, the memories and fears dragged up over the last few weeks.

Back in the office, as Neville headed off to the interview room with Lauder, Catrin brought Mark and Isabelle up to date. Mark would now have the job of watching the first set of interviews.

"So he says Nirupa Ranjani set the artificially low price, not him. How many dealers do you know work that way?"

Her two staff members didn't answer. Mark shook his head. "Perhaps the interview will bring out more detail; things that we can use to sort it out. You want me to go along and observe now?"

"If you would, Mark, please."

Howlett said, "I'm seeing Morley Kerswell shortly, just for an hour, ma'am; he is back from his holiday and flies out this evening to Washington. Can I ask him if the FBI has anything similar, in pattern? Not give him the case details, obviously. You never know."

"That's a good idea, Isabelle."

In the end, it was - but it didn't appear so at first.

26 STAIRS

It was later the same afternoon when Vicky came into Catrin's office and closed the door.

"There's a problem. Isabelle and this Morley Kerswell were taken to hospital, but were not badly hurt, I gather. Someone pushed them down a flight of stairs."

Catrin said, almost automatically, "What? Both of them?"

"Yes," said Vicky, "And Morley phoned using Neville's number. He asked for you to come over there. They were discussing something and you need to hear the information, something relevant to a case, about prices. He didn't say which one. He just said that it was Isabelle's request; she is not speaking too clearly at present. Her nose is broken."

"I will sort it out; which hospital are they in?" responded Catrin, picking up her things.

"At the Chelsea and Westminster."

The hospital was about fifteen minutes' drive away.

She called Mark. "Morley called. He and Isabelle have been in some sort of accident but they want to talk about the price variation in the paintings, I gather. This is more important than watching Pennywell."

It was carelessness and the totally unforeseen, combining to

190

look like stupidity, as these things often do.

Morley had enjoyed his holiday and had travelled back by train to London, due later to take an early evening flight from Heathrow. He met Isabelle at the George pub, supposedly for a drink, which they had in the bar. But once they started talking about the issue of painting price variability, it became more intense and time passed. Morley decided he needed food as he had missed lunch. The pub was downstairs; the Pig and Goose restaurant they had eaten at before Kerswell's holiday was up a flight of stairs in the old building, so they decided to check out the larger food selection there. Isabelle had pointed the way and Morley had started up the stairs, still talking about his theory.

Coming downstairs was a teenage boy with his mother behind him. It would have been easy enough to move past each other with care but Morley's head was turned sideways so that his voice carried to Isabelle. The boy was heavyset and, as they closed, he just lashed out, swearing about Americans blocking the way.

Off-balance, Morley went backwards into Isabelle and both ended up on their backs at the base of the staircase; him with a broken wrist and her with a broken nose where his head had collided with her face. As they looked up in shock, the woman was screaming at her son and talking about how sorry she was; her Adrian had anger management issues.

People came over to them from up and downstairs and in the melee, someone said that they should call an ambulance and the police. One of the people in the group said, "I am a police officer."

Through blood pouring through the tissues held to one side of her nose, Isabelle winced, "So am I."

They made the boy and the mother wait. As Isabelle and Morley went off in the ambulance, two uniformed officers had arrived and were talking to witnesses and the mother of the assailant. She was crying as the boy sat there, sulking.

They were both in pain, of course. Morley said, "I need to

cancel my flight."

The ambulance attendant said, "No doubt about that. You won't travel until a doctor clears it with the airline. Make sure you tell them inside ER so you get the right cast. Only certain types are allowed on aircraft."

Isabelle said, "Two police officers, beaten up by a teenage boy. I am not going to live this down. David won't let you back in the UK without an armed escort."

Morley laughed. "Let's get it classified as a hate crime, make it more serious; it will sound better for ego protection. I should have been looking where I was going. The kid looked to me as if he was claustrophobic; he just lashed out."

Being police officers didn't help a lot. They were triaged to wait. That was when Morley, at Isabelle's insistence, called Neville's number.

It turned out that of the two injuries, the nose was the more problematic immediately. It wasn't simply broken, the septum had deviated and the cartilage had fractured; it would need surgery.

"You will need to come back in tomorrow; we'll schedule it for then; it will be day surgery but you will need someone to take you home afterwards, as you need a general anesthetic."

For Morley, despite the ominous warning of the ambulance attendant, he was fitted with a two-part cast, told he should wait seventy-two hours to see how the swelling went down and if there were further problems. If not, and if the airline and his medical insurance company agreed, he could travel the following day.

It was impulse, but Isabelle said to Morley, "Do you want to go back to the hotel you stayed at last time? If not, I have a spare room in my flat, you see, and we can help each other."

He very quickly accepted her offer.

~~

Catrin and Mark found them in the coffee shop on the

ground floor; she had called Morley back on getting the news and told them she or Mark would drive Isabelle home and him to his hotel; it was the least they could do. Kerswell had passed the phone to Isabelle at her request.

She said to her boss, "We need to talk. It's about the prices of the paintings." It came over as, "Ith abowd der prithes od der paintin."

In the coffee shop Catrin tried hard not to focus too much on Isabelle's nose and the temporary dressing holding it, but it was the elephant in the room. Mark was fixated on it, she noticed. Catrin thought, thank goodness it's a hospital; anything goes here, in terms of people's war wounds.

Isabelle said, "God, it's awful, it feels like…"

She paused, lost for an analogy.

Catrin said, "Like a separate head stuck on the front of you?"

Isabelle nodded.

Catrin added, "When I had my face damaged, that's what my dressing felt like. I looked in the mirror and couldn't believe how flat it looked."

She looked at Mark then said, dead-pan, "When I came to Art and Antiques it seemed as if you two were leery of me because of my past incidents. Or so I thought. Now I have a team member in hospital. It feels as if the team is truly bonding."

Isabelle started shaking with laughter, complaining it hurt her nose further, as Mark responded, "It was the Welsh accent; very intimidating. DI Caldwell was a cricket fan and Isabelle used to ward off his invitations to matches. When you arrived we thought it would be Welsh choirs, interminable evenings listening to them."

Philip Caldwell had been Sayer's predecessor leading the Art Team.

Catrin smiled. "Interminable, Mark? You can't use that word with one of our choirs. Rapturous, delightful, perhaps."

Morley had been sitting quietly, following the banter. He looked at Isabelle and raised his eyebrows.

She said, "Why I called. I didn't go into detail with Morley obviously, but I asked him if he had encountered anything similar to our peculiar findings regarding Pennywell? He said yes. Morley, you tell it."

Morley cleared his throat. "I wasn't intruding, you understand; and Isabelle wasn't sharing details."

"Go on, Morley," said Catrin, having heard the disclaimer twice.

He said, "A gang member receives a series of paintings, all through the same dealer, who prices them down at the buyer's request. It seems to be more complicated than simple money laundering as you haven't found whether dirty money was used to make good the full price."

Catrin said, "That's where we are, yes."

Morley said, "The paintings could be a means of someone paying your man for other services or goods; disguising the payments in the price variation of the painting."

Mark nodded, following the logic. "And over time the true market value of the undervalued paintings would be restored anyway, which would be a bonus if they kept them; which they have."

"Payments for what, though; drug deliveries? We wondered about that," responded Catrin. "But the man is Bolan's right-hand man. He is already making a fortune from the trade. Presumably Michael looks after him well. Why would he be receiving payments disguised through paintings unless he was doing stuff behind Michael's back?"

Her question wasn't to Morley specifically; they understood that.

Morley said, "I gather that the value this man is netting per painting is about £25,000 to £50,000, give or take?"

Catrin nodded.

"They are not on a regular schedule, either, are they?"

Mark replied, "It doesn't seem so. That's the thing; there is no pattern consistent with known drug deliveries."

Catrin watched the FBI man focus in and saw he was thinking of something. Isabelle obviously knew what it was, but from her expressions she was anxious about how it would go down with her boss, it seemed.

Morley said formally, "DI Sayer, I suggest you check the man's travel patterns immediately around each transaction and look into his past, particularly any skills such as marksmanship or firearms. Also, check the records for any gang hits or professional assassinations in the regions he traveled to. It could well be a profile of a hit man's payments, it seems to me. And I do have some experience relevant to that suggestion; it's not simply a wild idea."

Isabelle burst in, almost indecipherable. "That's what Morley used to do before he joined the FBI Art Team; chase contract killers..." She trailed off.

She realized she shouldn't have spoken. It may not have been confidential, but he had told her in private.

Catrin first reaction on hearing the suggestion that it was related to firearms was, somewhat uncharitably she thought afterwards, Americans always turned to guns as an explanation for everything. His solution even sounded American.

She had been toying with the idea that Ranjani was sidelining drugs received from Bolan's suppliers and re-selling them. The variances around the paintings could be a method of covering that up. But running counter to it were two things; one, the quantities of drugs missing would stand out in a world which measures its product down to the milligram. Secondly, he was using the income for very visible and expensive art. Bolan would know of it at some time, she thought, and, if their value was inconsistent with his level of payments to Ranjani, Bolan would smell a rat.

So she needed to give Kerswell's suggestion a reasonable hearing, she concluded quickly. In her time as AC Hunt's assistant she had a bigger picture of the world of Met Policing activities and knew that expertise on contract killers resided somewhere in Trident, probably in the same group as

Inspector Entwistle, the triad expert. There was a specialist, she recalled, but she couldn't remember his name.

"Professional killers are hard to trace and convict," she said, "They don't leave much evidence."

Morley just nodded. "That's always been the problem; it's why the clear-up rate is so low."

Catrin said, "So you know about patterns of payments to contract killers, then? Would you mind popping over to talk with someone at the Yard for an hour or so? Is your arm up to it if I don't drive too badly?"

"He's coming back to my place," said Isabelle, defensively. "So I'll come along too. We can go home from there."

Catrin gave her a long look. "Are you sure?"

She reached into her purse and pulled out a small mirror.

"Oh my…" Isabelle said, "I can't go to the office like this! I look like a bloody panda."

Catrin said, "That's what I thought you would say. Look, Mark will give you a ride home. I'll steal Morley for an hour or so; let him run his idea by someone in Trident who is more knowledgeable than us and get him back to your place. We'll even collect takeout from somewhere for you both. You can rest up a bit. You have had quite a day already so you two can have a nice dinner at home."

A phone call later and a transfer to the extension of the man in Trident was productive; a DI Ewan Carstairs.

"Morley Kerswell, FBI? Yes, I know of him, please bring him along."

It appeared that DI Carstairs was happy to drop what he was doing and needed no persuading. On arrival at the Yard, she took him along and introduced them.

Carstairs said, quite eagerly, "I've been in this role only three years but I know your name, Agent Kerswell, so welcome. I didn't even know you were in the UK."

Catrin said, "He visited us recently, but he didn't tell us about his past role until today."

Carstairs looked at the FBI man. "So what's this about?

Have you seen one of our friends in London, by any chance?"

"No, just a hunch about some data DI Sayer has shared." He explained it with almost military precision.

Carstairs said, "So we need to work on dates; probably look for similar methods of kill. They would tie in to these sale dates on the paintings, I take it?"

Morley nodded. "Probably, but it is speculation."

What was interesting for Catrin was the way in which the Trident specialist didn't even pause at proceeding. She had half-expected that he would give the man a polite brush-off, but he didn't. She then thought it would be a long search but, in fact, the first two incident reports involving unidentified killers came within half an hour.

Carstairs said, "Two reported in Europe. They fit the window; both with a rifle at about 250 metres, single shot. I will work on seeing if I can find a fit for the rest. And I will start the check on travel records for this man Ranjani."

Kerswell looked at Catrin. "And I should get back to Isabelle. I can take a taxi…"

Catrin said, "No, I said I would drive you and pick up the dinner. By the sound of it, you have earned it."

While they left Ewan Carstairs working, Catrin took Morley to a deli and they bought a good mix of items for a meal at Isabelle's flat. As they pulled up at her block, Catrin asked, "Shall I bring it in, with your arm…"

But he was out of the door, shopping bags in his good hand. They had called to let Isabelle know they were arriving and she came out to the lobby. Catrin watched them meet up. She smiled as she drove off, partly at seeing the two of them, partly at Morley's parting comment.

He had said, ever the gentleman, "Thank you for listening to me, letting me help. I know it sounded weird at first."

Catrin responded. "It's us who should be thanking you for this lead. If it turns out to be solid, the FBI will be hearing about it, I guarantee. And I am glad Isabelle and you hit it off enough to get to the stage of talking about our case."

Morley said, "It's been some time… but I can sense when things come up involving contractors; I used to be able to, anyway. Perhaps I still can. It gives me something better to talk about with David Klintz when I get back than being beaten up by a teenager!"

By the same evening Catrin was informed that two Trident officers had been assigned temporarily to work under her direction and DC Derek Nkrumah, already seconded from a borough to the Antiques Team, had been reassigned to her also. Given Howlett's absence, they were needed. DCS Moore wasn't wasting any time and Chief Superintendent Matheson was keen to support the operation with Trident.

Catrin's instruction was to find out more about the undervalued paintings; who made up the difference to the sellers and how it was done. Moore wanted the paper trails, the owners and the payment details; preferably by yesterday.

Neville told her. "Five out of five assassinations in Europe are now linked to the same possible killer or pattern of kill. Each hit occurred within two weeks of a painting transaction. Even the countries line up in three cases. Circumstantially it's very strong; it's as if Nirupa chose a painting she wanted from a country in which her husband was happy to make a hit for whatever syndicate he is involved in."

Catrin said, "How will this affect the Pennywell deal?"

Neville said, "We are letting him talk away. Lauder has already some information to use against Michael Bolan. Anything further regarding a deal will need to wait on the outcome of the Ranjani investigation. When Trident gets on to Ranjani, they will break the news to his lawyer that Pennywell's engagement in price-fixing may be directly rather than indirectly linked to organized crime events. Belinda Strickland won't miss the significance of that and will tread very carefully."

He mused to himself. "I think Pennywell's wife would handle her husband fiddling around with painting prices; not be happy, but Simone Pennywell would pick up the pieces. If it breaks that he is knowingly involved in laundering the funds of a contract killer, he may find himself in the same boat as Brodie Shannon; his wife divorcing him."

~~

After their meal, a man with one working arm and a woman with a bruised face who ate very carefully and avoided anything crunchy talked of the strange day.

"I said we should stay in touch; now look. What a mess!" Isabelle said.

Neither could drink the wine that Catrin had bought; they were both on pain medication that couldn't be mixed with alcohol. Isabelle would have loved a glass of wine, not so much for the pain but to help her awkwardness. She was having second thoughts about her impulsive decision to invite Morley to her home and have him stay.

He stood up, taking his plate to the kitchen and returning to take hers, reaching over to the table as her hand shot out; partly to show she would do it, partly, she realised, to hold his. Her hand settled on his as it touched the plate and he turned his wrist round to hold hers as she looked at him.

"It's OK, isn't it; being here I mean? Do you want a hotel after all?"

He smiled. "It's perfect. Well, not perfect exactly. Not what I had in mind when I came to Europe but…"

He stopped talking and kissed her on the top of her head, impulsively." If I get any closer to your mouth you will roar with pain."

She laughed. "I can give it back, too. One slight turn of that cast and…"

She stood up from the table and leaned into him and gave him a gentle kiss. "Let's just be careful with each other."

Later, she asked, "How did it go with the Trident officer you saw, the one Catrin found?"

He nodded. "He knew my name, I didn't know him; he was

too new. We are a pretty small group of specialists. I had communicated with a colleague of his some time ago, it turned out, but that man had retired. But I think DI Carstairs bought into my idea and was working at it when I left. He knew it was different."

"Different?"

"Harder to track down. A lot of resources are focused on psychopaths, the serial killers. There is a lot of information, profiling, and so on. Contract killers are different, they are extreme sociopaths. They haven't got anything against their victim. It could even be their neighbour, or a schoolteacher or anyone. Then someone pays them a sum of money to kill and they... just do it; plan it carefully, execute the deed and go back to being Joe down the street. Harder to track down, as I said."

She moved closer to him. "Let's talk about art or something else. Paris perhaps."

27 TRUST

The following morning DCS Moore had assembled the teams and arranged also for DCS Strachan and her people to connect from Glasgow by videoconference. This time Sayer and Coltrane were accompanied by Mark Harper as they went over to the Trident operations room.

They had just reviewed the new findings. Strachan was initially showing her disbelief.

She said, "He has no need; he's family to Bolan now, as good as, you said. He's looked after. Even if he wants someone killed, he has the organisation and capabilities to have others do it."

Moore responded, "We know. The circumstantial evidence is strong and we have concluded it is not simply about the money. It is about psyche. He learned marksmanship in India and it wasn't about shooting big game; it was military training. He likes the challenge of being a sniper. And the prize is not a tiger head mounted on a wall, it is perfectly innocuous art. We see his wife's pleasure at their acquisitions; he sees his own successes; if you can call them that."

There was a moment's silence then Strachan said, "A hell of a hobby, Karen; a hit man for fun. The sale prices of the paintings you were concerned about had nothing to do with drugs, then?"

Moore replied, "No, we were off-base there, it seems, at least in part. The over-priced sales may still be to do with money-laundering; and one has to wonder what went on at different times in Cannes, if gang members had access to Pennywell's villa without it being traceable. But the five under-valued paintings appear to be hidden payments to Jalaj Ranjani to assassinate people. He is a busy man, it turns out."

"If we can prove it," interjected Superintendent Lauder.

She nodded. "But where does that leave us, Eileen, on the Connolly-Bolan link? I don't see it now. We had the Finisterre drug inventory in Bolan's distribution stream for a while, that's about it."

Strachan responded, "I don't get two things. First, when Sayer and Harper did the interviews we had that comment from Brodie Shannon on 'trust'. Then we had Dominic Connolly tensing up on the issue of us looking into the Ranjani paintings. Is Connolly aware of Ranjani being a hit man? If so, Bolan is, as well. Is it part of their business?"

Moore thought about it then said, "Gerry?"

Lauder replied. "I can't see it, to be honest. It's not Bolan's style. Like DI Sayer has said previously, Connolly considers himself to be a businessman. So does Bolan. They may occasionally have people beaten or killed but they aren't in the contract business themselves."

Hills piped up, "Perhaps Connolly wasn't worried about the link to payments for assassinations because he wasn't aware of them. He was worried about us delving into business arrangements between him and Bolan."

Catrin said, "Well Brodie Shannon wasn't, he was quite derisory about us being in the dark, wasn't he, Mark? We didn't understand 'trust', he said."

Coltrane suddenly sat up straight and said, "This may sound far-fetched, out of my area…"

Catrin noticed a couple of the assembled group working hard to keep their faces straight. They remembered the last team meeting, with his comment on Pennywell.

Moore looked at him.

"… 'trust' is one variant of the English translation of the word 'hawala', the Arabic money handling system; transactions that involve no long-distance transfer of funds. Perhaps there are no payments between Connolly and Bolan, just a running list of debts and balances. Nothing to track financially, because Michael Bolan and Dominic Connolly have some sort of understanding."

Moore nodded. "I see it. Could be a possibility. Hawala is a major issue for anti-terrorism investigations, we know. But internationally the system relies on brokers; they are the 'trust agents'. A broker in country A assures the broker in country B that he has received funds from a person wanting to make a transfer. The broker in country B pays the intended recipient the sum, less a fee. No documentation, no promissory notes, just a code word agreed between the donor and the recipient."

Coltrane said, "It's possible that a broker or brokers of some sort are involved - not banks, they keep records. But why couldn't it simply be an understanding between them, their own 'honour' system. Each keeps accounts. That would only work if the trade was two-way, obviously."

"We've not seen that," said Strachan over the video connection.

Moore countered, "Perhaps we haven't looked hard enough - either for two-way traffic or for people who would fit the bill of being brokers."

There was a lull.

Then Moore said, "Neville, you have come up with an interesting possibility but we are going to have to work out how to look into that separately."

Catrin thought that one or two of the Trident people were looking at her boss more thoughtfully now.

Moore's voice took on the tone of authority; as if a decision had been made.

"I will separate these investigations. Superintendent Lauder will now have two teams, one focused on the Connolly-Bolan business link; the second focused on the Ranjani case. We will look for cross-linking, of course, but we need to have focused investigations. I think Eileen and I need to discuss this new development and the Connolly-Bolan remit separately."

She listed out the key people in Trident who would work in core roles on each team. In passing, she made the point that the Art and Antiques Unit support would now logically link into the Ranjani development.

Finally, she said, "At this point let's discuss Jalaj Ranjani and his newly-discovered pursuit. Eileen, unless you see a need to be involved on this one I will call you separately and see where we go on the Connolly-Bolan link?"

Strachan said, "No, we are not involved in that side of it, so we will sign off. We'll talk separately, Karen. Goodbye all."

The connection went dead after a moment. That's the way big cases are, thought Catrin, most of the time. You are rarely in at the start and often not there at the end. You are brought in part way through and leave when they don't need you further.

Her mobile beeped and she checked it, unfortunately just as DCS Moore looked down the table.

"Sayer, hopefully that is not your mother-in-law wanting to know about a particular knitting pattern you stole from her some time ago?"

Catrin didn't think twice; perhaps she should have, when she saw Coltrane's expression. "No ma'am. It's your boss letting me know he wants to see DCI Coltrane and myself later today."

She had suddenly empathized with Loretta Hills on wanting to kick back at Moore's prods. Catrin looked down the table waiting to see if Moore was going to ask why, so she could tell her politely it was none of her business; she would need to ask Commander Barlow, who wouldn't tell her anyway, she was sure. Moore just looked at her for a moment then said, "Well, back to the issue of Jalaj and his gun."

Neville Coltrane finished reading the email he had also received and ostentatiously made a point of giving DCS Moore his undivided attention.

28 SOMERSBY

Barlow had called them to attend a meeting in Assistant Commissioner Sleiman's suite, a mirror layout of Catrin's former boss's office. She knew most of the people on Sleiman's team from her role working with Hunt.

They found Stephen Drew and a woman around the same age waiting, silent. As soon as Sayer and Coltrane arrived, Sleiman's assistant buzzed her boss and told all of them that they could enter Sleiman's inner office. Catrin noticed that Coltrane recognized the woman, but he made no comment.

Inside were Commander Barlow and the assistant commissioner. After seating themselves, AC Sleiman thanked them for coming and did the introductions. The woman with Drew was a Mrs. Clare Somersby and clearly she was the senior SIS officer present.

The assistant commissioner said bluntly, "We do not have a common operation under discussion here but we do have an issue that needs to be resolved. Commander Barlow?"

Barlow had pulled out a single sheet of paper, a reference list of points he wanted to make. Carefully but concisely he took them through the sequence of events from being first contacted by Stephen Drew, on to a discussion of an approach to DI Sayer regarding a penetration case of a triad group in

Hong Kong to the point where he passed on the decision by Catrin not to participate.

His final remark at that juncture was, "DI Sayer responded promptly and gave a logical and reasonable basis for her decision. I assumed the matter was closed. Then a little more than two weeks ago she alerted me to the invitation received by her and her artistic partner to participate in an event in Hong Kong. As Mr. Drew knows, I tried to clarify the significance of this event, given our earlier discussion, but I had no response before DI Sayer went to Hong Kong. Before I continue, I would ask DI Sayer to recount her experience there."

Carin summarized her encounter with Peter Griffiths and the brief discussion with him at dinner. Barlow jumped back in.

"DI Sayer reported that back to me and later told me, in confidence, that she had checked back through university photographs to find images of Griffiths at college. To her eyes, the man is similar in build but he is not the same man in her photographs. We haven't checked any further, although I suspect that we could find evidence to corroborate DI Sayer's observations."

So far both the visitors had sat in silence.

Stephen Drew spoke up. "Craig, you contacted me about this. I am not sure why we are regurgitating it now for our respective senior officers."

He didn't say it, but his voice conveyed, 'so what?'

AC Sleiman said, "Well, if the penetration operation isn't yours, some organization has picked up on the exact same idea that you put to DI Sayer, we think. Sayer, Mr. Drew did suggest one of the mechanisms to penetrate this triad was the idea of an art show of your work in Hong Kong, I believe?"

Catrin paused then said, "Sir, I was told I couldn't discuss these matters beyond Mr. Drew and Commander Barlow. I was told it would be a breach of the Official Secrets Act. No-one has yet told me otherwise."

The senior police officer smiled briefly. "Point taken. Let's take it that my question to DI Sayer has been answered in the positive."

Commander Barlow said, "The reason for the meeting now is this development."

He pointed at the slim box that Catrin had brought in, one that had caught the attention of the visitors already.

Catrin removed the lid and turned it around.

She said, "It's an art print by a Japanese artist - ."

"Utamaro." It was the first word that the senior SIS woman had uttered in the room after the introductions.

"Correct, ma'am. It is a gift to me from a friend of Jian Li Yeung's father, Michael Yau and his wife. My colleague received a silk item from him also, in appreciation of the fact we are mentoring his granddaughter, who was happy to have a work created by her displayed at the reception alongside our own.

"This print is called 'Ase o fuku onna', although I have no idea about the pronunciation. The selection of Utamaro, I believe, is because I used a different print by the artist as part of my tuition reference works with Miele Yau, this one - ."

She showed her iPhone image of the work she had used with Miele.

"I am getting lost," interjected Drew, although his tone of voice seemed to indicate otherwise, Catrin thought.

Catrin said, "The title of the work I was given translates as 'woman wiping sweat'. Jian Li Yeung said to me after the reception that it appeared I had seen a ghost - her words - when I met this man Griffiths. I tried to remain impassive but I was already on tenterhooks about the whole visit and the implications of the prior discussion with Mr. Drew. I thought I was neutral in my response, but my friend saw me otherwise."

Somersby said, "To be clear; you are saying, I think, that this man Yau spotted your discomfort with Griffiths at the time he was claiming to be a friend from college, establishing part of his bona fide?"

Sleiman said, "This officer is saying no such thing, Mrs. Somersby. She is simply presenting the facts. We don't have an operation in play, you told us, so you will need to take the information away and digest it."

Drew said, "This is very speculative…" He was clearly not on board with the message Catrin had passed on. But the woman beside him was lost in her own thoughts.

The assistant commissioner said, "Well, if…" He was looking around the table, a clear indication that he was about to wind up the meeting. The SIS woman held up one arm, stopping him.

"Tom, a moment please. Why would Yau do that, Stephen? Let's talk about it here, not later. Why?"

Drew remained impassive. Catrin thought that the man may decline to respond to his senior officer but instead he said, "To send a message, possibly. We know he claims to be retired. It could be that he spotted something wasn't quite right in the exchange between Sayer and Griffiths and drew the conclusion that he was a plant. He is telling us he wants no part of it."

The woman shot back, "Would that tie in?"

Drew said, "Yes. Griffiths has not had any follow up opportunity with Yau, but we weren't pressing it. We were treading lightly at this stage."

He looked across at Sayer. He was no longer the person who was encouraging her to assist his efforts; the look he gave her was, if anything, disdainful, dismissive. When he spoke his tone was accusatory.

"Griffiths reported that at the crucial point of meeting him, you looked angry momentarily. That was probably what ruined it."

Catrin flushed with anger. "You have the gall to - ."

Coltrane's voice overrode hers, the tone brooking no competitor. He ignored Drew completely.

"What 'ruined it', as your colleague put it was your arrogance, Clare. Giving this man authorisation to go ahead with an operation in which a police officer was co-opted after she had formally declined to be involved. And then he had the temerity to deny its very existence to Commander Barlow."

For a moment, it was as if there were only two people in the room, Somersby and Coltrane, centre stage; the rest were the audience. That Coltrane knew the senior SIS officer was clear to everyone, as was the withering glance from Coltrane that dismissed Drew as a minor player.

Coltrane spoke again, more pleasantly, before Somersby could respond. "But you may want to focus on the path forward."

Somersby's head dropped, either lost in thought or to acknowledge the accusation, Catrin couldn't tell. But the anger she felt dissipated in the public relegation of Drew to some sort of minor role. Drew's expression was wooden, betraying nothing.

Somersby said, "If it was an active member of Four Square who spotted Griffiths as a plant, they would probably want to fold him in, get him involved, knowing full well they could be selective on their feedback to us. They would play him, wouldn't they?"

Drew spoke quietly. "Possibly. Probably. Or keep their distance. But it is still early, too early to know either way, I feel. It could be simply the fact that Michael Yau selected this print for other reasons; that he liked it, or his wife did. You say it came from her also, DI Sayer?"

He was struggling to sound normal, business-like.

Catrin said as evenly as she could, "They were both at the reception. The covering note is in the box. You can see yourself that he is saying it is a gift from both of them."

Make your own assessment, she thought; I'm not doing it.

There was a moment or two of silence then Somersby turned to Sleiman and said, "Thank you, Tom. We will take the information into consideration."

She stood up, then realised that the box with the print was in front of her. "Nice quality and colour retention. The man chose well. Thank you, DI Sayer."

Her glance at Drew indicated that he needed to get up and start moving, which he did, obviously still lost in his own deliberations.

Catrin spoke up. "One more thing, please." They all looked at her.

"Commander Barlow may recall that in our meeting with Mr. Drew he alluded to a police officer being a better selection than 'say a lawyer'; his words. It could be nothing, but I took it at the time to be an inference that my friend Jian Li Yeung could be approached if I turned it down. I want her and her family off-limits."

Her focus was the SIS woman, not Drew.

"She is a Chinese national. If co-opting her went wrong, there would be far more serious repercussions than I would potentially face in similar circumstances. If she is approached by SIS she would report it to the relevant authorities, I believe. And if they heard, I suspect that other organizations, such as triads, could also hear about it."

"Believe or know?" Somersby asked.

Catrin said, "I am sure of it. I know her well."

I will make sure she does, thought Catrin.

Drew said dismissively, "She's too close, anyway, if Griffiths has been spotted. It wouldn't work."

Catrin nodded. Just so we understand each other, she thought. And it's not Griffiths, despite your charade.

DCI Coltrane had said nothing further. As Somerby left the table, she said, "Nice to see you again, Neville."

Catrin saw her boss nod, his face impassive. The look changed to a slight grimace as the backs of the two SIS officers moved away from the table. Somersby shook hands formally with Sleiman before heading out through the door. Drew followed his boss and closed the door behind him.

Assistant Commissioner Sleiman said, "Well, you will hear no more of that one, DI Sayer. Mr. Drew's gambit didn't work out, it appears. Obviously they already had Griffiths in place and were surprised by your rejection of further involvement, but they tried to finesse it anyway. I will mention this to the Commissioner."

Catrin acknowledged the comment, but knew, on the scale

of things, it would not get much further than a short sidebar discussion between relevant people at a future meeting. That was one of her insights from her prior role with Hunt, watching senior people patch interdepartmental squabbles. It may be a small matter between the Met and SIS, but for her it was a weight off her shoulders.

On the trip back downstairs, Catrin said to her boss, "You know Mrs. Somersby, I take it?"

Neville nodded. "I've not seen her for many years, to be honest. We were at Oxford together. She's a linguist. But we weren't close."

He paused. "Sylvia ran into her a couple of years ago. Clare Somersby mentioned she had seen that I was a policeman. She gave the impression she had a boring job as a bureaucrat."

Sylvia McNair was Coltrane's partner. Catrin and Jean had undertaken a commission for her some years ago, some table centrepieces.

Catrin said, "I suppose in their line, they can't say anything else."

Coltrane smiled. "They didn't even apologize for lying to us about the operation being active. But they got your message about Jian Li. Approach her and you would make sure that Yeung reported it."

"Was it that obvious?"

He smiled. "Oh, yes; to everyone in the room, I think."

29 PREPARATIONS

It took Catrin, Mark and the assigned officers from Trident the best part of a week to piece it all together as best they could; dates of sales of paintings in the originating countries; correlation with Richard Pennywell's statements as they came in, the travel patterns of Jalaj Ranjani and the details of the assassinations obtained from Interpol. The jigsaw bits were obtained individually, focusing on the art work in each case as part of a fraud enquiry, without at this stage declaring their full reasons to their police contacts overseas. After all, these were investigations from an art crime team to others engaged in similar pursuits.

Though they built a picture, it was incomplete; not every piece of the puzzle was there. In one case, Jalaj Ranjani was in the UK supposedly when the hit occurred, according to sources. They would need to find the chink in his alibi or eliminate him from that link. In two other hits, his wife had been with him on his trip and Lauder questioned whether that was the profile of a contract killer. If it was true, she definitely must be aware of his deadly sideline.

"She gets the paintings she likes," said Hills, "so she is OK obviously with the way they are bought, even down to the choice of paintings from the same country as the hits."

It was clear that in at least three of the paintings chosen, she had been active in their selection in the country of origin.

The one consistent and damning fact was that the art in each case had transferred to Ranjani ownership in the two-week period before the assassination had occurred. They may have fixed the price of each work of art to disguise the fact that Jalaj was being paid for a contract killing, but the terms of payment for the work were remarkably constant.

The Ranjani couple had missed that.

Catrin wasn't included in the senior level meeting that decided on the operational strategy. It was chaired by Moore and included Coltrane. Commander Barlow sat in on it. While it didn't take long it had important implications for the work of several teams, so quite a number of people were awaiting the outcome. Moore briefed the bigger team together afterwards.

"We considered whether to inform Interpol and the relevant authorities and wait it out, or not. The cheapest, easiest way is to do that, which resonated with some, but it means we do nothing but follow up once another jurisdiction develops the evidence that would lead to charges and an extradition request. Commander Barlow doesn't like the fact that a drug boss is moonlighting as a hit man and we do nothing directly to bring him down. Plus, we don't know when or where he may strike again and there is a need for proactive prevention of another death.

"So… we are going to have a go at him. At the very least, even if we get nowhere, it will take him out of the business. He will know that we will look at him every time a hit goes down."

Her voice softened. "The tipping point for us was the case of a Professor Elise Morin, a university scientist living near Lyon in France. She was assassinated on her balcony. A cancer researcher, she had witnessed a man run down by a car. Morin memorized the registration plate and identified the driver, who turned out to be the son of a mobster from near Marseille. For whatever reason, the local police didn't even think she needed protection before the trial. She was shot a week before it began. If we can bring in her killer, we can count on the French to go the extra mile to see this prosecution to fruition. Now, on to the details."

She looked at Coltrane and Sayer.

"The art team will handle the prep for the interviews that deal with the paintings; that will mean mainly focusing on Nirupa Ranjani. Lauder and Carstairs will handle Jalaj Ranjani once we tell him that his new vocation has become an interest of ours. I don't expect a wail of 'God, you found out! I confess, let me tell you all and clear my conscience'."

There were some smiles in the room. Everyone knew how hard those interviews would be. Ranjani would not be at all cooperative. Her gaze moved to a young officer in uniform no-one knew.

"PC Victor, what's your first name?"

He looked a little ill at ease. "Manny, ma'am. Emmanuel. People call me Manny."

"Well, Manny; you stay close to me during the interviews so I can understand what's going on once Superintendent Lauder persuades Jalaj Ranjani to talk about his guns and shooting people. I need an expert. You are it."

She looked at the room in general. "PC Victor is a weapons officer with SCO19. A sniper himself."

She pointed at Loretta Hills and then Mark Harper. "Hills and Harper, the two 'H's, will be in Brum ready to be nice to Nirupa's parents, Mr. and Mrs. Sengupta, to see what can be found out there that might help. Don't grimace, Loretta, just because you think being sent to Birmingham is like being sent to Siberia. Make Nirupa's mum and dad love you, tell you everything about their wonderful daughter and son-in-law. It could help, I think.

"The key people in all this are the search teams. We have twenty-four hours to hold the Ranjanis without charging them and in that time I want something solid, something as hard evidence, that Jalaj is a shooter. A sniper rifle with his prints on it and rifling marks that match some of the bullet fragments would be nice, but a day dream. We aren't going to find a weapon, DI Carstairs says; that's not the way these hits go down. But there will be something out there; find it. Even a bus ticket from Prague or another city the shooter was in when there is no evidence of Ranjani having travelled there would be good. But we have to get something other than the art into the evidence equation; from their home, from their boat, from the real estate business offices; wherever.

"Once we bring in the other authorities overseas there could be a lot more direct or corroborating evidence; CCTV of him surveilling the kill zone in advance, that sort of thing. But we want something here in the UK solidly linking him first, if we can. We can go talking abroad about our suspicions the moment they are in custody for interview. Calloway, you will lead that work. Then the cat will be out of the bag, anyway."

~~

Half-way through the preparations, Isabelle Howlett returned to work after her nasal surgery and some time off. With Morley Kerswell back in the USA, she had the job of completing the police follow-up interview for the Youth Court proceedings against the teenager who pushed them down the stairs. In reality, she knew she wasn't much help, but it had to be done.

"So you saw nothing other than your friend falling back on you?"

"That's right."

"And what did you hear?"

"A young, male voice saying, 'fucking Americans'; but I didn't see who said it. Then a woman was shouting and screaming."

The police officer looked at her. "And you say you couldn't identify the assailant? Why not? You are a police officer, after all; trained in observation."

"Have you ever had your nose broken?"

"No."

"That's why you asked the question. My eyes were full of

tears from the pain of it. By the time I saw the accused he was being berated by his mother and held by another person there. I concentrated more on the blood; I didn't want it on my clothes; it's a sod to remove."

The officer smiled. "Now that I do know about, in this job."

Isabelle was anxious about the state of her face on her return to work, only to receive warm support from the Art and Antiques Unit personnel. On the second day back she came in to find a foot-high furry toy panda sitting in her chair with a note saying, "If you need to take a rest, I'll cover for you."

Her zealous enquiries found the guilty party to be Derek Nkrumah. She threatened him with a permanent transfer to Art and Antiques so she could make his life a misery. They all knew he would stay in a heartbeat if the budget and headcount pressure was lifted; his period of temporary transfer from his borough was drawing to a close. She put the bear prominently on a cabinet in her workplace.

"He's called Morley," she said.

Her role for the next while was to continue the free port project and stick handle anything new that came in, Catrin told her. She and Mark would be full-time on the Ranjani thing until it unfolded.

"The first twenty-four hours after the arrests, we'll live in this place. After that we'll see."

Bringing in the Ranjanis and hitting them up with the circumstantial evidence was a risky strategy, everyone knew. But it was Moore's approach and she had senior buy-in for a fast closure. In Trident, only Lauder was circumspect about it; an investigator who liked his cat in the bag before the animal knew it was there.

~~

It was later that day that Catrin called Howlett into her office.

"Doing OK?"

"Glad to be back at work, ma'am. The people here have been good."

Catrin said, "How's Morley's wrist; do you know?"

"He saw a specialist on his return; it will take a while but they don't foresee complications. He went back into work today too."

"You like him?"

It was a question more than a statement.

"I do. We hit it off and… it's not clear 'what next', if anything. We are a continent apart. But he makes me feel good again."

Catrin smiled. "I'm glad. Just don't ask for a secondment to the FBI; we are up to our eyeballs."

Howlett smiled and nodded.

Catrin said, "Morley Kerswell is very well thought of regarding his old role, I heard from DI Carstairs. It was a very stressful one. Has he told you much, can I ask?"

Howlett said carefully, "He hasn't broken any of their rules, but he spent a long time working on contract killers, I know. He is now much happier with David Klintz's team working in art crime. And I saw in Paris how much they respect him. He had a medical issue come up…"

She didn't want to say, "breakdown', but she thought that was what her boss was alluding to.

All Catrin said was, "I hope it works out for you both, I really do."

Her mind was on the briefing session earlier when Moore hauled DI Carstairs front and centre.

"This is 'know your enemy' time. Ewan?" DCS Moore said, as introduction.

Carstairs stood by the screen showing the two lists he had prepared.

He began, "One of you has already told me that it is hard to rationalize why Jalaj would do this, take such risks. He has a good job, in a sense, a big income, nice flat, right? Think of it this way. If I, an eccentric millionaire, offered you employed people fifty thousand pounds to take a few days off and, expenses paid, fly to a European city to stick an Arsenal rosette on a particular statue - a 'thumbing the nose' joke at a rival football team just before an international game, would you do it? Into the square, or public gardens, a swift walk past, look around and 'pop', it's on the statue somewhere. Some of you; no - you must be Spurs supporters - but others, for the fun of it and the ready cash? Definitely. I see one or two Arsenal fans here were nodding all the way along."

There was some laughter.

"It's no more than that to Jalaj. He is used to operating in a more clandestine world anyway and to a contract killer it is no more mental stress than sticking the rosette. In fact, given his marksmanship skills, it's a boost to his ego to do it. He has a different perspective to 99.95% of the population, if he is the killer."

He pointed at the checklist of items on to the screen.

"Study these lists. The ones in red will probably never appear in your operation, but if they do, it will be a bonus - the right type of weapon, tracks on his computer of sniper chat sites, weapons, ballistics software or gun magazines - the paper sort, all the accoutrements of the gun enthusiast. The ones in blue are more likely but again, don't count on finding them. Evidence of hand-prepared ammunition is a dead giveaway but I doubt you will find tools or traces; they are probably with his armorer somewhere in Europe, whoever he or she is. But some snipers insist on packing their own ammunition.

"The one hope I have is that you find his scope. Telescopic sights are legal and very, very personal to a sniper. More so than the weapon at times. If we don't find a scope, there is a thing that Morley Kerswell came up with in a case in Arizona years ago we can try during the interview; it may create a break. I will get to that in a while. It's ironical that this line of enquiry started with him. When DI Sayer telephoned and said, "Do you have a moment for us - I am with a Morley Kerswell, a visitor from the FBI on holiday here - I was astonished.""

He stopped, realizing he was going off-track.

"A sniper at that level will have a local armorer or supplier; they are a team. For the list of hits we have, that will be someone in a Schengen country who can prepare and drive the weapon to the vicinity of the operation, find a suitable test site, set up the access and egress paths for the kill and if needed, the accommodation and drivers.

"The rifle barrel will be a one-time use or after the hit it will be re-distributed into the netherworld of illegal arms suppliers, ending up on a gun in the hands of a bozo who thinks he is a hot-shot. When he gets caught he is bewildered to find himself under investigation for a murder of a politician or policeman in a totally different place.

"The sniper will meet the armorer personally only twice, in general, during each operation. Once at the test location, to allow the shooter to assure himself of the weapon's capabilities and make his own final adjustments, and once at the kill zone. There, at the right moment, the sniper takes one shot and leaves; the armorer will have the responsibility to clean up. From the list of kills all of these shots fall into a 200-250 metre range under different elevations and wind conditions. Not truly long-range, the sort that causes all the hype in the newspapers about snipers. But it's a person who can place one round in a radius the size of a fifty pence piece, first time, consistently, knowing that it is not a roundel target, it's a person's head or heart."

As he walked back to his seat his final comment was, "You aren't looking for a gun lover, which is why you won't find the traces of one on his computer. You are looking for a cold-blooded killer who happens to use a rifle and, in this case, a man who earns his extra pocket money eliminating other people."

Which was the reason for Catrin's question to her team member; from a subsequent discussion with Ewan Carstairs in private she realised that FBI Agent Kerswell had a probably turbulent but distinguished past and she wanted to ensure that her colleague was not blind-sided about the apparently quiet man on David Klintz's team.

30 INTERVIEWS

The Trident and Arts Teams assembled at 8.00 a.m. the following morning. DCS Moore stood surveying people and checking the noise on the speakerphone sitting on the desk beside her.

She pointed over at DS Calloway and said loudly, "Let's get started. Calloway, you are all set for contacting Interpol and the relevant police departments?"

The officer simply looked at his colleague assigned with him to the task and they both nodded. "Ready to go, ma'am."

"Are you in place, Hills?" she asked, instinctively looking at the speaker unit as she spoke.

"Yes, ma'am. Sergeant Harper and I are ready." Loretta's disembodied voice came back loud and clear.

"Be nice now. Show the Sengupta's that we are a warm and friendly lot at the Met."

Several people in the operations seemed amused; it was not planned as a 'warm and friendly' day, overall.

"Yes, ma'am." The voice sounded amused then Hills added, "If you did this yourself, you could show them we even have friendly Mancunians in Trident."

That got a bigger laugh, for timeliness and pluck and it produced a smile from Moore. They were suffering from preoperation nerves, Catrin knew, and she liked Hills' response.

Moore said, "No, Loretta, I'm the big boss. I have to conduct the orchestra. Gerry, are your lot ready?"

"Yes, ma'am." Superintendent Lauder's voice came out of the speakerphone. He was with the arrest team and had insisted on supervising the operation in person.

"Then wake up Cinnamon Street and bring them in under caution; start the detention clock and make us busy."

There was silence on the phone after the acknowledgement. There wouldn't be a running commentary. They didn't think that the Ranjanis or their bodyguards would put up a fight. Tactical officers were there, just in case.

Several minutes later, DC Whitely, one of the team on site, called in. "Superintendent Lauder says we are leaving the home now, ma'am. We have both of them."

"Thank you. See you back here."

She closed the phone line and addressed the teams waiting for the Ranjanis. "They will be here in half an hour tops. By this time tomorrow we will have arrests for five open homicide cases to share with our friends abroad or we will be watching these two walk out with their lawyers. Give it your best shot. I'm off to update the commander."

Catrin had drawn the assignment to telephone the solicitor Donald Killam, as he had met her briefly but didn't really know her, so he couldn't read her responses so well. It was her first task in the day's plan. His office wouldn't be open yet, they knew so she dialed his mobile and found it engaged. When she called his home number she reached his wife.

"Is Mr. Killam there? This is Detective Inspector Sayer. We met regarding your painting, you may recall."

"Yes, inspector, he is talking with a colleague at present. No, hold on - I will pass him over, he heard the word 'inspector' I think."

After a moment's pause she heard the man's voice, "Killam."

"Mr. Killam. This is DI Sayer. We are bringing in Jalaj and

Nirupa Ranjani for questioning at New Scotland Yard; they will shortly be given access to phones to call for legal support. It would expedite things if you could ensure that you are available, or make available appropriate counsel for each person, rather than us resorting to duty counsel. They will be interviewed separately, of course."

There was no cry of anguish, no complaint about it interfering with his existing plans, whatever they were. He was a solicitor and understood the process. And clearly, Ranjani was a major client.

"They are in custody now, are they?" he asked.

"Yes, sir; they are on their way here as I speak."

"To Scotland Yard, not Bethnal Green?"

The Bethnal Green Police Station was the most likely interview location for Ranjani or his gang members on drugs issues, she knew.

Catrin said evenly, "That is correct sir."

After a moment's silence he said, "I can be there by nine-thirty, travel permitting. I will ask my colleague Lianne Mortimer to be present to represent Mrs. Ranjani."

"Thank you, sir; we will see you both then."

"One moment, DI Sayer. You are interviewing Mrs. Ranjani also. Is this about paintings again?"

"Yes, sir. It relates to a number of paintings. Where that takes us, we will have to see."

She closed the call and logged the time and completion of it. The case log would get a lot more entries in the next twenty-four hours.

~~

"Mr. Ranjani, good morning."

Catrin had walked in, sat down and switched on the recorder. DS Mahon from the Trident team also entered and sat down, but this phase was Catrin's show. Mahon was going to be watching Jalaj Ranjani on CCTV carefully throughout the main interviews; they had put him in with Catrin at the beginning to allow him a face-to-face, close-up encounter.

"For the record, please? This is Detective Inspector Catrin Sayer, and…"

"DS Gordon Mahon."

"Jalaj Ranjani."

"Donald Killam, solicitor acting for Mr. Ranjani."

Ranjani then said, "Where's Lauder?"

Catrin ignored the question.

"This interview is commencing at 0948. Mr. Ranjani, you bought the painting 'Loch Lomond, two houseboats' by Leslie Hunter for Lena Shannon at her request, you stated to us previously. Will you confirm that for the record, please?"

Ranjani looked surprised. "Still on about that? Yes I did. She wanted it; I bought it. We thought it was ours when she died because I paid for it. But you and Lauder told me it was hers, part of her estate. I am not contesting it. Why?"

"You bought it from a dealer, Richard Pennywell. Is that correct?"

"Yes."

"Were you aware when you bought it that the seller was a Mr. Garrard but that the painting had been previously owned by Dominic Connolly?"

Ranjani paused, looked at his lawyer, who nodded slightly. "Yes, I did. I believe Mr. Connolly or one of his businesses owned the painting previously, as you say."

"So your purpose in buying the work was to please Lena Shannon and possibly her father?"

Ranjani was looking puzzled. "Yes, I suppose so."

Catrin opened a file folder before her and pulled out a sheet of paper. She pushed it over so that both men could see the document, the filing with HMRC service for the transaction.

"For the record I am showing Mr. Ranjani the Revenue and Customs declaration filed under the Money Laundering Regulations by the dealer, documenting that you paid £20,000 in cash and a further £37,000 by bank transfer. Does it look correct?"

"Look, if you think you can start making an issue over me

paying in cash…"

Catrin interjected, "I'm not. Does it look right, is all I am asking?"

Ranjani perused it. "Yes."

Catrin pulled out a second sheet.

"For the record I am showing Mr. Ranjani a similar filing made by Mr. Pennywell, this time on a sale of a painting by Pierre Mignard for £184,000 listing you as the buyer. It came up in the same search at HMRC. Can you tell me where Mr. Pennywell found this painting for you?"

Ranjani stiffened. "No."

"No you can't or no you won't?"

Killam broke in, "Is this related to the same investigation, Inspector? If not, then I would like to confer with my client in private before further questions are asked."

She nodded.

"At this stage I am trying to ascertain whether or not this painting was also obtained indirectly from Mr. Connolly. After all, Mr. Ranjani was quite open just now about buying a painting Mr. Connolly had owned. This Mignard was obtained by Mr. Ranjani in the same twelve month period as the purchase of the Hunter. It is a reasonable link to draw."

The lawyer whispered to his client.

Ranjani said, "The only transaction I made to acquire a painting owned previously by Mr. Dominic Connolly was the Hunter purchased for Miss Shannon."

"So did Mr. Pennywell locate the Hunter? Or did you or your wife see it somewhere else and have Pennywell secure it for you?"

"I don't recall."

She nodded. "Mr. Connolly is in prison for illegal importation of Class A drugs and related crimes, as you may be aware. As is your colleague, Mr. Bolan. Have you purchased art works from other people directly or indirectly associated with drug crimes, Mr. Ranjani?"

Killam said, "Don't answer. That's it, inspector. Mr. Ranjani will not be subject to a poaching expedition by Art and

Antiques. If you have due cause for such inquiries, you can clarify them now. I am entitled to be made aware during preliminary disclosure of the issues involved prior to interview and then consult with my client. Being an art collector is not a crime; owning art is not a crime and I see no reason for this line of questioning to continue."

He doesn't know, she concluded from observing the man. His reaction is annoyance, not concern about the sources of the paintings. The lawyer doesn't know. At this stage it was what they were after. Ranjani was trying to look confident but his tension was building; his left hand was flexing, showing a nervous tic.

She pulled out the final document from the slim file.

"This is a copy of the warrant handed to you at your home earlier; you didn't look at it and just put it on a table there, I gather. I want to point out to you and Mr. Killam that we are searching your home and business premises and also a boat that you own."

"I have no more paintings," Ranjani responded.

Catrin looked him in the eyes as she said, "What we are specifically looking for are any items pertaining to a series of crimes committed outside the United Kingdom. We are also removing from your home a number of works of art we consider to be the direct proceeds of these crimes, including the Pierre Mignard. Mr. Killam, you will receive the further disclosure related to the specifics of this phase of the investigation from Superintendent Lauder now.

"Mr. Ranjani, you will be allowed time with Mr. Killam or another solicitor of your choice immediately afterwards. Then you will be questioned further by Superintendent Lauder and other officers."

She stood up, picking up her file folder, her eyes on the solicitor as DS Mahon stood also, his eyes not leaving Ranjani. Killam now realised that the art was an incidental element to another issue. Ranjani was now looking like he was made of stone.

Good luck communicating with him now, Catrin thought; he has switched off.

~~

Nirupa Ranjani's parents lived in Birmingham, in Angelina St., not far from the school at which Nirupa's father used to teach art. They had been surprised when the two police officers knocked on their door so early. Retired, they were in the middle of breakfast, but they invited them in and sat them in the front room.

The house was comfortable but not pretentious. The most striking aspects to Harper were the art; a range of images of India painted in acrylics and oils and some fine handicrafts; bowls, vases and relief work hardwood panels.

Harper looked at one in the hallway as they walked in, an Indian forest scene in fine and accurate marquetry. He said, "I know that wood, the red one, but the name escapes me..."

"Padauk," replied Mr. Sengupta, smiling. "What you mainly see in marquetry is African padauk but this, obviously, is Indian. From our home area - the woodwork, I mean; where my parents came from. The paintings are mine, but the handicrafts we buy over there. I wish I had such skills."

They sat down. Mrs. Sengupta offered tea. "We don't have coffee, I am afraid," she said.

"That's quite alright. We don't really need anything, thank you, but tea would be appreciated," said DC Hills, taking the lead. "We are currently conducting enquiries related to your daughter, her husband and some paintings."

Mr. Sengupta looked at his wife, the anxiety showing. He shook his head. "I am not sure how we can help and, to be frank, whether we should at all. It's our daughter. We have a dilemma about it, as you can imagine. Not that we have done anything wrong."

Mrs. Sengupta shook her head, whether in anger or sorrow wasn't clear, saying something in an Indian language under her breath. Hills, her face showing her to be the epitome of sympathy, just looked at her.

Mr. Sengupta said. "Disappointment, you see. Fine art, but bad money. You know why."

Drugs, he implied.

DC Hills said, "That's what we have come to talk about; the art, not the money. Or at least, DS Harper has. He is with the Art and Antiques Unit; an expert. You taught art nearby, we understand. Nirupa appears very knowledgeable herself but her art collection mystifies us, not only the significant value of it, but the selection of works."

Mr. Sengupta looked afresh at Mark Harper. Art was something he was happier to talk about than his daughter's lifestyle.

"You studied art then? I have heard of the Art and Antiques Squad; very prestigious, I understand."

Mark smiled and started his set of questions.

31 NIRUPA

Catrin took a peek through the small glass panel in the door of the interview room as she walked down the corridor to meet up with Neville Coltrane. Nirupa Ranjani could be seen talking with her lawyer, a young woman introduced as Lianne Mortimer. By habit, she had quickly checked the on-line background of the lawyer, as she did whenever she had the chance to do so before an interview. From the dates of Mortimer's LLB and LPC degrees, the solicitor had only three years post-qualification experience. The discussion between the client and solicitor was intense apparently, from the body language and facial expressions.

What concerned Catrin from the brief observation was the emotional variability of the lawyer, rising and falling with Nirupa. Good lawyers were stabilizing for their client, about to face the stress of a police interview; they weren't sympathizing and emotional.

Coltrane came along to meet her. "Ready?" he asked.

She nodded. "Watch out for the solicitor, Neville; it appears to me she's a bit emotional."

They entered the room and went through the ritual of identification for the record. This was Catrin's second interview session of what was projected to be a long day.

Nirupa Ranjani started off talkative, but it didn't last.

"I saw you on television, Mr. Coltrane. And my husband and I were at the 'Polish Art of the Nineteenth Century' gala, but didn't get to meet you."

Nirupa had prattled on for a good minute after formally identifying herself. Her young solicitor kept glancing at her. Neville let it roll on, maintaining a neutral expression, neither encouraging nor discouraging her. Catrin wondered when she would dry up and they could get started.

Coltrane looked down at his notes as Nirupa Ranjani paused, trying to think of other clever art conversation for social discussion.

Head down, he said, "The gala. Yes, there was a large turnout, it was a great event. You must have talked about your Mignard with people there, I suppose; you had owned it only two months at the time. It is very nice."

She beamed at the recognition. "Yes, it was finally back from restoration and -."

Coltrane butted in. "Restoration. Hardly that, surely? It shows no signs of that. I looked at it myself a little earlier. It has been cleaned, very carefully done, I must say."

"You saw my painting. How?"

"I was part of the team entering your flat under a search warrant that has been served. I wanted to see a number of the works specifically myself before talking to you."

Nirupa Ranjani looked as if she wasn't sure whether this was a threat or a compliment.

"What do you mean?" she asked.

This was the point where DCI Coltrane showed her that the meeting was an interview, not a conversation. He stared at her a long moment and then ignored her question.

"You paid a large fee for that 'restoration' after you purchased it, when it was simply a cleaning job. Why did you pay so much?"

The social graces went out of her demeanour. She said carefully, "It was the agreed price with a gallery we trust. Or at least, we trust the owner, Mr. Pennywell."

Neville said, "Did you check with other reputable restorers on the probable costs for cleaning the work?"

She ignored the question, saying, "We paid whatever was necessary to bring out its full potential. We left the details to Mr. Pennywell."

"You were aware that these costs were high, though, weren't you? You said to DI Sayer here, the first time she met you, 'Bought for a song and restored for a fortune'. Do you recall saying that?"

Ranjani looked at him defiantly then glared at Catrin. "Perhaps. I don't recall."

Coltrane looked down at the table, at his spreadsheet of figures he hadn't shared with Ranjani or the solicitor.

He sighed. "We haven't so far spoken to the seller in France. But once the investigation expands, we will show, I have no doubt, that somewhere along this transaction chain the price paid to the seller was about £40,000 pounds higher than the sums you transferred. That difference was paid by a third party for services your husband provided to them. Is that not so, Mrs. Ranjani?"

Ranjani's face was blank, but her eyes showed her concern. But she said nothing. After a long minute of silence, Coltrane ploughed on.

"But let's move our discussion to the charming landscape by Václav Jansa. You bought that about a year earlier through Pennywell also, did you not?"

~~

Mark Harper and Nirupa's father had got into an easy discussion about the merits and choices of the Ranjani art collection.

Mr. Sengupta said, "I can't say I understand her reasoning any more than you can. In fact, you have stated very succinctly the issues we have had with Nirupa's choices of art for many years. Intellectually, she can rhyme off facts about an amazing range of art works. You name it. But none of it moves her, I found. She has no passion for a particular artist or style or the life or experience that the art captures. She showed no interest in putting in the effort to study an art form herself, to determine her own potential. To me, her interest it is about the worst elements of art."

Mark asked, sensing the answer, "These being?"

"From your face, Sergeant Harper, I would say you know the answers already; possession and price. Ownership and flaunting to the world that she has the means and wherewithal to acquire them."

They had been talking about Nirupa's art collection, her education and background for about thirty minutes now, with Hills sitting silent, occasionally smiling at Mrs. Sengupta, who didn't join the conversation.

Mark nodded. "I do indeed."

Sengupta continued, "It's why she went out with and married Jalaj, I am sure. Not just about art but… wherewithal for everything. Money. It broke our hearts, to be honest. It still does."

Hills asked, "How did they meet?" glancing at Mark, signaling she saw the opportunity. From the background preparations, they both knew about Jalaj selling drugs in the area while Nirupa was a student.

Mrs. Sengupta, sensing it was the women's turn to talk, said, "BURC, that's how they met."

"Berk?" asked Hills, thinking it was some antiquated term they used for criticizing their son-in-law.

"Birmingham University Rifle Club," explained the mother. "He coached there, a volunteer thing for free use of the facilities, I gather. She was considering biathlon at the time but her skiing never made the grade. That's as important a part of it, as you know, I am sure. I thought it was too esoteric; why not some sport more British? She had been good at athletics at high school; a hurdler. But something about the Nordic sport struck her. It's very much a niche interest here, which she saw as an advantage; a way to rise fast.

"She stuck at it for a while. She was a good shot, though,

wasn't she, Amil? She has a trophy upstairs; she never took it with her when she left. We still keep it clean and polished. It's silver, you know?"

"And Jalaj coached her?" said Mark quickly.

"Oh yes, he was a fine marksman. He learned in the Indian army, I understand."

Mr. Sengupta spoke up. "He could volunteer the coaching time. His income came from different sources, as I suspect you know."

Mark said, "Could I see the trophy and anything you have on her biathlon interests, Mrs. Sengupta? DC Hills just needs to step outside and make a call."

Loretta was already pulling her mobile out as he spoke.

~~

Neville Coltrane was quietly and capably cutting a swath through the list of five paintings based on the investigative work of Catrin, Mark and the assigned officers. At each point where they identified the sales gap between real value and purchase value at around £25,000 to £40,000 Nirupa seemed to shut down. On several occasions, Lianne Mortimer interjected, mainly about anything with an overseas element. She stated that her client would only answer questions about acts and events in the UK. It seemed as if Killam had prepped her to make such interventions after the preliminary disclosure meeting between Lauder and the solicitors laying out the area where charges may be laid.

Each time, Coltrane swiftly moved on to speak about the next painting, often commenting on its quality or history. Nirupa was alternatively loving and hating the man, Catrin thought.

At one point Coltrane took issue with Mortimer.

"Miss Mortimer, you may address us on points of process or law but if you respond for her on a point of substance again we will have no recourse other than to file a complaint. Do you understand?

The lawyer just nodded, murmuring, "Please keep your questions to points of UK law, as I said."

Catrin's mobile vibrated. She checked it and showed the message to Neville.

He said, "We need to take a break. Let's say ten minutes, shall we?"

Outside, they saw Moore waiting. She said nothing until they followed her into another room and shut the door.

Moore said, "They are both marksmen. Harper and Hills found that out from her parents just now and we are re-running the travel pattern information. She must be using another passport if she is involved and if so, we can nail her on that domestically, but it will take time, even with facial recognition software. As best as we know at present, we can't account for Nirupa being in the UK when we need her to be overseas, assuming our new hypothesis that one or other made the hits. But it explains why Jalaj has a good alibi for one of them, at least."

Coltrane said, "She doesn't look a gunman to me. Could she hold a sniper rifle well enough? They aren't small weapons."

As expert as Coltrane was in art, his comment revealed his inexperience with weapons.

"Oh yes, one that was tailored to her build, it would be no problem," replied Catrin, thinking of several female officers she had met who were rated marksmen.

There was a knock at the door and a uniformed member of the team came in with a padded envelope.

Moore said, "Thanks, Betty."

She pushed the envelope to Catrin. "Another scope; I just commandeered it from the armory. You need to do what DI Carstairs is doing with Jalaj right now, and getting nowhere. You are AFO, after all; the Morley Kerswell trick he talked about. Are you up to it?"

AFO; Catrin's status as an authorised firearms officer had caught up with her again.

"Other than basic training years ago with a rifle; since then I only retrained in small arms, ma'am. Personal security, not -"

"I know. But we aren't putting someone new in with her at this time. You need to wing it. She was in the university rifle club; Jalaj was a volunteer coach. She is a good shot, her mother says, won marksmanship prizes. Nirupa was hoping to do biathlon but her skiing let her down, just like mine does. Don't you let me down, that's all."

She looked at Neville. "You are doing great, Nev. I want to slap that cow of a lawyer; she is totally out of her depth and screwing us up. But keep at it."

She looked at her watch. "Five minutes. Get prepared. I'm going back to see if Lauder has pulled Jalaj's head out of his shell yet. There's nothing from the search teams so far."

She went to leave the room and stopped. "And, just in case you missed it, if this is right, Nirupa the Shooter did Madame Morin in Lyon. Get her."

She went out without looking back. Catrin and Neville Coltrane exchanged glances.

Coltrane said, "Nev, indeed! I haven't been called 'Nev' since my fourth year at school. And she is mixing up skiing; she is down-hill, I know; biathlon is cross-country."

Catrin replied, "Don't look at me, Neville. I can translate from Welsh. You need Hills here to understand the Mancunian mind. She is getting quite wound up."

He sighed. "A break, then back in. Hopefully the coffee will energize the responses. Not the lawyer though, I hope. Do you need more time to prepare?"

His eyes were on the package.

She nodded. "It would help."

"Have your coffee in here. I will take Nkrumah in, have him sit there looking mysterious. Give him some experience. Once you are ready, just come in and he will jump out."

Catrin opened the padded envelope and pulled out the box. A Schmidt & Bender telescopic sight for a rifle. She had seen SCO19 officers assigned to sniper duties setting up scopes but she knew little else about the device. Yet she was now going to talk to an alleged assassin who would be an expert on their use.

In another interview room DI Carstairs was similarly teasing the interest of Jalaj Ranjani to trip up. She was now to do the same with Nirupa.

~~

Neville finished the preliminary question regarding a von Eckenbrecher painting, a nineteenth century German artist, just two minutes after Catrin walked in with her envelope. DC Nkrumah had stood up and left, as each officer noted their status for the record. As she sat down Catrin noted that Nkrumah had left a warm chair seat and sweaty hand marks on the table in front of her.

Coltrane said, "DI Sayer?"

Catrin reached into her package and brought out the scope box, opened it and placed the instrument on the table. A black cylinder with front and rear removable protective covers, connected by elastic. They all watched her. Catrin studied it without comment.

Coltrane said, "Let the record show that Mrs. Ranjani was shown a rifle telescopic sight."

He suddenly realised he knew nothing about it.

Catrin said, "It's a Schmidt & Bender Flashdot scope, to be precise. As issued to officers within the Metropolitan Police Service who have had specific training to be snipers. Compact, isn't it?"

The question was addressed directly to Nirupa Ranjani, who shook her head, not to deny the compactness of the instrument but rejecting the change in subject, it seemed.

Catrin asked her, "Did you ever use one of these - it's top quality - or one like it?"

"No!" said Nirupa sharply. "I don't have a gun."

"Not now, I meant. At university. You fired rifles then didn't you?"

The lawyer looked at Nirupa sharply but didn't say anything. Keep your trap shut, Miss Mortimer, thought Catrin.

Nirupa said, "No. Yes. I mean, I did fire a rifle for a while when I was thinking about biathlon. No, it didn't have a sight like that."

"Not needed," said Catrin, more an affirmation than a question.

Nirupa said, "The rules say you have a specific type of rifle, with a front and back sight, but not telescopic. I didn't own one. I used the club's guns. But not for long. My skiing wasn't up to it."

She was starting to recover her composure.

Catrin said, "Right, for fifty metres, the biathlon target distance, you don't need one of these really."

Nirupa answered obliquely. "It's a speed event. It's all about speed, how fast to ski, how fast and accurately you shoot the targets. But wind matters, not elevation. If the wind is gusty, or it's snowing or raining, weather is a factor."

Nirupa's voice was becoming tense again but it was if she couldn't stop talking.

"Here she goes," said Moore to everyone watching the CCTV. "Sayer may have her."

During the questions, Catrin had been removing and replacing the front and back lens covers almost absent-mindedly, it seemed, occasionally glancing at the scope but mainly looking at Nirupa. She put the scope down again on the table half-way between them, with one of the two dust covers left off. Then she put her elbows on the table, clasping her hands together beneath her chin, apparently thinking.

"Biathlon takes place under real weather conditions, as you said. You have to learn about ballistic trajectories, windage and point-of-impact adjustment, don't you?"

Nirupa responded, "As I said, it wasn't for long, so I don't recall clearly."

"Yes or no?"

"Well, the terms are not new to me, but I can't say I can explain them clearly, you know?"

"But you understood the term 'point of impact adjustment'

didn't you? I used that term a few seconds ago; the adjustment of the scope to counter environmental factors such as wind?"

Ranjani looked at her, thinking. "I don't recall clearly."

Catrin had come to the conclusion, as had probably Coltrane and her own lawyer that Nirupa Ranjani was not good at lying when under pressure.

She continued, "But these parameters would be much more important for say, a two hundred metres shot rather than one at fifty metres, wouldn't they?"

Ranjani said quickly, "I suppose so. Longer shot, but -"

Catrin interjected. "Why did you do that?"

"What?"

Catrin looked down at the table. Nirupa looked down at her own hands. She had picked up the scope and put the dust cap on the uncovered lens. Her eyes widened. She put the scope down as if it was burning her hand and started shaking her head.

In the CCTV room, Moore said, "Bloody hell, that Yank was right, wasn't he? Saying to do this. Shooters just can't keep their hands off a scope that's uncapped when it's not in use. Jalaj spotted Carstairs trying it with him and consciously pulled his hands back, but Nirupa went straight in."

Catrin said, "Cap the lens. Why did you pick it up and do that? We were talking and you did it automatically. I couldn't do it automatically. How could you?"

Nirupa said, "I don't know."

Catrin's voice was blatantly skeptical. "You've not used a telescopic sight yet you can cap one without looking? Really?"

The flow of questions was getting to the woman; that was clear. She was regretting touching the scope. Catrin pressed on, not waiting for an answer.

"167 metres, you would need to allow for drift, right? You would need to be sure of range, drop angle, wind direction and strength?"

"Yes, I suppose so. Yes, you would need to."

It was if she was grateful for a technical question she could answer.

"167 metres was the distance between the rifle and Madame Morin's head two stories lower down, so you would need to calculate all these things to ensure a kill, right?"

Nirupa had. "I -. I don't know. I - ."

Lianne Mortimer butted in, addressing Neville Coltrane, "My client will not answer questions about events outside the United Kingdom; they are outside your jurisdiction."

Coltrane said, "Answer the question, Mrs. Ranjani." His voice was firm and persuasive but his eyes were glaring at the solicitor.

Ranjani just burst into tears. "I'm not saying anything else."

The momentum had been broken for a fraction of a second, but it had been broken, nonetheless. The cavalry had rushed to Ranjani's defense.

In the CCTV room it went completely still. Then DCS Moore said, "Someone stop me. I want to go in there and kill the woman."

No one asked which woman Moore was talking about.

They moved on to her movements and alibi claims for the dates around the two assassinations that could be down to Nirupa Ranjani alone, but she was now isolating, they saw; evasive answers, claims of inability to recall, no recollection of appointments, visits to friends, anything like that. Catrin knew that the Trident team members would be ferreting through computers, CCTV and credit card information, trying to find things to feed the interview team. But she received no text; a sign that nothing was coming up that they could use.

An hour later, Coltrane said, nicely, "We are going to break now. Mrs. Ranjani will be taken back to a holding cell and given a meal. We will start again at 7.00 p.m."

He had just read a text sent to him directly from Moore.

"I'm tired," said the lawyer, candidly.

Neither officer said anything for a moment. Then Coltrane

said, "If you send a replacement solicitor, please let us know. We start at 7.00 p.m."

They walked out as uniformed officers entered to take Nirupa to the cells.

In the operations room, when they went in they received a few sympathetic grimaces. DCS Moore broke off her current conversation and walked over rapidly, heading for Catrin.

Tired as she was, Catrin's adrenalin flowed. She was in for a public bollocking, she was sure.

Moore grabbed her arm. "You almost had her," she said, excited. "Everyone! I told Catrin to wing it and it was almost there. She's a small arms officer; doesn't know one end of a rifle from another. And she was so close! It was lovely to watch. Now you sods, I want something else as pleasurable to watch in the evening session. Pizzas and soft drinks are coming in right now so get round the table and get your thinking caps on while you eat."

She turned, leaning into Catrin whispering, "I told them, I could gladly have strangled that stuck-up lawyer."

She walked off without a response, leaving Neville Coltrane, the archetypal 'stuck up' snob by reputation, without any acknowledgement for his grueling time leading the interview with Nirupa Ranjani. Catrin looked at him, half-smiling, half-amazed.

"It's not true, I know," said Neville quietly.

"What?" asked Catrin, equally quietly, although that was increasingly unnecessary in the noise around the arriving pizzas and cans of drinks.

"That you don't know one end of a rifle from another. Gravesend would have reported it, I'm sure. But I am grateful for her focus on you. Last thing I need now is a public statement by DCS Moore regarding 'our Nev' not succeeding."

Catrin snorted with laughter. "Sorry, but it's so funny. This is like Brixton nick after a hard Saturday, rounding up drunk football fans. Look at it!"

She was watching the food and drinks being collected.

Then she said, "Use your fingers. The plastic cutlery in that cup over there will be useless with pizza."

32 OIL

After the food had been rapidly consumed, in the main, Moore brought them back into focus.

"First, the analysts; DS Mahon on Jalaj, please?"

Each interview had an officer experienced in conducting interviews watching the event, not from the perspective of evidence-gathering but from the response and state of mind of the person being questioned.

Mahon said, "I think Jalaj started closing down as soon as DI Sayer finished with him this morning, as he realised that it wasn't about the art. From then on he has been totally uncooperative and largely unreadable. The one part where I felt that, while not saying anything, he started to show anxiety was the linkage issue to his other businesses; how he could takes such risks when he had both a drug business and a real estate business to run. I think he is worried about how Michael Bolan would perceive his man getting tripped up over these other activities. It's a point to work on."

Moore turned to Lauder. "Did you pay him to say that? That's more or less what you told me."

Lauder raised his eyebrows and smiled. "I claim the fifth, as they say across the water. Mahon and I are telepathic."

"Right!" said Moore. "Let's put that one on the board.

Howes? Nirupa; what's your assessment?"

The uniformed constable was a seasoned officer. She had a reputation for reading people.

"Well, it was close, as you said, over the scope issue. Earlier she was really upset with the suggestion that she could lose her art as proceeds of crime; that one hit home. So that may be something to work at. Second, she seemed happy to answer DI Sayer's technical questions only when she was in a bind after avoiding other questions about motive or process for the assassinations; so something that brings it back to a technical element may work. But she is backing out of responding now. Not, I think, in the same way as her husband, building a wall, but just shrinking into herself. I expect far more tears this evening with anything other than a soft approach."

Moore said, "If she shot people, I don't give a damn really. She could shriek her head off if we got something solid from it. Neville, assuming you and Howes aren't telepathic, it was your lead. What do you think?"

Coltrane said, "No disagreement with PC Howes, really. I agree particularly about the return to technical issues. I think we should go at it softly in general, with some hard hits, then switch immediately to something technical; see if she talks more then. We have to stay clear of anything that would have her solicitor say it is an issue to do with a crime outside our jurisdiction so she doesn't butt in again and ruin it."

Moore said calmly, "We will be watching. If Mortimer goes outside the guidelines once more, Commander Barlow has agreed to make a complaint to the law society; I went to him about it. She can challenge process or communicate with her client on how to answer but she can't do that again."

She went on down her list. Calloway confirmed that there had been a lot of questions following the contacts with the police departments overseas, but neither they nor Interpol had provided anything directly useful to assist the interviews yet. "But we do have a lot more specific information on two of the crimes coming in now, if needed."

The various search teams at the home, business and marina

reported in by phone; each had drawn a blank. One of the officers in the room asked, "Do they have a storage locker at the marina. A lot do, I think?"

The search team liaison replied, "Yes, they have one at the marina; it was checked."

Moore moved on. "Forensics; any joy?"

The lead forensics officer said, "The only thing that we found so far are small oil stains on the frames of two of the paintings at the home; fingerprint-sized but no prints, just smears."

It was as if Catrin woke up.

"What sort of oil? Which paintings?" she called out.

"We don't know the oil yet. It doesn't appear to be furniture polish or wood polish. It's on the Mignard and the Dyckman; the ones possibly associated with the assassinations attributed to Nirupa Ranjani, it now seems."

Catrin said, "Are they visible?"

"Not really, a very light stain fluoresces under UV light. We are still working on it."

Catrin pressed on, "What if she touched them; her paintings, her payments, really, during the firing test stage? Could it be gun oil traces if she has been setting up the weapon?"

Carstairs, the contract killer expert, said, "Unlikely, I would think, to take a valuable painting into a woods or a field; that is where it would be probably, the rehearsal scenario."

He was thinking as he spoke. "But, you know, the handover of part of the payment is often made at the proving stage, once the marksman is happy with the weapon and the client has seen that the contractor can do the job. But normally it is money in a briefcase or an on-line transfer completed on the spot. If the paintings are payments, you may be right after all."

Moore replied, "But it will be interesting to see if she explains it. Put it on the board. Sort out the questions to pose. We have an hour and ten until we start again."

~~

Coltrane spent a good ten minutes after they re-started the interview of Nirupa Ranjani on the issue of the paintings being 'alleged proceeds of crime', explaining carefully that even if only a part of each payment was directly linked to the crimes, the law was clear; although the other funds used in each case were legitimate, the paintings would be forfeited.

"The powers of the Proceeds of Crimes Act, 2002 are quite sweeping, you see; your solicitor can explain that more fully."

Mortimer listened carefully but made no intervention. Nirupa looked increasingly upset.

He then switched subjects. "Why did you select a painting from each of those countries, Mrs. Ranjani; can I ask that?"

Nirupa answered, "I like every painting we bought. Every one of them is a masterpiece in its genre."

He said in the same even voice, "I think you like them less for the art than what they represent; a visible display on your home walls of your prowess as marksmen and killers, each of you. They are trophies. Am I right?"

It was when he deliberately used the word 'trophies' her eyes revealed briefly his insight. She said nothing in response, but the video caught it; he was right.

He pressed on, "So in the Mignard painting, I see the image of a young woman from the seventeenth century celebrating her transition from youth to her life ahead; courtship, marriage and her own family. It is all caught in her facial expression. For you, it's a symbol of death, of your accuracy in dealing out death, to be specific. What do you say to that?"

Nirupa was looking angry now.

She replied, "I love the painting for its own sake! I own it; it's mine to enjoy."

Coltrane shot back, "And the Dyckman. And the others. You own them, you say. But can you explain your acquisition of each painting? How it ties in with a death of a person by rifle shot around the time you received it? You have seen the details."

She looked at him, but didn't answer. He waited a few seconds.

"More specifically, can you explain by any other means than extreme coincidence how every painting came into your possession within a two-week period prior to the deaths of the people we have identified in each of those countries. It's overwhelmingly clear, isn't it?"

Again, she said nothing.

Neville said, "And then there is the oil."

It was Catrin's signal. She added, sounding helpful. "The oil on the frames of two paintings, the Mignard and the Dyckman."

She had Nirupa's attention now.

"Oil, what oil?" Ranjani asked, getting a warning glance from the solicitor for asking a question.

"Oil residues. Not readily visible, but with the equipment our people have, they stand out. Our forensic people say they aren't wood polish. They are continuing the analysis as we speak."

She paused.

"I think it will be found to be gun oil; these oils have very specialized compositions, as I am sure you know. But we will see. Have you perhaps touched the frames after handling any machinery?"

"I take care of my paintings, so no. I wouldn't do that."

Catrin said, "So if there is the same gun oil residue on these paintings, two paintings obtained by you at different times from different countries, you will need to explain that, won't you? Why are you smiling, Mrs. Ranjani?"

It was as if the woman had recovered from the onslaught of misery of Coltrane's criticism. The smirk of superiority Catrin had noticed during the very first interview with the Ranjani couple had returned.

Nirupa said, "We have a biathlon rifle on the boat. We use it occasionally. Perhaps the oil from that is the trace on the painting if it stayed on my hands."

Catrin asked softly, "A rifle; where is it?"

Ranjani paused then said neutrally, "Ask Jalaj; he looks after it."

"Do you know the make?" she continued, carefully. She could see the lawyer getting concerned.

"It's an Anschütz 1827F Fortner, a standard biathlon piece. Nothing special. Kept from the old days."

"I thought you didn't compete at biathlon, your skiing let you down?"

Nirupa glared at Catrin. "It didn't stop Jalaj tutoring others did it? It is his rifle. I may have just picked it up from time to time."

The faint smile continued on her face as she gave the details.

Catrin was getting outside her own technical competence and looked at Neville who gave a quick glance at the CCTV camera.

In the operations room Moore couldn't stop talking.

"What the hell is she talking about biathlon guns for? She shoots people, not little targets. Is she going off her rocker? Call the boat search team; if they are on their way back, turn them round."

Manny Victor, almost forgotten in the events of the day, called out, "It's not about the power of the gun, ma'am, it's about marksmanship."

People looked at him, his excitement at seeing the answer.

He continued, "Professionals like these two wouldn't mix up the power difference of a .22LR round with that of a sniper bullet. What they have in a biathlon rifle is a highly adjustable weapon; stock length, cheek-pad position and trigger resistance are all easily adjusted. It's an ideal weapon for two people of different size to share; it can be tailored to each of them."

Moore nodded, taking in that the gun was more relevant than she first thought.

Trident team members were working out who was doing what, based on her instructions.

Moore sent a text to Coltrane; 'Finish the run on the gun details and call a break.'

"An Anschütz is an expensive gun, I take it?" asked Catrin.

"I thought you were a firearms officer, you said?" responded Nirupa.

Catrin said, "I am. But I don't know about biathlon rifles. What do you use it for?"

Nirupa nodded, "For pleasure, obviously. Target shooting. It's very good quality. Yes, it was expensive."

"For practice; you take it on the boat? Do you use it there?"

Nirupa Ranjani looked directly at her lawyer. "If I said yes that would admit to discharging a rifle over land covered by water, land we do not have shooting rights for. I could be charged for that, couldn't I?"

The lawyer looked baffled; she apparently knew nothing about that aspect of law. Obviously Nirupa did. Catrin wondered if the weapon was licensed, and to whom? Where, in fact, did they use it? Taking potshots at wildlife on the Blackwater, perhaps?

Nirupa turned to face Sayer. "No comment."

"We'll take a break," said Neville. Then he added, almost as a coda, "Your earlier comment, Mrs. Ranjani; about owning paintings. You don't. Neither do I own mine. The only person who owns it is the artist who conceived and produced it. Collectors are there to enjoy and cherish great art. What you own, I think, I wouldn't want."

The superior-looking smirk left her face, to be replaced again by one of hostility. Catrin thought that Nirupa would not be sweet-talking Coltrane about art galas again.

In the operations room, Moore looked at Lauder. He had caught the last bit after calling a similar break with Jalaj, who had continued stonewalling.

"What do you think, Gerry?" asked Karen Moore.

"Neville is provoking her hard enough, but she's playing with us. That smile… she knows we will play this gun thing back through Jalaj. But she isn't hiding her knowledge of weapons any longer. Let's get Carstairs in there after the break and talk about snipers, but keep Sayer in; she got her talking both times."

Carstairs said, "No she is not going crazy; just trying to be clever, I think. PC Victor is spot on. The weapon she is talking about is high-end. If she is right, for marksmanship practice she and Jalaj won't get confused over things like muzzle energy; they are entirely different weapons.

"Think of it as a scale difference; they are shooting people's heads at 200 metres with sniper rifles; they are probably shooting something the size of a thumbprint at 50 metres with that Anschütz. They still need to prepare with real sniper weapons but it could be part of the training program they follow."

Moore looked puzzled. "If we find this gun, is that going to be solid enough for an arrest, though? Is there a pattern of other snipers using these things for training?"

Carstairs gave a grimace. "No, as I said, I don't know, but I doubt it. I would need to ask around."

"When you do, ask that Yank, too. He seems a mine of information."

Manny said, "Ma'am, why would a sniper in America bother with a biathlon piece? The place is full of military grade automatic weapons."

"Ask him anyway," said Moore, looking at her watch. "It's not like you have to wake him up or anything."

Twenty minutes later, Lauder was back in with Killam and Jalaj Ranjani. The search team at the Horton Sailing Club denied missing anything on the boat but they were getting the locals to open the marina to search the vessel again.

"Mr. Ranjani, your wife has been talking to us. We now know about the biathlon rifle on your boat, the one you use for practice. It's a high precision item, I understand. Do you use it for marksmanship practice?"

He expected Ranjani to show some fear or concern about the break in his wife's interview. What he got was a smile.

"What's amusing, Mr. Ranjani, may I ask?"

"The first time I met my wife, superintendent, she was using a Steyr air rifle for marksmanship practice at the rifle club in Birmingham. It's a lot cheaper for students to use and the club had a limited number of official biathlon grade rifles. So I loaned her my Anschütz. It was how we met. Please let her know I am doing fine."

"Damn," said Moore. "She was playing with us, after all. We'll let Carstairs and Sayer stay at it."

Forty minutes later Moore called a stop to both interviews. Jalaj had gone back into his 'no comment' shell. Catrin and Ewan Carstairs were getting nowhere with Nirupa other than she could cite ballistic specifications for the Steyr air rifle Jalaj had mentioned. She would not discuss her whereabouts at the time of each assassination nor would she touch any question which related to other weapons.

When they had reassembled, Moore said, "Unless the search team sent back to the boat comes up with physical evidence or even this rifle, I think we are done. They have as good as told us that they are both marksmen and that they practice in the UK with a high-end sports rifle. Even if we find that, it's a minor charge at best and probably only for the registered owner or whoever has it in their possession; which may not even be one of the Ranjanis. And Nirupa will use it as an excuse for the oil stains on the paintings, if forensic analysis confirms the traces to be gun oil."

She puffed her cheeks out, mulling the options.

"Neville, Gerry; you two with me for a chat with their solicitors. Then we will call it a day."

The three officers sat across from the two lawyers. Catrin, Hills and several others watched on closed circuit television. Most other team members were taking a break. They needed it.

Moore began, speaking quite formally. "We will retain your clients in custody overnight and conduct one more interview in the morning.

"You have seen the case we have developed and presented

in its totality now. I emphasize our transparency on this. We have a strong circumstantial basis and the physical evidence of the paintings and their financial history. I admit we have little other physical evidence at present.

"We can tie some of their travel patterns with an unusual mix of locations and timings where a series of assassinations occurred. The Ranjani couple received paintings on a schedule that would support the explanation they are a means of payment for these crimes. In each case, these occurred through the involvement of a dealer called Richard Pennywell and his gallery.

"They have refused to answer questions about the numbered company that paid each seller the shortfall between the Ranjani payment and the sales price. We are convinced that it is linked directly to the syndicate that accepts the contracts for the killings but will leave that to the police in other jurisdictions to investigate.

"Finally, Jalaj and Nirupa Ranjani have admitted that they are both trained marksmen and Nirupa claims they own a sports rifle."

She stopped for a moment, assessing the reaction of the two lawyers before she continued.

"But these crimes did not occur in the United Kingdom, as you have constantly reminded us. Something we haven't shared with you so far is that throughout the day we have been in contact with Interpol and police departments abroad to share our findings and theories, including what we know about these financial transactions and the roles allegedly paid by the Ranjanis. Each jurisdiction has an unsolved murder case to pursue. Already our French colleagues are expressing an interest in interviewing your clients but are not yet in a position to do so; they, too, want to review their own evidence again first."

Catrin was watching the two solicitors, particularly the woman, who was looking exhausted and out of her depth.

Moore continued relentlessly. "Part of our purpose today was to try to get this sorted out cleanly; easily and cheaply you may say; a feather in the Met's cap; my cap. You'd be right. But we believed we had to act now as we have no idea when the next murder - indeed, that's what these are - is likely to occur.

"We knew the moment we filed our information with individual police services there was the potential for leaks to occur. The Ranjani names will be out there, sooner or later. With that comes the risk of retaliation from various quarters, for retribution or simply to silence them.

"We want to make it clear that if your clients choose to cooperate, there will be no deal-making to reduce sentencing for these murders, other than keeping them safely incarcerated. We will also acknowledge their openness to resolve these cases in a timely manner. Other than France, we will press for parts of sentencing to be served in the UK under EU transfer arrangements, if at all possible; we have support to offer that. We think we can keep Jalaj out of Italy but we won't keep Nirupa from France, if the French make the case. But we can keep him out of a Czech prison, we feel, which is no small thing."

She stood up, indicating the briefing was at an end.

"Tomorrow morning we will hold the final interview then we can decide our course of action. Unless they cooperate we will release them on police bail with the retention of their passports - and the art we brought in, for further forensic work. Doubtlessly you can take the matter to court, of course; it is a question of how soon we get evidence or requests from police departments abroad."

The younger female lawyer said, "So, on circumstantial evidence about a series of art irregularities, you have spread the name of our clients around a host of countries as a couple allegedly involved in assassinations, making them potential targets for revenge?"

Moore responded, "We have no choice. We have a series of facts, evidence that is pertinent to a number of on-going murder investigations, some in jurisdictions with which we have information-sharing agreements. Mrs. Ranjani has given us some inconsistent testimony that we could work away at.

Mr. Ranjani has given us nothing. It is their choice and your role is to discuss it with them.

"This all started, as you will recall, with the painting by Leslie Hunter found at the Stratford flat during the enquiry into the death of Miss Shannon. Well, in a different sense, your clients will be hunted - either by various police departments as we look to bring charges, or by others, as you now realise."

She left the room and Lauder and Coltrane picked up their files and followed her out without a further word.

Back in the operation room Moore thanked everyone and sent them home with the comment, "Tomorrow we will see. Goodnight, everyone. Gerry, you are going to have a word; right?"

She looked at Catrin after she put the question. Catrin had already been looking at Lauder, thinking back to a few minutes ago watching him on the CCTV, as Moore spoke to the solicitors about next steps. He had said something to himself, one word, as she finished. For some reason, not because she was a lip reader, but she thought she picked out the word - Galatians.

"Yes, ma'am."

He crooked his finger, calling Catrin over as people headed out and home.

Lauder smiled, unusual for him, and asked, "Hanging in?"

She responded, "Disappointed, but we gave it our best shot."

"A weird one, though," he responded. "They say that couples should find at least one pastime they should enjoy together. I never saw assassination as fitting that description."

He looked at her, ready for the item he had asked her to stay behind for.

"You have helped us a lot on this one. It's been noted. We would like you to do something else, but only if you want to. Niall Irvin. I was thinking back to our discussion in the car waiting for Pennywell to cave in. We'll fix it up for you to have a chat with him about the latest discoveries we have made, particularly about the relationship between Connolly and Bolan. See what he knows.

"It's not really your field but we thought you might consider doing the initial run-through for us? You can get Irvin's answers and put some of your own demons to rest in the process, is my view. We all need to do that at times in this job."

Catrin thought about it a moment. "Can I get back to you? I want to check with someone first; the psychologist who helped me, Dr. Herrington. I am also a bit tired now to make a decision, to be honest."

Lauder nodded, a little pensive, wondering if his offer had been a good idea after all, it seemed from his face. "That's no problem. So am I. I probably should have left it until then anyway. It's been a strange, long day."

"Sir? Galatians?"

He smiled. "Do you go to church, Sayer?"

"St. Paul's, the cathedral; I find peace there when I go, but I am not dyed-in-the-wool C of E."

He nodded. "It doesn't matter. Jesus never gave us any denominations anyway; they are a product of our own shortcomings. Galatians 6: verses 7-9. 'Be not deceived; God is not mocked: for whatsoever a man soweth, that shall he also reap'. I don't think, despite what Karen has planned, there will be much more to do on this now the news is out. Either they will confess or will be gone; they will go on the run or, possibly, they will be silenced."

He paused.

"I wonder who Michael Bolan will pick to run his operation if they do?"

~~

At 10.20 a.m. the following morning, Jalaj and Nirupa Ranjani were released on police bail. During the final interviews they had each elected to make no further comment. A police car followed Killam's BMW to Cinnamon Street where Mortimer and Killam dropped them off. They were met outside by their bodyguards and rushed into the flat.

33 HERRINGTON

The medical office in the block near University College Hospital had gone through renovation since her last visit years ago, after her final counselling session. When Catrin arrived and was shown into Herrington's office, she saw that it too had been remodelled. The layout was different. As usual, though, he placed his patients across from him in easy chairs, not at his desk. As she sat down, she saw the small vase on the bookcase, one she had given him in appreciation years ago.

The psychologist worked with both the Met and City of London Police services on trauma cases among police officers. Catrin had learned on her first visit that Herrington had first worked with emergency responders, particularly those officers responding to traffic accidents. It was the aftermath of a terrorist incident in London that resulted in his workload shifting exclusively to the police services. His workload hadn't diminished over the years. He had helped Catrin after the injury in Scotland and then again later, after the shooting incident in Kuala Lumpur.

He was watching her as she looked at the vase. "No, it wasn't put there especially for your visit; it's one of the survivors of the renovation. Cecilia went to town on that, as you can see. I don't think I like these chairs as much as the old ones."

Cecilia was his long-serving assistant who had greeted Catrin warmly on arrival.

Herrington began, "From what you told me on the phone, I was surprised you didn't call me earlier. Seeing Connolly, indeed!"

He had her file on his lap, closed.

She smiled at him. "Yes, I should, in hindsight. No excuses. The only other person who spoke against the idea with me was my current boss, DCI Coltrane."

He responded, "So you know the way we do this. Let's go through where you are; sleep patterns, new and old dreams and your fears. Then we can talk about moving forward."

It took most of the session to do that. Near the end he summarized his thoughts.

"The revelation that this man Irvin wanted you dead, not Connolly, is not to be easily dismissed. It's very personal, in part because he was part of the incident which caused your injury, which in turn led to the trauma we dealt with previously. Connolly may be the gang boss but he wasn't at Kinnington Church. Irvin was."

He asked, "When do you have to respond to Trident?"

"In the next few days. They need to keep the momentum up on the case."

He looked down at her file, lost in thought for a moment, then suddenly looked directly at her face.

"I suggest that you should do it, but only under certain conditions."

He was assessing her immediate reaction as he spoke, she thought.

"And they are?"

"You see me afterwards; the following day, in fact. Once you know the date, we will schedule that in as a priority. Secondly, who will be with you when you see Irvin?"

Catrin thought about it.

"I hadn't thought that through; probably my sergeant, Mark

Harper. He is physically capable in case - ."

She stopped.

Herrington looked at her. "I don't read a physical threat here. This man who suggested it, Lauder; I know the name but haven't met him. Tell me about him."

In a few sentences she described Gerry Lauder, as best as she could.

"I think he should be there; clearly he has some idea that this will help you. You should be part of it but not lead this interview, I think. I want your focus to be on your mental health, not Trident's information."

Catrin responded, "I can't tell a superintendent what to do, or ask him, really. He's a busy man, two grades above me!"

Herrington smiled, "But I can. What's his number? I will call him later and confirm with you."

He was looking at the wall clock, another survivor of the old office décor, Catrin saw. Her time was up.

As she picked up her bag she smiled. "When you talk to him say, 'Galatians'; he will know what it means. Having me interview Irvin was his idea. He can reap what he sows this time."

She stood up to leave.

"Thank you, Dr. Herrington."

He looked at her then said, "When we meet next time tell me about the other fears. I know you quite well now, Catrin, and when we finished reviewing the reasons why you came back to see me, I felt we hadn't touched bottom yet. Think about it, anyway; see if I am off-base or not."

34 MAGNUM

It took the police in Lyon three days to review CCTV coverage and check with witnesses, now they had photographs of suspects. In the process they turned up nothing new. The other jurisdictions were 'in progress' of re-examining the cases but had not responded further.

The French detectives asked for a videoconference call with the Trident team, which included Catrin and Isabelle, where they went over their findings. It was a sidebar comment from Isabelle to her boss that started it off; she mentioned she had not yet been to Lyon to see the art there. It came, ironically, as the French lead asked for any possible bright ideas.

Catrin said, "DC Howlett just put a thought in my head; is it possible to check any closed circuit records held at art galleries in the region in the period around the murder? Nirupa Ranjani is always interested in art she wants to collect."

The Frenchman nodded. "Probably most will not retain records for so long, but it's worth a try."

It was the weekend, ten days later. Catrin and Chris had gone down to Cornwall, to stay with his sister Jen in Falmouth. With some trepidation after a call by Chris to a family friend, Catrin allowed herself to be taken out in a dinghy, sailing in the harbour.

It turned out her reservations about her husband's capabilities with a small boat were unfounded; he seemed to know what he was doing and was as relaxed as she was tense each time they jibbed. For a moment it brought back her memory of sailing with Dafydd Powys and his wife on the Menai Strait during the Han Yeung investigation; the quiet competence of someone at ease with the vessel and the elements.

"You kept this talent well hidden," she said suddenly.

He smiled. "A talent; I don't know. A learned capability from others, yes, but I know sailors around here who are truly talented. But the prospect of a holiday with Li and James appeals and I could do my bit."

Catrin was shocked suddenly by the sound of Chris's mobile ringing. As he answered it she said, "You brought that on the boat? We could have capsized or got soaked. I left mine in the car."

He listened and then said, "It's for you; Isabelle. She's been trying to reach you on your office and personal mobiles; then she had the idea of looking up mine; she's at the office."

Catrin listened and said very little, then thanked her team member and closed the call. With only the sounds of seabirds, water and wind and a distant diesel motor drumming a steady beat she said, "The case I was working on; one of the suspects has been found murdered at their home in Cinnamon Street; the other is on the run."

Chris saw his wife was now lost in thought. "Shall we head back in then?" He knew better than to try to get more details.

Catrin was thinking back to Gerry Lauder's comment on 'Galatians' and how prescient the older detective had been.

"No," she said firmly, her attention back on her husband. "You proved you can sail still. Let's head out further, see how you handle rougher water."

He smiled. "Li will be proud of you!"

She responded, "And if we get soaked, it's your mobile that gets fried."

It was the cleaners that had discovered the body of Nirupa Ranjani. The two women were regulars and were used to being checked by the guards before they entered. It was unusual and intimidating, but the agency paid them double rate for this one, so it was worth it. They went to ring the bell, knowing that they were on a security camera anyway, and the polite young man would let them in. But there was no polite young man, or his colleague; then they noticed that the front door was open about a half-inch. Later, one said she wished they had simply turned around and forgone the pay. But her friend pushed the door open.

Nirupa had been shot in the reception room where the paintings had been displayed. The killer or killers hadn't used a rifle, preferring a .22 handgun of some sort. Powerful, quieter and less mess. There were no signs of torture or extraction of information, just the injuries associated with a shot to the heart with a further two shots into the head at close range. A professional elimination, a business deal; the sort the Ranjani couple did themselves.

That it wasn't to do with Bolan's drug business was made abundantly clear. Nor was there any evidence of revenge; a note, a photograph of one of their victims, that sort of thing. A single .338 Lapua Magnum bullet, not from a handgun but from a rifle, was left by her head. It had no fingerprints or DNA traces. The ammunition was a standard sniper round.

Ironically, the formal request from the police authorities in Lyon for assistance in interviewing Nirupa Ranjani came in the same day. The people who arranged the hit hadn't taken long to set up, really; they didn't face the same bureaucracy and protocols as governments.

In the ensuing investigation, during the interviews with neighbours, a Caucasian woman with a backpack had been seen approaching the flat with a man and, later, a woman fitting the same description had been observed approaching a car then driving away with a man beside her and an Indian man in the rear seat, witnesses claimed. The timing seemed to fit the window of the probable time of death given by the pathologist.

One person interviewed thought she recognized the Indian man.

"He lived at the flat the police are at, or nearby. But I didn't know him," she said.

DS Calloway was asking the questions. "Did he seem co-erced, or show any signs that he was under any pressure at all?"

She paused, thinking about the question. "Not that I could see. They were just walking together, not talking or friendly, like; but no-one was forcing him, I thought. Just walking along together. He had a brown leather bag with two handles, one of those stylish, expensive grips. I liked it, that's why I can recall it. The bag seemed full, the way he was walking. That's all I can say."

Calloway made notes and added, hopefully, "And the car?"

"Black, an SUV. I didn't take in the make or number, to be honest. No reason to, really. It was the bag I liked."

No, thought the detective. No reason to at all. You had no idea that they had just walked out of a flat where a cold-blooded murder had taken place.

The two bodyguards were found at their respective homes and had solid alibis. Both men had made sure they could account for their time with witnesses covering the previous day. Jalaj had told them not to come in, each said. There was to be a meeting with people at the flat and they were explicitly told not to return to the house until called.

The older man said, "I told my partner that we should ensure we have proof that we weren't there. I don't know who they were meeting, but I thought they were planning to leave. You had their passports but, frankly, that wouldn't slow them down. My expectation was that we would be called to babysit an empty flat for a while until Mr. Killam told us that it was for sale, or something."

"Didn't you have concerns? Your job was to protect them." Lauder asked him.

"No. I was simply following instructions," the man replied,

his face revealing that he had considered other outcomes, probably not much different to what happened.

Lauder sat thinking as Hills piped up, "If Mr. and Mrs. Ranjani thought that there would be a risk in the meeting, why didn't they have you and your colleague present for their protection?"

The man looked at her, pondering his answer. "I'm not sure, to be honest. I have thought about it, obviously. Perhaps with the people they were meeting, we might not have been much use. We are capable, trained; but not armed."

"And perhaps," Lauder added, "It was in recognition that either way, you two would be dead, right?"

The man looked away, revealing he had already been thinking along that track. If they were there when Mrs. Ranjani was killed, they would be killed also. The syndicate would want no-one left behind who could identify their members.

"Mr. Ranjani treated us fairly," was all he said in response.

All that came out from the initial investigation by Trident was that Jalaj had taken a call from a throwaway phone, talked with Nirupa and then given the security guys their instructions. Why the Ranjanis took the risk, they couldn't explain.

Gerry Lauder told Coltrane and Sayer later that he had first suspected it was someone in Bolan's organization who had arranged the hit but changed his mind.

"To stop Nirupa doing a deal; offering information on Bolan's gang in trade for immunity?" Catrin asked.

"That's what I thought. After talking to the two security people, I think it was the contract syndicate cleaning up, tidying up loose ends. Nirupa Ranjani became a liability."

"And what about Jalaj?" asked Coltrane.

Lauder said, "We suspect that Jalaj was told he would be spared if he co-operated. He is probably now under cover and will stay off the grid, one way or another, unless he is caught or killed."

"That won't be that easy, these days; staying undetected," said Catrin, thinking of the systems in place.

Lauder shook his head. "He's from India. He could be anywhere the syndicate wants him; back in his home country, or in Africa, you name it, complete with a false identity. But not here; we will be looking for him."

Catrin replied, "So you think he was complicit in eliminating his wife?"

Lauder said, "Ewan Carstairs thinks so. So do I. She was the one pushing for the paintings and they were the route to their downfall. She talked to us when Jalaj said nothing. Resentment at that, I think. Ewan says it is simply the nature of extreme sociopaths; either one of them could give up the other if the circumstances dictated it."

'They didn't even ask us for protection," said Mark, hearing the update later.

Catrin replied, "We couldn't do that unless they admitted to the murders. We never offered them an immunity deal; the assassination of the woman in Lyon made that a 'no go' at the very least. Politically, the UK doesn't want to be in a position where it had to turn down an extradition request from France."

She said, "The only thing that they had to offer was the Bolan gang and their links. Trident never asked because they couldn't grant immunity from prosecution, only protection, as I said. In the end, the Ranjanis took their chances."

Neville Coltrane walked in, wanting to talk to Catrin. Mark stood up to leave as Coltrane clued in on the discussion.

He said, "We did our bit; that was all we could do, Mark."

Harper nodded.

Coltrane continued, "The thing I missed; well we all missed really, was her; not that she was an assassin, but her perception of art. By putting it on her walls and talking knowledgeably about it we thought it meant something to her. Other than its trophy value and price; it didn't."

He shook his head and continued, "At least with the free port owners, we know they keep their art in storage lockers so they have little interest in it other than money. Nirupa Ranjani threw us on that one."

Mark suddenly smiled. "You said 'at least'... you mean you encourage people to keep art in storage lockers, sir? Can I quote you?"

Catrin laughed at the comment and at the face on Coltrane when he realized what he had just said.

Neville smiled. "DC Hills smart remarks are rubbing off on you, Mark. Perhaps I should see about transferring you to DCS Moore's team?"

Harper left the office shaking his head and warding off the suggestion with both hands.

Neville said, "The freeport update. That's what I am here about. Let's go through it before I have to work out my briefing for tomorrow's meeting with Bob Matheson's team."

35 FAVOUR

"They made the call; it was to be expected, Michael."

Dominic Connolly was speaking carefully, factually. Michael Bolan had called him with the news.

"You were right earlier, Dom; when you had that feeling about the Met focusing on Jalaj's paintings. That unraveled it all. I did what I could, gave him the offer but... he said he would sort it out himself."

Connolly replied, "No fault of yours. Just have to move on..."

There was a short sigh from the older man, genuine or not, Connolly couldn't say, then Bolan said, "The next shipment is due; same terms as usual, I know. But my delivery costs have increased and afterwards, I want to talk about it, for the future."

"All our delivery costs are increasing, Michael. For the cocaine, the production cost is dropping, at least for the short term, so I think it balances out. But let's get the accountants going through the numbers, as usual."

As Coltrane had suggested, the business arrangements between Connolly and Bolan did not involve money transfers, in cash, on-line or in kind; they hadn't operated that way for a long time. One or other handled the orders abroad; they covered each other's needs and the two accountants kept track. They would have denied that it was a Hawala-type operation, as there were no fees involved between them. The bond went back a long way.

When the painting issue developed, Bolan and Jalaj had talked; he hadn't hidden his 'pastime' from his boss. In fact, both Bolan and Connolly were aware of it and the syndicate that Ranjani had joined. Bolan had, in fact, used it some years earlier, a contract dealing with a gang member who had fled the country with significant funds. His only stipulation was that it was a totally separate issue and Jalaj and Nirupa did nothing on UK soil.

His only thought when Jalaj came out of custody was whether the man or his wife had traded any information on the Bolan operation. Ranjani claimed that he hadn't and Bolan believed him.

In the meeting with Bolan, Jalaj had said, "Nothing about it was raised with Nirupa or me. You know Lauder; it would be in his mind but, until he broke open something on our activities overseas, he would keep it shelved."

He had waited for his boss's pronouncement.

"Not my issue, Jalaj. The best I can do is to fix a new name and life for you both. Not in London or the UK, obviously; but everything would be left behind; you know that. You would be working for people upstream, but not in the UK; where I don't know, yet."

Jalaj Ranjani had replied that he and his wife had talked, they were of one mind. They would hold their ground and resolve it with the syndicate; try to convince them that they would stay silent. The police would get nothing from either of them, even if it went to trial and went against them. They were of the opinion that there was no basis in evidence for charges to be laid.

Bolan said to Connolly, "Even then, I thought he was holding something back. It wasn't the only option he was considering."

As the two gang leaders closed the current call, Bolan said, "Once again, thanks for the help. It was easier to talk with Jalaj. From what I hear, it was a nice touch."

Connolly demurred, dismissing it before signing off. He handed the phone to Tony, to make it disappear wherever his team hid such items. It was visiting time soon and he was looking forward to seeing Joan.

He mused on Bolan's last comment. After Ranjani's visit to see him, Michael Bolan had asked Dominic Connolly to talk to their contact at the syndicate, to make it clear that there were no impediments to whatever solution they chose although Bolan's preference was to leave the Ranjanis in place. Dominic agreed to pass that on, as Jalaj was reliable, Bolan felt. But if they chose to shut one or both of them down, it couldn't reflect on Bolan at all; that was the only stipulation.

The magnum round found by Nirupa was the result of that conversation. It wasn't Jalaj, the message came back afterwards; it was Nirupa they worried about.

It had been Killam who gave Bolan the basis for that message; Lianne Mortimer would never at this stage of her career breach trust on a client. But Killam knew who his client really was; Bolan, not Ranjani. He had expressed his misgivings to Bolan, which had led to part of Bolan's message passed on to the syndicate by Connolly.

Killam was no fool. He suspected his message would seal the fates of the Ranjanis; Nirupa, at least. He would lose out on fees working for Jalaj Ranjani, of course, but he was Bolan's solicitor for the long haul.

36 CRIME SCENE

"How was it?" asked Catrin.

She had sent Howlett to the Ranjani flat, at the request from Trident that someone from Art and Antiques accompany the HMRC representative. It would be a chance for Isabelle, nose now back to normal size, to get from behind the desk and meet her contact, Howard Potter, in person again.

Isabelle said, "Chief Superintendent Moore almost lost it, but not quite. She made her point and we stuck it to Killam. But his junior threw up. Superintendent Lauder looked like the Second Judgement had descended. He didn't say a word. He didn't need to."

Catrin thought it might come to something like that.

Moore had called Killam at seven thirty a.m. and insisted that he and Lianne Mortimer be at the Ranjani flat at 10.00 a.m that morning. The lawyer objected, but she made it clear if they didn't comply she would send cars for each of them. She reminded him they were still bound by professional standards to represent their deceased clients in the absence of other instruction, as if the lawyers weren't aware of the fact.

The two solicitors were shown into the flat by Howlett when they arrived. DCS Moore was standing by the window, looking out. Superintendent Lauder was sitting in a chair looking in; introspective and lost in thought. Howard Potter from HMRC was pacing, revealing his nervousness.

DCS Moore turned to face the lawyers.

"Good morning," she said, apparently brightly, but there was an edge to her tone that made Donald Killam wary.

He just replied, "May I know what this is about? You insisted on seeing us, Chief Superintendent."

"Certainly. First, we are closing out the crime scene here today. Miss Mortimer, we will of course continue to look for your client's killer or killers. And for your client, Mr. Killam, wherever he is, particularly as we haven't ruled out that he was the killer. We just wanted you to see room before we finished."

Moore pointed at the body marker flags and the dark stains on the floor. The young solicitor was already staring at them. Killam kept his eyes on Moore, occasionally glancing at Lauder.

Karen Moore said evenly, "In my job I don't lose much sleep when people who live outside the law go after each other, but we will be diligent, I assure you, in pursuing whoever did this. What I think about most is that we were almost there, solving five premeditated murders committed by Nirupa and Jalaj."

She had told Howlett in the drive over that she was going to use only the first names. "It makes it more personal, you know?"

Moore continued, "But Professor Morin. She was just a good citizen, doing her duty. She saw a crime and was prepared to testify in court until Nirupa blew her brains out. And the Giuliani girl in Italy was seven. Her grandad may be a villain, but Jalaj knew the bullet could fragment the way it did; it was designed to. The granddaughter was standing just beside him."

"Two days ago, the police in Lyon came up with CCTV of Nirupa in an art gallery there the day before Madame Morin was killed. As you recall, Miss Mortimer, she claimed she was at home during that period. Come here, please."

She beckoned to the young solicitor to join her as she dropped down in a crouch close to the body marker for the head, near the stain, her willpower forcing Mortimer to do likewise. Karen smiled at her, invitingly.

"It won't bite. It's a crime scene. Not even smelly and wet at present. This is what your best legal advice got for you client, you see?"

She kept her eyes on the young woman as her hand pointed out her explanation. At one point Donald Killam started to interrupt and her voice rose momentarily in volume to almost a shout, then subsided to her normal level, but she didn't stop speaking.

"She was shot first from a distance, over there, we think. Nirupa took one to the heart and went on her knees, falling forward. From the powder marks, the two other shots were close, from the same weapon. From the spray pattern, one went into the left temple and the final shot into the base of the skull. A professional hit, just like she did herself; just a little more intimate. Then they would have waited."

"Waited?" asked Mortimer automatically.

"For death to occur, to be sure. The bathroom is over there, don't puke here."

Howlett watched the young lawyer run, hand to her mouth. She saw Killam draw in a breath, about to unleash his objection to this treatment and heard Lauder's voice say simply, "DC Howlett?"

Isabelle was on stage.

"Mr. Killam, I am here regarding your McTaggart painting."

The lawyer stopped what he was about to say and said, "What?"

"Detective Constable Howlett, with the Art and Antiques Unit, sir. We believe that the valuation of the painting from your firm transferred to your wife's personal property was highly irregular. We can see no basis, in terms of our expert opinion, for the painting to have dropped in price so far. It's tax fraud, we believe."

He looked surprised, almost amazed, at the change in topic. "Is this really something to talk about now? I have just witnessed the most flagrant -"

His eyes were on Moore.

Isabelle said loudly, "It is relevant now, sir. We have informed HMCR of this irregularity and Mr. Potter represents them."

She looked at Howard as Killam finally noticed the rotund man.

Howard Potter said in a quiet monotone, "We looked into the matter raised by the Art and Antiques Unit, Mr. Killam, and we consider it a deliberate misrepresentation during your tax filing."

"Then send me a bill," Killam said forcefully, "with interest, no doubt."

Potter replied firmly, "No sir, it's your business filing that is incorrect, not your personal return. You are a solicitor; there are professional standards. We have made today a formal complaint to the Law Society about an apparent irregularity in your business practices. No doubt they will be following up with you and we are pursuing our own audit of your accounts. Our team is arriving at your office around now, sir. So when you get back, I would appreciate your full and open cooperation."

He handed Donald Killam a sealed envelope with the audit notice.

Killam said nothing as Lianne Mortimer came back, looking pale. The older lawyer looked across at Moore and saw that her eyes were gleaming. A tax audit and a review by his professional body were going to tie Donald Killam up in time and cost far more than any charge of petty fraud would, they both knew. And, if validated by either investigative body, it would have repercussions that could bring the police back into the picture.

He looked again at Superintendent Lauder, sitting like Solomon in judgement. Dealing with Trident was going to become a lot more difficult for him in future he suddenly realised, and wondered why. Then, from Lauder's expression, he understood. He had crossed a line; they saw him no longer just as a solicitor, despite their distaste for his clients. He had seen it before with other defense counsel; the sense of loss of professional respect, the looks which say they think he is now part of the criminal world.

Killam was working out how to test this when Lauder suddenly stood up, his full height causing Killam to tilt his head back a little.

"It was too soon, you see?" Lauder said to the lawyer.

Too soon for this to arise from a leak overseas, he meant, but deliberately didn't explain it further. He was watching Killam's face for signs; puzzlement, understanding or denial, but the lawyer remained impassive, unreadable.

Lauder added, "We know you went to see Michael Bolan and then Bolan talked to Jalaj."

He suddenly turned away, looking directly at Mortimer, who was clearly uncomfortable, wanting to leave. "You should tell your colleague that he should say 'no comment', don't you think? As he advises the criminals he represents to say. Not that we are accusing him of anything, mind."

"At present. Other than tax evasion," said Moore, brightly.

Howlett finished her feedback to Catrin with, "DCS Moore hummed as she drove on the way back; it must have been quite motivational for her. I can see why Superintendent Lauder insisted on driving himself there and back. I wish I had gone with him, but you can't say no to a DCS, can you?"

Catrin smiled, thinking about turning down the offer from Commander Barlow to work with SIS.

"It needs to be done carefully, if you do," she replied.

37 MARINA

It was two weeks after the murder that Nirupa Ranjani's father, Amil Sengupta, called the nice detective, Loretta Hills, who was in the middle of doing her laundry on one of her precious days off.

"Yes, Mr. Sengupta, I do remember you, of course. What can I do for you?"

His voice sounded distressed.

"Well, I am now the executor of my daughter's estate; the only will they could find is one she drew up some years ago mentioning me. I should call someone with the police but... I met you and had your card."

She waited a moment allowing the man to decide what to say. She hadn't seen him since the visit to their home. The feedback in the daily briefing, she recalled, after the Sengupta couple had been informed about the death of their daughter was, 'they were devastated'.

From his voice and background noise, he wasn't at home, he was outside somewhere.

"Is there something you want to tell us?" she asked. Loretta was getting anxious about the stress level the man seemed to be under.

Sengupta said, "I am at the marina in Essex, now getting

275

Nirupa's belongings from the boat. The solicitor I am using arranged access for that, even though the boat is in Jalaj's name. The man who works here we are talking to showed us also a locker rented to my daughter. There is a gun inside, like a biathlon gun, I think."

The thought of her laundry went out of her mind.

"Are you there now?"

"Yes we are; looking at it."

"Have you touched it?"

"We just opened the case, so we have touched that, but not the gun."

"Then please don't. Close the case again and I will get someone with you as soon as possible. Please wait there. Let me know exactly where you are."

Nirupa's father did so, then started crying and she could hear another man with an Essex accent trying to calm or console him, it appeared.

After a moment, Amil Sengupta said into the phone, "It makes it all true doesn't it, what you suspected, once you found out they were both marksmen. It wasn't about drugs, was it? It was about guns; that is why she was shot."

Loretta wanted to get off the line and call it in, but she realised she couldn't. No-one had mentioned the discovery of a sniper round next to the body, which was a bigger giveaway. The news release had said only that Jalaj Ranjani was wanted in connection with breach of bail and clarification of his role in the death of his wife, whatever that may be.

Instead she said, "It means Nirupa told us the truth, that they had a rifle at the boat. We will need to take it as evidence, I'm afraid. Mr. Sengupta, I should have said earlier, I want to express my condolences. Whatever she was involved in, I know she was still your daughter and how much it must hurt you and your wife."

She was talking over his sniffles, as the man tried to control himself.

"I will wait here. Please call back and let me know how long it will be and… thank you for your kind words. After you and

Sergeant Harper left my wife said why couldn't we have a daughter like you? Leading a proper life."

"I have to go now, Mr. Sengupta, to call for assistance so you can get on your way as soon as possible once the other police officers collect the gun and inspect the locker. Please touch nothing else there."

They made their goodbyes and Loretta closed the call. She pulled up Sengupta's mobile number to pass on. She found her eyes were blurred with tears. As she called Lauder, she silently cursed DCS Moore.

'Be nice', Moore had said, and she had. And it came at a price.

~~

The Anschütz had been handled by both Ranjanis. The forensic examination revealed that the stock adjustments showed two particular combinations of settings, consistent with the bodies of larger and smaller framed marksmen. Also in the case, not mentioned by Sengupta, was a high-end telescopic sight and mounting.

Catrin was briefing Mark and Isabelle, passing on down the chain the information received at her own briefing.

"How did they miss it first time, during the search?" asked Isabelle.

"Everything about the boat was in Jalaj's name, including the locker. The separate locker had been registered to Nirupa; it was in the name of N. Sengupta. They missed it. It's a large marina."

"Shouldn't the marina staff have linked it - pointed it out?" asked Mark.

"The person did, when the executor turned up. The same man was away on holiday when the search was conducted. The person on duty then wasn't aware of the second locker. It just fell through the gap. It was an oversight, as DCS Moore was quick to point out."

"Well, that closes out that case," said Isabelle, with some

finality. "And for us, the benefit of not even having a trial to prepare for."

Catrin smiled and said nothing, indicating by picking up a file that she needed to get back to work. It wasn't quite true; she had one more job to do, something that couldn't be shared with her team. Tomorrow she would be in Lyme Regis and no-one else was to know. She was out on a case, simple as that, they had been had been told.

Mark had a training course that day, also.

"I'll cover things; unless I get invited at short notice to join the FBI," Howlett declared.

"Don't hold your breath," said Catrin. "And stay out of pubs with stairs."

38 LYME REGIS

The Royal Lion Hotel in Lyme Regis was the venue selected for Lauder and Catrin to interview Niall Irvin; not by the Met but by UKPPS, the group responsible for keeping Niall Irvin safe. Part of the National Crime Agency, the UK Protected Persons Service provided security and relocation for everyone from innocent witnesses, akin to Professor Morin in France, through to hardened criminals who have become informants. In Irvin's case, they worked closely with their Police Scotland counterparts.

All Catrin could draw from that selection of location was that Irvin had not been re-settled in the West Country. She was thankful for that; they went there quite a bit, given Chris was Cornish and she now had family and friends there.

She hoped it wasn't Wales, either.

Lauder had driven; they took motorways to Exeter, staying there overnight. The following morning they headed back east, to Lyme Regis. Lauder had been provided with a location, a room number, a name and a time. All had to match up.

Lauder had told Catrin, "Don't expect to see or have contact with the UKPPS people, but if they have concerns they will intercept us and identify themselves, they say. In the times

279

I have done this previously, it has never happened."

Catrin wondered if her counter-surveillance training during her role as AC Hunt's security officer would allow her to spot the NCA staff.

She led the way out of the elevator, checking the room numbers before knocking on the correct door.

"Mr. Townsend?"

It was the agreed name.

Niall Irvin opened the door and stepped back, taking in the woman and man as he said, "Come in."

Then the realization hit him. Lauder closed the door behind him.

Irvin was dressed in grey slacks, a casual shirt and a V-necked sweater; not the formal dress of a lawyer, the suit and tie she had last seen him in. His hair was dyed and had some grey streaks to make him appear older. Other than that, they had taken no particular steps to change his appearance.

In fact, she had second thoughts on the grey streaks. As she assessed him carefully, he was looking older, with more lines around the eyes and throat. He was still the man of her... not dreams, no. With Colin Cheney, the two men of the occasional recurring nightmare.

Irvin said, "They said representatives of Trident were coming... I thought you were -."

Lauder interrupted. "I am with Trident; Superintendent Lauder." He showed Irvin his warrant card.

"This is Detective Inspector Sayer, with the Art and Antiques Unit. And we are a long way from Kinnington Church, in more ways than one. We have some questions for you, ones within your immunity deal agreement."

He made it sound neutral, professional, as if he was just any old informer they didn't really know.

But Catrin was trying to put out of her mind the image of Irvin by that car outside the church in Glasgow when she was feeling bloody and beaten up, about to pass out. That was their last encounter.

Irvin gestured, offering bottled water, coffee or tea; a tray standing on the side dresser had recently been sent up from room service. Catrin took in the details of preparation for the meeting.

The room was a bedroom with a bay window, but it appeared that the bed had not been slept in. The bay window gave a view of the street and the café and higher floors of the building across the road. Net curtains let in the light but protected privacy. Even so, the round table that had sat in the bay and its three chairs had been moved into the room by re-positioning the sofa. The chairs around it were set neatly at 120 degrees, in preparation for the meeting. She moved one chair closer to another across from the one they wanted him to use. It was their interview, after all. Lauder had told her how he wanted it set up on the drive down.

Catrin pulled out her pad and the recorder unit. She was to take notes, as would Gerry Lauder. Irvin didn't seem bothered; he had spent many days divulging the secrets of the Connolly gang in settings similar to this one, Catrin thought and interviews were stock-in-trade for a lawyer.

If Connolly ever located Irvin, she knew he would be a dead man. Connolly hadn't conveyed that in his remark during his interview comment, 'I still don't feel charitable to him, actually' but she was sure that would be his intent.

Irvin didn't need a solicitor with him; he had immunity. He was also once one of the sharpest defence lawyers in Glasgow. He may have been Dominic Connolly's lifelong friend until the split, but Connolly wouldn't have kept him as his legal counsel for so long unless he was that good.

As he sat down and waited for the questions, she took in the 'new' Irvin. A new life perhaps, but the strain of a new identity and the threats from the old life had all taken their toll. With Dominic Connolly, Catrin had the passing thought that the devil looks after his own, the shape he was in; Irvin looked as is the devil had forgotten him and God hadn't found him.

Lauder said, "We have questions in several areas. We will start first with the relationship between Dominic Connolly and

Michael Bolan and the deals between them struck around the time of Operations Finisterre or earlier; ones that you would have some knowledge of. Secondly, we know that Jalaj Ranjani and Brodie Shannon were quite good friends prior to Brodie's arrest and conviction. You haven't given details of anything about that previously. We want to know more about the working relationship between them and also about the relationship between Shannon and a man called Paul Farrar, the accountant for Bolan."

Irvin nodded, indicating either that the subjects mentioned were 'fair game' or were areas he had some information about.

Lauder added, "Ranjani has fled bail and his wife was killed recently. You may have read about that?"

"Yes, I did."

"Thirdly, both Ranjani and his wife sidelined as contract killers themselves, although this is not yet public, nor will you reveal it to a third party. We want to know if he did any work of this nature for the Connolly gang or the Milne gang. Again, you have made no mention of that."

Irvin interrupted. "Jalaj and Nirupa; both killers? No, I - ."

Lauder interrupted him back. "I am to remind you, before we get into the details, that the terms of your immunity deal are clear. If it can be shown that you have knowingly lied to us based on evidence currently in our possession or that we may become aware of, the Crown Prosecution Service will be informed."

The immunity deal could be scotched, wholly or in part, he was inferring. He would still be protected, but could be tried in camera and sentenced on a slew of crimes to which he had already confessed.

"I will ask the first set of questions, regarding Connolly and Bolan. Inspector Sayer will cover the questions regarding Shannon and Ranjani and the issue of a painting that came up during our investigation. I will come back on the issue of the Ranjani couple's roles as assassins."

He looked at Catrin. They were off to the races. As Lauder put the first question Catrin sat back listening actively, taking in the facial expressions of the man that had wanted her dead.

~~

It took three hours, with only one break for the bathroom and some coffee. Irvin had lost none of his erudition or ability to formulate clear messages. Catrin could already pick up elements that would need further probing and analysis. Most significantly was the reluctant revelation of a single exchange at a social gathering between the Connolly gang team and their Edinburgh counterpart, the Milne family. It wasn't much, but it was a chink.

Irvin had mused a little in response to a series of questions Lauder had put to him about use of contract killers. Initially he repeated that domestically, Connolly rarely killed people and when he did, he used his own enforcers. He had covered that ground already with Strachan years ago, he said.

"And betrayals or issues abroad, if he faced them?"

There was a pause then Irvin said, looking at Catrin, "I often think that if I had known that Daniella Milne was a psychopath, I would never have started the Colourist deception with her. If I hadn't, I would still be practicing law in Scotland and giving Strachan a run for her money."

The Met officers waited.

Irvin continued, "The subject came up at the gathering at the Fonab Castle Hotel of the Milne and Connolly leadership. Strachan knows about that in detail other than... Steve Milne and Dominic had a discussion one-on-one. I came into it at the end, to tell them something - dinner, the kids, I forget what. Steve Milne said, 'I will send Martin along anyway, to introduce himself; you can talk one on one. He has no problem with overseas assignments'. That's Martin pronounced the French way; could be a surname."

Lauder asked, "Martin - do you have more details?"

Irvin shook his head. "Not even whether it's a first name or surname. Nor, in my remaining time with Dominic did I hear it further. It's only that there was someone in the organization who had recently skipped off abroad; but I don't recall the name. Hence the assumption of the topic, but I could be wrong."

It was a slim link. It could mean nothing but Lauder would need to assess that, Catrin thought. This would be the first tier of questions on these subjects. Moore and Strachan's teams would work through them assiduously and Irvin would find himself in more interviews as they tunneled down the details, particularly the new avenue of the relationship between the Connolly gang and Bolan gang accountants, Shannon and Farrar. Neville Coltrane appears to have been right about the 'Hawala'-type relationship. It now appeared that Shannon and Farrar arranged family holidays annually in a coordinated fashion, always choosing the same location. Three times it had been Disneyworld in Florida.

When questioned about the financial details, Irvin claimed he had none.

Finally, as they realised they were finished and silence descended on the room, she glanced at Lauder. He nodded and they noted the closure time and he switched off the recorder.

She felt tired and assumed Superintendent Lauder was too. If Irvin had looked worn at the beginning, he looked totally wrung out now. He wasn't aware that the Ranjanis had been contract killers it seemed and, to her, that seemed genuine.

During her phase of the interview, one question which struck her that she had added in on the fly came back. She had said, "Dominic Connolly tensed up when I mentioned we were looking into Ranjani's art collection. Why was that, do you think?"

She expected a simple response, a denial of any knowledge of events after his own departure into witness protection, but he thought about it and said, "I don't know, of course, but I suspect something was off about it. Dominic has an incredible ability to sense - I can't describe it otherwise - other people. When I made the decision to defect, for want of a better term, I went straight to Strachan. I knew if I even went back to see

Dominic thinking about it, he would tune into it. So the only suggestion I have is that he sensed you were on to something once you started investigating Ranjani's art."

He waited a second then said, "You saw Dominic recently?"

"Yes, I did," she answered in a tone that made it clear that she would say no more on that subject.

Catrin dearly wanted to ask him why he thought Connolly had gone to the trouble of telling her that it was Irvin, not himself, who had wanted her dead, but it would throw off the flow, she thought. In her own mind she had the answer anyway. She had hit Connolly hard with it at the beginning of the interview in Shotts and he had partly wanted to drop Irvin in it, get at Strachan in the process. But he also wanted to set the record straight; that 'sixth sense' Irvin had just commented on.

The best parts of Irvin's information would need more work but she saw it could help Trident build their case against Bolan; their special surprise for the man's parole hearing.

They were putting their notepads away and moving the chairs back when Irvin said, "I teach part-time; but not around here. A new life."

Neither officer commented. I don't want to know, Catrin thought. You aren't supposed to say.

Then Lauder simply said, "Thank you for the answers, we will leave now."

Catrin saw Irvin look across to the phone on the table beside the bed. He had probably been told to call his handlers on it as soon as they left. At the door she hesitated. It was too much of a burden to hold in what she wanted to say. She turned back as Lauder was about to open the door.

"Connolly told me that it was you, not him, who wanted me dead. Is that true?"

He looked at her, then down at the phone he was about to pick up. "Yes, at the time; yes. Everything was going wrong and…"

He stopped. "No excuses. Dominic didn't say no to my request at the time. Nor did he say yes. He was focused on the Finisterre operation loss and his ire was directed at the French police agent; he would have killed him, I think, given the chance. The whole thing got wrapped together. I told Strachan all this."

Lauder was looking impassive. If he wasn't happy with this impromptu coda, he didn't show it. He, after all, had said this meeting would be good for Catrin.

She said, "Someone at the Kelvingrove stays in touch with your cousin Elizabeth. Mary Gault passed away without ever being told the whole truth; just that you had been involved with the Connolly gang and turned Queen's Evidence when you disappeared. Did they tell you that?"

He shook his head. "UKPPS never talk about those aspects with me; it's one of the rules about a clean break for a new life. It's... it's something, I suppose. Less pain for my aunt while she was alive."

Catrin fired back, "Not really. Elizabeth relayed that Mary told her she knew that you must have been involved with your uncle's death if his heart tablets had been substituted with ineffective copies. I met both women during the investigation into Reverend Gault's death. Mary didn't miss much, did she? Anyway, Elizabeth wanted you to know that your aunt forgave you, as she was sure that Alexander forgave you, too. When I heard this, I had no idea we would ever meet."

She left it hanging that Elizabeth had not included herself in this message. The emotions running across Irvin's face as she talked revealed a lot. He had been such an arrogant bastard; now she saw the suffering. There was pain, but she wasn't sure about what; probably self-pity about his ruined life.

She looked at Lauder and nodded. She hoped her expression conveyed that he had been right in his assessment of the value to her of doing the interview. Irvin at Kinnington church would be replaced by this memory of the man. She could live with that.

Gerry Lauder opened the door and left the room without

looking back and Catrin followed him out.

They used the stairs down to the lobby. Catrin noticed two people there who were talking, totally disinterested in them, it seemed. She ignored them and walked past, heading for the main door. Then she stopped and checked back. One was on his mobile and they were now heading up the staircase. Hopefully they were Irvin's handlers - or Townsend, or whoever he was called now.

"What now? You are thinking of something, I can see," asked Lauder, once they were outside.

"A hunch. The name Martin. Cross-linking, I think DCS Moore called it, when she separated the Bolan-Connolly and Ranjani investigations. I am thinking back to my interview with Anne Shannon. She said that Jalaj and Nirupa Ranjani had visited Brodie in Glasgow and taken the Shannon family out to dinner."

She paused, musing. "We need to find the location; a restaurant in a hotel, I recall ... I need to check my notes. Shannon said Ranjani broke away to talk with a man he clearly hadn't expected to be there; a Frenchman, who was there with some people Brodie knew."

Lauder said, "Good catch! This man Martin, perhaps?"

Catrin nodded. "We know that the Fonab Castle gathering of the two gangs took place sometime before Operation Finisterre. Irvin just told us that the hotel was the location where Steve Milne mentioned a contract killer with that name. What if, later on, one of the Milne gang was on his way to see Connolly with this man Martin and by chance took him to the same high-end restaurant where the Shannon family and the Ranjanis were eating? Or the man was staying in the hotel, if the restaurant was there? There would be records..."

They had walked as they talked, heading down the street to the Marine Parade. Lauder pulled out his mobile, pointed to Catrin to sit down at an outside table at the fish and chip restaurant at the sea front as he dialed Moore's number. It didn't take him long.

As he closed the call he said, "They are on to it. Karen is getting people to check with Police Scotland. She also says they will check with the Indian authorities, to see if a Frenchman called Martin was in the country around the time Jalaj was in the army or shortly thereafter. Perhaps they met before he came to the UK?"

"It's a big country, a lot of people," replied Catrin.

Lauder was checking his screen, pulling up a map of India. "Indore, was where he came from, wherever that is."

He prodded away at his phone. "It says here that it's in the middle of the country, about two million people. That's not big for India, you know? Who knows? Now, the important bit. How do you feel now; about seeing him?"

Catrin said slowly, "Better, I think. Like, he is cut down to size, if you know what I mean? More pathetic now; the immunity deal is no pushover, I can see, despite my wish to see him in jail for what he did. And... he still has Connolly on his mind, that's clear. I will talk to Dr. Herrington about it but thank you for pushing it. It was the right thing to do."

Lauder smiled, a rare thing for him, she thought. "The right thing to do, I think, is have fish and chips here, by the sea, before we head back."

39 FEARS

Once Catrin and Gerry Lauder returned and reported their detailed observations, Moore thanked them and Neville Coltrane for his unit's support and wrapped up the meeting. Within a short time, the Art and Antiques Unit were back on their own agenda and Coltrane was lost in the critical interviews of suspects in an antiquarian book theft case being investigated by DI Madder and his Antiques team.

Coltrane heard some days later from his boss Matheson, who had seen Moore at a meeting, that Trident was busy; still focused on the Bolan gang activity. Michael Bolan had named his second oldest son, Michael Junior, as his outside man, keeping the job in the family this time.

Coltrane later told Catrin. "Apparently, Mickey J, as he is affectionately known by some and disparagingly referred to by others, doesn't have his father's talents or Jalaj Ranjani's skills. There is discontent in the Bolan world and the Trident team is making the most of it."

Catrin had called Dr Herrington on return from Lyme Regis. He suggested that, given her positive report, they hold off a week before he saw her next.

"Let it settle a little. And remember my parting shot. What else is troubling you?"

The following day the Arts team found themselves immersed in an investigation into a theft of a painting from an auction held in a hotel at Canary Wharf.

"No drugs and deaths, thank God," said Isabelle. "Just plain greed and bare-faced effrontery. At least it is worth a lot - a lot more than the stuff we have been messing about with for Trident. Neville will be happier."

There had been more than one time in recent weeks that DCI Coltrane had grumbled about the time and cost of the support work for Trident. He was always one for chasing expensive art thefts.

The week went by quickly and the appointment with her psychologist came round before Catrin had time to think too much.

"I've given it some thought; what you said," Catrin began almost as soon as she was settled, while sitting across from Herrington. "It's nothing to do with Scotland or gangs or work, really."

He nodded but said nothing.

She continued, "The case starting with Lena Shannon's death tended to push my other concern to the background, but it pops back. I'm nearly thirty-one, married and torn over whether I want a baby or not. What do I want to do with my life? What do Chris and I want to do? Have a family? Balance our careers? I don't know."

She sat forward, on a roll with her explanation. "From early on, I wanted to do art and then I wanted to be a police officer and I worked hard, studied hard and now I have what I wanted. Here I am, leading the Art Team at the Met. If you had told me I would do that when I was eighteen, I would have laughed at your daydreaming. That's what I am torn over. If Chris and I are going to have children, we shouldn't dawdle but -."

She smiled. "I don't think it is an issue for you, as a police psychologist, I know. It's something many couples go through. But you did ask."

Herrington replied, "I did. And you have just told me about the issue, the big decision facing you and your husband. But you haven't told me about the fears beneath it, have you? That's what I was asking, really as that is the only thing I can comment on."

She paused, thinking.

"Just say it, Catrin. Don't polish it up."

"Would I be a good mother? Would I enjoy being a mother at all? If I don't do it, am I depriving Chris? How could I manage a job like mine and be a mother? It's all these things - and more. If I decide no, now, in twenty years will I - ."

She stopped. "You get the drift, I think."

Dr. Herrington looked at her, appearing pleased. "Now, why don't you remember those, develop them further, then go and ask your husband about his fears and hopes about this matter. Not to talk about the decision to be made, but about how each of you feel. And then decide together what is going to make each of you - and hopefully both of you - feel fulfilled and happy, as best as you can assess? Because I am sure, knowing you, whatever you decide to do, you will do it well. Agonizing over how you will feel in twenty years isn't going to help, believe me."

She nodded, suddenly looking at the problem from a different perspective.

"Now," he said, "how have you been sleeping and how do you feel about Niall Irvin and Dominic Connolly?"

40 BAD PENNY

The Trident case resurfaced for Art and Antiques three weeks later, like a whale suddenly dumping itself on Brighton Beach. Matheson, Coltrane and the Arts team were hauled in, briefed and Catrin found herself on the train north again the following day.

This time the meeting at HMP Shotts wasn't informal. Dominic Connolly had his solicitor present and the man had already been pre-briefed about the reason for the interview. Sitting across from them were DCS Strachan and DI Sayer, the record showed.

Strachan began, "Mr. Connolly, we are investigating to what degree you were involved in the death of Nirupa Ranjani. We have a few questions."

Connolly said nothing, his face remaining impassive. He hadn't seemed surprised to see Strachan, but his first look at Sayer reflected that he wondered why she was back here.

"Three days ago, the French police arrested in Poitiers, France a man called Xavier Martin. Do you know this man?"

She held up a photo of a man in his late fifties or early sixties, it appeared, obviously a mug shot.

Not receiving an answer, she added, "Whether or not you

knew the name; have you met this man in person? Were his services referred to you?"

Again, Connolly didn't comment.

"During the raid they found evidence of his expertise as a gunsmith, a very specialized gunsmith, according to reports. Yesterday he was charged in relation to the murder of a Professor Morin in Lyon. He didn't pull the trigger but did just about everything else, I gather, from the French police. I am sure it will be the first of a number of charges. That news will become public today."

Catrin was carefully watching Dominic Connolly; from his expression he was wondering what this meant for him. Strachan pressed on.

"Apart from some interesting equipment and tools, he also had a computer and a phone."

So far, Catrin had been told, the French police had found records of payments that tie in closely to the known assassinations. And also it had details of two recent payments to a UK account just before and after the assassination of Nirupa. But that wasn't for Connolly's ear.

Strachan paused, waiting, eyes focused on Connolly's face.

"On the mobile phone there was a call received from another mobile. Tracing it back, it appears to have originated through a tower close to HMP Shotts. It was made in the period between our interviews with the Ranjani couple and the date of Mrs. Ranjani's murder. Did you speak to a Mr. Martin at that time?"

The caller's phone was unlisted and had not been traced, but she said nothing about that.

She waited. "I believe it was you making that call. Do you deny it?"

Strachan stopped. From her expression, it was clear she wasn't going to say anything else until she had a response of some sort. She had reached the end of the area of questioning shared with the solicitor. It was this man, Niall Irvin's replacement, Catrin thought, who broke the silence.

"My client refuses to answer any questions without a clear

indication of the charges you wish to make. Even then, he may exercise his right to remain silent."

It was as if the lawyer wasn't present. Connolly stared impassively at Strachan and she didn't waver in looking at him.

"Did you advise Mr. Martin that it was acceptable to Mr. Bolan for the Ranjanis to be eliminated, one or both of them, if the syndicate so chose?"

This time neither the solicitor nor Connolly said anything in response. Then the solicitor said, "Charges?"

Strachan replied, "Section 59, 'incitement'; or Section 45; 'encouraging' a crime; unless you give us better answers to make it a trivial matter, such as use of an illegal phone to call an old friend?"

She was referring to the Serious Crimes Act provisions. The solicitor, who had been given time to talk to Connolly privately after receiving the initial briefing, said, "It should be interesting to see the evidence if charges are made. A crime committed in London while my client is locked away, a 'Category A' prisoner in a high-security prison, without access to mobile phones."

Strachan looked combative but simply addressed Dominic Connolly. "Do you have anything at all to say?"

Connolly let his breath out slowly, as if he was tired of the meeting. He turned to face Catrin, ignoring Strachan and asked, "Why are you here?"

Catrin looked at him; then at Strachan, who nodded slightly.

She replied carefully. "The Metropolitan Police are currently interviewing Michael Bolan, asking similar questions. One of DCS Strachan's officers is assisting in that interview; reciprocity, you see?"

Connolly wrinkled his nose in annoyance at the answer.

"Not why the Met; why you specifically? What does this have to do with art?"

Catrin didn't answer, but Strachan said, "I invited her specifically."

Then Catrin added, almost as an answer with a deeper

reason, "And I wanted to come. Your final comment at our last meeting was correct and, in fairness, I wanted to let you know that."

That it was Irvin who had called for the hit on Catrin, not him.

Connolly's lips parted, slightly amused. He looked at Strachan and said, "So you told her after all?"

Strachan replied, "I did. But you heard it from the horse's mouth, too, didn't you, DI Sayer?"

It sounded as if she was taking a jab at the man, from her tone of voice, understanding the significance of the remark. Catrin looked at Strachan, but did not answer.

After a moment, Connolly said, "So, you talked with Niall?"

It was a statement more than a question, by the tone of it. Again, Catrin made no answer. She was watching him, his mind playing over the implications.

Then he said to her, "You really are like the proverbial bad penny, aren't you?"

The coin that causes problems always turns up in your change at exactly the wrong time.

Not waiting for an answer he looked at his solicitor and then at Strachan. "I have nothing more to say. If you have charges, lay them. Otherwise, move on."

Strachan just said, "Interview terminated at 11.42 a.m." and switched off the recorder.

She said, as her final volley, "I'm working on them Mr. Connolly, believe me. As is Trident with Michael Bolan."

She looked at Catrin and they got up, picked up their notebooks and left the room.

They watched Connolly on CCTV taking advantage of time alone with Niall's replacement prior to being taken back to his unit. The solicitor had asked for time to consult.

"He bit, I think," said Catrin.

Strachan replied, "I know him well; yes he did. The 'bad penny' reference. You turned up six years ago on Irvin's forgery and one thing led to another and eventually to his current imprisonment. Now you turn up on the Hunter painting and are back as Martin's name is mentioned. And you talked to Niall Irvin. He was working out the link. Like Irvin, he may have even recalled the Fonab Castle meeting when Stephen Milne mentioned the man's name."

She smiled.

"Unless Martin turns, we'll never have a sufficient basis to charge Bolan or Connolly; their solicitors are banking on that. And there is near-zero chance that the Frenchman will talk. He hasn't so far."

The arrest of Xavier Martin had been carefully planned. A tactical unit went in the front and back of the house in Poitiers. The man was in the shower. They took him in the bedroom; his hand on the handle of the drawer that was later found to contain a machine pistol, Lauder had said. The arrest was just in time to prevent further bloodshed.

"It went by the book; he was caught dead to rights. They should have no trouble putting him away on a life sentence," he claimed.

It wasn't quite that way. The French officers hadn't actually moved to restrain him as the naked gunsmith stood there. They waited, a man and woman with their own weapons trained on him, to see if he chose to open the drawer. In the background brief, the alleged role in the Morin assassination had been mentioned.

Martin had slowly let go of the drawer handle and raised his hands, so the team took him swiftly into custody. They had given him the option, knowing the background. But that was kept within the team.

Lauder had said, "They don't know much about him, at present, I gather; nor is he co-operating. He has no record and has been off the radar so long it's proving difficult. He was born in Paris, I gather, or near there and they can track him to the age of twenty-three. He worked at a Renault plant, on the production line. After that he went abroad. I am sure they will fill in some of the blanks in due course."

What the UK authorities told no-one, in their turn, was that it was not the information from Niall Irvin, with the vague reference to the name Martin, which provided the lead. It was Anne Shannon. The woman recalled the dinner in Glasgow where Ranjani got up and spoke to the man. One of Strachan's most experienced interviewers had gone along this time with PC McKinnon.

"Yes, the name Martin is right; I recognized it was French. His features were typically French, I thought at the time. His first name was one of the unusual French ones, began with an X, or, J, or perhaps a Z, I think. I recall one of the others used it once. As I said to Inspector Sayer and her colleague, Jalaj Ranjani didn't introduce him, which was… suspicious to me; too secretive. Xavier, I think, its coming back now. With an X, isn't it?"

It took no more than a day to locate a Xavier Martin in Poitiers; and to discover that he had been in India. The French authorities provided a photo. Anne Shannon picked him out of a photo line-up without hesitation, saying, "This was taken before I saw him, he was older, more lines under his eyes. But it's him. That was the man in Glasgow."

Unlike the French with Madame Morin, they were taking no chances this time. The information flow to Interpol and others was that the name arose from a 'major informant' on the Connolly gang; a clear reference to Niall Irvin. The basic purpose of the interview with Connolly was to reinforce that perception. Nothing would be traceable back to Anne Shannon, Moore and Strachan decided.

The interview report was classified accordingly. Catrin was briefed on a 'need to know' basis. As much as she had no wish to see Connolly again she felt that for this purpose, it was worth it. As she said to Dr. Herrington when she told him she was going to do this visit to HMP Shotts, "I have a good reason to see him this time, from my perspective, not just the Met's."

"How do you feel about Connolly?" he replied.

"I think he is everything I stand against; drugs, gang life, almost feudal power over people, all driven by money for him and his empire. At the core of it, he is a primary reason why police services exist. If I can help protect an innocent person by seeing him again, I have no hesitation. Does that sound OK?"

"Yes," he replied unhesitatingly, "It does. But Catrin, don't get hooked on the Trident banner; or Chief Superintendent Strachan's banner either. I see the outcomes of that never-ending grind, too."

She laughed, thinking back only weeks ago to her decision to turn down Commander Barlow's offer regarding SIS, which would have also fitted that 'never-ending grind' scenario.

"I have no intention of doing that, I promise," she said.

EPILOGUE

It was the Met communications people who flagged and circulated the piece, a feature article in the Saturday edition of 'The Scotsman' entitled, 'The Crack beneath the New Hunter'.

On the Sunday afternoon Susan Hetherington called Catrin to talk about it.

Catrin said, "I only read it in detail this morning; I was busy at a friend's wedding yesterday. I was a bridesmaid."

The feature was about, at a superficial level, the Leslie Hunter painting of a Loch Lomond scene donated recently to the Kelvingrove Museum in memory of Lena Shannon, a local girl. 'Lena's Hunter', the writer called it. It took the story of Anne Shannon and her family from their domestic bliss as a hard-working, well-off couple with a daughter and followed the spiral down, describing the discovery of Brodie's true accounting work, the backlash against Anne and Lena, then Lena's move to London and her death high on drugs in E3.

People were named. The writer noted that Malav Rai, who hooked Lena on drugs and was in the room when she died, would be eligible for parole in eight months. Once the Colourist painting had been determined to be their joint property, Anne Shannon and her ex-husband had argued; he was against donating it to the Kelvingrove Museum and wanted to sell it. In the end the painting had gone to the museum in memory of Lena. Anne was quoted as saying she would 'have no truck with drug money'.

It revealed that Brodie's business friend was a Jalaj Ranjani who had disappeared, believed to have fled the country after his own wife had been killed in their home, implying it was all part of the underworld of drug dealing. Anne spoke about the burdens on her life; seeing her husband as being 'up there with the drug lords' and her daughter as one of their many victims. The underpinning message was that Shannon had no answer to the way that street drugs had overwhelmed her life, but she felt that the government's response to them was too fragmented and compartmentalized. It was oblivious to the suffering of family and friends.

Her final quote was, "If I had my way, I wouldn't leave Brodie hiding away in prison with his cronies. Nor his boss, Dominic Connolly. I would have them face their victims in a public room so that people like me can come along with our stories, our photos and our pain and tell them to their face what they have done to hurt us. That's what I would do. But we can't do that; they have rights. We inherit their actions as our sorrows; they keep their rights."

The writer finished the chastening article on a relatively warm and upbeat element. Joseph Tarrant, a noted artist and copyist in Edinburgh, had offered to paint three copies of 'Lena's Hunter', to be sold in support of 'Last Call', a frontline help group for people in Glasgow struggling with drug problems. He had met with Anne Shannon and Lena's former school friend, Nina Trew, a student at Glasgow University. Nina volunteered with the charity in memory of Lena. The first painting would be auctioned at a dinner event, the annual Glasgow gathering of members of the Strachan clan. Apparently someone in Clan Strachan had said it would sell for a hefty price, she was sure.

Catrin said to Hetherington, "Put Connolly in a place with public access a few days running, the next thing you know he would be on a private jet to South America. But I feel for her. And I see Eileen's hand behind the scenes, although she kept out of the limelight."

"It made me think of you," said Susan. "We've not talked since you went back home."

"Why's that? I mean, the article making you think of me?"

"Well, you've been to Scotland twice - ."

"Three times," interrupted Catrin. "I came up to be a witness at Colin Cheney's murder trial; the prisoner he killed in Barlinnie. They tried to say that it was a byproduct of me kicking him."

She wasn't going to mention the most recent visit.

"Three then, but the third only illustrates the point I was about to make. None of them have been pleasant; each has hurt you in some way. So I was talking with Audie, my husband. We still have his family's old house in Oban; it's used as a holiday home for us and our relatives. I know you've been to Oban already to see Mary and Elizabeth Gault but that was in the past. We thought you and your husband might like a holiday on the coast there this summer. Not to talk to Eileen or anyone else, not about work. Just to enjoy Scotland, for a change."

Catrin was touched by the thought and told her so. She would talk to Chris.

Susan continued, "It's where Audie's family lived and all the kids grew up but it's a tiny place really; just fine for two. Let me know when and I will block it for you. The only thing I can guarantee is the weather."

"In summer?" Catrin's mind was already looking ahead.

"Anytime really. You can't rely on it at all in Oban. You were a bridesmaid, you say?"

She deftly changed subject back to Catrin's Saturday.

~~

Catrin had been Jean's bridesmaid. A woman who was a long-time friend of Melanie from her home town of Yeovil was her bridesmaid; she had helped a lot during the early days of Melanie identifying as gay. Parents, friends and relatives were present and Catrin's parents, who had known Jean since her toddler days, made the trip up from Pontypridd with Jean's family.

The registry office ceremony was over with quite fast. Jean and Melanie had chosen to wear formal suits with skirts, both in pale blue. The only person who cried was the curate at St. Stephen's. She had attended, but was suddenly angry that the formal vows couldn't be taken in their church, so much so that she fell apart.

But that evaporated when they went on to St. Stephen's Church. Jean and Melanie had started attending there after moving to London, brought in by other people they had met in the LGBT community and both were now an active part of the congregation. Though formal blessing of same-sex marriage was still not allowed in the Church of England, St. Stephens, like many others, had derived their own form of service of celebration. That and the reception afterwards in the church hall was all they could wish for in a congregation celebrating its own.

At the end, by prior arrangement, Catrin and Chris drove Jean and Melanie home. That's what they wanted; no honeymoon, no hotel, just home to their flat as a married couple.

Catrin and Chris spent most of the Sunday with Catrin's parents before they went back to Wales by train. In the middle of it she took the call from Susan Hetherington. Whatever it was, the chemistry of the weekend, the sense of the rituals of life or the recent experiences at work, it was hard to say. But she reached a decision.

She and Chris went to a restaurant in Paddington after seeing her parents off.

During the meal Chris said, "Work tomorrow; I forgot; I will be back late." His hours were more predictable than hers, generally.

She nodded but said nothing.

He looked at her. "Penny for them?"

She looked serious. "Jean told me that they are now going ahead and will try to have a baby; at least Melanie is going to. They don't want to wait any longer."

He said nothing, interpreting her comment but not sure what to say. She reached across and took his hand.

"Neither should we, I feel. I'm ready. What do you think?"

NOTES

As stated in previous novels, the Metropolitan Police in London has an Art and Antiques Unit within its Specialist Crime Command that was established back in 1969. Its structure and activities as described herein are entirely my own creation. During the course of writing this novel it was reported that the officers assigned to the real Art and Antiques Unit had temporarily been reassigned to other duties.

The 'Art Crime Unit' in the Met described in these novels is an invention that has no real-life counterpart.

The elements of the role of contract killers and their modes of operation are not based on any specific cases or real-life examples, but I should acknowledge that I recalled reading years ago Martin Booth's novel 'A Very Private Gentleman' and was influenced by the world of assassins it created.

It was a lunch in the Lyceum Tavern on the Strand, a few yards from the George pub shown on the cover, which gave the idea for the events in Chapter 26.   Both old pubs contain upstairs restaurants. The George dates from 1723, the Tudor façade being a later addition.

Finally, I want to thank my wife Gill and my friend Jack Soule for reading the draft manuscript at different stages; their comments have been invaluable.   Any remaining errors are entirely my own, of course.

ABOUT THE AUTHOR

Allan Jones lives in Ontario, Canada. He was born and grew up in Merseyside, England. By profession an industrial chemist, he worked for many years as a consultant on international chemical regulation. He has lived in or travelled to most of the regions featured in the Catrin Sayer novels.